Breaking STONE

THE STONE SERIES: BOOK FIVE

Dakota Willink

DAKOTA WILLINK

AWARD-WINNING AND INTERNATIONAL BESTSELLING AUTHOR

PRAISE FOR THE STONE SERIES

"There's a new billionaire in town! Fans of Fifty Shades and Crossfire will devour this series!"
— **After Fifty Shades Book Blog**

"This read demanded to be heard. It screamed escape from the everyday and gave me that something extra I was looking for."
— **The Book Junkie Reads**

"Hang on to your kindles! It's a wild ride!"
— **Once Upon An Alpha**

"Heart wrenching and undeniably sexy! This series is going to my TBR again and again!"
— **Not Your Moms Romance Blog**

"A definite page turner with enticing romance scenes that will make you sweat even during those cold winter nights!"
— **Redz World**

"I would gladly hand over my heart to Alexander Stone!"
— **Crystal's Book World**

BOOKS BY DAKOTA WILLINK

The Stone Series
(Billionaire Romantic Suspense)
Heart of Stone
Stepping Stone
Set In Stone
Wishing Stone
Breaking Stone

The Fade Into You Series
Untouched (New Adult Romance)
Defined (Second Chance Romance)
Endurance (Sports Romance)

Take Me Trilogy
(Billionaire Romantic Suspense)
Take Me Under
Take Me Darkly
Take Me Forever

Standalone Titles

The Sound of Silence
(Dark Romantic Thriller)

Please visit www.dakotawillink.com for more information.

BREAKING STONE

THE STONE SERIES: BOOK 5

DAKOTA WILLINK

DRAGONFLY INK PUBLISHING

TRIGGER WARNING

NOTE : This book discusses pregnancy loss and infertility, and may be difficult for some readers.

"History, despite its wrenching pain, cannot be unlived, but if faced with courage, need not be lived again."

— MAYA ANGELOU

1

Alexander

The thump, thump of bass filtered up from The Dungeon of Club O below. The sound was faint but could still be heard in the private suites located two floors above. I envisioned a sea of twisting bodies on the dance floor and knew the smell of sex was sure to be heavy in the air. The sweet and tangy scent practically oozed from every wall in this place. It was hard to believe I was back here—at the club I swore to never set foot inside again.

I looked around the slate gray walls of the private room in Club O. Restraints lined the walls alongside other various BDSM equipment and pleasure tools. Suspension gear hung from the ceiling, casting shadows over a bed covered in black satin sheets. There was no headboard or footboard, only four tall posters at each corner. A large window was parallel to where I stood, its curtains closed tight to block the view of any on-lookers. I wouldn't have it any other way. I may have considered exhibitionism for a time, but everything was different since meeting Krystina. It was mutually decided that my wife was too possessive of me, and I was too protective of her. I was hers, and she was mine. The intimacy between us would never be shared with anyone else.

My gaze traveled over Krystina's naked body sprawled over the black satin. A red band circled one of her wrists, symbolizing that she was only available to me. It was a safety measure provided by the club to prevent any unwanted advances from other Doms while we visited. Her chest rose and fell, her breathing heavy in anticipation as she waited for my next command. Until that point, the only thing I'd ordered her to do was get undressed and center herself on the bed.

Moving along the wall of crops and whips, I ran my hand over each as I decided what to use. After settling on a black and scarlet red leather flogger, I glanced over at the narrow table pressed against the wall. A Bluetooth speaker rested on top of the glass surface. Sidestepping over to it, I pressed a few buttons to sync my cellphone, waiting a beat until Sarah McLachlan's "Possession" drowned out the distant sounds of the club. I wanted there to be no distractions, making it so that my wife's sole focus was only on what was happening in this room.

The melody was sad, but Krystina and I lived in a sad time. I wanted her to feel the haunting lyrics and remember the reason we were here. Coming to Club O had been her idea. I'd resisted at first but ultimately conceded after another failed attempt to dominate her in the playroom at our home in Westchester. There were just too many memories in that room —memories trapped in time that I just couldn't seem to get past. But I didn't want to think about that. At this moment, all I wanted was to fulfill my angel's every desire. It was time to let go of the past. She craved my domination, and that's what I would give her.

Stepping up to the bed, I ran my fingertips along the smooth skin of Krystina's bare shoulder. Moving down, I trailed my touch over the curve of her breast, stopping only for a moment to pinch the hardened point of her nipple. She inhaled sharply, but I didn't linger, just continued south. When the tips of my fingers felt the slightly raised skin of a tiny stretch mark near her hip, my jaw tightened, but I didn't stop my exploration. I didn't want anything to get in the way of what needed to happen tonight, including the scars that were permanent evidence of her pain.

When I reached her ankle, I used the flogger handle to push apart her legs and expose her sex before working my way back up her body. Rounding the corner so I was standing at the head of the bed, I let my fingers slip through the lush, chestnut brown curls that fanned over the pillow and looked down at her. She stared up at me, her eyes swirling with passion and longing. Her tongue darted out to lick her bottom lip, causing my cock to jerk. I shifted uncomfortably in my jeans, anxious to be rid of the restrictive denim.

"Tell me what you need, angel," I demanded.

"Pain," she replied without hesitation. "I want the pain and all the pleasure that follows. Please don't hold back, Alex."

Krystina's voice was pleading, and I found it both arousing and concerning at the same time. I loved giving her both pain and pleasure, but lately, she seemed to want pain for all the wrong reasons. It was almost as if she were searching for it.

I studied her face a moment before responding. The darkness that was so often present wasn't there tonight, only red-hot desire. Perhaps coming here was exactly what she needed to make everything disappear. There was only one way to find out.

"Flip over onto your stomach," I ordered.

She did as I'd instructed, giving me a full view of her backside. Leaning over her, I slid my hands down her spine and cupped both cheeks. Her heated flesh molded to my palms. Krystina's ass was always a glorious sight to behold.

Reaching between her legs, my finger found her wet slit. I pushed until I breached her opening, groaning when her slick heat sucked me in. A moan escaped her as she began a slight pump of her hips against the bed. However, almost as soon as she started giving herself over to the pleasure, I felt her body stiffen.

"No, Alex. I need the pain first."

Instinctively, I bristled from her attempt to take control. I pulled my finger from her body, then used that same hand to place a well-aimed slap to her right cheek with the intent to hurt. The place where I'd hit her instantly began to turn red.

"Don't try to top from the bottom," I said firmly. "I didn't just slap you because you asked for pain, but to remind you of your place. You'll take what I give you, and if I want to show you pleasure first, you'll accept it without question. Do you understand me?"

"Yes," she whispered.

I smiled with satisfaction as I reached to finger her opening once again. Gently I circled, spreading her moisture as I waited for her to tremor with excitement. However, after several minutes of stroking her inner walls in all the places that were sure to get her off, Krystina remained stiff and unmoving on the bed. It wasn't long before I realized she was deliberately denying herself the pleasure I'd ordered her to take.

"I want your orgasm," I demanded gruffly. "Relax your body so I can feel your pussy pulse around my fingers."

Pushing a second finger inside her heated well, I flexed against her G-spot. Her sex instantly tightened, but I knew she was still fighting off her imminent orgasm by the way she clenched her fists. Indentations creased her palms from where her nails bit into them. It was the exact thing she did when I ordered her to hold back, only this time, that was the opposite of my command. But before I could begin to fathom why she would torture herself in such a way, I heard a sob break free from her lips.

"Alex, please," she whimpered. "The pain. I need that first."

There was no denying the quiver of emotion in her voice. I angled my head to read her expression. Her eyes were shut tight, but there was no mistaking the tear I saw rolling off her cheek and onto the black satin.

Damn it!

I wanted to unleash my dominance more than anything. I wanted to own her—to demand that she fall to her knees and suck me off. I wanted her fingernails digging into my flesh while I fucked her rough and unrestrained. I wanted her cries, her pleading, her pain, and her pleasure. I wanted to take it all without consequence.

But not if she was crying.

After everything we'd been through, Krystina's tears trumped any ideas of dominance. I realized then that her idea to come here tonight had nothing to do with hurdling past painful memories. She didn't want me—she only wanted an escape. Knowing this caused my chest to constrict. I knew it wasn't personal. Everyone was allowed to work through difficult emotions in their own way. I just wished Krystina had found a different way to channel her feelings.

My jaw ticked, and my hand flexed around the handle of the flogger. If she wanted pain, I would give her what she needed—but only for tonight. Tomorrow we would discuss who was ultimately in control when we were in the bedroom.

Raising my hand, I delivered the first blow. The snapping

sound of the leather on her flesh was an incomparable aphrodisiac, and my cock instantly went rock hard. Bringing my free hand to the waistband of my jeans, I unfastened the button and slid down the zipper. My erection sprung free, anxious to feel one of Krystina's tight holes.

Bringing the flogger down a second time, I hit her in the same place as before. Normally, I'd spread the blows evenly over her backside, but she wanted pain tonight—real pain— and this was a sure way to deliver just that. When the third and fourth lash came, Krystina's hands gripped the edge of the bed until her knuckles turned white. I hadn't held back at all and knew this was hurting her, but she didn't utter a single word.

I took in the beautiful lines of pink that had blossomed over her ass. My dick throbbed from the sight. I wanted inside her sweet well of honey more than anything, but not yet. My pleasure, and hers, would come soon enough. Gripping the base of my cock, I stroked it and brought the flogger down for the fifth time.

By the time I'd reached the tenth blow, the shade of pink had developed into a bright red. Welts had begun to raise and I wasn't sure how much more she could take before blood was drawn. I paused, waiting for her to utter her safeword, but the word 'sapphire' never fell from her lips. Given her behavior as of late, I didn't know if she would use it to stop me. All I knew was that I wasn't going to wait and find out. She'd wanted the pain—which was precisely what I'd delivered—but enough was enough. Now it was time for her to experience the pleasure.

Setting the flogger down, I stepped out of my pants and climbed on top of the bed. Then, shifting onto one elbow to make sure my full weight wasn't resting on her, I reached down to notch the head of my cock at her opening.

"Alex, no!" she cried out, clamping her legs closed as she did so. "Not yet. I need more. Hit me again."

"You've had enough, angel."

"I'll know when I've had enough. I'll use my safeword if it becomes too much."

"I'm not convinced that you would, and I won't make you bleed, Krystina. I would never do anything that could leave permanent marks. You know this, so why are you asking me to?"

"I'm fine. I'm not going to bleed," she insisted, and shimmied her body slightly to the left so she was no longer directly under me. "Go again."

I pressed my lips together in a tight line, thoroughly annoyed over her petulant attitude—but also concerned.

Very concerned.

She's not herself. This is all wrong.

Climbing off the bed, I picked my pants up from the floor.

"We're done here," I told her.

"Wait—what?" She flipped over onto her back and tossed me an incredulous look.

"You heard me, angel. Put your clothes on."

"No. We're not done," she challenged.

"Yes, we are. This was a mistake. Coming here was never the answer."

Scrambling to the edge of the bed, Krystina picked up the flogger and held it out to me.

"I need this, Alex—we need this. Please."

"Don't look at me like that. This isn't healthy, and you know it."

"You're going to talk to me about what's healthy and what isn't? That's rich coming from the king of everything that's fucked up," she lashed out angrily. Her pupils flared, and icy goosebumps raised on my arms. I knew she didn't mean what she said. Her words came from a dark place—a place where I couldn't reach her. I needed to save my wife from the black abyss she was falling into, but I didn't know how.

"You don't want to go down this path, Krystina."

"You have no right to judge me. Wasn't it you who tried to escape life through BDSM? I might not know all the details about that time in your life, but I know who does. Maybe we should reach out to her. What do you say, Alex? Should we see if darling Sasha is still a member of Club O?"

"That's enough!" I snapped. I refused to do this with her—not now. Not in this place. "Physical pain is not going to erase your emotional pain."

"Don't try to psychoanalyze me. I'm perfectly aware of that!" she bit out. "I don't need you reciting lines from your college textbooks."

She was right. No psychology degree would help me now. She needed more than anything I could give her.

"Get dressed. We're leaving," I stated bitterly, not bothering to disguise my disgust over our current situation. "First thing in the morning, I'm making an appointment for you to see Dr. Tumblin."

"And what should I tell him? That after more than five years of practicing BDSM with my husband, he's suddenly afraid to whip me?"

"Don't play games. You know it's more than that," I said and tossed her clothes at her. When she didn't begin to put them on right away, I stepped up to her and picked up the black satin button-down shirt. Draping it around her shoulders, I attempted to put it on for her.

"Stop it," she protested. "I don't even have my bra on. I need to—"

"Fuck the bra," I interrupted. I just wanted her covered enough to get her out of here. We engaged in a tug of war of sorts, her pulling on one sleeve of the shirt and I the other. Using my free hand, I tried to pry her fingers from it.

"Alex!" she yelled, jerking out of my grasp. "Please. Don't make me leave here. I just need... we just need...."

Her voice cracked. I looked up and saw a deep well of tears pooling in her eyes. She blinked, and the tears spilled down her cheeks. Dropping my hold on the shirt, I reached up to touch her face. I ran my finger over her forehead, wishing I could read her mind. Her agony was in plain sight, but the solution to what ailed her was out of my reach.

Leaning in, I pressed my lips to hers, using my mouth to express everything words could not. I ran my hands up the base of her neck and into her hair, gathering the thick mass and holding her head still while I plundered her with my tongue. The salty taste of her tears blended with our saliva, and I strengthened the kiss. She responded with a violent passion. Her breathing went from quivering to panting in desperation. This woman—the very essence of her—was my weakness. I would do anything to chase her demons away.

"Alex," she breathed. The cracked vulnerability in her voice made me pull back to look at her. Using my thumb, I traced the line of her bottom lip that was swollen from my kiss. She stared up at me for a long moment. When she eventually spoke, her tone was dripping with remorse. "I'm so sorry."

"Angel, don't apologize. You've been dealing with a lot, and—"

"No. That's no excuse. I shouldn't have lashed out so cruelly and thrown your past in your face. No matter what I'm going through, you didn't deserve that. I expected tonight would...." She trailed off, seeming at a loss for words. "I guess I don't really know what I expected. Let's just go home."

She bent to retrieve her clothes without another word, and we both hurried to finish dressing in silence. Then, when we were ready to leave, I snaked my arm around her waist and led her from the private suite to the hallway. The pulsating music was louder out here but not so loud that I couldn't be heard over the bass.

"We can come back another time, angel," I suggested as we walked down the long corridor to the steps that would take us to the main vestibule. I wasn't sure if returning was the best idea, but seeing her defeated expression was almost too much to bear. I had to give her hope—to make her believe that we would be okay again. "Let's revisit the idea once we... once we sort through everything."

"Maybe," she replied quietly.

Before we exited Club O, we walked by the marble statue of Venus. The Roman goddess was wrapped in a loosely draped cloth with one breast exposed, alluding to her full, erotic beauty. I'd always appreciated her attributes—beauty, persuasion, seduction, sex, and fertility. Yet, seeing her today of all days felt bittersweet. Her alluring expression just seemed to mock my very existence.

2

Krystina

I blinked, my vision slowly adjusting to the moonlight sliding across the ceiling. I shifted and felt Alexander's warm body next to me. Instinctively, I rolled to curl into him, but stopped myself at the last minute. My hand reached out, wanting to touch him. I only held back because I was afraid that I'd wake him, and I didn't want to talk to him this morning. It had been a strenuous weekend after what happened on Friday night at Club O. We'd barely spoken since, and now here we were on Monday morning, and I still wasn't sure what to say to him.

Returning to my backside, I stared at the high ceiling. Despite the darkness outside, I knew dawn was approaching by the sounds coming from the open bedroom windows. Birds were coming to life, their low chirps mingling with Alexander's slow and steady breathing. The cool August night temperature had been comfortable when we'd gone to bed, so we opted to keep the balcony door to our bedroom open. The late summer air filtered in through the privacy screen, promising a pleasant morning.

Turning my head, I looked at the clock. It was nearing five in the morning. Alexander would be stirring soon. I knew his routine like I knew the back of my hand. First, he would go downstairs to our home gym. After completing his morning workout, he would come back up to shower before going to work. He always started his workday well before I did. While he was typically in the office no later than seven, I didn't get in until after eight. There was no need for me to get there earlier because most Turning Stone Advertising clients didn't open for business until nine anyway.

A moment later, the low sound of Alexanders cellphone alarm went off. I felt a shift in the bed as he moved to silence it, then got up. I laid perfectly still, pretending to be asleep. Judging by his footfalls on the bamboo hardwood floor, he was approaching the his-and-her closets on the opposite side of the room. Peering with one eye, I watched his gloriously naked form illuminated in the dim light. A nude Alexander was always a sight to behold. The chiseled, rock-hard lines of his body would make any sculptor itch to mold his impeccable form.

When he entered his closet, there was a faint click of the handle right before a tiny sliver of light darted out from the bottom of the closed door after he turned the interior light on. When he emerged a few minutes later, he was predictably in a pair of gym shorts and a T-shirt. He turned my way and I quickly closed my eyes, feigning sleep once more. Alexander was always so in tune with me, he most likely knew I was awake. But if he did, he didn't say anything before exiting the bedroom to begin his daily workout.

This was the third morning in a row where I'd awoken this way—carefully studying my husband in silence, longing to touch him. I craved his warmth and his embrace, but we seemed to be on opposite ends of the world lately. We were two souls lost in grief, yet I couldn't talk about it. How could I when there wasn't even a way to explain to myself how I felt? It wasn't that I didn't want to open up about my feelings—I wanted to scream about them. The problem was, I couldn't find the words.

Rolling to my side, I ignored the tear that slid down my cheek and closed my eyes. I pulled the blankets up tight around my shoulder, feeling thankful that I didn't have to be up for another hour. I needed sleep to take me so I could escape into the blackness and get away from all the hurt—even if only for a little while—before facing the day once again.

TWO HOURS LATER, I sat in the backseat of a black Maserati Quattroporte as Samuel Faye, my security detail, backed out of the garage. I never ended up falling back asleep like I'd hoped. It was why my travel mug contained my second cup of coffee for the day. I treated the caffeine as if it were my lifeline.

We passed through the black wrought iron gate at the end of the driveway and turned onto the main road. The low rumble of the engine was the only thing that could be heard on the quiet residential street. The Maserati was Alexander's latest acquisition after he decided the BMW that Samuel used to drive was no longer good enough for my safety. My husband insisted that the paparazzi obsession with me dictated the need for an armored vehicle. I'd argued that the Italian-made luxury car was eccentric at best and wasn't necessary, but I gave up when he started talking about ballistic proof body shields—

whatever that meant. My upbringing made it so that car facts were like a second language to me, but military grade vehicles were well out of my wheelhouse.

Less than ten minutes later, Samuel turned toward the main entrance for Westwood Hills Cemetery. I knew the route by heart and barely noticed the things passing by as he navigated the narrow asphalt road. After all, I'd been coming to the cemetery daily ever since we buried our precious baby girl here.

The day I told Alexander I was pregnant with her seemed so long ago—a fairytale Christmas that didn't see through to a happy ending. I'd lost our baby after twenty-eight weeks of pregnancy and there were no words that could be used to describe that kind of pain. Time just seemed to stop. All we were left with was hollow emptiness. It didn't matter if four and a half months had passed since fate cruelly snatched everything away from us. Alexander and I felt trapped in time. We'd fallen still—stagnant in the most inexplicable ways—and I didn't know how to move us to a place where we were wholly together again.

It was part of the reason I came to the cemetery every day. I never wanted to forget how precious life was. It was a gift, one that could easily float by unnoticed as we went through our daily routines. It was only during life's most extreme moments, whether it be unmeasurable joy or heart-shattering grief, that people tended to feel the most alive. In a way, coming here was my therapy. It reminded me that I was alive despite the debilitating numbness.

Samuel slowed the car to a stop in front of an all too familiar towering maple. When he came around to open the car door for me, I swung my legs out and moved to stand on the side of the road. I kept my head down, staring absently at the blades of green grass as I waited for Samuel to hand me a solitary lily. It was another part of my daily routine, so when I saw it appear in my peripheral, muscle memory propelled my hand up to take it. My jaw clenched as I wrapped my fingers around the stem, trying to fight the visions flashing before my eyes.

For some reason, the same memory always came to me at this precise moment each day. No matter how hard I tried, I couldn't push my thoughts away, and I felt every emotion just as I had on the day I'd originally felt them—that feeling of elated joy being violently ripped away, leaving a gaping black hole when there should have been nothing but love and devotion. It was the day my fate was decided for me.

I'd given birth to our daughter after a long, hard labor that started much too soon. The doctors had tried to stop my laboring, but it was to no avail. After her birth, I'd cradled her tiny form in my arms. Alexander and I stared at her and placed her delicate little hands in ours. Her eyelashes were barely visible against her translucent skin, and what little hair had begun to grow on her head was dark. If given the chance to grow out, I envisioned her to have long, nearly black locks that matched Alexander's sister, Justine.

Our baby was perfect—so tiny—but perfect, nonetheless. We were able to hold her for what seemed like the shortest of minutes, only to lose her before we could ever possibly be ready. A knot in her umbilical cord had robbed her of much needed nutrients, and in the process, robbed us of our future with her. Every precaution we'd taken to ensure a healthy pregnancy had been for nothing. The pain of birthing her had been for nothing.

But the worst was being forced to accept the reality of my situation. I could still see the pity in the eyes of the maternity ward nurse when she introduced Alexander and me to the grief counselor who would help us through the burial process. I'd been in shock. Even though it was the natural course of things, the idea of a burial had never occurred to me as they wheeled our tiny angel away. The idea of holding a funeral for a baby who had so few moments on this earth seemed foreign to me. The entire experience had felt out of body.

I didn't even remember the name of the grief counselor who spoke with us. I only remembered her handing me two brochures. One brochure presented a selection of miniature caskets and the other explained cremation. I couldn't stomach looking at either. The sudden realization of what lay ahead had caused me to vomit off the side of my hospital bed.

If we weren't already processing enough, my OBGYN had delivered us another blow. Not only did I lose our child, but I was told I'd most likely never be able to conceive again. Her brutal words tore through my flesh and bones, leaving me flayed and bloodied and feeling as if I would never be whole again. Hearing phrases like 'inhospitable uterus' in the midst of everything was too much to bear. Between the placental abruption that occurred when I was giving birth and the uterine scarring from my previous miscarriages, the damage to my womb was too great. Attempting another pregnancy would be dangerous and life threatening.

All hope for the future was gone, and I'd felt as if a vital part of me had died. There were some days when I still felt that way. There was no way to easily get past so much pain. In fact, I didn't think I ever would. All I knew was that I wanted to escape it any way I could. When people would assure us that we could try again soon, I wanted to scream. I didn't have it in me to explain why we couldn't. Instead, I'd give a fake smile and a nod, a part of me still refusing to believe my reality.

Taking a deep breath, I focused on putting one foot in front of the other. I tried to embrace the serenity around me as I approached my daughter's grave. Stopping in front of her headstone, I slowly lifted my eyes to read the inscription.

Liliana Lucille Stone
Held for a moment, loved for a lifetime
April 9, 2022

I'd come here so many times that I no longer choked up when reading the engraved marble. All I felt now was numbness. I was told that everything happens for a reason by so many. It was a motto I used to believe in, too—but not now. There was no reason for this—for this pain that wasn't deserved.

Squatting down, I replaced yesterday's lily with the fresh one and returned to a standing position.

"My dearest, Liliana," I whispered. "We will never know your wit, wisdom, and personality, but I know you would have made our hearts full if given the chance. Every moment we had with you was a gift. Life evolves, forcing people to change with it. You changed your father and me in the most inexplicable ways. You'll always be a part of us. Until we meet again, baby girl..."

Pressing two fingers to my lips, I brought them down to touch the cold, marble headstone.

It was strange to think about how much my life had changed since meeting Alexander. I barely recognized the woman I used to be—a naïve recent college grad who'd slipped on a spilled latte, leading her to fall hopelessly in love with a mysterious billionaire. I'd adjusted and grown so much since then, and in some ways, those days had been the end of my innocence. I wondered if our tragedy was the result of poor choices or if it truly was just fate. I had to believe it was the latter. Thinking otherwise would cause me to go mad from questioning every move I'd ever made.

Glancing over my shoulder, I saw Samuel waiting patiently by the car. I'd been standing in front of Liliana's grave for fifteen minutes and I knew it was time to go. Still, walking away was never easy. My chest would always tighten when I took that first step. Today was no different.

As I headed back to the car, a single tear slid down my cheek. I brushed it away, drew a deep breath through my nose, and whispered a reminder to myself.

"Time to face the day. You can do this."

3

Krystina

Traffic was terrible as Samuel drove us through the city. I sighed with impatience as we approached the financial district. As much as I abhorred the delays, I also felt grateful for them. The congested streets were a sure sign that everything was ultimately back to normal. It took a while, but all of New York had finally moved on from the pandemic, and she was once again the bustling city that I'd come to love.

When we came to a standstill near the corner of Trinity Place and Rector Street, I rested my head back against the seat and ran my hands over the soft Italian leather seat. Closing my eyes, I breathed deep. My mornings at the cemetery were always emotional, and I sometimes required a quick reset before attempting to tackle the day. It was one of those days.

Counting to ten, I concentrated on my breathing. I inhaled and exhaled slowly, trying to push out my anxiety every time I breathed out. It was an exercise Dr. Tumblin had given me to calm the overwhelming waves of anxiety after losing Liliana. He'd prescribed anti-depressants to help me through the worst of it, but I didn't want to be on them long term. The simple counting exercise allowed me to find peace without medication so that I could focus.

Eventually, traffic began to move again and we continued our way. By the time Samuel came to a halt at the curb in front of Cornerstone Tower, I felt relatively calm and more like myself. I waited as he climbed out of the driver's seat to open the passenger door for me.

"Thanks, Samuel," I said as I stepped out onto the pavement.

"Ma'am," he replied with a short nod as he took my elbow and led me to the main doors of the building.

I breathed deep when I caught the smell of honey and sugar permeating the air. Glancing to my left, I saw that a street vendor had set up shop on the sidewalk and was selling roasted almonds. I made a mental note to come down and grab some at lunch time as I looked up at Cornerstone Tower. The impressive structure towered before me. From my place on the sidewalk, the sleek ornamental spire loomed high above, piercing the low hanging stratus clouds above and seeming to go on for infinity.

By the look of the sky, rain was sure to hit before noon. The humidity that always came with summer showers would undoubtably be brutal, and I was thankful I'd decided to wear my hair back today. There was no taming my curls after a New York summer rain.

Samuel and I approached the revolving glass doors and pushed through to the main lobby. Once inside, he followed his familiar routine of looking around for anything out of the ordinary. After deciding all was clear, he gave me a half salute, then made his way back to the car. It wouldn't be long before he returned. After he parked the car, he'd be back to stand guard outside the offices at Turning Stone Advertising.

As much as I appreciated feeling secure, always having someone over my shoulder felt stifling at times. Still, I understood the necessity. After a sleezy photographer had stolen a picture of me in a bikini laying by our pool in Westchester, I'd felt so violated. Even though the incident happened a couple of years ago, I still got goosebumps when I thought about it. Alexander had lost his ever-loving mind when he saw me plastered all over the front pages of the local tabloids. That picture had sparked a sudden interest in me that hadn't been there before. The tabloids didn't seem to care about Alexander at all anymore, having found a new obsession with the billionaire's wife—me. Because of that, Alexander vowed that I'd never again be without protection on the streets of New York.

Crossing the large vestibule, I passed the security desk and headed toward the bank of elevators. My black high heels echoed across the blue-veined marble floors. When I reached the elevator, I typed my floor number into the keypad. A moment later, the doors opened, and I was surprised to see Alexander on the other side.

"Alex!" I said in bewilderment. While he frequently left the office for business meetings, it was unusual for him to leave the fiftieth floor this early in the day. "Where are you headed so early?"

"Just down the block to Billy's Bagel Shop. I skipped breakfast this morning and I want to grab a bagel and an energy drink," he explained.

Sidestepping to let him pass, I frowned as he exited the elevator. He typically had Laura, his assistant, do things like that for him.

"Where's Laura?"

"Her mother is having surgery, so she's out today and tomorrow. I told you last week, angel."

My frown deepened. I had a vague recollection of him saying something about Laura, but I didn't recall the details.

"It must have slipped my mind."

"That's been happening a lot lately. It's unusual for you. Are you feeling alright?"

Not particularly.

But I couldn't tell him that without providing an explanation I wasn't able to give. I didn't know how anyone could explain feelings of emptiness.

"I'm good," I lied.

Alexander frowned as if he didn't believe me. "Did you go to the cemetery this morning?"

I stiffened.

"Of course, I went to the cemetery," I replied. I tried to keep the rigidness out of my voice because I didn't want to spark an argument.

My daily visits were a sore spot between Alexander and me. He didn't like that I went so often, and insisted it was the reason I couldn't get past losing Liliana. But he didn't understand. In fact, he'd refused to return to her gravesite after we'd buried her. I tried not to judge him too harshly. Everyone was allowed to grieve differently, but I couldn't help but think he was just trying to mask the pain. So, I went to the cemetery alone—and it was hard not to resent him for it.

"I assumed," he said with resignation. Pursing his lips, he shifted his weight from one foot to the other. "Do you want me to get you anything from the bagel shop while I'm there?"

"I'm set, but thanks," I told him and held up my travel mug of coffee that I'd made before leaving the house.

Alexander took a step closer to me, and although he didn't

touch me, it was impossible to ignore the heat that radiated from him. My husband was always just so *there*. It never mattered what sort of turmoil we were going through. Nothing seemed to stop the sexual, kinetic energy from bouncing between us.

"Angel," he began and placed his hand on my arm. "I skipped breakfast this morning because I didn't have an appetite after I saw you weren't in the kitchen for the third day in a row. You and I always take breakfast together in the morning, no matter what our schedules look like. I'm certain Vivian thought it was odd, too. What's going on with you?"

"Alex, now isn't really the time to—"

"Then when is the time, dammit!" he bit out harshly. He dropped his hand and took a step back. His teeth were clenched as he raked his free hand through his dark waves. "I'm sorry. I shouldn't have snapped. It's just that... I don't know."

I hated the look of helplessness that flashed across his face —hated that I was the reason for it.

"It's fine, really. It's been a strange few days. Maybe we can talk later?" I suggested.

Alexander's expression softened as he stepped closer to me once more and snaked both arms around my waist.

I reached up and gently cupped his cheek with my free hand. His sapphire blue eyes turned hypnotic—spellbinding and alluring. For a long moment, we simply stared at each other.

"I love you, Alex," I whispered.

Leaning in, he pressed his mouth fully to mine. I felt a current charge down my spine the moment our lips connected. It was electric. Energizing. That was how it always was with him. No matter what was going on, love and lust were never an issue with us.

The kiss was short, and when he pulled away, there was no

denying the heat in his gaze. But there was something else there, too. If I wasn't mistaken, I thought I saw a flicker of sadness.

"I know you love me, angel. And I love you. You've always been my light, but you've gone dark on me and I'm worried."

"Alex, I don't want to hash this out here. Like I said—"

"I know. Later. You're right. This isn't the place." Leaning down once more, he pressed a light kiss to my forehead. "I'll see you after work."

When he walked away, a feeling of melancholy came over me. My body seemed to move on autopilot, and I was a little jarred when the elevator doors opened up on the thirty-seventh floor. I'd barely recalled getting into the elevator. Alexander was right about me forgetting things lately. I'd been a total space cadet. It had to have been from all the stress I was under.

Stepping out of the elevator, I put on my game face and made my way to my office at Turning Stone Advertising.

"Morning, Regina," I said to my secretary as I passed by her desk.

"Good morning to you, too. It's already shaping up to be a busy day," she remarked.

"No matter how much we prepare, it always seems that way when we launch a new campaign, doesn't it?"

"It sure does."

"Is Clive in yet?" I asked. "I want to review the new online campaign for Sheppard's Cuisine with him before it goes live."

"He's here. I saw him poking around here a few minutes ago. He already looked frazzled," Regina added with a laugh.

I shook my head. "If he's all wound up, maybe I won't go over it with him yet. Clive needs to relax. This is hardly our first launch. Considering all the hoops we had to jump through during the pandemic, this should be a breeze. If he starts acting like City Hall is burning, send him to my office.

Having him all hopped up on nerves is never good for anyone."

Leaving Regina to her morning routine, I continued to my office. Once there, I slung my purse over the back of the desk chair and sat down behind the computer. Just as I shook the mouse to wake the monitor, I heard my cellphone vibrating in my purse. Reaching down, I retrieved the phone and saw Allyson's name on the caller ID.

Smiling, I slid my finger across the screen to answer it.

"Hey, you," I said.

"Hey, yourself. What are you up to?" she asked.

I laughed. "It's five minutes to nine on Monday morning. What do you think I'm up to, Ally?"

"Okay, smart-ass. Let me clarify. What will you be up to at lunchtime? I'm going to be doing a photoshoot near your office later today and I thought we could grab a bite to eat."

"I wish I could, but it will be a working lunch for me today. I have too much on my plate. We're launching a new ad campaign and prepping for another one that's set to drop next week."

"Bummer. I feel like I haven't seen you in ages. I miss you."

"I know. I miss you, too. Our schedules just haven't aligned lately. I could really use some girl time."

"I hear you. It's been a rough few months. Are you hanging in there?" she asked softly.

"Sort of. Alex and I... well, we've been off lately. I can't explain it."

"Krys, you guys went through hell. Of course, things will feel off for a while. Have faith. You'll find your groove again. Unless, of course, something else happened that I'm not aware of."

"Yes and no," I said, biting my lower lip. I debated whether I should tell her about Club O. While Allyson knew about the club's existence, I'd never discussed my experiences there with her. I wasn't sure why I hadn't but talking to her about the underground club while sitting in my office at work would undoubtably be inappropriate conversation. My office had a door, but the walls were thin and the risk of someone overhearing me was too great. Despite the unending press probes, Alexander's history with the BDSM club had miraculously stayed out of the news cycle and I didn't want to do anything that could potentially change that.

"What do you mean, yes and no?" Allyson prompted.

"It's kind of long story—one that I can't get into at work."

"You sound tired, Krys. Are you sure that you're okay?"

"Yeah, Ally. I'm fine." I pressed my lips together in a tight line. I felt as if I'd been saying that a lot lately.

"Do you know what I think? I think you've been working too much. You and Alex are workaholics. It's no wonder things feel off with the two of you. You need a vacation."

I laughed. "A vacation? How will that solve anything?"

"It's a break from life! And I can't think of two people who deserve it more. In fact, now that I think about it, I haven't taken a vacation since before the pandemic. We should all go somewhere together. Maybe..." She trailed off before suddenly exclaiming, "That's it! Vegas!"

My stomach sank. Allyson wasn't talking about a staycation. She wanted to travel, which meant I would have to be away from the city—and Liliana.

"Vegas?" I repeated slowly.

"Yeah! Why don't you, me, Alex, and Matteo go to Vegas for a few days. Labor Day is coming up and Matteo was just saying how it's usually a slow weekend for the restaurant. I'm sure he'll be able to sneak away for a bit. It's the perfect time for us all to take a long weekend. This could be so fun! What do you think?"

I shook my head. She sounded so excited, and it was hard to shut her down.

"I don't know, Ally. I suppose I could talk to Alex, but—"

"Perfect! And I'll talk to Matteo. Oh, my gosh! Vegas!" She squealed and I had to hold the phone away from my ear or risk a ruptured eardrum. "Let me know what Alex says. I've got to run. The model I'm supposed to take pictures of will be here in ten minutes and I have to finish making up the set. Talk to you soon!"

Before I could say another word, the line went dead.

What the hell?

I was used to Allyson's whirlwind antics, but that was a little much—even for her.

Vegas, huh?

I'd never been to Las Vegas, and I had to admit that the idea sounded appealing. The last time Alexander and I took any kind of break was when we vacationed in Vermont a couple of Christmases ago. I just wasn't sure if I'd be able to leave Liliana for any length of time. The daily visits to her gravesite had become a coping strategy, and the idea of not being able to go made me anxious.

However, I couldn't deny that Alexander and I needed a break. And who knew? Perhaps I'd finally get to the bottom of what was going on with Allyson and Matteo. The two of them insisted there was nothing, but I wasn't blind. You could practically cut the sexual tension with a knife whenever they were around each other.

I leaned back on the chair and pushed my brows together in thought. Perhaps going to Vegas was exactly what Alexander and I needed to get out of our funk. I wouldn't know unless we went. I mused about what we could do while we were there. We weren't much into gambling, but I'd heard there was so much more to Vegas than just that.

Deciding to present the possibility of a vacation to Alexander later on that night, I turned back to my computer. I flipped on the stereo system in my office and began sorting through emails to a Kelly Clarkson song. As I filed each email into the appropriate inbox folder, I tried to talk myself into the idea of not visiting Liliana for a few days.

But as the day progressed, the more I was convinced that it wasn't something I'd be able to do.

4

Alexander

I climbed into the driver's seat of my late model Tesla feeling satisfied. It had been a productive and lucrative day, the result of striking a praiseworthy deal with Empire State Innovation. Their focus was on creating new jobs across the state. I'd worked with them frequently ever since they directed me to Wally's Grocery Store, a worthwhile investment in more ways than one. If it weren't for their referral, I never would have met Krystina.

Today, we struck a deal that would produce good paying union jobs and generate revenue for both the city and Stone Enterprise. Stone Arena, the first Major League Soccer complex in New York, had been my vision. I was the primary investor and had purchased the naming rights, but the arena had been a money drain since the day we broke ground. It wasn't sustainable with just soccer alone.

The pandemic had only amplified that money stress. We needed other events—concerts, trade shows, and the like. That's why the deal with ESI was so monumental. After months of negotiation, handshakes, knowing grins, and way too many raised glasses of expensive booze, we finally signed a contract that gave ESI sole control over concessions. They would keep all the profits, and in return, would coordinate with city government on scheduling major events at Stone Arena, making the venue competitive with places like Madison Square Garden. Their guarantee of a pre-determined number of events would not only keep Stone Arena in the black, but also make it an extremely profitable investment in the long run.

It was like a game of chess, and I'd just successfully navigated my way to calling checkmate. The press release would go out next week, announcing the partnership. Even my accountant was beyond thrilled. Bryan, who was typically a financial pessimist, was excited. It was contagious, and it was the reason I still had a smile on my face as I pulled out of the parking garage of Cornerstone Tower. Now, I was just looking forward to getting home to Krystina. After what happened this past weekend at Club O, I was prepared for an emotional discussion tonight, but I didn't care. I would be near her and that was all that mattered.

A light rain was falling, causing the automatic windshield wipers to turn on. Glancing in my rearview mirror, I saw Hale following closely behind me in the Porsche Cayenne. It was unusual for us to drive separately, but he'd said he had someplace to go for a few hours this afternoon and wasn't sure if he'd be back in time to drive me home. He hadn't volunteered where, and I wished I'd asked him. When I saw him return late in the day, he couldn't mask the worry etched into the lines of his face. I'd been so wrapped up with the Stone Arena deal that I hadn't had a chance to ask what was wrong.

Reaching forward, I pressed the small arrow on the bottom of the display screen of the Tesla to activate the menu. Selecting the phone icon, I called Hale.

"Boss," he said after the first ring. "What can I do for you?"

"I just wanted to touch base about the errand you had to run this afternoon. I noticed that you seemed distracted when you got back—worried almost—but I wasn't able to talk to you about it given everything that was going on. Is there anything you need to tell me?"

"Yeah, but I didn't think I should get into it at the office. I was going to bring you up to speed when you got home."

"It's an hour drive to Westchester. Let's talk now."

When he spoke again, there was no denying the hesitation in his voice. Red flags instantly raised, and my jaw tightened as I prepared for whatever it was he was about to say.

"I've got a development on Michael Ketry," he slowly began. "You aren't going to like it."

"Ketry? Refresh my memory."

"Krystina's biological father," Hale reminded.

I pressed my lips together and frowned. When Hale first told me about Michael Ketry, I'd been surprised. Krystina only mentioned him once, and not by name. I wasn't even sure if she knew what his name was. In Hale's effort to protect me when I first started dating Krystina, he'd completed a thorough background check on her and her family members—including any estranged family members. That's how he'd learned of Ketry, but Hale had only mentioned him to me last December after he discovered Ketry moved to the city. I hadn't heard his name since, so I assumed he was a non-issue. However, Hale's tone said otherwise.

"What is it I'm not going to like?" I asked cautiously.

"I told you his new apartment was within walking distance

of Cornerstone Tower, but that it may be nothing. A coincidence."

"I remember."

"As it turns out, I was right to keep an eye on him. I've had a tail on him since early January. At first, everything seemed normal, but now it looks like he's here for Krystina after all."

"What do you mean he's here for Krystina?" I demanded.

"The PI who was following him said he's been seen lurking outside Cornerstone Tower several times. I also have security footage of him downstairs in the main lobby of the penthouse. Obviously, without a keycard to access the elevator to the floors, he didn't stick around long. He was also spotted lingering in La Biga."

My hands gripped the steering wheel so tight, my knuckles turned white. Krystina and I no longer lived in the penthouse, but we'd decided to keep it for convenience purposes. We'd also kept Hale's old apartment so our security detail had someplace to stay. It just made sense. Our home in Westchester was an hour away and the penthouse came in handy if we were ever late in the city.

Still, Hale's mention of La Biga is what caused a million warning bells go off in my head. La Biga was Krystina's favorite coffee house. Ketry's presence there, as well as the downstairs lobby of the penthouse, couldn't be a coincidence. He was looking for something—or someone. He had to be following her, and just the mere thought of it sent chills down my spine.

"Have you alerted the appropriate people?"

"Of course, boss. I spoke to Angelo at La Biga personally about it, increased security at the penthouse, Cornerstone Tower, and around the house in Westchester. I even bumped up patrols around *The Lucy* at the marina. Everyone of relevance has been given a photo of Ketry, including Jeffrey."

Jeffrey, the doorman for the penthouse, had a history of

absentmindedness. While he'd improved over the years, he wasn't the most alert individual. It was highly unlikely that he'd pick up on anything suspect, and I felt better knowing Hale had beefed up security there.

"This guy, Ketry, is nothing to Krystina—a sperm donor. What's your take on why he's suddenly hanging around?" I asked.

"Most likely, he found out Krystina is married to you and is looking to cash in. With the amount of media attention she's received over the years, it wouldn't be surprising. But my best guess is as good as yours. I really have no idea."

"Your guess is probably right. Goddamn gold-digging vultures," I cursed. "Find out what he wants, Hale. I want to know everything there is to know about this guy. And in the meantime, I want you to take over Krystina's security detail. Samuel does a fine job, but you and I both know how unpredictable she can be at times. Until we can figure out if this Ketry guy poses a serious threat, I only trust you with my wife's safety."

"I understand. If I'm going to be with Krystina, you'll have no coverage. Should I reassign Samuel to your detail?"

"No, I'd rather him be at the house keeping an extra eye on Vivian and my mother in case Ketry decides to loiter around there, too."

"But that will leave you alone. At the very least, I can bring on another member of the team and see about—"

"It's fine. I don't need anyone," I interrupted. Hale had been off my detail for only a short time after we moved to Westchester. I'd assigned him to the house because I wanted someone I trusted to be close to my mother. I'd tried to bring on somebody else to replace him, only to learn that Hale was irreplaceable. Nobody else had lasted more than a week. I'd rather be alone than have someone I didn't trust ambling about.

"As you wish. Krystina has already left Cornerstone Tower for the day. According to the GPS on the Maserati, she should be home in about twenty minutes. I'll advise Samuel of the situation and begin Krystina's detail first thing tomorrow."

"I'll tell her about the security change, but I don't want her to be worried about this, Hale. If she asks you—which knowing Krystina, she inevitably will—make up some excuse for why you need to take over without telling her about Ketry. At least not yet. Let's figure out what's going on first."

"I understand your reasoning, and I don't mean to question your judgement, but..." He hesitated.

"But what?"

"We're talking about her biological father here, and we both know how your wife can be. Are you sure keeping this from her is wise?"

"No, I don't. But what else can I do? She's been through so much over the past year." I paused and ran a frustrated hand through my hair.

"I know. I was there."

"She doesn't need any more heartache, Hale. We need to know more about Ketry before I tell her about this. I can't protect her from the unknowns."

"Understood, boss."

I pressed a button on the car's touchscreen, ended the call, and contemplated the situation. Perhaps I was overreacting. Maybe the man just wanted to talk—to get to know the daughter he'd abandoned.

Fuck that.

Any man who gave up his child was no man in my book. He forfeited the right to talk to her years ago. Anyone who would try to come back after nearly three decades had to have an agenda. What that agenda was, I didn't know, but I'd be damned before I allowed him to waltz back into Krystina's life without asking any questions. I needed answers, and until I had them, I would do everything in my power to protect my wife.

I turned onto the I-87 ramp towards Westchester and opened the Tesla's glass panoramic roof. Turning up the volume of the radio, "Gold on the Ceiling" by the Black Keys blasted through the speakers as I hit the accelerator. Embracing the blistering force of the vehicle, I was happy to leave the chaos of the city and head toward the tranquility of home.

WALKING INTO THE HOUSE, the savory aroma of rosemary filled my nose. If my sense of smell served me right, I'd guess Vivian was making a roasted chicken for dinner. Heading down the hallway that led to the kitchen, I found my housekeeper layering a baking pan with quartered red potatoes.

"Good evening, Mr. Stone," she greeted when she saw me come in.

"Smells good, Vivian."

"Oh, just keeping it simple tonight. Nothing fancy. I've got a chicken roasting in the oven, with salt potatoes and green beans almondine on the side."

"Sounds perfect. Have you seen Krystina?"

"Yes, sir. She got in about thirty minutes ago. She said something about being happy the rain had cleared, poured herself a glass of wine, and headed out into the backyard."

Nodding my thanks, I hurried up to the master suite and stripped out of my suit and tie. The humidity left behind after the rain was brutal and the last thing I wanted to do was lounge in the yard in woven cashmere.

Once I was dressed more comfortably in shorts and a T-shirt, I made my way to the backyard. Walking out the door, I heard Adele's melodic voice coming from the garden speakers surrounding the inground pool. I found Krystina relaxing on a chaise lounge, staring at the view of the breathtaking thirty-six-acre lot. Lush pines and tall maples dotted the landscape, following the gentle slope until becoming so thick, we were unable to see the large retention pond near the back of the property from this vantage point.

Krystina glanced up when she heard my approach. She offered me a small smile, took a quick sip of her wine, and then stood. She was dressed in a loose tank and a pair of cut off jean shorts. She looked comfortable and casual, yet still sexy as hell. I couldn't help but admire her long legs, golden tan from our weekends spent on *The Lucy*. I imagined her lithe body wrapped around mine, and I could suddenly no longer wait to touch her.

Closing the remaining distance between us, I circled my arms around her waist and pulled her tight, my need for her as fierce as ever. Leaning in, I pressed my lips to hers. She gave in, setting her drink on a nearby side table and bringing her hands up to clasp the back of my neck. Her fingertips toyed with the ends of my hair, and I growled my appreciation. I kissed her deeply, noting the crisp flavor of wine on her tongue as our mouths slid and clashed. I savored this feeling of homecoming —the taste of her lips, the press of her body against mine. Everything about her was vital and real every single time we were together.

Although she kissed me back, it felt different—emotionally detached in a way. It was as if her body was here, but her mind was someplace far away. Reluctantly, I pulled back to look at her. Wide chocolate brown eyes stared back at me. Reaching up, I traced the hairline near her temple with my finger.

"Where are you?" I asked.

"What do you mean?"

"You're here but you seem lost in thought."

She took a step back and sighed. It wasn't a sigh of exasperation, but more like one rooted in confusion. It was as if she were trying to sort something out in her mind.

"Ally called me this morning," Krystina began. "She wants us all—you, me, her, and Matteo—to go to Las Vegas."

I raised my eyebrows in surprise.

"And what did you say?" I prompted when she didn't elaborate further.

"I told her I'd talk to you about it, but if I'm being completely honest, I'm not sure if I want to go."

I wasn't entirely thrilled with the idea of going to Las Vegas. While some people loved it, it wasn't for me. Perhaps it was because I knew about its darker side. While tourists and high rollers lived for the flashiness and exaggerated decor, the seedier side of Vegas was right under their noses. From the camps of homeless people living under the casinos to the penthouse orgies orchestrated by drug-dealing bellhops, Sin City wasn't nearly as glamorous as everyone liked to believe.

Still, I'd never expressed my distaste for Vegas to Krystina. Putting my thoughts aside, I was curious about her reluctance.

"Why aren't you sure about going?" I asked.

"Because I don't know if I'm ready to..." She trailed off, seeming to struggle to find the words as she turned to walk back to the chaise lounge. Lowering her body, she settled back, and I noticed the way her hands twisted in her lap.

"You're fidgeting," I said, pointing to her tell. "What's making you nervous?"

"I don't think I'm ready to take a break from visiting Liliana, even if it's only for a few days," she admitted. "Just the idea of not going to see her in the morning makes me anxious."

I allowed her words to percolate for a moment before

responding. A distraction and a break in routine might just be the right medicine for Krystina. Plus, the idea of getting her out of New York while Hale figured out what Michael Ketry was up to certainly had its appeal. I just wished Allyson had suggested going someplace else.

"Krystina, I can't say Vegas is my favorite place in the world. However, what I think about it is hardly relevant. I'm more concerned with why you don't want to go. I know why you visit Liliana's grave every day, but I think a break in routine will be good for you. I've been thinking that for a while. As time goes on, you seem to retreat further into yourself, and I think it's a direct response to reliving all those painful memories at the start of every day."

"Is that your professional diagnosis?" she questioned dryly.

"No. That's my concerned husband diagnosis."

Her face softened, losing a bit of the anxiousness that seemed to be present before.

"I don't mean to worry you, Alex. And maybe you're right. Perhaps this will be good for me. But what if it's not? What if, after we get there, I go into a full-blown panic the first morning I can't go see her?"

Moving toward her, I sat on the edge of the chaise and took her hand in mine.

"If you're upset or find yourself starting to panic, I'll be there to help you through it. I've got you, angel. I always do. You need to trust that."

She looked up at me with wide eyes that slowly glassed over as tears began to form. She blinked them away and squeezed my hand as one corner of her mouth turned up into a small, sardonic smile.

"I do trust you, Alex. It's me I don't trust."

I pressed my lips together and frowned at the gravity of her tone. There was so much emotion swirling in her expressive eyes. It was so hard to unpack because I didn't know where to begin.

"Angel, we need to talk about Club O. What happened to you while we were there?"

"I don't know," she said quietly with a shake of her head.

"I think you do. Help me understand this desire you have for me to hurt you—to inflict permanent damage. That wasn't the first time you pushed me to do it. This slow path to self-destruction is..." I paused as I tried to summarize how she'd been behaving. "You've been slipping away from me a little more each day for months now. Physically, you're here. But mentally, you're someplace else. I can't help if you keep shutting me out. Talk to me, Krystina."

She took a deep breath and averted her eyes, seeming to collect herself before looking at me once more.

"I just hurt all the time. I don't talk about it because what's the point? Nothing will change the fact that a vital part of me died with Liliana. I don't know if I'll ever feel whole again. At Club O, I just wanted to escape those feelings by any means necessary. It was foolish—I know. I just wish I could explain the ache I live with every waking moment."

My eyes began to burn, and I blinked. I didn't have the luxury to give in to a single tear—not now. Not when Krystina needed me to be strong.

"You don't need to explain, angel," I said, unable to keep the rasp out of my voice.

"But I do, Alex."

"No, you don't. I know exactly how you feel because I feel the same emptiness every goddamn day. I miss her so much and..." I trailed off, knowing that if I continued talking, I wouldn't be able to hold it together. The horrendous ache she spoke of was something I was all too familiar with.

Liliana Lucille was pure and innocent, just like the meaning of her name. We had named her for Krystina's favorite flower, the Lily, in combination with my grandmother's name. It was perfect, just like she'd been. She was the most precious thing I'd ever laid eyes on—so small that she'd fit right in the palm of my hand. I didn't think it was possible to feel so much happiness, love, and sorrow at the same time. When Krystina and I lost our tiny miracle, the pain I'd experienced was like none other. It was as if the devil himself had risen up from the fires of hell to tear my heart from my chest.

"If you miss her, then why don't you come with me to the cemetery?" Krystina asked. "I haven't missed a day since we buried her. I go every morning all by myself."

I heard the hurt and accusation in her voice, and that's when it clicked.

She thought I'd abandoned her.

Was that why I felt as if she was emotionally retreating from me?

"Angel," I began, knowing she needed my honesty more than anything else right now. "I don't go because I'm afraid if I see her grave again, the hole in my chest that was left after she died will be blown wide open. I can't afford for that to happen."

"Why not?"

I stared deep into her eyes, committing to giving it to her straight.

"Because if I give in to it and let the pain consume me, I won't be able to give you the support you need. As hard as I try to protect you from anything that might cause you harm, I can't shield you from your own emotions. The only thing I can do is make sure I'm strong enough for you to draw on my strength. This might sound melodramatic, but I know what will happen if I allow myself to wallow in grief. I'd become a shadow of myself, and in effect, become useless to you. I would rather die before allowing that to happen."

Krystina shifted in her seat, maneuvering her body until she was straddling my lap. Wrapping her arms around my neck, I stared into her tear-filled eyes. When a single tear rolled down her cheek, I kissed it away.

"I'm sorry, Alex."

"Sorry for what?"

"I know Liliana's death was hard on you, but you just seemed to get over it so quickly. I was so mad at you for not coming to the cemetery, for not showing emotion, for not... well, I suppose it doesn't matter now. I had no idea you've been holding it together all this time just for me."

"I'll do anything for you. You know that."

"But you need to grieve, Alex."

"I have, and I will continue to do so for the rest of my life. But for now and always, you are my priority. We can mourn the dead, but we must live for the living—and that's exactly what I'm doing."

"I love you so much it hurts," she whispered.

"Ditto, angel."

Leaning in, she pressed her lips to mine. Her kiss was somewhat chaste at first—hesitant almost—yet it made my heart race. My tongue darted out to trace her lower lip, coaxing the sensual curve until she opened for me. When she gave in, her tongue met mine with a heated craving that shot straight to my groin. The kiss was packed with emotion—sadness, understanding, desire. I felt everything as I ran my hands up her back, plunging my fingers into the lush curls of her ponytail. My wife had the ability to turn my blood into molten lava, and I was on fire.

When she eventually pulled away, I traced a finger along her swollen bottom lip.

"I love kissing you," she breathed. "And as much as I'd like to continue this, I'm sure Vivian will be popping her head out here any minute to let us know dinner is ready. Continue this later? Maybe in the pool?" she added suggestively.

"Only if you're naked."

"Sounds like a plan," she said with a knowing smirk as she untangled herself from my lap. Once she was standing in front of me, she pulled her phone from the back pocket of her jean shorts and frowned.

"What is it?"

"It's a text from Ally letting me know Matteo is a go for Vegas. I suppose we should talk more about that."

"What's there to talk about? Let's go," I said with a shrug of indifference. I'd already worked out the travel details in my mind, however. A private plane was a given. I'd have to arrange for a car service since I planned on having Hale and Samuel stay behind. I'd assign Samuel to keep watch over the house and my mother, and I would tell Hale to take advantage of our time away to find out what Michael Ketry was up to.

"You think it's a good idea?" Krystina asked.

"I can't say Vegas is one of Allyson's more brilliant ideas, but yes. I think we should do it. Like I said, I think a break from the everyday will be good for us. And if you find yourself struggling, I'll help you through it. I'll get with Hale in the morning and have him see about booking us a plane."

"Well, I guess it's settled then. Vegas, here we come." Her tone was flat and held little emotion. There was no excitement or anticipation for a weekend getaway, and I couldn't help but wonder if this trip was only going to be one big, disastrous mistake.

5

Krystina

Alexander and I walked out of the house on Friday morning and headed toward the black Cadillac SUV limousine parked in our driveway. Traveling to the airport via a car service felt strange to me. I was so used to Hale or Samuel behind the wheel of our own vehicles. One of them always seemed to be with us wherever we went. The only time they weren't was during the pandemic, a time when keeping physically distant—even from our security—was essential to our safety. When Alexander told me we'd be traveling to Las Vegas without them, I was surprised. He'd said it wasn't necessary since we were less recognizable outside New York, and it would be easier to stay off people's radar.

I didn't question it, choosing to appreciate the rare occasion of being truly alone with my husband once we got to Vegas. While I appreciated Hale and Samuel, not having them hovering about would be nice—even if only for a little while. I never really understood the need for twenty-four-hour security. Despite the occasional creepy paparazzi treating me like a local celebrity, I'd often thought Alexander's concerns were a bit over the top.

We approached the limo and a young male driver holding open the passenger door. Alexander put a hand on the small of my back as we stepped up to him. My husband's hand was possessive and claiming, controlling the direction of my body. I smiled to myself, loving the message behind his touch. He never wanted anyone to question who I belonged to—and apparently, that included the limo driver. I considered myself strong and independent, but Alexander's possessiveness was still absolutely thrilling to me. It was a constant balance I maintained.

When we were both seated inside, the driver closed the door. Alexander sat angled to the right of me, facing the rear of the car. I took the bench seat that spanned the length of the vehicle. When the driver climbed into the front, Alexander turned his head to speak with him.

"Do you have the addresses?" he asked.

"I do, sir. Your head of security gave them to me," the driver responded.

The corners of my mouth turned up in a small smile. We could almost always count on Hale to be one step ahead.

"Good," Alexander said with a slight nod. "We'll pick up Allyson first in Greenwich Village, then get Matteo before going to the airport."

"Yes, sir,"

The limo began to move around the semi-circular driveway down toward the street. It was an hour-long drive to Allyson's apartment, so I settled back and looked out the window, content to enjoy the peaceful ride.

We rode in silence for a bit, and I used the quiet time to think about my morning. As was routine, I'd visited Liliana. Leaving her was always hard, but today was more of a struggle because I knew I wouldn't be back to visit until Tuesday morning.

Just thinking about it caused my stomach to tighten and roll from anxiety. Worry over whether I could actually leave New York took root, and I seriously thought about telling the driver to turn around.

After a while, I had the sense of someone watching me. I turned my head, and my eyes caught Alexander's.

"Stay with me," he said quietly.

"I'm here."

"No, you're not," he insisted. "You're fidgeting. Just relax, angel. Everything will be fine."

I looked down to see my hands twisting in my lap. I quickly pulled them apart as Alexander reached over and traced a finger up my thigh. With his other hand, he grabbed hold of my calf and brought it up to rest my leg across his lap. Then he began to massage my ankle. His sapphire blues narrowed, conveying an unexpected message, and I raised my eyebrows in surprise. I knew that expression all too well.

My husband was aroused.

I wasn't sure what brought this on, and I took a moment to consider him. He was dressed in blue jeans and a white dress shirt. A navy Brunello Cucinelli sport coat completed the outfit. Even when dressed casually, Alexander was a visual feast oozing with sophistication and prestige.

His shirt was unbuttoned at the neck, giving me just a tiny glimpse at the hard chest underneath. I imagined unbuttoning his shirt and running my hands along the muscular lines of his body. That thought caused me to smirk. Alexander knew I loved it when he dressed this way and I couldn't help but think his unexpected desire was planned. His ability to read me should never come as a shock, and I was sure this sudden display of desire was his way of distracting me from thinking about missing Liliana.

If that was the case, it was working. I felt a stirring low in my belly, and it wasn't long before our sexual tension weighed heavy in the air. I didn't know what it was with limos. Something about them always turned me on.

Or perhaps it was just the way Alexander was looking at me.

He didn't just look—he studied me as if analyzing every subtle move I made. I could feel my face heat as my chest began to rise and fall. I had no idea what he was planning, but I knew I wouldn't be disappointed.

However, after a short while, it became apparent that he wasn't going to advance our situation further. I frowned. I thought for sure more was coming. I couldn't possibly have imagined that hot, dangerous glint in his eye. I'd seen it way too many times in the past to have mistaken it.

What are you about, Mr. Stone?

I mused over Alexander's intent before deciding there wasn't any reason I shouldn't take matters into my own hands.

Shifting my foot, I kicked off a Louboutin ballerina flat and slid my toes along Alexander's thigh. Because of my position, the forty-five-degree angle that my body sat to his didn't allow me to put pressure on his groin as I wanted. Still, he knew what I was hinting at. His hand roamed over my knee and higher up my leg. His expression remained stoic as he pressed his thumb to the apex of my thighs. I sucked in a sharp breath when he began to lightly massage me through my designer jeans. His gaze was intent and never left my face.

I glanced over at the driver of the limo. The privacy glass was down. I wanted to straddle my husband's lap and ride him here and now, but I didn't want an audience. I looked over at the button that would close the glass, and Alexander followed my gaze.

"I'm not raising the glass, angel," he preempted before I could give voice to my thoughts.

"Why not?"

Lowering his voice to a whisper, he said, "Because what I want to do with you requires more time, and we'll be at Allyson's apartment in less than thirty minutes."

"I can think of a lot we can do in thirty minutes," I countered, already feeling breathy. Then, to my satisfaction, a slow smile spread across Alexander's face.

"You might be right. Sit here, Mrs. Stone," he said firmly, beckoning me by patting the seat beside him. I glanced at the driver behind him, and Alexander tsked. "Ignore him and do as I say."

His low voice reverberated through me. He had that tone— that dominant tone that made my toes curl.

"Yes, sir," I whispered.

Moving quickly, I followed his command and slid into the seat beside him.

Alexander leaned in close to my ear and whispered, "I don't want you to make a single sound. Your screams are for me and me alone. Do you understand?"

In other words, we weren't alone, and no matter what happened, I needed to be quiet. The driver was within earshot, and for some reason, the possibility of being heard or caught was an instant turn-on. My breath involuntarily hitched, and I nodded my agreement.

Alexander snaked his right arm around by back, slipping under my shirt until his hand cupped my breast. Pulling down the lace cup of my bra, he began to roll my nipple between his fingers. I nearly groaned, but quickly remembered his orders about staying silent. However, his next move made that near impossible.

Looking down, I watched as Alexander used his free hand to unsnap the button of my jeans and lower the zipper in one seemingly fluid motion.

"Lift your hips," he ordered.

I did as he asked, allowing him to shimmy my pants down just enough to give him easier access to my most sensitive region. Then, before I had a minute to react, his fingers were searching my folds for that tight bundle of nerves only he knew how to command. When he found his mark, I whimpered.

"Shhh. Stay quiet." His hushed words were barely audible against the shell of my ear.

Pushing his hand further, he found the opening between my legs and traced the slit. I was already wet. Alexander hummed his approval so only I could hear, then breached me with two fingers, sinking in to the second knuckle. My slick, greedy flesh sucked him in, flexing as he stroked my inner walls.

I stared down as he worked his magic. My jeans were just barely around my hips and there was something incredibly arousing about seeing the rise and fall of denim covering his hand. He fingered me with expert precision, sliding deeper and curling his fingers until I thought I might combust. I pushed my head back against the seat, keeping it still even though I wanted to thrash it from side to side.

Staying as still as humanly possible, I focused solely on his touch. My moans were low and quiet, just as he'd instructed. When he pushed a third finger inside and quickened the thrust, those low pants became near silent, breathy gasps. I wasn't going to be able to keep this up for much longer. I was desperate. I needed to come—and now.

As if sensing my need for release, Alexander pinched my

nipple, rolling it hard between his thumb and forefinger. The jolt of pain ignited a spark that sent me off like a rocket. My body stiffened and I slammed my eyes shut tight. Within seconds, I exploded around his skillful fingers.

"Just in time," Alexander whispered as he slowly pulled his fingers from the spasming clutches of my body.

I lazily opened my eyes to see we had long since arrived in Greenwich Village and were turning onto Bleeker Street. Allyson's apartment was just up the way. Suddenly at full attention, I huffed out a breath, unable to believe I had less than two minutes to compose myself. We'd cut it close—too close.

"Damn you, Alexander," I cursed as I scrambled back to where I was seated at the start of the drive.

"Wait until later, angel," he said with a chuckle. "That was just a taste. I'm not even close to done with you yet."

Ignoring him, I hurriedly fastened the button of my jeans and shifted by bra back into place. Once my clothes were back in order, I pulled my compact from my purse, snapped it open, and looked in the mirror. My eyes were dilated, and I cursed Alexander again what I saw how flushed my face was. I'd always hated how easily my face reddened. I glanced at my husband. He looked like a sex God as usual while I looked like I'd just run a marathon. I applied a new layer of powder foundation and hoped I'd covered the worst of the blush at least.

When I tossed the compact back into my purse, my cell screen lit up and I saw there were two missed calls. I pressed my lips together in a frown when I didn't recognize the number.

"What is it?" Alexander asked.

"I just had two missed calls in a row from an unknown number. It's probably a sales call or something like that," I said dismissively, dropping the phone back into my purse as the car pulled to a stop.

I looked up to see we'd arrived at our destination. Allyson came bounding down the steps from her apartment building wearing ankle jeans and a black crop top with her blonde hair pulled back into a stylish ponytail. She didn't bother waiting for the limo driver to open the door for her, but yanked the door open herself and poked her head inside. Silver hoops bobbed at her ears as she flashed us a huge smile. Then, pulling her hand out from behind her back, she produced a bottle of champagne and four plastic, long-stemmed glasses.

With an excited waggle of her perfectly shaped brows, she chimed, "We're going to Vegas, baby!"

6

Alexander

Eight hours later, we arrived at the Florentine Resort in Las Vegas. As we walked through the main doors and across the lobby, I took note of Krystina's bright expression. The flight had been long, but she'd slept for most of it. Now she looked more rested than she had in months. The shadowy rings that always seemed present under her eyes were gone, and her smile was a like a sunbeam lighting up the dark aura that had encompassed us after we lost Liliana. A content smile tugged the corners of my mouth, and I could almost feel the tension in my shoulders loosening.

After we checked in, it was discovered that our suite was in a different tower from where Allyson and Matteo's rooms were. It was only a minor inconvenience, but I was still irked. When I'd made the reservation, I'd been explicit about making sure our rooms were close. Pressing my lips together in aggravation,

I turned my attention to Krystina and our friends. They were discussing dinner plans.

"I'd like to freshen up if I can," Allyson said. "I always feel grimy after being on a plane—even swanky private ones like the one Alex booked for us. Is there time for me to change?"

"Plenty," Matteo told her. "Don't forget about the time change. We gained three hours on the way here. I already know the perfect place to eat. Amore Tuscan Steakhouse. One of my customers told me about it. He said their food rivals the food I serve at Krystina's Place and swears it's *delizioso*! I can call and make a reservation. How does seven o'clock sound?"

Krystina glanced up at me. "That sounds good to me. Alex, where do you want to meet up with them?"

"The main entrance to the hotel is fine."

"Sounds like a plan," Allyson agreed.

We parted ways and followed the bellman to our suite. However, in typical Vegas style, we were forced to walk through a large section of the hotel's casino on the way to our room. It was a ploy used by all the hotels to try and get every dime they could from their patrons, and I hated it. In fact, there wasn't much I liked about Las Vegas. So many loved to get lost in the sea of glitter, reveling in the cacophony of stacking chips and shuffling coins. It was mystifying to me.

I glanced around as we weaved through the throngs of people, keeping my hand on the small of Krystina's back as we went. Those we passed all wore mixed expressions. Some looked happy, obviously high on their luck or possibly just enjoying a well-deserved vacation from life. Others looked frustrated, many having an almost manic look in their eyes. It was if they were holding out hope that the next spin of the roulette wheel would be *the* one.

We passed a middle-aged couple arguing in a loud whisper. I only caught wind of part of their conversation, but I heard enough to know they were wondering if their last five bucks would serve them better at the Blackjack table. I only hoped they didn't have any young kids. If they did, he or she would most likely be found sleeping in an alley somewhere outside of the casino, a hopeless derivative from a gambling addiction.

Right before we reached the elevator that would take us up to our suite, I spotted a trio heading in our direction—two women on the arms of a man in a pinstriped suit and fedora. The women wore skirts designed to be much too short for legs that stretched on for days, and their bright red painted lips were curved up in knowing yet sultry smiles. Despite their heavy makeup, I was able to see the hardness beneath their façade. The man carried a small black box, and it wasn't hard to imagine what might be inside. It didn't take more than a transient glance for me to assess the women as sex workers and he was their pimp. Most likely, he was escorting them to their next client.

Krystina and I paused to let them pass, and I inwardly sighed. This was Vegas—and it was exactly as I'd remembered it. Sex, sin, and sickness was everywhere I turned.

Why did I agree to come to this godforsaken place?

After a short elevator ride, the bellman opened the double doors to our suite and stepped aside for Krystina and me to enter. I followed behind her, my gaze sweeping the surrounding area as I took in our accommodations. Unfortunately, being so last minute, the Penthouse Suite was already booked, and I'd had to settle for the Executive King Suite. Thankfully, the rooms seemed to emit every level of comfort one would expect from a luxury resort. The Italian marble of the foyer boasted elegance and grace, and the plush, sprawling suite that proceeded it did not disappoint.

"Sir, where would you like your luggage?" the bellman asked in a thick Ukrainian accent.

I looked back to where the young, dark-haired man stood in a crisp black shirt. He'd been with us since we arrived at the hotel from the airport, and he'd been ever the gracious host. Glancing down at his name tag, I made sure to address him by name. It was a practice Krystina had gotten me into before we were married, insisting it was a show of respect toward a staff member charged with our care. Despite our life of luxury, my wife was anything but pretentious.

"Nykolai, please take the bags to the bedroom," I told him.

"Shall I unpack them for you, sir?"

"No, thank you. We can unpack ourselves," Krystina chimed in.

"As you wish, ma'am."

After Nykolai deposited our bags, I passed him a generous tip for his service before he left. Once I closed the door behind him, I made my way to the living area where Krystina was waiting. I'd had champagne, a charcuterie cheese board, and chocolate-covered strawberries delivered to the suite in time for our arrival. Krystina glanced back at me when she heard me enter the room, and I saw her eyes alight with pleasure.

"I can't tell you the last time I indulged in chocolate-covered strawberries," she said.

I smiled, still reveling in seeing her so relaxed. Perhaps she'd been right about taking a trip to Vegas. Despite my initial resistance, I was beginning to think Sin City might be the distraction we needed to help us get past the pain we'd been through after all.

"After the long plane ride, I figured we'd want a snack to hold us over until dinner," I explained.

Moving over to the lounge chair in the corner of the room, I bent to take off my shoes. After removing my navy sport coat and untucking my shirt, I walked barefoot in jeans over to the coffee table where the food had been spread out. Plucking one dark chocolate-covered strawberry from the tray, I turned to Krystina. Her head was tilted to the side, and she wore a curious expression.

What's going on in her head?

After five years of marriage, one would think that I'd know what was going on behind those big, beautiful brown eyes. Unfortunately, Krystina was always a puzzle. Sometimes the pieces fit, and sometimes they didn't. Understanding her mind was a rare intimacy, and I hated not knowing what she was thinking.

Stepping up to her, I snaked an arm around her waist and brought the strawberry to her lips.

"Bite," I told her. "Then I want you to tell me what you're thinking."

Bringing her eyes to meet mine, she wrapped her lips around the strawberry, slowly bit down, then lazily sucked the juices. I raised my eyebrows in surprise. There was no denying her deliberate attempt at seduction as she gingerly ran her tongue over her bottom lip. While it wasn't unusual for Krystina to tease me in such a way, I'd assumed she'd be tired after our flight. Apparently, I'd been completely wrong.

"I was just trying to remember what time Matteo said he was going to make the dinner reservation for. Do you remember?" Krystina asked with feigned innocence as she took another bite of the strawberry. Juice trickled at the corner of her mouth, prompting her tongue to dart out to catch it.

My breath immediately caught in my throat before rushing out in a growling exhale. There was nothing but heat in my wife's eyes. It matched the smoldering look she'd had when I gave her a tease during the limo ride to the airport, and I knew we were about to finish what we'd started there.

"We have to leave here in two hours." Even to my own ears, my words sounded hoarse.

She pressed up on her tiptoes and leaned in to capture my lower lip between her teeth. She suckled it in one long, drawing pull, before tilting her head up to meet my gaze.

"There's a lot we can do during that time, Alex," she whispered seductively. Taking a step back, her hands moved to unbutton her shirt.

Standing completely still, I watched her undress, mesmerized by her stunning beauty. Every inch of her was perfection. It was all I could do to keep myself from throwing her over my shoulder, hauling her to the bedroom, and possessing her like a ruthless beast. Desire clawed at me, and I suppressed a groan.

Krystina walked to the bedroom doing a slow striptease, leaving a trail of clothes in her wake. I followed behind, my clothes dropping next to hers as I went. When she reached the bed, she wore nothing but a red thong. My eyes ran up the length of her flawless legs and settled on the curvature of her impeccable ass. A vision of my wife's lithe limbs wrapped around my hips consumed me.

I slowed my steps, wanting to touch her yet savor the vision before me at the same time. After climbing onto the bed, she crawled on her hands and knees toward the pillows. This time, I didn't bother to suppress my groan. All willpower was thrown to the wayside.

Climbing onto the bed, I flipped her over onto her back then leaned in to claim her mouth. I pushed my tongue in roughly past her open lips and devoured her. She moaned, the vibration from her lips sending an electric shock straight to my groin. I worked my way down her neck, appreciating the pounding of her pulse beneath her skin as I breathed in her scent. She smelled like vanilla and strawberries, an aphrodisiac that was potent to my senses.

She wrapped her long, glorious legs around my waist and

pulled me tight to her. I felt the heat of her sex through the red lace as she pressed her pelvis against me and began to grind. Her need was hot. So hot.

I twisted her nipples and she gasped her pleasure. I relished the weight of her bare breasts in my hands before taking a ridged peak into my mouth. I sucked and rolled the hardened areola around my tongue and gave a silent thanks to everything divine for making this woman mine. I was desperate to be inside her—to feel her velvet heat.

But not yet. She'd taken the lead, and now it was time for me to take back control. Thinking quickly, I concocted a plan that would bring my wife the most pleasure in the limited time we had.

"Wait here and keep your eyes closed," I whispered into her ear.

Sliding from the bed, I walked over the corner of the room where Nykolai had left our bags. I knew Krystina's reasons for wanting to unpack the suitcases ourselves went beyond her dislike of strangers touching her things. More than likely, she'd predicted that I may have packed questionable items. She was right. While I didn't have a plethora of sex toys at my disposal as we did at home, I'd packed enough to get creative.

I grabbed a necktie and a coil of silk rope, then went back to the living space to get the bottle of champagne. Returning to the bedroom, Krystina lay still and waiting with her eyes closed.

Setting the items down on the nightstand, I crawled over her body. My tongue traced circles on her skin like a needle rotating on vinyl. Carnal, sensual sounds elicited from her with every revolution, creating heady music for my greedy ears. Slowly and deliberately, I pulled her panties down her legs, worshiping every inch of her skin as I went.

Once she was completely naked, I climbed off the bed once

more and retrieved the necktie. I fashioned a knot with a few quick twists and slipped it over Krystina's head to form a blindfold. After ensuring the knot was secure at the base of her skull, I uncoiled the rope.

"I want you immobile. I'm in control, angel. I will do whatever I want to your body, however I want to do it. Do you understand me?"

"Yes, sir," she breathed. I smiled to myself, pleased to hear the tone she only used when in a completely submissive state. I could have buried my cock in her right then, driving into her like the wild animal she made me. And I would—eventually. But my wife deserved my adoration first.

Taking the rope, I wrapped the soft woven silk, my movements slow and deliberate as I tied each wrist. Once her hands were bound, I dragged the ends of the ropes to the top corners of the bed and secured each end to the side rails. With her hands tied tight above her head, her body stretched out before me like a feast just waiting to be devoured.

Grabbing the champagne bottle, I straddled Krystina's body. My thick cock weighed heavily on her abdomen, anxiously waiting to be buried inside her as I worked to remove the cork from the bottle. After a moment, I heard the familiar cork squeak, followed by a loud pop. Champagne bubbled out of the top, dribbling onto Krystina's torso. It dripped over her sides and onto the bed, trailing down between us to the apex of her thighs.

Shifting down so that I was positioned between her legs, I pushed her thighs up so that she was fully open to me.

"Oh, angel," I whispered as I stared down at her glistening sex. Sliding down, I pressed my cheek against her inner thigh. Her lush lips were pink and inviting. There were so many possibilities. "What do you want me to do to you?"

When she didn't answer, I nipped hard at her thigh with my

teeth—hard enough to make it hurt. She squirmed slightly with discomfort before pushing her hips up to silently communicate her fiery need. I smiled to myself. A little pain was a sure way to arouse my wife instantly.

"I want whatever you'll give me."

"Do you want me to make you come?" I teased as I tilted the champagne bottle until bubbly liquid began to slowly pour from the top.

"Yes." The single word was barely a whisper. She sucked in sharply, her breath stolen from her lungs as the cool champagne hit her mound and slid through her folds.

I pressed the glass neck of the bottle against her wet heat, gently prodding her throbbing bundle of nerves. She began to pant. The sound of her ragged breathing was nearly enough to make me come, and I couldn't wait any longer. I had to taste her. Leaning in, I crushed my mouth against her desire. Burying my face in her soaking wet heat, her back arched and she cried out, the persistent motion of my tongue provoking soft cries and moans from her lips.

I pulled away only for the briefest of moments to set the bottle back on the nightstand. When I returned to her, I shoved her legs up roughly to spread her even wider and devoured her like a starving man who would never get his fill. And I wouldn't. Until the day I took my last breath, I would never have enough of Krystina.

The taste of tangy champagne mixed with her essence was driving me wild. Her breathing was ragged as her head tossed back and forth in the throes of passion. Her clit throbbed beneath the merciless flicking of my tongue, and I knew she was close. So close.

Within moments, her body stilled, and she cried out. Her juices, the sweetest of all nectars, exploded over my tongue and coated my lips. I felt a tremble course down her legs, and I smiled in satisfaction. I suckled every last drop until she began to squirm from sensation overload.

Reaching up, I shoved the blindfold over her forehead so I could look Krystina in the eyes. Her cheeks were flushed, and her gaze was desperate. Desire pooled in the depths of her eyes, and I knew what she wanted.

Me. All of me.

She wanted me to fill her without holding back. She didn't want my fingers to prepare her first, stretching her before my invasion. She didn't want a moment to adjust to my girth. She wanted it hard and fast, and no holds barred.

"You want my cock deep, don't you?" I said huskily.

Her lips parted slightly, and her eyes went dark with want. "So deep. Fuck me, Alex. Don't hold back."

Positioning myself at her slick entrance, I pushed in. I moved slow, but I wasn't gentle. Her breath caught, and her mouth went slack as she absorbed each stab of pleasure as I stretched her. I rocked into her over and over again, working her into a desperate frenzy.

"Come again for me, angel."

I kissed the sides of her face and the shell of her ear, moving down to her neck and shoulders. I continued to push into her hot well until she began to tremble from the pressure of me being so deep. Grabbing her right leg, I brought it up over my shoulder and pushed forward until the tip of my cock was pressing against her very core.

"Oh, god!" she gasped in shock.

And that's when I felt it.

White-hot pleasure shot through my veins as the walls of her vagina began to constrict around me. She sheathed my cock in heat, pulsing with desire. I pulled back slowly, then drove home, again and again, needing to feel her orgasm more than I needed my own. Her body writhed with pleasure, taking all I could give.

With her lush brown curls splayed over the pillow and her breasts bouncing as I rode her, she looked like a sensual, fiery goddess. Pushing her leg up higher, I gave her bottom a sharp slap.

"Yes!" she screamed out. "Again!"

I hit her again, this time a bit harder. Her pussy tightened more with every smack until she began to vibrate around my cock. She matched my every thrust, pulling at her restraints, moaning as I possessed her. When she screamed, the visual she created of her climax rocketing through her body compared to nothing else. Her eyes rolled back, and her sex tightened like a vice. I knew I wouldn't last much longer.

"It's my turn, angel," I hissed through clenched teeth as I gripped her hips.

"Yes. Let me feel it deep. Please, Alex!"

Krystina's spectacular plea sent me straight over the edge. Everything fell dark before a bright-white awareness overcame me. I plunged deep, allowing my seed to eject into the most intimate place in her body. Our connection was complete.

Panting and sated, I collapsed down, shifting slightly to the side so that I didn't crush her. When our breathing returned to a normal rhythm, I moved so I could untie Krystina's hands. There were marks on her wrists from her straining against them. The marks weren't the usual pink that often happened after she was tied up, but an angry red. The skin wasn't broken, but it had come damn close. I frowned and cursed silently, making a mental note not to use that kind of rope again.

Climbing from the bed, I retrieved a bottle of aloe from my small bathroom tote. Popping the cap, I sat on the edge of the mattress and began to massage the ointment into Krystina's wrists. She watched me as I worked, waiting patiently for me to finish. When I finally settled back against the pillows, she shifted to lay against my chest and let out a sigh of contentment. She traced small circles on my chest with her fingers and, within minutes, the motion became lax and her breathing slow and even. I glanced at the clock. We had less than thirty minutes before we had to meet Allyson and Matteo for dinner.

"We should probably get ready to go," I suggested to my sedate wife. If we laid here for much longer, I was sure she'd fall asleep.

"Mmmm," she murmured, then flipped onto her back. "I wonder what Ally and Matteo were doing while we were..."

"Doing it fast and dirty in Vegas?" I finished for her.

"You could say that," she said with a quiet laugh. "After our plane landed, they went their separate ways—or so it appeared. I can never quite tell with those two."

"I know," I mused. "I often wonder if there's more to them than they let on."

Saying that I wondered about it was an understatement. If I were a gambling man, I'd bet there was something more than friendship happening between our two best friends. However, I'd made a conscious choice not to express how strong my suspicions were to Krystina. Their relationship was none of our business, and I didn't want speculation to get in the way of our time here. We were in Las Vegas for one reason and for one reason only—to get away from months of agony and rediscover what it meant to live again.

Krystina wanted to escape—to let it all go. So far, we'd managed to do a pretty good job of achieving exactly that.

7

Alexander

Krystina and I stepped out of the elevator and walked across the main lobby of the hotel. Making our way to the exit, we were forced to walk through a large section of the hotel's casino once again. When we stepped outside, the summer heat assaulted us. It was a different heat than what I was used to in New York. Here it was dry and not nearly as sticky, but still every bit as stifling.

The valet had pulled up the Audi R8 convertible that I'd rented, and he stood patiently by its side waiting to hand me the keys. I looked around for Allyson and Matteo, but they weren't here yet. It would be miserable standing outside in the heat, and I half wondered if we should go back inside until they joined us.

I was about to say as much to Krystina but paused when I saw her eyes wide with wonder. She was smiling—really smiling—as she took in everything around her. She was clearly caught up in all the glitter and glam that I detested.

"Beauty is in the eye of the beholder," I remarked.

"Why do you say that?" she asked absently as she continued to look around.

"You're regarding everything around us with awe, but I barely see it. I can't look beyond your beautiful smile. It's a refreshing sight, angel."

Looking up at me, her smile widened. It was so breathtaking, reminding me that she was the reason I'd come to the city of sin. And I'd come back a million times more if it meant my wife kept beaming like that.

"Hey, guys!" called a familiar voice from behind me.

I turned and saw Ally and Matteo approaching. Matteo's mouth was cocked up in a lopsided grin. It was almost a smirk —an expression I'd seen many times before, although not recently.

Shit.

Matteo and I had been best friends for as long as I could remember. He had a terrible poker face, and I'd always been able to easily read his moods. There was no denying that freshly fucked look he was sporting. My friend had clearly just gotten laid, and I was fairly confident it wasn't with someone he'd just met, either. For starters, that wasn't his style. Plus, we'd only just arrived. The probability of it being a random hook-up was slim to none. That left only one other possibility.

I quickly glanced at Allyson. She was smiling and leaning in to hug Krystina. Allyson was clearly the better liar because she appeared as though nothing was amiss. Turning back to Matteo, I firmly gripped his shoulder and leaned in so only he could hear.

"I hope you know what you're doing, man," I whispered. "Just don't fuck it up. Krystina will have your balls if you do."

Matteo leaned back and tried to look surprised.

"What are you talking about?" he feigned.

I smirked.

"You can't bullshit me, Matt. I know you too well. I'm not sure why you're hiding it, but it's your secret to tell. I'll keep quiet for now but take my warning. Krystina isn't naïve. She'll figure it out soon enough and it's best if she hears it from one of you first."

"Are you ready, boys?" Krystina asked, coming up behind me on my left. "Ally is already in the car. We're just waiting on you two. By the way you have your heads together, it looks like you're scheming. What are you up to?"

Glancing down at her, I slid my arm around her waist. I tossed Matteo a knowing look as I pressed my lips to the top of Krystina's head.

"We aren't up to anything. Come on, angel. Dinner awaits."

THE DRIVE to the restaurant was an animated one. Despite the heat, Krystina and Allyson had insisted I keep the top down to better see the sights on Las Vegas Boulevard. While I found the mash-up replicas of famous places around the world to be a bit gaudy, I couldn't deny them from seeing the iconic Strip. It was home to the city's most famous hotels and casinos. From the dancing fountain shows and life-like volcanoes to the singing gondoliers and roller coasters, the women had their cellphone cameras at the ready to take pictures of it all.

During the short drive, music blasted from the car stereo and I found myself softening a bit toward Vegas. Perhaps it was Krystina's musical laughter ringing through the air whenever she saw something that delighted her. I couldn't be sure. All I knew was that by the time we reached Amore Tuscan

Steakhouse, the reluctance I'd had about Allyson's choice of vacation spot seemed to dissipate.

After we were seated and our drinks were ordered, Krystina and Allyson began discussing potential plans while we were here. Allyson wanted to see a Cirque du Soleil show, and Krystina wanted to find a trendy nightclub for dancing. They left little room for Matteo or me to have an opinion, so I just sat back and listened while Matteo scrutinized the menu. I was sure he was making comparisons to his menu for Krystina's Place. Whether he was critiquing or getting fresh ideas, I couldn't be sure.

The waitress returned with our drinks and placed them before each of us. I picked up my bourbon and seven and took a small sip, feeling content for the first time in a long while. As much as I loved my work, it felt good to be away from Stone Enterprise for a bit. I had competent employees and knew I could trust them while I was away. It made me appreciate how selective I'd been when hiring each and every one of them. I also knew that if one person stepped out of line, Laura would be right there to put them back in place. My secretary was a godsend, and there were days when I wondered if anything would get done without her.

"Are you all ready to order?" the waitress politely asked, interrupting my musings.

I gave a nod to Krystina, but she waved me away and said, "I haven't decided yet. Everything just looks so good. You guys order first."

The waitress moved on to Allyson, who ordered a Caesar salad and the Atlantic Salmon. I settled on escargot as an appetizer and a porterhouse steak for my main. Matteo, on the other hand, seemed to order enough food to feed a small village. He didn't skip one part of the traditional Italian courses —*antipasti, zuppe, pasta,* and *secondi.*

I snorted a laugh.

"What can I say? I need to know my competition," Matteo said somewhat defensively.

"I would hardly consider this place competition to your restaurant in New York," Allyson replied dryly.

The waitress just raised an eyebrow, appearing slightly amused, before turning her attention back to Krystina.

"Have you decided what you'd like to order, Miss?"

"Yes," Krystina began as she pointed to the menu. "I'd like to start with a cup of *zuppa di fagioli*, with the petite filet mignon for my main dish."

"Yes, ma'am. How would you like that prepared?"

"Medium well, please. And can I have—" She stopped short and looked down at her cell phone sitting on the table in front of her. The screen was lit up and it was vibrating. Looking back up at the waitress, she shook her head and apologized. "I'm sorry. Can I please have sauteed mushrooms with that?"

"Absolutely," the waitress replied.

After she walked away, I asked, "Who was calling?"

"I don't know." She shrugged. "I keep getting calls from an unknown number. That's the third one today. I hesitate to answer it after the paparazzi debacle we went through a few years back."

"That was awful," Allyson agreed.

"That was after the sleezy photographer snagged a picture of you in a bathing suit, right?" Matteo asked.

"Yes," Krystina said with a disgusted shake of her head. "Then he leaked our address and my phone number. After three days of perverts leaving me voicemails, I decided to go through the hassle of changing my number—not that I had much of an option. Alex just about lost his mind once he heard some of the messages."

I remained silent as the three of them discussed more

details about the incident, my concern growing by the minute. I couldn't help but wonder if the unknown caller was Michael Ketry. I would need to get with Hale about it as soon as we got back to New York. I couldn't bear the idea of Krystina being confronted with more turmoil.

I sat back in my chair and took another sip of the bourbon and seven, considering the potential situation. My wife had gone through enough over the past couple of years. She didn't need any more pain. It wasn't that I didn't think she couldn't handle the possibility of meeting the father she never knew— my wife was the one of the strongest people I knew. I just didn't want her to have to deal with it. After all the heartache, she more than deserved a bit of peace.

8

Krystina

My face scrunched tight, and my stomach felt like there was a lead ball in it. I had been dreaming of something, but I couldn't recall what it was. I only knew that whatever had haunted me in the night left me feeling empty. Slowly, I opened my eyes and looked around. The room was dim with a subtle glow coming from two ornate nightlight sconces positioned on the wall opposite the bed. I felt disoriented, and it took me a moment to remember I was in Las Vegas. Once I remembered, a terrible feeling of dread settled over me.

I won't be able to see Liliana this morning.

My heart constricted and my face pinched up again. I couldn't stop the tears from welling even if I tried.

I abandoned my little girl.

If I stayed in bed, Alexander would eventually know I was

crying, and I didn't want him to see my tears for reasons that were hard to explain. I knew it was ridiculous to hide from him —he was my husband, after all. But a part of me was ashamed to cry. Carrying on at this point was silly. No amount of crying would bring my baby back. But another part of me wanted to be selfish with my tears. It was as if they were a symbol of the grief that I needed to keep all for myself. It was a twisted and weird thing to think, but it was how I felt all the same.

Tossing off the blankets, I slid out of bed and made my way to the bathroom. A quick glance at the clock told me it was just after four in the morning. I wasn't sure if Alexander was awake, and I didn't look back to find out. Instead, I entered the bathroom and closed the door behind me. Leaning against the door, I slowly slid to the floor, dropped my head into my hands, and let the tears silently fall.

Unexpectedly, the room began to spin, and a sort of tunnel vision occurred. I blinked rapidly, struggling to regain focus. My narrowed sight remained, and my heart began to race. I wasn't sure how much time had passed. It could have been minutes or hours and I wouldn't have known. I could only focus on the heavy weight pressing down on me, robbing me of precious oxygen. I clutched my chest, struggling to find breath.

"Krystina," I heard from the other side of the door.

Alex.

The thought of him seemed to make my heart pound faster. I gasped for air, feeling as if I might suffocate, and I wondered if this was what it felt like to die.

There was a knock on the door. It was quiet at first, and then it became more persistent.

"Krystina!" I heard Alexander call again.

A moment later, I felt myself being pushed.

Who is pushing me?

Am I having a heart attack?

I want to throw up.

Who is pushing me?

"Krystina, move away from the door so I can come in."

Alex.

He's the one who's pushing me.

With the door.

I'm in the way.

Need to move.

I shifted to the side, absently following Alexander's request as fragmented thoughts swirled in my mind. I clawed at my chest. It was as if I were having an out-of-body experience. I could see what was happening, but it felt like a silent movie with only the sound of my heart pounding in my ears. I seemed to watch rather than feel Alexander as he picked me up and carried me over to the toilet. Lowering the lid, he set me down and began to rub his hand up and down my back.

"Christ, you're fucking shaking like a leaf," he cursed.

Was I?

It was strange that I hadn't noticed until he pointed it out. The only thing I could focus on was my racing heart and the nausea. I clutched my stomach and began to rock, trying once more to regain my focus—to rid myself of this terrible tunnel vision. I only succeeded in breaking out in a cold sweat.

Am I going crazy?

"Alex, make it stop," I choked, but I wasn't sure if a sound had even come out.

"Krystina, I think you're having a panic attack," he said in the calmest voice I'd ever heard him use. "Please concentrate on your breathing. Deep breath in, and then slowly exhale."

I did as he asked, repeating the action on Alexander's command. At some point during the exercise, my racing heart began to slow, and my vision returned to normal. I'd been staring at the floor, and when I raised my gaze to look at my husband, worry lines marred his beautiful face.

"I don't know what happened," I began. "All I remember is waking up from a dream, but I don't recall what it was about. Then I was in the bathroom, and I couldn't breathe. Then you were here and..."

Suddenly, the reason I'd been upset in the first place came rushing back.

Liliana.

Tears instantly sprang into my eyes and my heart pounded at an almost painful staccato.

"Shhh," Alexander soothed as he ran his thumb over my cheek to brush away a tear that had spilled over. "Whatever it is, it will be okay."

"No," I disagreed with a vehement shake of my head. "It won't be okay. Coming here was a mistake. I should have known I wouldn't be able to leave her."

I didn't have to explain who I was referring to. He knew. His sad expression said as much.

"Come on, angel. It's barely dawn. Let's crawl back into bed. I have something I want to show you."

Without waiting for my response, he slipped an arm under my knees and another behind my back, cradling me to his chest once more. Carrying me from the bathroom as if I weighted nothing more than a feather, he brought me back to bed. Once I was settled, he climbed in next to me and pulled me close. I was exhausted. I'd never had a panic attack before, and if that was in fact what I'd just had, I never wanted to experience anything like it again.

"Do you think I should call Dr. Tumblin once it's a reasonable hour in New York?" I asked quietly.

"You can if you'd like, but I want you to watch this first."

Reaching over to the bedside table, he picked up his

cellphone. Raising his arm, he held the phone up horizontally so we could both view the screen. Clicking on his camera roll app, he pulled up a video and pressed play. It was a video of the backseat of the Maserati with Samuel in the front seat behind the wheel. Then, suddenly, the screen flipped, and Alexander's face came into view.

"I know this won't be the same," he said in the video. "My hope is that this might help on the days you can't go in person. I love you, angel. I love you so much that it hurts."

I frowned, feeling momentarily confused, until the screen flipped around again to show the car passing under the gated archway of Westwood Hills Cemetery. My breath caught.

"Alex, what is this?" I whispered.

"I asked Samuel to recreate your morning routine."

I couldn't tear my eyes away from the screen as I watched Samuel navigate the narrow asphalt road that led to Liliana's grave. When he slowed the car to a stop in front of the giant maple, Alexander reached for my hand and gave it a soft squeeze.

Samuel came around to open the car door for Alexander, and I watched our trusted driver hand my husband a solitary lily—just as he did for me each morning. My throat clogged with a million emotions. I almost couldn't believe what I was seeing. I recalled everything Alexander had said to me about why he didn't go to the cemetery. He thought it would rip him apart, yet here he was recreating this precious moment—all for me.

I expected him to start walking toward the headstone, but he stood still with the camera pointed straight ahead.

"I have to ask you something and I want you to be honest," Alexander asserted. "Samuel told me that you don't walk to the gravesite right away but stand silent near the car for a considerable amount of time. What do you think about?"

Still unable to take my eyes off the screen, my response was automatic but hushed. It was as if speaking too loud would somehow ruin the moment.

"I relive those brief moments of joy I felt when I got to hold our daughter. It's the best part of my day. But then I remember all the pain that followed. Losing her, and then remembering how the doctor ticked off all the reasons I couldn't bear another child, with each explanation falling like wicked dominoes. And well... It might sound like torture to you, but I just keep hoping that one of these days I'll leave the cemetery only recalling the joy. I don't want to remember the bad stuff."

"Krystina, I—"

"Shhh. Don't. Let me have this moment you created for me."

I continued to watch the video, staring mesmerized at the screen as Alexander walked through the serene cemetery toward Liliana's headstone. When he reached it, he replaced the lily from the day before with a new one—just like I did each day. Then he stood up, allowing the camera to focus on the headstone's inscription. The trees rustled in the background, and I could almost feel the warm breeze on my face. And if I imagined hard enough, it could be like I was really there. Alexander was right. It wasn't the same as being physically present in the cemetery—but it was something.

And at that second, I felt as if my heart might burst from the onslaught of emotion. I'd felt so alone for so long, yet Alexander had been there the whole time just waiting for the moment I needed him most. My husband—my everything, my white picket fence—he got it. In my loneliness, I hadn't given him enough credit. He really understood me after all.

9

Alexander

Krystina and Allyson had packed the day with sightseeing. After the emotional morning, the full schedule had been a much-needed distraction. From the Shark Reef Aquarium to driving a Lamborghini around the Speed Vegas Motorsports Park, the women had planned it so there wasn't a minute to spare. Krystina had understandably seemed off for most of the day. She was trying her best to keep up her smile, but I saw beneath the façade. It wasn't until we sat down to dinner that she seemed more like herself.

Still, the day was far from over, and by the time we returned to the hotel to get ready for a night on the town, I was exhausted. Krystina had managed to fall back asleep this morning after her panic attack, but I hadn't. I'd been too consumed with worry. The state I'd found her in on the bathroom floor was extremely concerning. She wasn't prone to panic attacks, and I hoped this wasn't a sign of something more serious.

Despite having no desire to go back out, Krystina and Allyson were excited to try out the nightclub Krystina had found online, and I didn't want to deflate their enthusiastic bubble. I'd never heard of the club they wanted to go to, and if we were in New York, I would have vetted it before stepping foot inside. Letting my guard down was typically never an option because there was almost always a tabloid photographer lurking in the shadows waiting to catch me in a compromising position.

I considered this as Krystina and I rode the elevator down to the lobby.

"What did you say this club was called?" I asked.

"The Red Door."

"Hmm," I mused. While the press frenzy was once something I'd taken in stride, everything changed after marrying Krystina. I never wanted to take chances with her safety, and I was kicking myself for not running a check on the establishment we were about to go to and see what sort of security measures were in place. Everything about this trip had been so last minute, there just hadn't been time to conduct any research. "I should call Hale and have him run a check on the place."

"Oh, no you don't," she replied with a small laugh. "Hale doesn't need to do any such thing. You need to trust me. I know the risks. Put that controlling monster living inside you away before he wreaks havoc on our night."

I raised an eyebrow and smirked as the elevator doors opened.

"Controlling monster?" I teased.

"You know exactly what I'm talking about."

"I just worry about—"

"I know what you worry about, Alex. May I remind you that we're in Vegas? You said yourself that we aren't as recognizable here."

I pressed my lips together and decided not to push my concerns.

When we exited the hotel, I spotted Matteo and Allyson standing near the curb. I was pleased to see the Audi already waiting for us as well. As we approached, the valet opened the back car door. Allyson climbed in first. Krystina stood by waiting to follow Allyson, and it wasn't hard to miss the valet's eyes traveling up my wife's legs.

Down boy. She's all mine.

Making my way over to her, I placed a possessive hand on the small of her back and guided her inside the car. The valet handed me the keys and quickly looked away when he caught my cool stare. I couldn't help it. Krystina brought out every possessive bone in my body, fueling my compulsion to make sure everyone around us knew who she belonged to. But I also couldn't blame the valet for gazing upon my wife for just a little too long. With those sky-high fuck me heels on her feet, she looked like a goddamn sex goddess tonight.

After taking nearly two hours to primp and prune and do whatever it was women did in the bathroom for a ridiculous amount of time, she'd exited the bathroom of our hotel room with darker than normal makeup. The smokey shadow and sultry pink lips gave her a mysterious allure. She wore a short black skirt and a royal blue satin tank top. The plunging neckline was revealing, but not overly so. Rhinestones studded the thin straps, accentuating the slender curve of her shoulders. Around her neck was the triskelion necklace that I'd purchased for her back when we were dating. The sight of it made my cock twitch, and all I could think about was tossing her on the bed like a violent sex fiend and fucking her so hard, she wouldn't be able to walk tomorrow. The five-inch stilettos on her feet just amplified that urge. They emphasized the shape of her long legs, sending a very clear signal that any hot-blooded male couldn't ignore.

While the outfit sent all sorts of messages to my groin, it had been her hair that had given me pause. Gone were the lush curls I'd come to love. She'd straightened them completely, and I wasn't sure what I thought about the absence of her thick waves. She looked damn hot, that was for sure. But she also looked different—dangerous almost, like a sexually-charged vixen on the hunt for her next victim.

I was tempted to tell her to change but knew from past experiences that she rarely responded well to extreme possessiveness. Instead, I resigned myself to keeping her close by my side tonight.

It was a short drive to The Red Door. When we pulled around the circular drive to the VIP parking area, I glanced up and down the row of cars waiting to be driven away by a valet. Every vehicle had a six-figure price tag, and the passengers climbing out of them were dressed to match. Clearly, this was an upscale place. I forced myself to relax. Krystina was right. The club was probably fine, and I needed to learn to trust her judgement.

After I handed the car key over to the valet, the four of us climbed out. Keeping my wife tucked to my side, we made our way toward the building. Allyson and Matteo fell into step beside us as we walked toward the club's main entrance. The women spoke animatedly to each other, excited to enjoy our second night in the city.

"I'm dying to see the inside of this place. I hope it's as good as you said. Your hair looks amazing, by the way!" Allyson gushed as she reached over to finger one of Krystina's shiny locks.

"Thanks. I decided to take advantage of the dry Nevada air and do something different for a change," Krystina said with a shrug.

I heard their chatter, but I was barely listening at the same time. For some reason, the closer we came to the building, the more anxious I became. Something seemed off but I couldn't put my finger on what it was. The hairs on the back of my neck stood on end as the foreboding feeling grew.

When we entered, we were immediately confronted with yet another casino that we'd have to walk through to get to our intended destination. It didn't matter where you went in Vegas. The opportunity to gamble was smack in your face at every turn. Even the airport had slot machines.

The casino crowd at the club was livelier than it was at our hotel. At first, I'd attributed it to the late hour, but quickly realized all the commotion was due to a Let-It-Ride tournament.

"Hang on," Matteo said, placing his hand on my arm and then pointing to the card table. "The game looks like it's in the final round. Let's watch for a minute."

I was about to protest, but Allyson and Krystina already seemed enraptured. I pursed my lips with annoyance, wanting to be anywhere else. I didn't know what it was about gambling that bothered me so much. Perhaps it was because I saw glimpses of my abusive, alcoholic father in the eyes of too many gambling addicts. I recognized that raging, manic need all too well. At the end of the day, addiction was addiction, whether it was the Blackjack table or the bottle. Both ruined lives.

Ten minutes later, the crowd around the table had grown considerably. It was down to the final two players. In the end, there would only be one man left standing. Judging by their bets, I could make an educated guess on who it might be. One man was all in, stacking every last one of his chips into three neat piles. Either he had something really good or he was just incredibly stupid. Either could easily be the case in this city.

The community hand was revealed one card at a time, showing a ten of spades and a jack of spades. Neither player had pulled back a bet. The lively crowd had fallen silent and the tension in the room was palpable. When the man who'd put forth all his chips finally flipped his hand over, he had a queen, king, and an ace—all in spades. A royal flush.

Lucky bastard.

There were several gasps in the room, but other than that, everyone remained silent. Even though the first man couldn't possibly be beat, any celebration had to wait until the other player revealed his cards. When he tossed out three aces in an angry huff, the game was over. The gathering crowd erupted in applause, many congratulating the man who had the royal flush with pats on the back.

Krystina laughed, the sound a high succinct reverb. I hadn't heard her laugh quite like that in far too long. It was music to my ears, and no matter how hard I tried, I couldn't stop the corners of my mouth from curving up in a small smile. It didn't matter if I detested gambling. Her laughter and energy were contagious. I followed her eyes to see what was amusing her and saw that a blonde woman had weaseled her way onto the winner's lap. She was currently planting a long and exaggerated kiss on his lips.

"Round of drinks on me!" the winner called out to everyone after the woman had pulled away. This incited the crowd further.

"I think we can buy our own drinks once we're inside the club, don't you?" I suggested to my group, hoping to persuade them to get moving.

"That was fun to watch, but I agree," Krystina said with a nod.

We continued until we passed an A-frame sign with an arrow directing us toward the club entrance. I looked ahead and saw the words The Red Door in bright neon letters. As we approached the red double doors, obviously painted for the club's name, the ominous feeling returned. I didn't know why, but something was telling me we shouldn't enter.

Before I could voice my concerns, Matteo pushed through, motioning for Allyson, Krystina, and I to pass as he held one of the doors open.

"Matt, I don't think—" I began as I walked past him, but I was cut off by the sudden sound of a loud drumbeat. Almost instantly, we were surrounded by women in grass skirts and coconut bras. One of them came up to me, placing a silk petal lei around my neck.

"What the hell. Must everything be so exaggerated in this town?" I muttered.

Krystina, on the other hand, squealed with delight.

"This is so great!" she announced.

I turned toward her. "Krystina, what is all this? I thought you said this was a nightclub."

"It is, sir," said one of the women sporting coconuts and a grass skirt. "Follow me to the club room where you can dance and mingle. Tonight is luau night. Everyone gets lei'd."

Then she winked and gave me a knowing look. I'd caught the woman's play on words, and was almost certain she wasn't referring to the flowers around my neck. However, everyone else seemed oblivious. Allyson laughed, and Krystina looped her arm through mine.

"Don't look so serious, Alex. Come on. I've been looking forward to dancing with you all day."

My jaw flexed but I didn't say anything. Instead, I stayed silent as our group followed the animated woman into the club toward the VIP booth Krystina had reserved for us.

An attractive blonde with olive skin and a tight black dress walked past us. She looked Matteo up and down as she sauntered over toward the bar, shaking her round ass as she went. My brow furrowed, bothered by her for some odd reason, and I glanced at Matteo. She was exactly his type and I'd expected him to notice her. However, when I looked at my friend, he appeared engrossed in whatever Allyson was saying and didn't seem to catch the come-hither side-eye the blonde had given him.

I exhaled heavily, just imagining the pending doom that was sure to come between Allyson and Matteo. They were just too different. Matteo was a hopeless romantic. He loved women —all women—but he'd insisted that when he found the one, that would be it and he'd cherish her for the rest of his life. I worried because I'd never seen Matteo look at another woman like he was looking at Allyson. The problem was that she was entirely too flighty. Pinning her down would be near impossible. They would never work.

Once we were seated, my sense of foreboding about the nightclub intensified. There was a feel in the air—an unmistakable sexual vibe that I was familiar with. It was a feeling I only felt when I was in Club O. While Matteo and Allyson debated over individual mixed drinks or bottle service, I preoccupied myself with assessing our surroundings.

The club was circular with a high, steel-beamed ceiling and curved walls surrounding a large dance floor. A decent crowd had gathered there, comprised mostly of couples dancing. After watching them for a few moments, it appeared as if everything was normal. Still, that strange feeling of something being amiss refused to abate. My eyes traveled the circumference of the room, noticing several red doors lining the walls. Upon closer inspection, the alarm bells that had been quietly ringing in my head went on blast.

Something really isn't right.

I quickly pulled my phone from my pocket and looked up the website for The Red Door. At first glance, everything seemed legit—enticing actually—and I could see why it had appealed to Krystina. However, the site clearly stated that this was an *adult* nightclub. That one word gave the club a whole new meaning. I clicked on the site menu and saw there was a members-only link. I opened it and discovered there was a five-hundred-dollar fee to access the content.

Fuck it.

I hurriedly went through the steps to pay it, needing confirmation for my suspicions before voicing them aloud. Krystina, Allyson, and Matteo would think I'd gone mad with paranoia if I was wrong.

As soon as the payment went through, I was granted access to the restricted area of the site. It took me less than thirty seconds to confirm what I already knew. I glanced up at my wife and our two friends. Allyson and Matteo were still discussing drink options. Krystina tapped her foot in time with the music, looking around with anxious excitement. All three were completely naïve to the precarious situation we were in.

"Shit," I hissed and shook my head.

"What's wrong?" Krystina yelled over the loud music in the club. She pulled her hair to the side, allowing it to drape over one shoulder to reveal the curve of her neck. My stomach clenched. My wife was fucking gorgeous, and she was prime meat in a place like this. I had to get her out of here.

"We need to leave."

"What do you mean? We just got here."

I pointed to the doors along the walls of the circular room, mentally kicking myself for not following my normal precautions. I always listened to my instincts, and I knew I should have had Hale run a check.

"Look at the names painted on the walls above the door frames. This isn't a normal dance club, Krystina," I said irritably.

Allyson and Matteo seemed to have taken note of my tone. They stopped haggling over what drinks to order and turned to where I pointed.

"The Basement, The Multiplier, The Fountain, The Watcher, and The Bare Room," Matteo read aloud. "So what?"

I couldn't believe how blind they were to something that was so obvious to me.

Shaking my head, I looked pointedly at each of them and said, "We are currently VIP guests at the hottest swinger's sex club in Las Vegas."

10

Krystina

I raised my eyebrows and laughed.

"Alex, be real. I think I would know if I booked us a VIP table at a sex club," I dismissed.

"Apparently not, because that's exactly what you did," Alexander quipped.

"I'm not that naïve. I read the reviews online. Nothing was explicit, but..." I trailed off momentarily, recalling the subtle innuendoes that I'd read. "I suppose a part of me knew there was something a little risqué about the place. But I just figured, what the hell? We're in Sin City. I just hadn't anticipated exactly how naughty the club would be. I certainly didn't know it was a swinger's sex club—if that is, in fact, what this place is. I mean, everything seems pretty chill. I honestly think you might be overthinking things."

"I'm not. Look," Alexander said, thrusting his phone in my direction.

I took it from him and immediately recognized the website I'd been on when I first discovered the club. However, I was looking at an area of the site I hadn't seen when making our reservation.

Allyson came to peek her head over my shoulder to see what I was looking at. I glanced up at her, bit my lip, then quickly scanned the internet pages depicting all the rooms Matteo had just read off.

The pictures of the room called The Basement reminded me more of a medieval dungeon with whips, shackles, and chains hanging from cinderblock walls. I'd seen some interesting things at Club O, but the paraphernalia here was more extreme than anything I ever saw there.

The Fountain room looked to be nothing more than a shallow wading pool surrounded by carefully constructed waterfalls. It was reminiscent of a Roman bathhouse, but I was fairly certain it wasn't as innocent as it appeared.

The images of the other three rooms weren't as primitive, but more whimsical with a strange sexual allure. Scrolling down to the room descriptions for The Watcher, The Bare Room, and The Multiplier, I saw the name accurately fit their purpose as well. The Watcher was for voyeurs, and there were no clothes allowed in The Bare Room. The Multiplier was basically a big orgy room, something that had never been of interest to me—and it never would. Just the idea of so many naked, sweaty bodies made me want to slather my body in hand sanitizer. I scrunched up my nose, realizing how acutely aware of germs I'd become after living through a pandemic with Alexander.

"Holy shit," Allyson said, then let out a low whistle. She

took a step back, tossing her long blonde hair behind her shoulders with the flip of a hand and scanned the room. She appeared to be seeing everything with new eyes, just as I was.

I pressed my lips together and tried to decide how to handle the current predicament. Frowning, I looked back up at Alexander.

"Clearly, this place isn't quite what I thought it was going to be," I explained again with a shrug. "I did a search for adult nightclubs in Las Vegas. This one looked the most interesting, so I booked it."

"The keywords you used in the internet search was your problem. There's a huge difference between a Las Vegas nightclub and an *adult* nightclub," Alexander pointed out sardonically. Leaning in so only I could hear, he quietly said, "I'd be a hypocrite to condemn what goes on here, Krystina. My issue is you being in a sex club that I haven't vetted. This isn't like Club O. There are rules there, and I have yet to see anything like that here. To me, it's about safety."

"Honestly, as crazy as that website looks, does it really matter if this place is some sort of kinky club?" Allyson asked, unaware of the concerns Alexander had just voiced to me. "Everything seems alright. I mean, aside from the outlying side rooms, this place is basically just a dance club—and a killer dance club at that. It's exactly what Krys planned for us. Plus, it's getting late. Do we really want to waste time finding someplace else to go?"

Matteo, who had been silent and contemplative up until this point, nodded his agreement.

"I'm with Ally on this one," he agreed. "Nobody is making us go into the other rooms, and if anyone approaches us, we'll just let them know we aren't interested. We're all adults. Let's just hang out here for the night like we planned."

Reservation was apparent in my husband's eyes, so I placed a reassuring hand on his arm.

"Alex, it will be fine. You'll see."

"This isn't like back home," Alexander insisted. "In New York, I know what to expect in the so-called underworld. Vegas is different. It's seedier and more dangerous."

The ominous tone of his voice sent a chill down my spine, but I ignored it. I needed this distraction tonight. I'd play-acted all day, pretending to enjoy myself even though all I wanted to do was burst into tears every time Liliana came to mind. I couldn't let Alexander's need to control everything ruin the night. It was just like Allyson and Matteo had said. The club only had to be what we made it of it—and we wanted to dance. Nothing more.

"You worry too much, Alex" I brushed off, determined to make the best of our situation. Turning to Allyson and Matteo, I asked, "Did you guys decide on drinks? Are we doing bottle service or a la carte from the bar?"

"A la carte. They have quite a few luau themed drinks that I want to try," Allyson said.

"Perfect. Then let's go get a drink, shall we?" Looping my arm through hers, Allyson and I made our way toward the bar.

THIRTY MINUTES LATER, Alexander had seemed to relax a bit, but I would still catch the furtive glances he'd toss around the room every so often. He was wary, and rightly so. As the night wore on, we definitely witnessed some questionable behavior. Thankfully, none of it was directed toward any one of us. Still, despite Alexander's many reservations, the nightclub was absolutely amazing—the best I'd ever been in. Sure, New York had some great hot spots, but no club that I'd visited had quite the same vibe that this one did. The music and energetic atmosphere were intense in all the best ways.

"I don't care what this place truly is once you pull back the curtains. The way the DJ is mixing the steel drum island vibe with modern house music is awesome! He's killing it!" Allyson praised, echoing my thoughts as she spun past me. Matteo caught hold of the lei around her neck and yanked her in his direction. Then, to my surprise, she shimmied down his body as if he was her own personal stripper pole.

I arched an eyebrow as Allyson worked her way back up, gripping his hips as she went. Matteo wrapped an arm around her slim waist and pulled her in close. He began to gyrate his hips against hers, and she reciprocated in kind. The way Matteo was looking at my friend had to be illegal in some countries. I decided right then and there that I would corner Allyson about Matteo as soon as we got home. I knew there just had to be something between them. I was sure of it. Their visible chemistry was undeniable.

As the night wore on, the DJ transitioned from Hawaiian sounds to an eclectic mashup of alternative indie rock and house music that oozed sexiness. Alexander held me close, and we moved together. I wasn't sure why we didn't go out dancing more often. My husband was as skilled on the dance floor as he was in the bedroom, his assertive lead no different than his dominant side when we were intimate. He moved with fluid strength, using his familiarity with my body to his every advantage.

I got lost in the rhythm, using the way it made me feel as an escape from everything and anything. I felt like myself for the first time in so long. I'd needed this more than I'd realized.

"Do you like this song?" Alexander asked, taking a step

back to cast an appreciative look up and down my body. His gaze was hungry.

"I do. Why do you ask?"

"Because I need to know if I should find more songs like this to add to your playlists. I like seeing your ass move like that. You're a red-hot, fiery goddess—my goddess," he added with a gruff, possessive edge in his voice.

My core tightened at his words. Gripping my hips, he pulled me close once more. I stared into his heated eyes. Our impassioned connection was almost more than I could take, and I forced myself to look away from his smoldering gaze before I did something scandalous.

"I don't know about fiery, but I'm definitely thirsty," I said breathlessly. I held up my glass. "I could use a refill."

"What would you like?" he asked.

I pressed my finger to my lips and looked down at what remained of the pineapple and vodka concoction in my glass. I was usually a wine drinker, and I was unaccustomed to the stronger alcohol content in a mixer. Nevertheless, I couldn't deny that the fruity drink Allyson had ordered for me was delicious.

"This Maui Island Breeze was tasty. I'll have another one of these, please."

Alexander began to step away, but something behind me caught his eye and he paused. Turning, I spotted an attractive couple dancing. The male had white-blond hair and was dressed casually, yet stylish. He looked familiar to me, but I couldn't quite place him. The woman wore a dress that left little to the imagination. The silver fabric clung to her body, pouring over her like liquid. They moved gracefully, completely in sync with one another. Pushing aside the woman's long mane of red hair, the man leaned in to say something into her ear. Whatever he said made her grin and she tossed her head back in laughter. But a split second later, her face turned serious when he wrapped his fingers around her neck and squeezed. She quickly brought her arms up and gipped his forearms tightly.

I gasped.

Was he choking her?

I nearly shouted for him to let go of her. However, my natural concern that he might be hurting the woman melted away when he unexpectedly dropped her into a low, sweeping dip. With her back straight as a board, her long hair skimmed the floor before he swung her back up until they were nose to nose. His intent was anything but vicious. The sultry gleam in her eyes told me there was nothing nefarious about the chokehold at all. They had timed the drop perfectly with the song's crescendo, and I found myself gaping at the pure, unadulterated sexual vibe that emanated around them. I felt my face flush as heat spread through me. There was something so very primal about their actions, and you'd have to be numb to not be affected by it.

"What was that?" I asked, more to myself than anyone else.

"Choke drop," Allyson replied.

I turned and saw that she and Matteo had stopped dancing to watch the couple as well. Matteo released a slow whistle and shook his head in amazement.

"I've never heard of it," Alexander said with a frown.

"No, I don't imagine you would have since you and Krys aren't on social media," she explained. "A choke drop was part of a dance someone did on TikTok a few months back. They hash tagged it as a choke drop and the video went viral—and rightly so. That move is sexy as all hell."

I glanced back at the couple with renewed interest. The male dancer caught my eye and tossed me a flirty wink. I flushed at having been caught staring, and quickly glanced over at Alexander. Thankfully, he was looking at Allyson and didn't seem to have noticed the man's flirtations. The last thing I wanted to deal with tonight was my husband's jealousy.

"I'm going to get Krystina another drink from the bar. Do you want one?" he asked Allyson.

"Sure. I could use a refill," Allyson replied.

"I'll come with you," Matteo offered.

Alexander looked toward the bar. I followed his gaze and spotted a long line of people waiting to get drinks. He seemed to have noticed it as well because he frowned and shook his head.

"We paid for a VIP table, yet we haven't seen a single waiter or waitress since we got here," Alexander said irritably. "Matt, that line is massive, and I don't want to leave the girls alone for too long. You should stay here."

"You can't be serious," Allyson admonished and rolled her eyes. Then she winked and added in an exaggerated southern accent "Bless your heart, Alex, but I think us fragile wallflowers can handle ourselves for a short while."

I stifled a laugh, then reached over to place an assuring hand on Alexander's forearm. However, before I could touch him, Allyson grabbed hold of my wrist and yanked me in the direction of the dance floor.

"Ally, wait. I—" I faltered, glancing back at a very annoyed looking Alexander.

"Come on!" Allyson insisted. "It's Taylor Swift's latest. I love this song. Let's dance!"

There was no stopping my friend once she set her mind to something, so I just went with it.

We both moved to the rhythm on the dance floor. I wasn't typically a Taylor Swift fan, but the sensual vibe of the current song was great for dancing. Apparently, a lot of other people liked the song too because the dance floor seemed to crowd relatively fast. I glanced up to see if I could spot Alexander, but there was no way to see him through the throng of twisting bodies. Assuming he and Matteo had gone to the bar, I went back to swaying to the music.

We'd been on the dance floor for less than five minutes when I felt a hand wrap around my right arm. Turning, I came eye to eye with the man who'd performed the so-called choke drop with the red-headed woman. He was tall and muscular, and his blond wavy hair was cut long, leaving it to touch the tops of his shoulders. His eyes were ice blue, almost cold, and undeniably calculating.

I hadn't thought he looked intimidating before, but without the protection of Alexander by my side, a wave of anxiousness hit me. This was a swinger's club after all. I'd have to be careful to not give the wrong impression.

"We saw you watching us earlier," he said, and then lifted his chin in the direction of his dance partner. "It was when we did the choke drop. We could teach you how to do it if you want."

"Oh, gosh no," I said with a laugh. "I can hold my own, but a move like that would only show everyone that I secretly have two left feet."

"Oh, I don't know. Your moves look pretty good to me," he told me with a teasing wink.

I smiled awkwardly, already sensing how quickly this conversation could turn if I wasn't careful.

"Um...thanks, I guess," I said as I glanced over toward Allyson. She looked curiously at me and danced her way closer so she could hear the conversation over the music. The man's dance partner did the same until all four of us were in a huddle of sorts.

"I'm Logan and this is my wife, Cherise," he introduced, and they both extended a hand to Allyson and me.

"I'm Ally and this is Krys," Allyson replied.

"Have you been here before?" Cherise asked.

"No. It's our first time. We're from New York," Allyson explained, and I wanted to kick her. The last thing we should be doing was giving out personal details about ourselves in a place like this.

"Ah, newbies," Logan said with a knowing look. "I thought so when I saw you earlier up near the bar."

And that's when I realized where I recognized him from. He'd been in line at the bar when we first came in.

"That's why you look familiar," I said. "You suggested the Maui Island Breeze to Allyson."

"I did. It's the best drink on the menu," he confirmed, winking at me again for the third time tonight. He did it so often, and I half wondered if it was a nervous tick.

"I'm not a fan of pineapple, so I ordered that for Krys," Allyson said as she continued to bop along to the music. "I got a Mai Tai instead."

"Oh, really?" Cherise remarked. A look of surprise appeared on her face, but it disappeared so quickly, I thought I'd imagined it.

"I'm sure both drinks are great," Logan quickly added, and then pointed upward. "Song change. This is a good one for couples dancing, too. Since you're new here, the best advice I can give is to just relax. Let things come as they may."

"That's what she said," Cherise said with a smirk, causing Allyson to laugh.

Logan grinned and I just smiled awkwardly, not wanting to give the couple any encouragement. There was something unsettling about them and we'd already engaged with them long enough. Allyson, for as worldly as she was, was showing her naivety. From my time with Alexander and the few occasions I'd been to Club O, I'd learned a lot about the dos and do nots in places like this. The moment Logan and Cherise first started talking to us, I'd noted how they were standing just a little too close for comfort. I had no doubt they were testing the waters to see if we were interested in more than just friendly conversation.

Logan reached up and placed his hand on my waist. Instinctively, I recoiled and pushed it away.

"I'm sorry, but I'm here with someone. My husband, actually. He's up at the bar—"

"I know. I saw him standing with you earlier. When he returns, he can join us," Logan said easily, allowing the corners of his mouth to turn up in a suggestive smile. "The more the merrier."

It wasn't hard to decipher the true meaning of his words. I had to shut this down—now.

"Oh, no. We aren't here for that. Really," I insisted.

"Aren't you, though? The dance floor is the best place to find others who want to play." He reached for me once again and I took a step back.

"I'm serious. We aren't here for that," I repeated nervously, glancing behind me to see if I could see Alexander. I spotted Allyson engrossed in a conversation with Cherise, not noticing that anything was amiss with Logan. "Look, my husband will be back any minute and—"

I stopped short when he stepped closer, slid his arms around my hips and cupped my behind. Yanking me close, he squeezed.

"A firm ass. Cherise will like that," he growled.

"Hey, get the hell off me!" I said, pushing at his chest. "I already told you—"

However, I didn't get to finish my sentence before I was

roughly pulled back by Alexander. Once I was safely out of Logan's clutches, my husband moved to stand in front of me. He was holding my drink, and I half expected him to slam it to the floor—either that or into the face of the man who dared to touch me.

Alexander angled his body to look back and forth between Logan and me, his jaw set tight.

"Fuck off," he growled at Logan, causing the man to put his hands up in surrender and slowly back away.

Shit.

We'd been here before—and I was *not* going to let it happen again. I recognized the expression on Alexander's face. He looked murderous, and I had no intention of bailing him out of a Las Vegas jail cell simply because he didn't trust me to handle myself.

Just as I was about to step forward and stop my husband from hitting Logan, he rounded on me.

"This is exactly why I didn't want to be here. You're too naïve," Alexander lashed out harshly. "I don't know what you were thinking by choosing this place for us tonight. You're practically inviting people to grope you. Or perhaps that's what you wanted."

I blinked, shocked that his anger was directed at me—as if I somehow asked for a strange guy to touch me inappropriately. I glanced over at Logan in accusation, only to see he had discreetly melted into the crowd.

Rounding back on Alexander, I narrowed my eyes. "Wait a minute. You think I planned this on purpose?"

His jaw tensed as he stared at me with a confused look on his face. Then, taking my arm and angling my body toward our table, he led me in that direction. Once there, he set down the drink and rounded on me.

"I honestly don't know what to think, Krystina. I saw you

watching that couple earlier. There's no denying your curiosity. It was written all over your face. Then, the minute I walked away, you started dancing and getting all loquacious with them. I don't understand you. This dark path you're on..." He paused and shook his head with apparent frustration. "You seem to be searching for something that I can't give you."

"What are you talking about?" I demanded in pure bewilderment. "I came here to dance. Nothing more."

"Were you intrigued by all the equipment in The Basement room, Krystina? Did you think maybe that guy would dominate you in ways I won't? Maybe even hurt you?"

"Now you're being an egocentric jerk for no reason. Knock it off, Alex," I snapped. I didn't know what had gotten into my husband, but I was appalled that he would even think such nonsense.

"I'm the jerk? I wasn't the one who let a stranger grope me," he retorted. "But I'm not going to get into an argument about it here. We're leaving."

My face fell and I glanced behind me to where I'd left Allyson on the dance floor. She was talking to Matteo, a fresh drink in hand, smiling. Cherise and Logan were nowhere to be seen, and my friend seemed oblivious to what had just gone down with Alexander, me, and Logan.

"We barely just got here, Alex. I don't want to ruin the night for Ally and Matteo."

"They can stay if they want. Let's go."

Without giving me another second to protest, he wrapped his arm around my waist and all but dragged me toward the exit. I started to struggle, but the action made my head spin, and I wondered if I'd underestimated the strength of the first drink. It was part of the reason I rarely drank mixers—you never knew how much alcohol was actually in them.

"Alex, stop—"

"Don't. Just don't," he barked gruffly.

Once out of the club, Alexander pulled me through the small casino back toward the main entrance. We passed the Let It Ride table where we'd watched the tournament earlier. The table was empty now and all the excitement I'd felt from watching someone's luck unfold seemed like a lifetime ago. I badly wanted to wrench my arm out of Alexander's grip and go back to the dance club, but I knew doing so would only cause an unwanted scene.

When we got outside, I finally did yank myself free, infuriated over being manhandled in such a way. Alexander didn't fight to hang on to me but made his way over to the valet instead. I clenched my fists, feeling as if I was about to go nuclear on him in a way I never had before. I only didn't because of the sudden wave of nausea that came over me. I felt like I might be sick.

What the hell?

I knew I was a lightweight, but still. I shouldn't be drunk after only one drink—even if it was a strong one.

I stepped toward the side of the building. I was starting to feel lightheaded, and I needed something to support my weight. As I leaned against the brick wall, I felt my cell vibrating in my purse. Assuming it was Allyson wondering where we had gone, I unlatched my purse and removed the phone from the inside pocket.

However, it wasn't Allyson. It was the same strange number that had been calling me when were on the way to the airport. It was a 718 area code. Whoever it was on the other end of the line was calling from Queens. I looked at the time on the top left-hand corner of the screen. I blinked a few times, struggling to focus on the numbers. Once I did, I saw it was after ten, which meant it was past one in the morning in New York. Whoever was calling kept odd hours.

Hitting the ignore button, I shot Allyson a quick text to let her know that I'd catch up with her in the morning and deposited my phone back into my small clutch. Alexander stood about twenty feet away talking to the valet. After a few moments, he walked back to me.

"The valet has instructions to let Matteo take the car back to the hotel later on," Alexander explained. "I've arranged a car service to bring us back to the hotel. Our ride should be here in about fifteen minutes."

I quickly realized it was a settled matter and knew there was no point in arguing about it on the street. The last thing we needed was a public disagreement which, knowing our luck, would somehow find its way into the press. It didn't matter if we weren't as recognized in Las Vegas—there was always someone with a cell phone. Any argument I wanted to have with Alexander would have to wait until we were back at the hotel. Perhaps by the time we got back there, I would be feeling a bit better, too.

"Fine," I bit out, not wanting to engage further. I looked away from him, the action making the ground tilt. I reached back to find purchase on the wall.

"Krystina, are you okay? Your eyes are glassy. How much did you drink?"

"Apparently not enough," I quipped, hoping to avoid the sort of lecture only Alexander could give. It undoubtably would include something about owning responsibility for my safety.

My cellphone began to vibrate again. Exasperated, I took it from my purse only to see the same unfamiliar phone number. I had no interest in talking to whoever was calling, but it was a welcome excuse to avoid conversing with Alexander. Sliding my finger across the screen, I brought the phone to my ear.

"Hello?" I blinked, hoping the word didn't sound as slurred as it felt.

"Hi. Um, yes. Is this Krystina Stone?" said a woman with a heavy New York accent.

"This is she. Who is this?" I asked.

"My name is Madilyn Ramos. I'm a friend of Hannah Wallace."

I frowned.

Hannah?

My hazy mind thought about the woman I'd met years earlier at Stone's Hope Women's Shelter. She'd been knocked down by life's adversities one too many times. In her desperation to survive, she'd stolen money from the shelter, and it resulted in a series of unfortunate events—including holding me and several others hostage. I'd been able to defuse the situation, and I'd used my connections to help her through the legal trouble that ensued as a result of her impulsive mistake.

Everything had been settled months ago, and I couldn't rationalize why Hannah's friend would have a need to call me after all this time. Whatever the reason, it had to be important based on the sheer number of times she had tried to contact me.

I reached up and rubbed the back of my neck. I tried to connect the dots, but I had trouble concentrating. It was hot all of a sudden. So hot. We needed to leave soon. If I stood out in the Vegas heat much longer, I was sure to vomit all over the sidewalk.

"How can I help you?" I asked, my words sounding slow even to my own ears.

"Look, I'm really sorry about the late call. I work nights, and I haven't had much success reaching you during the day," she explained. "When I saw in the paper that you were in Vegas, I figured it might be okay to call now. You know, with the time difference and all, I thought you might still be awake."

So the paparazzi knows we're here, after all.

I sighed and glanced in Alexander's direction, concentrating until he came into focus. He was staring straight ahead and there was that telltale tick to his jaw, signaling he was angry and stewing. I turned away from him, splitting my attention between the caller and my roiling stomach.

"Well, you've got me on the phone now, Miss Ramos. What can I do for you?" I asked again, somewhat absently.

"It's about what you can do for Eva, Hannah's daughter. Hannah trusted you, and I just... I'm just beside myself. I don't know what else to do," she choked out.

"Do about what?" I prompted, feeling genuinely confused by the strangeness of the call.

"Mrs. Stone, Hannah is dead. She killed herself."

"What? Dead? I..." I trailed off, unable to complete the sentence as the earth seemed to tilt on its axis. Madilyn Ramos continued to talk but I was barely hearing her. She was saying something about CPS and a promise...

My mouth went dry, and my stomach pitched. I gripped the wall behind me to try and steady myself.

God, how much alcohol was in that drink?

I looked around to find Alexander. I needed his help. Something was seriously wrong with me. As I searched for him, all I saw were blurry faces. Nothing seemed in focus, and I felt detached from my very being. The only thing cutting through the haze were flashing headlights from the cars parked along the curb. Somewhere in my subconscious, I knew this feeling wasn't alcohol induced.

I took a step, but it felt as if my shoes had led in them. In fact, I couldn't move my limbs at all. Everything felt heavy. So heavy. My heart pounded in my chest and the edges of my vision began to go dark. I heard a clatter and realized I'd dropped my phone. I hoped the screen wasn't cracked. And then I smiled—remembering the last time I'd had a cracked cell phone screen. It was the day I'd first met Alexander.

That was my last thought as the concrete ground came up to meet me. And then, for the first time in a long time, I felt nothing.

11

Alexander

I glanced down at the GPS tracker on my phone to see how much longer until the car service arrived. The blinking little icon said seven minutes.

Too many fucking minutes.

I just wanted to get out of here—away from the club and far away from Vegas. I hated this city. It had the ability to turn the most prudish individual into a fiend, and that was exactly what had happened to my wife. There was no mistaking the look on her face. I barely recognized her. She was intrigued by the couple on the dance floor, and I wasn't about to stick around long enough to see if she'd act on her curiosity.

Adrenaline surged through me, all rational thought escaping me as I envisioned the way I'd seen that cock sucker grinding up against Krystina. I never should have walked away from her in a place like this—not for one minute.

I turned to look at her, intent on asking her why she allowed that to happen but stopped short when I noticed she was swaying awkwardly. Krystina had a natural grace about her, so to see the clumsy way she grappled at the wall was alarming. Her movements were slow and uncoordinated as she searched for stability.

Is she really that drunk?

I didn't think she'd had that much to drink. In fact, I knew she didn't. Something was wrong. I took a step toward her and noticed how glazed and unfocused her eyes were. I'd seen Krystina intoxicated before. This wasn't that. Whatever was going on, I didn't believe it had anything to do with alcohol. I'd seen enough drug use in my lifetime to recognize it when I saw it, and if I wasn't mistaken, Krystina was on something. I just didn't know if she'd taken an illicit drug herself or if someone had slipped her something. It was disturbing to realize I was even questioning it.

She wasn't a recreational drug user—but she hadn't been a lot of things until recently. All I knew was that she'd been laser focused on escaping the emotional agony only a tragic loss could bring. She had literally begged me to help her erase that agony with physical pain. But never did I think she'd use drugs when I refused to deliver. I didn't want to believe it.

"Krystina, what's going on with you? You look—" Before I could finish the sentence, her knees buckled.

Instinctively, I moved toward her, catching her just before she hit the ground. I brought her to her feet until she was in a standing position. She could barely support herself, so I wrapped my arm around her waist to endure most of her weight.

"Alex," she slurred.

She felt so small and frail slumped against me. Panic consumed me. There was no doubt in my mind—Krystina was experiencing the effects of drugs. No matter what was going on, I'd have to determine whether the drug use was a conscious choice another time. All that mattered now was getting her out of here.

"Move the fuck out of my way," I snapped at the bystanders. I couldn't wait another fifteen minutes for the car service. I needed to get back to the hotel now and get water into Krystina. The sooner I could flush her system, the better.

Moving to the side of the road, I raised an arm to signal one of the cabs waiting by the curb while still using the other to support Krystina. One of the taxis came around to where I was standing. Moving quickly, I opened the back passenger door and positioned Krystina inside. Reaching over her shoulder, I secured her seatbelt, and then moved around to the other side of the car to climb in.

"The Florentine Resort. And don't stop until we get there," I barked at the driver.

"Um, is she okay, mister?" he asked hesitantly while looking back and forth between Krystina and me in the rearview mirror. He seemed unsure about the situation. I couldn't blame him. I was sure he saw a lot in his line of work, and I could only imagine what this might look like to him.

"No, but she will be. I'm her husband."

His face visibly relaxed, and then he gave me a short nod before shifting the car in drive and heading out toward the road.

Once the cab was in route, I settled back and clung tightly to Krystina. I couldn't help but notice how shallow her breaths were, and I contemplated taking her to a hospital. However, I knew all they would do was give her IV fluids. Not to mention, checking in to the local ER would draw unwanted attention. Until I knew if Krystina had taken something herself or if someone else had slipped her a roofie, I couldn't chance the media. The last thing my wife needed was public speculation over whether she was a drug user.

I felt sick to my stomach. I never should have let her out of my sight. I knew staying at that club was a mistake. At the very least, I should have had Matteo stay with Allyson and Krystina while I went to get the drinks.

Shit. Matteo and Allyson.

My eyes widened when I remembered our friends. I'd gone from furious to frantic in the blink of an eye, and I'd barely given them a second thought. If someone had, in fact, slipped something into Krystina's drink, they may have done it to Allyson as well. Reaching into my side pocket, I pulled out my cell phone. There were two text messages and a missed call from Matteo.

Today

10:24 PM, Matteo: *Where did you go?*

10:31 PM, Matteo: *Krystina texted Ally. She said we'd catch up in the morning. Is everything okay?*

I contemplated what to say. If Krystina took drugs, it wasn't anyone's business. It was something we would work out in house as husband and wife. We had enough emotional strain as it was and certainly didn't need any outside influences. However, if there was a person running around the club dropping Rohypnol in drinks, Matteo and Allyson needed to be aware.

10:47 PM, Me: *Everything is fine. I left the valet instructions so you can take the car back to the hotel tonight. How is Allyson feeling?*

I waited, staring at the screen until I saw the three little dots that signaled Matteo was responding.

10:48 PM, Matteo: *She's good, why?*

10:50 PM, Me: *Krystina isn't feeling well. I'm not sure if it was the drink or if there's something else going on. Somebody might have slipped her something.*

10:51 PM, Matteo: *Shit. Are you serious?*

10:52 PM, Me: *Yes. Again, I'm not positive on anything. I just wanted you to know just in case. You might want to pick a different place to hang out tonight.*

10:53 PM, Matteo: *Noted. Is Krystina okay? Should we come back to the hotel?*

I looked down at my wife's face. She would have appeared to be in a peaceful sleep if it weren't for the slight sheen of sweat covering her brow. I closed my eyes and took a deep breath. Never in my life did I think I would wish to see my wife suffering the effects of a roofie, but it would almost be a comfort to know that's what it was. The idea that she might have done this to herself was just too much.

Turning back to my phone, I typed out a quick response to Matteo.

10:55 PM, Me: *No need to come back. We're good. Just enjoy the night. And be careful.*

10:57 PM, Matteo: *Okay, my friend. Text if you need anything.*

I pocketed my phone once more and pulled Krystina a little tighter to me. By the time we reached the hotel, she was barely conscious. Rather than attempt to get her to walk, I carried her lifeless body to our suite. There were several curious onlookers, but I paid them no mind. After all, this was Vegas. I was sure they'd seen stranger things.

I fumbled with the door to the suite for a moment before entering. Bringing Krystina to the bed, I gingerly laid her down and began to slowly undress her. After stripping her down to nothing but her panties, I retrieved one of my t-shirts from the armoire and slipped it over her head. Propping up the pillows, I shifted her body back until she was angled against them in a half-sitting position. Confident that she was comfortable, I went to the bathroom and filled a glass of water.

When I returned to the bed, Krystina's eyelids were fluttering. I couldn't tell if she was trying to wake up or if she was dreaming.

"Angel, I need you to wake up and drink this," I said, giving her shoulder a gentle shake as I brought the glass of water to her lips. It was imperative that she drink something.

"Alex," she murmured, my name sounding almost unrecognizable as she spoke. "Why do I... can't feel..."

Her eyes rolled but she parted her lips enough for me to tilt a bit of water into her mouth. She swallowed it easily, so I tilted the glass further to give her more.

"Krystina, did you take some kind of drug?" I whispered. She shook her head so subtly that I might have missed it if I hadn't been watching her intently.

"No. I think... I think it might..." Her words were slurred, and I could barely make them out.

"What, angel? You think it might what?"

"Choke...drop...dancing... I think he..."

Our eyes locked briefly before her head lolled back. She was out cold, but she'd said enough for me to begin to make sense of it all. She hadn't willingly taken any drugs. It was that guy—the one who thought he could get all handsy with my wife.

I was a powerful man. I had money, connections, and means. Yet it seemed as if I still couldn't turn away from my wife for one minute without her landing herself in some sort of trouble. It didn't matter if she wasn't looking for it. She was a magnet for it, and she made it all but impossible to protect what I cared about most.

Her.

The worst thing in the world would be losing her, and the mere thought of it terrified me. I was about five seconds away from leaving the hotel, going back to the club, and beating the shit out of that asshole. I would have done exactly that, but Krystina needed me. I had to stay with her. She had to sleep off whatever was in her system, and I refused to leave her side until I knew she was okay.

As I stared at her sleeping form, guilt flooded me, ashamed that I thought Krystina would deliberately take drugs. Even if the thought was short lived, I didn't know how I could have been so incredibly wrong. Yes, she seemed on a path of self-destruction as she tried to learn ways to cope with losing our daughter, but I knew better. I knew my wife.

Moving back over to the bed, I knelt beside her. Sweat covered her brow and her breathing was still too shallow for my liking. Her coloring was a bit better, but not great.

"I'm so sorry, angel. I'm so sorry. I never should have doubted you."

12

Krystina

I smile when I see a red cardinal land on a tree branch just outside the family room window. Its musical chirps add an air of cheerfulness to the beautiful spring day. The house smells of lilacs picked fresh from the trees near the pond. They were a pleasant surprise brought to me by Alexander's mother and her nurse after their morning walk.

It's nearing five o'clock and Alexander will be home soon. I smile again as I think about what he will do after he walks in the door. It's the same every day so it's not hard to predict. I picture him removing his suit coat, hanging it in the closet in the foyer, and walking up the grand staircase to Liliana's nursery. Just as he does every day, he'll pick her up, rousing her from her late afternoon nap. Seeing my husband bond with our daughter is always my favorite part of the day.

I hum to myself as I step away from the family room window,

intending to go to the kitchen and see if Vivian needs help preparing dinner. I pause when I hear a tiny cough. I look to the baby monitor on the end table.

Liliana.

It sounds like she's coughing. No—it's not a cough. It sounds like she's choking.

My heart sinks as I hurry out of the family room, rushing up the stairs to my baby's nursery. When I look at her tiny pink form swaddled in the basinet, I stare in horror at what I see.

A metal wire is protruding from her mouth. Her little fists flail as she chokes and coughs. I want to remove the wire from her throat, but my arms are glued to my sides. I can't lift them. They are heavy. It's as if they are made of lead.

I scream.

"Liliana!"

I am helpless as I watch her choke. Her eyes widen and her lips turn blue.

Somebody has to hear me. My baby needs help.

I scream again and again. My throat becomes raw with the effort.

Nobody comes.

I can't save her.

MY EYES SNAPPED open as my legs frantically kicked under the blankets. I reached up, clawing at my throat, expecting it to feel raw from screaming even though my mouth was only gaping like a fish with no sound coming out. My heart pounded and a cold sweat covered my skin. I forced myself to still, my consciousness slowly creeping back in and making me realize that my frenzied and fearful state was the result of a terrible, horrific dream.

The room was nearly pitch black, the only slivers of light

coming from the sides of the blackout shades. I sat upright and shivered, then began trembling uncontrollably as the images from the nightmare resurfaced. I rubbed my eyes in an attempt to fully wake and escape the gruesome night terror, only to discover that my cheeks were wet with tears. I choked back a sob as my heart constricted with an overwhelming grief I couldn't put into words.

I reached to my right where Alexander should have been laying but all I felt were cold sheets. Turning to my left, I felt for the lamp on the nightstand and turned on the switch. I squinted from the sudden flood of light and allowed my eyes a moment to adjust. When they did, I saw Alexander sleeping in a chair in the corner of the room.

Why is he in the chair?

I propped myself up on two elbows and glanced around. My head was pounding. The clothes that I'd worn the previous night were tossed haphazardly over the settee on the opposite side of the room. Everything felt hazy in my mind. I remembered what happened last night, yet I didn't at the same time. It's as if I were viewing everything through a fog. I remembered dancing and...

I squeezed my eyes shut tight and tried to sort out the flashes of memory. I'd felt a sense of euphoria from being at such an amazing club—a swinger's club if my recollection served me right. Nobody had really cared about the swinger aspect of it because we just wanted to have fun dancing. We hadn't been at the club very long—at least I didn't think so. I remembered a man coming to talk to me. I had become disoriented, and I'd gone outside—no, *we'd* gone outside. Alexander had made me. He was angry about the man.

What was the guy's name?

I couldn't remember.

When Alexander and I were outside, I'd gotten a phone call and...

The phone call. Hannah.

Hazy details from the call slowly crept into my mind. A woman by the name of Madilyn Ramos had called to inform me that Hannah Wallace was dead. The specifics of the call were fuzzy, but I remembered the gist of what Madilyn had said. Hannah had committed suicide and Madilyn was reaching out because she wanted me to fulfill a promise I'd supposedly made to Hannah.

My brow furrowed. I ignored the pain the small action caused and forced myself to remember the conversation I'd had with Hannah not so long ago. It was the day she held me and many others hostage at Stone's Hope.

"*I* DON'T KNOW *what's going to happen after I walk out of here*," Hannah said. "*I know you think you can use your connections to help me, but knowing my luck, I'll still face time.*"

"*You don't know that. I can—*"

"*No, listen. Please. I know I fucked up, and I'll do whatever it is I have to do to make it right. If a judge wants me to volunteer my time dancing in a chicken costume in Times Square, that's what I'll do. But if he gives me prison time, I have no family to take care of my daughter. I grew up in foster care, and that can't happen to Eva. She's too good—untainted. So, if I have to go away for a bit, I need to know she'll be somewhere safe. Can you make sure of that?*"

"*I can try, Hannah. I don't know if I'll have much sway with Child Protective Services, though.*"

"*I doubt CPS will dare tell someone like you that you can't take Eva into your home.*"

"*Wait. Me? You want me to take her in?*"

"*Only if I have to spend time in jail. I need to keep Eva out of the system. You can understand that, can't you?*"

"*I understand your concern. I'll do what I can, but let's just hope it doesn't come to that.*"

IT WASN'T a promise per se, but I had given Hannah my word to see what I could to keep Eva out of foster care. But I'd only been talking about a few days. Madilyn Ramos had made it seem like I'd promised more. Squeezing my eyes closed tight again, I tried to remember the conversation I'd had with her last night. Eventually, the fog in my brain seemed to clear a bit until I could hear Madilyn's words replay in my head.

"*HANNAH OFTEN SAID that Eva would be better off if you were her mother but I never took her seriously. I should have. One of her final acts was to write a note that outlined her wishes for Eva. Mrs. Stone, you made a promise, and Hannah wants you to make good on it.*"

I DIDN'T REMEMBER what my response was to Madilyn. Shortly into the call, everything went dark. Looking back, the entire day seemed surreal. From the rough start in the morning to unintentionally going to a swinger's club, just trying to recap all that had happened made my head spin.

But why did I black out?

I didn't recall having that much to drink, and it was infuriating to realize I couldn't remember more about what may have been the most important phone call of my life.

"Alex," I muttered groggily and brought my hands to my temples. My head throbbed.

"Angel, you're awake." His voice sounded hoarse from sleep,

but if I wasn't mistaken, I thought I heard relief in his tone. "How are you feeling?"

"My head hurts. What time is it?" I asked as I struggled to get my bearings.

Alexander looked down at his watch. "It's almost eight."

Eight?

I might choose to sleep in on occasion, but my husband never slept that late.

I glanced down and noticed I was wearing one of Alexander's t-shirts—always my favorite to sleep in. If I was dressed, that meant we probably didn't have sex. Not that it mattered. I was more alarmed that I didn't even remember putting the shirt on.

"Alex, what happened last night?"

He dragged a hand across his face, then leaned forward to balance his elbows on his knees. He appeared exhausted, as though he had barely slept more than a wink. That's when I noticed he wore the same clothes that he'd had on last night. When he looked at me again, his expression was wary.

"I think you were drugged."

I sat up straight, but almost immediately regretted the sudden action. My skull felt like it was about to burst wide open as I looked pointedly at Alexander.

"Drugged?" I asked, even though a part of my subconscious remembered thinking exactly that last night.

"I suspect Rohypnol. It might have been slipped into your drink by that guy who was trying to dance with you while I was at the bar getting drinks."

I closed my eyes and recalled the face of the man in question. I had no idea if he was capable of doing what Alexander claimed, but I would probably never know. None of that mattered now anyway. All that mattered was the call from Madilyn Ramos.

"Alex, about last night," I began.

"It also could have been the bartender," he interrupted gruffly as he stood up from the chair. He began to pace, suddenly seeming wide awake. "When I consider the timeline, I don't recall you ever putting your glass down. It was always in hand, which means the bartender was the only other person to have access to your glass. While you were asleep last night, I called the club and demanded to see their CCTV footage. I got the owner on the phone, but he insisted they didn't have security cams. He said something about needing to protect the privacy of the patrons. I told him that was bullshit and—"

"Alex, wait," I interrupted, barely able to keep up. I needed to tell him about the call I received last night. "Something happened and—"

"You're damn right something happened. And I'll sue the ever-loving—"

"You will not sue anyone!" I yelled, way too forcefully for my head to handle. It damn near exploded from my outburst. "You have to listen to me. I have something to tell you— something that's more important that any lawsuit that would probably go nowhere without any proof of malice anyway."

"Fucking Vegas," he swore, acting as if I hadn't spoken and continuing to pace. "When I think about what could have happened..."

He didn't need to finish his statement. I could hear how mad he was by the tone of his voice. His words were laced with a venom I rarely heard but was almost always reserved for occasions when my safety was in jeopardy. He could go from zero to one hundred in an instant if he thought I was in harm's way—and this was one of those times.

I grew up hearing the warnings about the date rape drug and knew the seriousness of it. But in all honestly, assuming that's what was given to me, I found myself not all that concerned about it. I'd been with Alexander last night, and I knew he would never allow anything terrible to happen to me.

"Alex, calm down. I only have a headache. That seems to be the worst of it," I assured him, beginning to feel impatient as I swung my legs over the side of the bed.

"You shouldn't have a headache at all."

"I'm fine. Nothing really bad happened to me last night because you were with me."

"But what if I hadn't been?" he insisted stubbornly.

I pinched the bridge of my nose and mentally counted to ten. Alexander watched me, waiting for me to speak. I looked at his beautiful face. He appeared tired and angry, and I knew I would have to choose my words carefully if I wanted to get through to him.

Shaking my head, I stood up from the bed and made my way to the closet. I ignored the way my heart was oddly palpitating in my chest as I grabbed an outfit to wear today off one of the hangers.

"Alex, I need you to listen to me," I reiterated as I tossed the clothes on the bed. Then, without skipping a beat, I pulled out my suitcase and began putting all my other clothes into the luggage. "You have to book us a flight home."

"Good idea—especially after last night. I hate this godforsaken town anyway. I'll see about moving the flight from Tuesday to Monday and—"

"No. Not Monday. It's an emergency. I need to get home today," I explained more forcefully.

Alexander angled his head curiously, seeming to finally hear the urgency in my voice.

"An emergency? You said something happened. Is it your mom? Or is it something with Frank?"

"It's not my mom or stepdad. They're fine as far as I know. It's about Eva."

"Eva? Who's Eva?" he asked, sounding genuinely perplexed. I stopped packing my suitcase and looked up at him. His expression matched his tone.

Damn it.

We didn't have time for long explanations, but I knew I had to give him more.

"Do you remember Hannah Wallace from Stone's Hope?"

I saw the moment he recognized the name. His gorgeous sapphire eyes flashed angrily before he tightly pressed his lips together. I knew the mere mention of her would spark his fury. After all, she'd been the woman who'd held me hostage at gun point. Alexander never understood why I forgave her so easily, or why I'd helped her with the legal ramifications after everything went down.

But my husband hadn't been there to see the look of desperation on her face. Hannah was a single mother, barely hanging on by a thread, and her expression had mirrored something from my past. It was reminiscent of a look belonging to my mother once upon a time—back when the electricity had been turned off because she had to choose between paying the utility company or paying the hospital copay when I'd fallen and needed stitches. I was young then, but I clearly remembered the piles of bills and the sounds of her sobs. She'd been desperate—just as Hannah had been.

I studied my husband for a moment, noticing the way his brows pushed together in obvious irritation before sudden realization came into his expression.

"Krystina, is Hannah the person you were on the phone with last night?"

"No, it wasn't Hannah. But I wish it was." I sighed and shook my head. Sadness washed over me, and I couldn't stop tears from welling up in my eyes.

I turned away before Alexander could see them and resumed packing. However, he wasn't having it. A moment later, I felt his hands on my shoulders. Turning me to face him, I raised my eyes to meet his. Gone was the anger over last night and the mention of Hannah. All I saw now was genuine concern.

"Angel, who was on the phone?"

"It was her friend, Madilyn Ramos. Hannah is dead, Alex. She killed herself."

My husband's eyes widened as he slowly exhaled.

"Jesus Christ. She had a kid, right?"

"Yes. That's Eva," I stated.

"But why? You practically moved mountains to get her out of legal trouble after the kidnapping. I thought everything was fine now."

"So did I."

"Was she suffering from anxiety or depression?"

"I don't know," I admitted, annoyed that I hadn't been with it enough last night to ask questions. I bit my lower lip, suddenly nervous about how my husband would take the rest of the news—at least as much as my clouded mind could recall. All I knew was that the pounding in my skull was killing me and I wanted a clear head when explaining the little I did know about the situation to him. Aspirin and a shower were in order before I said or did anything else. "There's a lot to explain. I'm going to take a shower and try to rid myself of this headache. I'll tell you everything I remember from the call when I get out. In the meantime, can you please see about getting us a flight home today?"

"Krystina, I'm not booking a last-minute flight until you explain what all the rush is for," he stubbornly stated.

"Alex, please," I pleaded once more, hoping to convey with my tone how much I needed him to do as I'd asked.

After a moment, his eyes softened, and he shook his head with resignation.

"Fine," he muttered. He was thoroughly annoyed over having to wait for an explanation, but I was grateful for the reprieve—at least for the moment.

13

Krystina

I grabbed the clothes that I'd lain out and went into the bathroom. Once there, I nearly gasped at my reflection in the mirror. Dressed in nothing but a lace thong and Alexander's T-shirt, I was anything but sexy. Not only did I feel like I'd been hit by a semi, but I looked like it, too. The T-shirt sagged limply over my shoulders and my face was pale from exhaustion. The paleness emphasized the dark circles under my eyes. My hair was an absolute disaster—which wasn't all that unusual for me in the mornings—but today the ends seemed to be in more disarray than normal.

Sighing, I stripped out of my clothes, pausing to breathe in the scent of Alexander's shirt. It smelled like him—that familiar sandalwood cologne that never failed to turn me inside out.

After turning on the faucet, I adjusted the water temperature and climbed in. Resting my head against the marble tiled wall, I stayed there for a long while and considered what I remembered Madilyn saying to me over the phone. I *had* given my word to Hannah, even if it was in a moment of desperation. I'd said I would take care of Eva if anything were to ever happen to her. Now that something had happened, I had to consider how to explain it to Alexander. Just thinking about the monumental decision that I might have to make rocked me to my very core.

If it comes down to it, do I want to take care of this innocent little girl?

I'd only met Eva a couple of times when Hannah had brought her into Stone's Hope. I barely knew her, but I knew the answer to my own question before I'd even asked it of myself. It was undoubtably, yes. I would take care of Eva if that's what was needed.

Madilyn hadn't explained much about the situation over the phone from what I could recall. Death by suicide was the only thing that really stuck out in my mind. Once it was a reasonable hour on the East coast, I would have to call her back, apologize for last night, and have a more coherent conversation.

Still, apologies and details didn't seem to matter. My focus had zeroed in on one thing—Eva. I couldn't help but think that this was fates way of *finally* shining a light on me. After so much pain, suffering, and endless nightmares like the one I'd experienced last night, maybe this was the end. Perhaps this was how I was meant to become a mother.

Don't get ahead of yourself, Krystina.

I brushed off the warning voice in my head. I already wanted Eva more than words could describe, but I knew I had to pump the brakes. I knew next to nothing about the situation. Taking her in might not even be an option for more reasons than one. This was a human being we were talking about after all. A child was a huge commitment, and I had no idea how Alexander would feel about it.

As the water streamed over me, I thought about everything Alexander had told me about his childhood. He'd spent most of his youth living in poverty. If his grandparents hadn't taken him and Justine in after the tragedy with their parents, he might have ended up lost in the foster care system, just as Hannah feared Eva would be. Given the burdens Alexander carried at such a young age, who knew how he would have fared?

At the end of the day, I knew Alexander would want me to do the right thing. I just wasn't sure if he and I would agree on what the right thing should be.

Climbing out of the shower, I wrapped a towel around my body and stood in front of the mirror. As I began to towel dry my hair, I started to feel more like a human being again. Not great, but a bit better at least. Dark circles still cast shadows under my eyes. My head no longer felt like it was about to split open and had transitioned into a throbbing ache behind my eyes. Reaching into my makeup bag, I pulled out a bottle of aspirin and swallowed a couple of the pills, hoping to alleviate the headache. Coffee was definitely in order as well, but I wanted to at least look somewhat presentable before exiting the bathroom.

Alexander came in as I applied the last touches of my makeup. He just stood there, watching me through the mirror with a curious expression on his face.

"What?" I asked.

"Nothing. I just... I don't think I'll ever tire of looking at you. You're beautiful."

I glanced at my reflection and nearly laughed. While the makeup had helped cover up how tired I was, it didn't perform miracles.

"I've had better days," I joked, trying to keep my tone light despite the serious set to his jaw. He may have just given me a compliment, but his tone was reserved—strained almost. And if I wasn't mistaken, I also thought I heard a hint of regret.

The room began to feel tense. Looking for a distraction, I reached for the brush to comb out my hair, but Alexander grabbed it before I could.

"Let me," he said.

He placed the brush at the top of my head, pressing down slightly near the roots before dragging the bristles slowly over my scalp and all the way down the tresses to the ends. Then he began again, the deliberate motion almost mesmerizing as we stared at each other through the mirror. The non-sexual touch was relaxing, yet incredibly erotic, and the tension that was present just a moment before seemed to melt away. I half wondered if it had only been my imagination.

"Alex, the phone call I received last night," I began. "I don't remember a lot of the details. Or perhaps Madilyn didn't offer them. I can't be sure. Do you remember the day when everything happened with Hannah at the shelter?"

Alexander pursed his lips.

"That's not a day I'll soon forget, angel," he said dryly.

"Of course, you remember. I should have been more specific. Do you recall me talking to her when she was in the back of the police car?"

"Yes," he said, albeit hesitantly.

"She was terrified that her daughter would end up in the foster care system, and I'd promised to make sure that didn't happen. Her friend, Madilyn, called last night to remind me of that promise."

"Let me guess. She wants you to find this orphaned child a home now that Hannah is dead," he replied coolly.

I blinked, taken aback by the callousness in his voice.

"Sort of..." I trailed off, suddenly uncertain about my words.

"Hannah obviously wasn't in her right mind. If it was depression, she hid it well, and I can't help but think it was actually desperation—not depression—that drove her to take her own life. Alex, you didn't see the look on her face while she held an entire room of people at gunpoint. That look never quite went away—even weeks later after I worked to free her from all her legal trouble. Madilyn said something about Hannah thinking I'd be a better mother to Eva. I'm not sure what all that was about. I just know I can't sort this out from Vegas. I have to get home. Plus, I owe Madilyn an apology for my response last night—or lack thereof. I have no memory of saying anything to her after she told me about Hannah."

Alexander frowned.

"Speaking of last night, I asked you this before you fell asleep, but I don't know if you remember. I have to ask again because I need to be sure. You didn't take anything, right?"

I cocked my head to the side in confusion. "What do you mean?"

"Drugs. You didn't willingly take something, did you? Like, ecstasy or something like that?"

I stared at him incredulously through the mirror, not sure what had brought on this ludicrous abrupt turn in conversation.

"Of course, I didn't take anything! Why in the world would you think that?"

"No reason. I just wanted to double check. That's all," he replied calmly.

I rounded to face him. The extent of my drug experience only went as far as breathing in the skunky smell of someone else smoking marijuana. I'd never even held a joint in my hand, and I certainly never entertained anything hardcore. Alexander knew this. There had to be more going on. He wouldn't just randomly ask me something like that. But now the damage was done. I'd heard him loud and clear and there was no way to mistake the accusation in his tone.

"No, Alex. It's not 'that's all.' Why would you think I took drugs—and ecstasy of all things?"

He sighed and set the brush on the counter.

"Look, you've been trying everything to get away from the pain of losing Liliana. I didn't believe you'd resort to drugs but I had to be sure just so I knew what I might be dealing with."

"You're joking, right?" I all but demanded. This wasn't just a normal insult. It somehow felt like betrayal—as if he didn't think he could trust me.

"It's no joke, Krystina. I don't find any of this remotely funny. Put yourself in my shoes. It was just a week ago when we were at Club O, where you practically begged me to cross a line that I wasn't willing to cross. You had a full-blown panic attack yesterday morning, and the next thing I know, we're in a questionable swinger's club in Vegas—that you booked—only to be mysteriously drugged. I think it's only natural to ask questions. But like I said, I didn't believe you would. I just wanted to make sure."

He spoke so calmly, not seeming to understand how much sting his suspicion carried. Turning away from him, I exited the bathroom. I didn't know how to respond or how to react to what he'd said. The fact was, his words hurt.

Badly.

Alexander followed me into the bedroom, but I didn't speak. Moving to the nightstand, I saw I had a missed text from Allyson.

"Did you get us a flight out today?" I asked Alexander as I unlocked the phone to read my friend's text.

"Not yet. I was waiting to hear what the reason was first."

"Don't trust me?" I quipped bitterly as I pulled up Allyson's text. I read it quickly, feeling confused by the string of heart emojis that proceeded the text, and then looked up at Alexander. "Ally and Matteo are already at breakfast. Apparently, they have something to tell us, and they want us to meet them in the hotel restaurant as soon as we can."

My tone was cool and detached. Alexander stared at me with the oddest expression. My stomach twisted with anxiety. I hated fighting with my husband, and I knew if we stayed in this room together for much longer, that's exactly what would happen. I was hurt, and when I was hurting, I lashed out. Alexander was suspicious and angry about last night—a bad combination that would undoubtably lead to him saying irrational things.

I was sure he was having similar thoughts because he simply nodded and said, "Give me ten minutes to shower. After that, I'll call about getting us a flight home today, and then we can head down to meet them."

———

WHEN ALEXANDER and I entered La Cena, one of the restaurants in the resort, I spotted Allyson and Matteo seated at the opposite end of the room at a table covered in white linen. I pointed them out to Alexander, and we headed toward them.

They didn't appear to have ordered breakfast yet, but both had a cup of coffee in front of them. Allyson absently stirred hers while she scanned the room. She was biting her lower lip, and when her eyes landed on me, a nervous smile flashed across her face. I shifted my gaze to Matteo and saw he was tapping his thumb anxiously on the rim of his coffee cup. He wore the same apprehensive expression that Allyson did but there was something else there, too. Excitement maybe? I couldn't be sure.

I glanced up at Alexander and whispered, "Why do they

both look like they were just handed a warm cup of tea that they can't wait to spill?"

"I was thinking the same thing," he murmured. "Whatever it is, I'm sure we'll find out soon enough."

When we reached the table, Matteo stood. "*Buongiorno! Sleep well?*" he asked.

"Not particularly," Alexander said dryly as he held out a chair for me to sit. "You do recall the text message I sent to you last night, right?"

Matteo cringed guiltily.

"Yeah, sorry. How are you feeling, Krystina?" he asked.

Before I could answer, Allyson spoke up. "Why wouldn't she be feeling well?"

"Krystina was drugged last night," Alexander stated matter-of-factly.

"What? Drugged!" Allyson exclaimed in disbelief. Then, turning to Matteo, she said, "And you knew? Why didn't you tell me?"

Matteo shrugged. "Alex made it seem like he wasn't sure. By the time he told me, we'd already made the decision to leave the club and I knew there was no harm to you. We were having a good time and I didn't want you to worry."

"You should have told me," Allyson admonished.

"My apologies. In hindsight, I guess I should have mentioned it. I just wasn't concerned because she was with Alex. If I had told you, then maybe..."

He trailed off and quickly glanced my way, then back at Allyson. The irritated look on her face instantly melted away, replaced by the anxious expression she and Matteo had when Alex and I first approached the table.

I narrowed my eyes.

"Maybe what?" I prodded. "Why do you two look like the cat who swallowed the canary?"

Allyson glanced apprehensively between Alexander and Matteo before settling her eyes on me.

"Don't be mad," she said.

"I can't say I won't be mad until I know what it is, Ally. What's going on?"

"Well," she began as she reached for a sugar packet. Tearing the top, she dumped the contents in her coffee. "Do you remember that episode of *Friends* when they all go to Las Vegas?"

"Vaguely. Isn't that the one where Monica and Chandler almost get married?"

"Ah, good. You remember. You see, 'almost' is the key word. They didn't actually go through with it, but other people did."

I frowned, not knowing where she was going with this as I watched her tear the empty sugar packet into tiny pieces.

"Spit it out, Allyson," I pushed.

She tore the paper into more tiny pieces but didn't immediately answer.

"Oh, for Christ's sake!" Alexander's voice was laden with irritation, and he leaned back in his chair. "I've had a long night and I don't have a lot of patience at the moment. Matt, what the fuck is going on?"

"Ally, you said you wanted to be the one to tell them. Do it now or I will," Matteo warned, but I could see his trepidation.

I glanced back and forth between them, unsure what to think. All I knew was I was starting to get nervous.

"What's going on?" I demanded.

"Matteo and I pulled a Ross and Rachel," she blurted out.

"Ross and..." My eyes widened, and I gasped as soon as I realized what she was saying. Almost involuntarily, I began to shake my head in disbelief. "No. You didn't. In that episode, they... You didn't really..."

"We did," she confirmed. She glanced at Matteo and smiled.

He reached up, removed whatever was left of the sugar packet from her hand, and intertwined his fingers with hers.

"Oh, shit," I breathed.

"I've never seen a single episode of *Friends*," Alexander said, pressing his lips together to form a thin line. "Clearly, I'm missing something."

I turned to look at my husband, barely able to wrap my head around what Allyson just admitted to doing.

"Alex," I said slowly. "Apparently, Ally and Matteo got married last night."

Alexander went from looking irritated to stunned in an instant. His eyes darted to their hands before he whipped his head to the side to look at me.

"Oh, shit," he said, parroting my words. Because there really were no other words to describe the situation. While we both suspected there had been something between Allyson and Matteo, neither of us ever would have expected this. Looking back at Matteo, Alexander shook his head. "When I asked if anything was going on, I didn't think it was anything that serious."

"You knew there was something going on with them?" I asked incredulously.

Alexander angled his head to look at me, and I struggled to read his expression. I wasn't sure if he was annoyed by my disbelieving tone or if he was feeling just as confused as I was. His lips pursed as he studied me.

"No, I didn't know. Not really, anyway. Like you, I only suspected, and had asked Matt about it on our first day here. He didn't confirm or deny because you came up and interrupted the conversation," Alex explained. Then, turning back to Mateo and Allyson, he said, "I guess congratulations are in order."

"Congratulations?" I asked in confusion, and then laughed.

"They aren't really going to *stay* married. I mean, nobody gets married in Vegas for real. Even Ross and Rachel planned on getting an annulment. Well, at least Rachel did, but that's beside the point. I'm sure Ally and Matteo—" I stopped dead when I saw Allyson shaking her head.

"No annulment, Krys," she said.

"We want to make a real go at this," Matteo added.

I blinked.

"Seriously?" I asked, unable to help myself even though deep down I knew this was for real. I could see it in her face.

My best friend had gotten married—and I'd missed it. Allyson had always been flighty and impulsive, but I never would have predicted this. She'd been my Maid of Honor, but now I wouldn't have my turn at being hers. There would be no bridal showers, a bachelorette party, or any of the wedding traditions that best friends typically shared together. Hell, she hadn't even told me there was something between her and Matteo. Now they were a done deal. Married. For better or for worse.

And for the second time that day, I felt incredibly betrayed.

"Krys, have you ever been so physically attracted to someone that you can't think straight?" Allyson asked, seeming to notice my silent shock. "I know you have because I've seen the way you and Alex look at each other. That's what it's like for Matteo and me."

"*Destino*," Matteo murmured.

I looked pointedly at both of them.

"Marriage is a hell of a lot more than just physical attraction," I said dryly, thinking of the many challenges Alexander and I had experienced over the years. Even now, the tension between my husband and I was palpable, and I could feel the brewing argument simmering just beneath the surface —and all because he didn't trust me.

Apparently, that was the theme as of late because Allyson hadn't trusted me either.

Am I the problem in these equations?

I didn't know the answer. In fact, I could barely wrap my head around anything that had happened lately. Never in my life had I felt as isolated and separated from everyone who was important to me as I did at that moment. It was incredibly lonely.

"I know marriage isn't always easy," Allyson said, and then paused. She seemed to consider me for a moment before cocking her head to the side. "You seem upset, Krys, and I'm sorry. It was just so spur of the moment and I—"

"It's fine," I interrupted, noticing how high-pitched my tone sounded. When I spoke again, I plastered a fake smile on my face and made a conscious effort to keep my voice from wavering. "I'm happy for you. Really, I am."

14

Alexander

T he flight home had been relatively quiet. I was exhausted from being up worrying about Krystina most of the night, and I'd slept for much of the journey back to New York. When I was awake, Krystina hadn't said much—about Allyson and Matteo's unexpected nuptials or Hannah's little girl. I didn't know what she was thinking, but turmoil was plainly written all over her face.

We'd left our friends behind to "honeymoon," but I knew my wife, and I knew the marriage had hurt her. She and Allyson confided so much in each other, and I was sure Krystina was experiencing feelings of betrayal. However, I thought it was more than just Allyson that was bothering her. She seemed upset with me as well. I just didn't know why. Rather than ask her, I tried to assess her unusually subdued behavior.

Her silence spoke volumes, and after a while, I wasn't convinced the raging hurricane in her eyes was all because of Allyson or possible anger at me. While we were walking through the terminal at LAS, Krystina had been engrossed in her phone. She'd stepped away and out of earshot from me, talking animatedly to someone. I didn't know who it was, but I suspected it was Madilyn Ramos. That suspicion was all but confirmed after we boarded our plane. I'd caught a glimpse of her cell phone screen just before she powered her phone off, and I saw that she'd been looking up private elementary schools in New York City.

Instinct told me there was way more to the story about this little girl than my wife was letting on, and it was extremely troubling. This went far beyond a random call from a distraught friend of Hannah's, or a promise my wife made in a moment of desperation. I'd wanted to demand Krystina give it to me straight right then and there, but I'd hesitated. A part of me knew what she would say, and I wasn't ready to have that conversation.

By the time we walked through the doors to our house in Westchester, I'd decided that had given her ample time to work out whatever she'd been thinking about. Now I wanted answers.

"Come with me," I ordered as she hung her coat in the front closet.

"Alex, I have stuff I need to take care of and—"

"No. I've given you space to work through whatever it is that's going on in your head, but now I deserve answers. You owe me that much after the way we rushed back to New York. You will do what I tell you to do, Krystina. Now, follow me."

Without giving her a chance to argue further, I took her by the elbow and led her into the living room. My grip wasn't rough, but it was firm—firm enough for her to know I meant business. I hated games and this was starting to feel like one.

Once Krystina was seated on the Nieman Marcus sofa, I walked over to the custom crafted liquor cabinet and poured myself two fingers of Johnnie Walker Blue Label, then turned to look out the window at the thirty-six-acre lot. I barely noticed the lush pines dotting the landscape.

"Krystina, I know you made a promise, but what exactly does that mean?"

"I don't understand."

"How far are you going to take this?" My gut churned, and instinct kicked into overdrive. A part of me knew what she was going to say before I even asked the question. When she didn't answer right away, I prodded her with my suspicion. "I hope you aren't planning on bringing the child here."

"What if I was?" she responded, somewhat indignantly.

I turned to face her. She was standing now, and had one hand on her hip, appearing posed for a fight. However, the worry lines on her face made me realize she was also genuinely concerned about my response—as if she desperately needed my approval. I had to shut this down.

"Then I would say it's out of the question," I replied. My tone was matter of fact, leaving no room for debate.

"I have to do something, Alex. I promised to make sure Eva was cared for. She's currently staying in Brownsville with Madilyn, a single mom of two who works third shift. She has a hard enough time finding childcare for her own kids without adding Eva into the mix, and she can't afford another kid for more reasons than one. She flat out told me over the phone that she was going to have to turn Eva over to the State if nobody else steps up. Hannah has no other family that I know of, so where else can she go but here?"

"I won't bring a kid from Brownsville into this house, Krystina. Have you been there? The crime rates are brutal. The girl will be carrying a lot of baggage."

"I said Brownsville is where she was currently staying. She's not actually from there."

"Then where is she from?" I asked. Krystina hesitated and I knew I wouldn't like whatever the answer was going to be. Narrowing my eyes, I asked again. "Krystina, where did this kid live before Brownsville?"

"Hunts Point. But—"

"Hunts Point! Fuck, Krystina. That's even worse. She's probably seen more prostitutes and drugs in a week than you've been able to imagine your entire lifetime. I grew up in it, remember? You didn't. The answer is still absolutely not. The girl can't come here."

"Alex, stop being so pretentious. Where she lives should have no bearing on anything. If you'll just listen to me," she said in a pleading tone. "I thought that maybe...well, since we can't have a child of our own..."

She trailed off and my eyes widened. There was no mistaking her hopeful expression. My worst fears were realized. She actually wanted to keep the child—a stranger's child—long term.

Permanently.

"No. I won't foster someone else's kid, Krystina."

"It wouldn't be fostering. We'd be her permanent legal guardians," she said quietly as she returned to sitting on the sofa.

"That's a ridiculous idea." I scoffed and shook my head. "Doesn't she have a father?"

"Hannah told me last year that he was in prison. Madilyn didn't say, but I'm assuming he's still there. He's never had anything to do with Eva, so whether he's in prison or not, I'm not worried about him causing a problem for us."

For us?

I stared at her incredulously, somewhat shocked that she'd literally thought of everything without consulting me once. It made me wonder what else she discussed over the phone with Madilyn while I wasn't listening.

"You already have this all worked out, don't you? And without talking to me. Krystina, we have no idea what this little girl has been through, and I refuse to inherit someone else's problems. Who knows what she's been exposed to and what kind of emotional trauma she could bring. I mean, her mother killed herself. Her father is in prison. Her entire short life was spent living in hell on earth. I've come too far to be associated with that life. I've gotten away from all of it, and I will not willingly step back into it."

"This isn't about you, Alex."

"You're wrong. It is all about me—and you. It's about us, and I am not willing to risk everything we have by bringing that into our home, Krystina. We are better than gutter trash."

My wife gasped as shock registered on her face.

"Gutter trash? Eva is practically a baby—only five years old. How can you be so cold?" she whispered. "You've said it yourself. You know what it's like to grow up in poverty—and it wasn't a life you chose. You had no choices back then, just as Eva doesn't have any. She's only a child, and your judgement is unwarranted."

I closed my eyes, the hurt in her voice cutting me to the core. While she was right about the lack of choices, she didn't understand. I pictured the rundown cinderblock building that I'd spent my childhood in—the projects in the Bronx—with bars on the windows and the paint chipped walls of the stairwells where foul odors never seemed to dissipate. The people there were the lowest of the low. I'd seen crime and drugs, and witnessed both gun deaths and overdoses before the age of six. It had stolen my innocence and hardened me to the world. It made me suspicious of everyone and everything. This little girl would come to us the same way and it just wasn't something I wanted to take on.

Turning back to look out the window, I took a short swig of whiskey. My jaw tightened in determination.

"No, it's not unwarranted," I replied. "You haven't seen what I've seen. It's why you don't understand. This isn't up for debate, Krystina. The child is not our responsibility."

"But I promised, Alex."

"And the woman you made the promise to is dead. She won't know the difference if you break it."

"But I will—and what about Eva? I told you that she can't stay with Madilyn. I can't just let her go to a foster home. She'll be lost in the system within a year. You know that."

"I'll repeat. It is not our responsibility. The child—"

"Eva. Her name is Eva. Say it," Krystina demanded through gritted teeth.

"Saying her name isn't going to make me change my position. I'm not budging on this."

"You don't know me at all, do you?" she whispered. "If you'd been paying attention over the past few months, you'd know why this is important to me."

I cringed. I knew exactly why she felt compelled to make good on her promise. I just didn't agree. My wife was doing this for the wrong reasons. This little girl would never replace Liliana, and as soon as Krystina realized it, the sooner we'd be able to move on from this outlandish idea.

"Taking in someone else's child isn't going to bring back what we lost," I said quietly.

"I know, Alex—trust me on that. But everything happens for a reason."

"You said you hated that expression—that you didn't believe it anymore."

"I thought I didn't. But now, nothing else makes sense. It's like my meeting with Hannah was fated, and I've realized that if we can't have a child of our own, I'm okay with accepting what was clearly meant to be instead."

I closed my eyes and shook my head, pushing away the sadness that washed over me.

"This wasn't meant to be, Krystina. This is nothing more than a terrible tragedy—one that is not our responsibility to fix."

"Maybe you're right, but I need to follow this and see where it takes me. Instinct is telling me that taking in Eva is the right thing. Perhaps it will be a mistake, but I have to try. I'm going to pick up her up from Madilyn's house first thing in the morning."

"And do what with her?"

"I haven't decided yet. But Alex, you should know that I'm doing this with or without your support."

I spun around to face her once again.

"You wouldn't dare."

She angled her chin up in defiance. "Watch me."

"Krystina," I said in a warning tone.

"Don't, Alex. Please. I want to do this together, but if you can't support me on this, it might be..." She hesitated, seeming to weigh her words carefully before she spoke. "It might be best if you stay at the penthouse for a bit."

I scoffed. "Are you really kicking me out of my own house simply because I don't want to take in a stranger's child? That's a bit irrational, don't you think?"

"No. In fact, I don't think I've ever felt more rational in my life. I want this, Alex, but I won't fight with you over it nor will I expose Eva to the conflict. That's why I think it's best for you to stay at the penthouse—at least until we work through things. Or, you can choose to stay here and we do this together. The choice is yours."

"No, you've already decided. It's your way or no way."

She shrugged. "If that's how you want to see it. You know how I feel and where I stand. Now, I'm tired and I have an early morning. I'm heading to bed. Goodnight, Alex."

Stepping up to me, she extended up on her tiptoes, kissed my cheek. A smile of regret flickered like a hologram, and I wasn't sure if it had only been my imagination. Then, she turned and exited the room.

"Krystina, wait," I called out when she reached the door. She didn't stop. Instead, she left me staring at her back until she disappeared from my line of sight. I cursed aloud to the empty room. "Fuck!"

I tossed back the rest of my drink and contemplated my next move. I felt sick. It was as if a massive pit had opened between us, and everything we'd built was falling inside it. The idea that Krystina thought she could make me leave was ludicrous. What she needed was a good sense-fuck.

I left the room, crossed the large foyer, and began to climb the grand staircase toward the master bedroom suite. However, I paused halfway up the steps, rethinking my next course of action. The more I thought about it, the more I began to think going to the penthouse wasn't all that bad of an idea. My wife was stubborn as hell. She would need to figure this out on her own, and I was confident that she'd eventually see I was right. Let this be a lesson to her. As much as I didn't want to be apart from her, perhaps spending a week alone with a child—a child who was certain to be psychologically damaged—would make Krystina see sense.

Reaching into my pocket, I pulled out my cellphone and dialed Hale.

"Boss," he said after the first ring.

"Get with Samuel and tell him to pack a bag. He and I are going to stay at the penthouse for a few days."

15

Alexander

I hadn't been to the penthouse in months. The last time was when Krystina and I had stayed here after the Met Gala this past May. Our stay had been planned, knowing we would most likely be out late and wouldn't want the long drive back to Westchester. We'd asked Vivian to stock the refrigerator with the essentials, but of course she went above and beyond what we'd requested of her. She knew the empty penthouse would have a cold feel to it after being vacant for so long between visits, so she sought to add little touches to make us more comfortable. Her addition of fresh lilies for Krystina and the current edition of *The Times* for my morning reading had given the place a more lived-in feel.

When I walked in today, all I smelled was lemons from the organic furniture polish used by the cleaning company that came in once a month. There wouldn't be any food in the refrigerator, and I wasn't going to find flowers in a vase on the tigerwood dining room table. The penthouse was as empty as ever.

I looked around, shocked by how remarkably impersonal it was. I didn't know how I never noticed it before. I thought back to when I'd first purchased the Manhattan penthouse. It had been a blank canvas for my interior design engineer, Kimberly Melbourne. While her work was superior, it lacked the feminine touch Krystina had eventually brought to the inexpressive space. Before then, my home shared the same vibe one would get in a museum.

Krystina and I had only lived here together for a short time. The house in Westchester was built and move-in ready shortly after we were married. Any personal touches she'd added to the penthouse moved with us to Westchester. Gone were the pictures of us together at various events, including my favorite picture of all—the one of Krystina with all her glorious curls blowing in the wind on *The Lucy*. The penthouse felt like a sterile museum once again and its lifelessness was suffocating.

Crossing the foyer and going into the living room, I didn't bother to turn on any lights. I used the moonlight streaming in from outside to guide my way. I tossed the small duffle bag that I'd packed onto the sofa and turned around to address Samuel. The young guard stood in the entrance to the foyer waiting for instruction. The security light on the wall behind him was the only one on in the penthouse. The gentle glow left Samuel cast in shadow so that I could only make out his silhouette.

"I'll be fine for the night," I told him. "It's late and I have no intention to go anywhere. You're free to crash in the guest room or downstairs in Hale's old apartment."

"I'll head downstairs and give you your privacy if that's okay with you, sir."

"That's fine. I'll see you in the morning."

Samuel turned on his heel and made for the door. When it clicked closed behind him, the silence that fell didn't feel like welcome solitude, but rather something loud and intrusive. I should be used to being alone. After all, I'd been alone for years before meeting Krystina and I'd managed just fine. There had been women, but nobody serious. I never saw the point. My work precluded a lot of things, including close relationships. Plus, my not-so-conventional preferences in the bedroom made keeping any woman around for long a serious risk. So, I'd made sure to find ways to discreetly satisfy my desires, yet always made sure to keep my eyes on the prize— building my empire. I'd never wished for anything more.

My life had been perfect as far as I was concerned. But then I met Krystina, and everything turned upside down. Now she was my world, my obsession, and my whole reason for living. I didn't know how to be alone anymore. I wanted her—and only her—with me all the time. This rift that had been slowly building between us had become a gaping canyon after tonight, causing an ache in my chest that was wholly foreign. I didn't know what to do with it. I didn't even know who was to blame for it—her or me. Perhaps it was both of us.

I walked over to the window, stared out at the millions of lights dotting the skyline, and gave in to a good stretch. The nighttime view was breathtaking, but it felt like an indulgence I didn't deserve. I couldn't believe I'd walked out—that I had actually left.

What kind of an asshole did that make me?

Yes, it had been her suggestion, but I shouldn't have taken it.

"I should go back and make things right," I said aloud to the empty room.

A part of me wished Hale had accompanied me tonight instead of Samuel. I wouldn't have dismissed him as quickly as

I had Samuel but would have bounced ideas off him and sought his advice. Hale undoubtably would have had indirect words of wisdom that might help me right now. He knew my wife almost as well as I did.

However, it was better that Hale was in Westchester. There was nobody I trusted more with Krystina's safety than him, and if she was determined to head to Brownsville in the morning, I needed his keen eyes on her.

Turning away from the windows, I walked over to the mahogany bar and poured a shot of Jamison. I tossed it back, then set the glass down a little too forcefully on the bars surface. The loud bang of glass on marble echoed in the silent penthouse. I needed noise of some kind—anything that would cut through the loneliness surrounding me.

I thought about ordering the voice activated sound system to turn on music, but immediately decided against it. It didn't matter if I'd spent a fortune on it. Any sort of music right now would just remind me of Krystina. Instead, I sat in a cushioned armchair positioned in front of the floor to ceiling windows and looked out over the city skyline once again. I was shrouded in darkness, but I didn't turn on any lights. I wanted the obscurity of night to mute any distractions as I considered all that had happened.

I knew what Krystina was planning even though she hadn't said it. Eventually, she'd want to adopt Hannah Wallace's little girl. While adoption worked for some people, it just wasn't for me for more reasons than one. I had told Krystina it was because of the emotional baggage the child was bound to come with, but it was more than just that. I truly believed my wife was misguided. This child could never replace all that we'd lost.

But the biggest reason of all, and the one I couldn't bring myself to voice out loud, was that I didn't care for the idea of having to share Krystina with someone else—someone who wasn't created by the two of us. I knew I'd never be able to look at the child as my own, and it wouldn't be fair to Krystina or the little girl. All around, we would all be doomed to nothing but heartache.

Glancing down at my watch, I saw it was after one in the morning. I was running on fumes and needed sleep. Perhaps after a good night's rest, I'd be able to think about everything more clearly in the morning.

Getting up from the chair, I made my way to the master bedroom. I stripped down to my boxer briefs, climbed into bed, and stared at the ceiling. Never in my life had I felt more alone. Despite my commitment to stay away for a week or so, I couldn't carry on like this. I needed Krystina like the air I breathed. We rarely fought, and when we did, it never lasted for long. We always found a compromise. But if I were being honest with myself, I had left no room for compromise this time. I'd shut her down the minute she suggested taking in a stranger's child.

Rolling onto my side, I stared at the vacant space where my wife should have been. I reached up and touched the pillow, imagining the lines of her naked body disappearing under the sheets. I missed her already and I'd only been gone for a couple of hours. Perhaps I'd been too quick to react.

Closing my eyes, I vowed to go home and talk to Krystina first thing in the morning. I may not concede to her wishes, but I would at least hear her out. There had to be a middle ground, but we'd never find it as long as we stayed a part. She was mine —the better half of my soul—and she belonged by my side.

Always.

THE SUN IS HOT. *My house will be even hotter. I don't want to go inside. He gets angry when he's hot.*

I look at my bike lying in the ugly dead grass.

I should pick it up, so I don't get yelled at. Mom says Grandma bought me that bike and I should take better care of it.

I'm too sweaty. I'll put it away later.

I go into the apartment building and pinch my nose. The hallway always smells like a toilet. I need to get to my door where it doesn't smell so much inside.

I hear yelling. Is that him?

No. It's the crazy lady down the hall.

My backpack is so heavy.

I can't wait to put it down.

Not on the floor, though. He'll get mad if he trips.

I look at the numbers on the doors I pass. Ten. Eleven. Twelve. Three. The one is missing. I think it is supposed to say thirteen.

Almost there.

I reach the door that has the number fifteen and place my hand on the knob.

MY LEGS THRASHED and I bolted upright. Shaking my head as if to clear it, I blinked rapidly until my sight came into focus. I turned, reaching for Krystina, but the only purchase my hands found were cold sheets. That's when I remembered where I was.

The penthouse. Alone.

I took a deep breath and sighed, waiting a beat for my heart rate to return to a normal rhythm.

Jesus. What the fuck was that?

I tried to will away the images of the night. The putrid smells in the dream seemed to linger in my nostrils. I hadn't had that nightmare in years—not since we found my mother.

After that, the terrible visions that had haunted me while I slept had suddenly stopped. I had no idea why they would resurface now.

But a part of me knew exactly why the dream had returned. It was all the talk about Hannah Wallace's daughter—the little girl who spent the first five years of her life living in the same hell hole that I once had.

Hunts Point.

I'd lived in that very section of the Bronx, where prostitution, drugs, and violent crime were commonplace. It was, and still is, considered one of the worst places for a child to live in New York City. The families who lived there had no future, many of them trying to survive on less than fifteen thousand dollars per year. I made more than that in a day. As an adult, I quickly learned the impact of growing up in an impoverished community. The affects were far-reaching and I knew I was one of the lucky ones who had been able to break free of the cycle.

Through fundraising efforts at the Stoneworks Foundation, I'd had the project housing I once lived in torn down, replacing the decrepit building with new, low-income housing. We'd also built a small multigeneration community center in the middle of the housing complex and called it Hunts Point Garden. It gave the residents a respite from the streets, designed to inspire hope where there was no hope to be had for the people of Hunts Point. It was also a learning center where adults were empowered through educational tools to become advocates for their families. Stone's Hope Women's Shelter was actively involved with the center, and they coordinated regularly to help the women in Hunts Point escape domestic abuse.

I frowned, suddenly remembering something Krystina had said to me about Hannah.

"A little over a year ago, I had convinced Claire to take a chance

on one of the young mothers who had been a frequent flyer at the shelter. The mother's name was Hannah. She was constantly leaving her abusive boyfriend, only to go back to him because she couldn't support her daughter on her own."

If Hannah had been going to the shelter, there was a strong possibility that she learned of its existence through the Hunts Point Garden community center.

Reaching over to the nightstand, I grabbed my cell phone and pulled up a blank internet search tab. Then I typed "Hannah Wallace Hunts Point NYC" into the search bar. The first things that popped up were social media profiles, but I skipped past those until I came to a White Pages link. Clicking on it, Hannah's basic information immediately populated, including her last known address.

"There's no fucking way," I whispered to myself after I read it.

Swinging my legs off the side of the bed, I sat up and rubbed my temples. Hannah Wallace had lived on the same street and in the very building that was constructed to replace the one I used to live in.

It had to be a coincidence.

Whether it was or not, one thing was clear. Any thoughts I may have had about working through this with Krystina were now gone. There was no way I could live with a child who was a living, breathing reminder of the place I grew up. I'd worked my whole life to forget about that time. I'd buried it, and I wouldn't go back. The nightmare I'd had was a warning sign— a warning sign provided by instinct.

And my instincts were rarely wrong.

16

Krystina

Unable to sleep, I lay awake most of the night, fighting to keep the tears at bay. I didn't have time or energy to waste on crying. Alexander would come around. He had to. I needed this—no, we needed this. I knew in my heart that bringing Eva into our home was the right thing. I pictured her little face with those wide, expressive eyes. I only saw her once, the day Hannah first came to Stone's Hope, but I hadn't forgotten her. I knew I needed to do this—with or without Alexander.

As was routine, I'd made my daily stop at Liliana's grave. Hale had driven me and didn't know to bring a fresh Lily as Samuel usually did for me. Saddened by this, I tried not to look down at the wilted Lily laying at the base of the headstone. The last time a fresh one had been placed there was Friday. That fact made me feel like I'd let Liliana down somehow—as if not having a fresh flower each day would make her feel as though I didn't care.

During the drive from the cemetery to Brownsville, I couldn't help but wish there was someone I could talk to about everything. I felt so alone and isolated from everyone I held dear. I hadn't expected Alexander to really leave last night, and I had no idea if we were even on speaking terms now.

I thought about calling my mother, but we weren't really the type to have heart-to-heart conversations. Besides, I didn't know where she would land on the subjects of fostering, legal guardianship, or adoption. The last thing I needed was for her opinions to make an already complicated situation worse.

Then there was Allyson. I normally would have spoken to her about this. I told her near everything, but I couldn't call her —and it wasn't just because she was on a honeymoon. It was because I felt like I didn't know my best friend anymore. I half wondered if it was the result of the pandemic. We hadn't seen each other nearly as much during that time. Perhaps our friendship wasn't designed for video conference calls. Whatever the reason for keeping the secret about her relationship with Matteo, I felt incredibly betrayed. I never thought she'd keep me in the dark about something like this. Until I sorted everything out, maybe it was best if I just kept my distance.

As we drove through Queens on our way to Brownsville, I people watched through the tinted windows. Everyone passed seemed to walk with purpose, many looking down at their smartphone with coffee in hand. Because of the time of day, I could only assume they were on their way to their perspective jobs.

However, people watching did little to occupy my mind. By the time Hale pulled up to Madilyn's apartment complex in Brownsville, my nerves were shot. When I stepped onto the curb, I glanced up and down the street. Everything was quiet, with only a few passing cars, and there wasn't a soul to be seen. It was a stark contrast to the streets in Queens.

Turning back toward Madilyn's building, I looked up at the five-story complex. Considering Alexander's concern about the area, the apartment building didn't look bad or dangerous. In fact, everything looked fairly new. The grass and landscape were well-maintained, giving the building an inviting feel despite the sterileness of the red brick building. Shiny bicycle racks lined the front of the long building, and although the bikes chained to the racks looked a little beat up, they appeared to be in working order.

However, across the street looked like another world. The rows of tall brown buildings looked more like prisons than residential housing. While most of the surrounding area appeared harmless, I reminded myself that it was nine o'clock in the morning. I was sure the evening hours would tell an altogether different story.

I could hear Hale's footsteps falling behind me and I paused. Turning to face him, I considered what his presence might look like to Madilyn and Eva.

"Hale, you might want to wait in the car. I appreciate you being here, but you can be a bit intimidating. I don't want to scare Eva."

"With all due respect, ma'am, I'm going to deny that request. You don't know what you're going to walk in to. It's best if I stay close. I won't interfere. I promise. You won't even know I'm there."

Stubborn as a mule.

I shouldn't be surprised by Hale's insistence. Still, I took in his large, brooding form and raised my brows skeptically. No matter how hard he tried, he would never be able to shake the commanding ex-military stance he always carried.

"Right. You'll just blend right in," I said with a nervous laugh, but I didn't argue. I didn't have the energy. All my energy was zeroed in on keeping my composure for what may be the biggest moment of my life.

I only wished Alexander were here with me. Still, I'd come to accept the things I couldn't change. Alexander was one of those things. He would have to come around in his own time.

And if he didn't?

I pushed the troublesome thought aside. I had to focus on the present and not dwell on the what ifs.

Stepping up to the door, I pressed the black call button for the apartment number Madilyn had given me. We'd arrived about twenty minutes early. Madilyn told me she worked nights and I worried she might not be home yet from her shift. I waited for what seemed like forever before a voice came through the intercom.

"Yeah," a female said.

"Hi. Is this Madilyn Ramos?"

"It is."

"It's Krystina Stone. May I come in?"

"Sure. Come on up. Second floor. First door on the right," she told us in a thick accent that seemed more prevalent than I'd remembered from our phone conversations. The word 'sure' sounded more like *shore*, and she'd dropped the *or* sound in 'floor' and 'door' to end them with an *aw* sound instead. I couldn't help but smile. That strong New York accent wasn't as ubiquitous in Manhattan or Westchester. One had to venture deep into the boroughs if they wanted a dose of it regularly, and it was one of the things I loved most about the city.

A moment later, the door buzzed. Hale pulled on the handle and stepped inside first, motioning for me to enter after he seemed satisfied all was clear. Sometimes I'd swear that he saw boogeymen in every shadow.

As we ascended the stairs to the second floor, our footfalls were silent against the thinly carpeted steps. The air was thick from lack of airflow in the stairwells and hallways, and I couldn't help but think how stifling it would be in here on hot and humid days. Thankfully, today was only supposed to reach the mid-seventies with mild humidity. There was an odd stench in the air as well. The faint yet unpleasant odor smelled like urine that someone tried to mask with a flowery air freshener.

When we reached the door to Madilyn's apartment, I raised my fist to knock but the door swung open before I could connect.

"Oh!" I said, somewhat startled. "Hello."

A waif, thin woman with thick curly brown hair stood on the other side of the threshold. Dark circles cast shadows under her red-rimmed eyes. Her clothing hung loose on her body, and I couldn't be sure if it was a style she was going for or if it was from weight loss. Fatigue lines sagged on her features even though she couldn't have been more than twenty-five-years-old.

She gave me a slow once over before bringing her gaze to meet mine.

"So you're Krystina, the rich girl Hannah used to babble on about. You're early," she said flatly.

I blinked, not sure how to respond, and glanced down at my attire. I wore flat sandals, capri jeans, and a casual purple cap sleeve top. Nothing about my appearance screamed wealth. I'd made sure of it when I got dressed that morning because I had no idea what I was walking in to. I didn't want anything to intimidate or influence the situation.

"Um, yes. I'm Krystina Stone. And this is…" I trailed off and glanced hesitantly behind me at Hale. If my appearance wasn't intimidating, he made up for it. I silently groaned, wishing that I'd pushed harder for him to stay in the car. "That's Hale, a friend of mine. You must be Madilyn."

"In the flesh. I guess you should come in so we can get this over with."

She turned and motioned for us to follow but I hesitated, knowing that Eva would be inside.

Am I ready for this?

My heart began to pound, suddenly finding myself a nervous wreck. I fought the urge to fidget and pressed my damp palms to my sides. Taking a step forward, I followed Madilyn through the doorway with Hale closely behind.

Madilyn took a seat at a small kitchen table. Following her lead, I sat across from her while Hale stood conspicuously a few feet behind me. I took a quick moment to assess my surroundings. The apartment was tiny, probably no more than a thousand square feet, and I could see most of it from my vantage point. Everything appeared clean, but not tidy. It was as if Madilyn had time to dust and vacuum but couldn't keep up with the everyday clutter. Toys were scattered on the floor in the family room and dishes were piled high in the sink. I took note of the toys—Marvel action figures, a remote-control Sonic race car, and tiny pegs from a Battleship board game that was left haphazardly unfinished on the floor.

Boy toys.

I didn't see anything that might be for a little girl.

I looked out the back windows and saw a community courtyard of sorts. Like the front of the building, everything from the child play area to the gardening plots looked well cared for.

"This place is nice," I remarked, trying to cut through the awkward silence that had fallen.

Madilyn scoffed.

"I'm only here because my name got picked in a lottery. If it weren't for that, I'd still be livin' in Brownsville Projects. But don't let this place fool you. It's low-income housing, too. You can put lipstick on a pig but it's still a pig. The people here are no different than the people in the projects. The walls are just fancier here. But give it time. It won't be long before this place resembles the building on Osborn Street. I just hope I can get my boys out of here before then."

"How old are your boys?" I asked.

"Alejandro is seven and Enzo is nine. They get along okay with Eva, but they're the rough and tumble type. Eva is so meek and mild, they tend to run roughshod over her. I think she's a lot like her mother."

"Oh?" I asked, my curiosity peaked. I didn't know Hannah well, so any insight I might gain from Madilyn could only help me with Eva.

"Hannah was always so passive—at least from what I saw. I wasn't very close with her, but there were some things that were obvious. We used to work together at Jacobi's Pizzeria."

Not close?

That seemed odd to me. Hannah made it seem like they were good friends. Or maybe I just assumed that was the case since Hannah had left her daughter in Madilyn's care.

"I was under the impression that you and Hannah were good friends," I casually mentioned.

"Not really. I mean, we kept in touch after Hannah stopped working at Jacobi's, but it was mostly just to help each other out with babysitting or shit like that. Neither one of us has family to rely on." She paused to yawn, then shrugged. "I liked Hannah, though. Sweet girl. I just didn't hang around with her much because of Dante. I never liked that guy."

"Dante?" I prodded with a raised brow, working to keep up with her unexpected narrative. I needed to be a sponge, absorbing every bit of information I could get.

"Dante is Eva's daddy. He deserved everything he got."

"What do you mean?"

"He was killed last month in prison. Didn't you know? Gang fight."

"No, I wasn't aware," I mused as I tried to process the information. If Alexander and I decided to go as far as adopting Eva, it seemed as if there would literally be nobody standing in our way.

"Hannah got the call about his death because she was still listed as next of kin. After that, she seemed... I don't know. Off, I guess you'd say. She seemed distracted all the time. Talked about you a lot. I didn't understand why she obsessed over you so much. This letter explained some to me, though."

Standing, she took a few steps to the kitchen counter and retrieved a folded piece of paper. The ends were tattered, as if it had been read over and over again. When she handed the letter to me, her expression was cold and hard. I took it from her outstretched hand, unfolded it, and began to read.

To whoever finds this, please deliver it to Mrs. Krystina Stone.

It went on to list my contact information, but I paused from reading to look up at Madilyn.

"Who found her?" I asked.

"Her neighbor." I nodded, but before I could continue reading, Madilyn pulled a silver key from her pocket, placed it on the table, and added, "I don't want to forget to give you this. It's the key to Hannah's apartment. The landlord plans to empty it at the end of the month, so if you want to go poke around and see if there's anything you can use for Eva, you'll need to do it before then."

I eyed the key for a moment. I didn't know Hannah all that well and the idea of going through her things was unsettling to me. It seemed intrusive. Still, everything seemed to be happening so fast. Until I figured out my next steps, it was probably best to have the key just in case. Reaching forward, I picked it up and dropped it into my purse.

"Thank you, Madilyn."

Then, focusing my attention back on the letter, I began to read.

Mrs. Stone,

I'd like to say that I'm sorry to do this to you, but I'm not. I have to do what's right for Eva, and I know that I'm no good for her. I just hope this letter helps you understand and, maybe someday, you'll be able to tell her how much I love her.

Eva would never have nice things with a mother like me. I couldn't even afford the shoes on her feet. I had to steal them from the local Payless and just hope I wouldn't get caught. I didn't, but me snatching a pair of shoes without paying for them didn't make much of a difference. We still had to eat—she still had to eat. So, I took advantage of someone's weakness and stole again.

You see, there's nothing worse than a child's hunger cry. It's not anything like whining because they haven't gotten their way or crying because they fell and skinned a knee. Her hunger cries cut through my soul, and I was helpless to make her stop. A few days after the crying began, the tears stopped. Eva started to sleep a lot and dark shadows appeared under her eyes. I knew I was failing as a mother. My inability to feed her was slowly killing her. I had to do something. I didn't have any food stamps because I'd sold them for cash so I could pay the rent. It would be two more weeks before I could get more. So, I took Eva and we went out to see if I could find food.

We ducked under the gates to the subway and took a train to

Midtown. When we got off, we made our way up to the street and spotted a food cart vendor closing up his stand for the day. There was a homeless person walking by. He was elderly and frail. I'd wondered how someone like him had made it this long on the streets. The vendor took pity on him and gave him a few scraps—a hot dog and a handful of fries that had strayed from the fryer. I viewed that as an opportunity. I instructed Eva to go back into the subway stairwell where we'd just come from and stay there until I returned. After the vendor pushed his cart away and was out of sight, I seized the moment. Without the tiniest bit of guilt, I walked up to the homeless man and stole the food he'd been given. He didn't even protest.

I went back to Eva, gave her the food, and watched as she ate. With every bite she took, the more awful I felt, and I knew she deserved more than what I could give her. I always tell her she can be anything she wants to be when she grows up, but that's a lie. People in this life never get out. She'd grow up poor, caught in this endless loop that people like me never escape from.

After she finished eating, we lingered in the subway tunnels, waiting for a train back home. Eva wasn't crying anymore, but I knew it wouldn't be long before the hunger cries would start again. Just the thought of it made me consider pushing Eva onto the train tracks. Yes, I really did think about killing my own daughter. But at that moment, all I could think was that death had to better than the life I was forcing her to live. I thought about hurling us both onto the tracks—to end our misery at the same time. Then I began to cry. We ended up riding the subway almost all night. I didn't want to go home to the graffiti buildings and streets littered with needles and cigarette butts. Eva slept in my arms as we rode, and I knew the only way to give her a better life was to remove myself from it.

I love my daughter so much. Eva is a gift to me—one that I don't

deserve. But you do. Maybe this is a cowardly way out. I don't know.
I just know in my heart that my baby will be better without me.
Take care of her, Mrs. Stone. Love her as much as I do and give her
everything I could not.

Hannah

My eyes were glistening with tears as I set the letter back onto the table. I looked at Madilyn, expecting her expression to match mine. However, my gaze only met an icy stare.

"Selfish if you ask me," Madilyn said.

I shook my head sadly. "No. Desperate. Just desperate. Perhaps even depressed."

"Call it what you want, but you weren't there to get the call from Hannah's neighbor. She saw Eva outside after dark and became concerned. Hunts Point ain't no better than Brownsville, and it's certainly no place for a kid at night. The neighbor knocked on Hannah's door, and when there was no answer, she let herself inside. She found Hannah hanging in one of the closets. Just imagine if little Eva had found her? So, I'll say it again—Hannah was selfish. Now that poor child is homeless with only a few belongings to her name." Madilyn paused and pointed to a tattered duffle bag on the floor. "That's it. No mother. No father. Nobody to care for her like she deserves."

Madilyn's tone was unforgiving, speaking like a person who truly understood the harsh realities in the world. I wanted to scream that I would take care of Eva, but I knew this had to happen one step at a time. For all I knew, Eva wouldn't want to live with Alexander and me. We were strangers to her. There was also the State to consider. I would need to file a petition in family court, but that didn't mean I'd be granted guardianship. Perhaps there were grandparents in the picture. I literally knew nothing about the child outside of our brief meeting more than two years back and the few things Hannah had told me.

"Madilyn, when can I meet Eva? Is she here?"

"She's here. Probably sleeping in the bedroom with the boys. Or maybe she took over my bed. I didn't check after I got home. Who knows what time they went to sleep last night after I went to work. I'm telling you, I can't wait for school to start back up so these damn kids get back into a routine. At least I won't have to worry about them during the day if they're in school."

"I'm sorry," I said, unsure if I'd heard her correctly. "Don't they go to daycare or something like it while you work?"

"You're funny. I'm lucky to have a bank and a grocery store within walking distance. Some people in town don't even have that. This area is what they call a food desert, but you probably know nothing about that. Daycare is even more scarce— especially for people who work second and third shift like I do," she retorted harshly.

"I didn't mean to imply... I just meant..." I stumbled, trying to find the right words. "They are just so young to be left alone."

Sighing, she shook her head.

"Look, it's been thirty-six hours since I last slept. When I got home from my second job, you rang the bell ten minutes after I walked in the door. I haven't even had a nap. I won't apologize for being a little snippy. This whole thing with Hannah and her kid was unexpected but life goes on. I know what you're thinking, but I had no choice except to leave her here with my other two while I worked. I don't need your judgement."

"I'm not judging."

She smiled wryly. "Yes, you are, sweetie. I can see it in your eyes. I know things are different for you, but the world never pauses for the poor. The people in Brownsville say if you make it to twenty-five, you're either dead, in jail, or done with gang life. The young teen mothers around here can get their hands on a gun easier than they can a box of Pampers. We've got babies raising babies, each one locked and loaded. I don't want that for my boys. They ain't got no father to help us out, so if I want out, I gotta work. Eva is just another mouth I'd have to feed when I can barely feed my own flesh and blood. She has to go."

As if on cue, a little girl walked out of one of the bedrooms rubbing her eyes. She was wearing a nightgown that seemed a bit too short on her. It skimmed the middle of her thighs, and when she raised her arms to stretch, pink polka dot underwear could be seen. She had a sweet round curve to her pale cheeks that were rosy from sleep. She was tiny with skinny shoulders, appearing to be much younger than five-years-old. If I hadn't already known her age, I wouldn't have guessed her to be more than three.

Her hair was in complete disarray, the curly light brown ends sticking up every which way. I smiled to myself, all too familiar with that sort of bedhead. Her overall appearance was a disheveled mess—but she was also the most beautiful thing I'd ever set eyes on.

"Eva," Madilyn said. "I want you to meet Mrs. Stone. You're going to live with her now."

17

Krystina

M adilyn had made little fanfare about saying goodbye to Eva. There wasn't even much discussion with Eva about who I was outside of the initial introduction. Madilyn just didn't seem to care. She'd simply instructed Eva to change from her nightgown, and then handed me the duffle bag containing Eva's limited personal belongings.

"Good luck in family court, Mrs. Stone," she'd said as she shooed us toward the door. "And Eva, you behave now. I don't ever wanna see you back in this part of town, you hear?"

Eva had nodded, although she probably had no idea why Madilyn would say such a thing. After that, the thin, tired woman had shown us the door, muttering something about trying to get some shut eye before her boys woke. It was at that moment I knew, without a shadow of a doubt, that I was doing the right thing. This child deserved so much more than what

Madilyn could have given her. It went beyond material things, such as food and clothing, to include emotional needs as well. They had very little connection. She just passed Eva off to me —a virtual stranger—without any questions whatsoever. Madilyn never would have been a mother to Eva.

But I could be.

The proverbial angel on my shoulder nodded her head encouragingly, but I was still apprehensive. I glanced down at the wide-eyed child, unsure what she'd been told about her true mother. It was such a delicate subject, and I didn't know how to ask her about it. So, as we walked hand-in-hand back to the car, I decided to let Eva take the lead. She hadn't spoken a word since she exited the bedroom in the tiny apartment, and I didn't want to push her too much. Everything was new to her, and from her curious expression, she seemed to be trying to sort it all out in her young mind.

Hale opened the back passenger car door and waited for us to get inside.

"Climb in, Eva. There's a booster seat in the back just for you. I bought it this morning." She looked up at me with furrowed brows and I smiled. "Everything will be okay, peanut. I promise."

Her unsure frown turned into an instant look of surprise.

"My mommy called me peanut," she said quietly. "She said it's because I'm small."

That was the exact reason I'd called her that, too. I wasn't sure what to think about the coincidence. I cast a brief, worried look at Hale before hurrying to respond to Eva.

"Oh, I didn't know that. I won't call you peanut if it bothers you. We don't need to use nicknames."

"No, I like being called peanut. Madilyn said you're going to be my new mom, so it's okay if you call me peanut just like my old mommy did."

Now it was my turn to have a look of surprise.

"Ma'am, we need to get you two in the car. I don't like the look of things," Hale said in a warning tone.

I looked up and followed Hale's gaze down the street. The once quiet and empty block was starting to come to life for the day, and we were receiving more than just a few curious glances. When a couple of teenage boys began to slowly make their way toward us, I saw what had caused Hale to become concerned. Although the boys were a good distance away, I'd caught the glint of something shiny in the hand of one of them. I squinted and my heart rate increased.

A knife maybe?

Or perhaps I was imagining things and it was just the glint of a ring in the bright sun. Whatever it was, I had no intention of waiting to find out. Never in my life did I think I'd actually be grateful for Alexander's insistence on using a bullet proof car for my transportation—until this moment.

Note to self: stop watching Criminal Minds.

I hurried Eva into the vehicle, closed the door, then quickly slid into the passenger seat of the blissfully air-conditioned car. Hale wasn't far behind me, sliding into the driver's seat and starting the engine. Within seconds, we were driving away, leaving the desolate world behind. I shared Madilyn's sentiment. Eva would never come back here again, and I would do everything within my power to make sure of that.

Turning in my seat, I glanced back at Eva. She was watching out the window, not seeming to realize anything had been amiss. She angled her head to look in my direction, and pale blue eyes met my gaze. Her eyes were lighter than Alexander's sapphire blues, but no less stunning. Her wintery irises were rimmed with a faint tinge of violet, reminding me of a Husky— beautiful, captivating, and extremely observant.

"So, Eva. Where would you like to go today?"

She shrugged. "I don't know. Where can we go?"

"Lots of places. We're going to go back to my house later, but I thought we could spend the afternoon doing something fun. Maybe tell me what you like, and we can decide from that where to go."

She pressed her pointer finger to her adorable pink lips and furrowed her brow as if she were deep in thought.

"I like animals. Elephants are my favorite."

"Hmmm, elephants," I mused, trying to think of an activity that would give me the opportunity to learn more about Eva. "We can go to the Central Park Zoo. They don't have any elephants, but there are plenty of other animals we could see."

"Okay. Maybe they have monkeys. Those are my second favorite animal."

I smiled.

"I'm pretty sure they have monkeys." Glancing at Hale, I gave him a quick nod. "You know the way, Hale. Central Park Zoo it is."

SUNLIGHT FILTERED through the trees as we passed by the clock with the mechanical animals in Central Park. We paused when Eva screeched in delight upon seeing them to life. I'd forgotten about the clock that animated only every fifteen minutes, and upon seeing Eva's bright smile, I felt fortunate to have walked by at the right time.

We walked through the entrance of the Central Park Zoo, and Eva looked around excitedly with wide eyes. I'd only been here once before, after I first moved to New York City. From the looks of it, not much had changed since then.

We walked from exhibit to exhibit. I explained what each animal was, and Eva listened with rapt attention, seeming to soak in every word I was saying. And when we reached the snow monkeys, her joyful laughter as she watched their silly antics sounded like music in my ears.

I glanced behind me at Hale. He'd been following behind us, keeping his distance but never allowing us out of his line of sight. A rare ghost of a smile played on his lips, and I knew Eva was the reason for it. Even though we barely knew her, it was hard not to smile at her innocent excitement. It was as if she was seeing everything around her for the first time. Perhaps she was. I had no idea if Hannah had ever taken her to the zoo before. If I had to guess, she probably hadn't.

"Did you know that some monkeys store food in their cheeks?" Eva asked.

"No, I didn't know that."

"Yep. They store it and then eat it later when they have a safe place to rest."

"Well, that's a fun fact to know," I said with a smile as I watched one of the snow monkeys contort it's face in weird ways. It almost seemed as if it was trying to communicate with the monkey across from it.

"Are there any Howler monkeys here?"

"Oh, gee, Eva. I'm not really sure."

"Howler monkeys are the loudest kind," she informed me.

I chuckled. "You sure do know a lot about monkeys."

"Not as much as I know about elephants," she boasted. "They are the largest animal on the land. They take mud baths so they don't get a sunburn. And did you know they can use their trunks as a snorkel?"

"I didn't. But that's pretty cool. How do you know so much about animals, Eva?"

"From books mommy would read to me at the library. The elephant books were my favorite because I want to be like them."

"You want to be like the elephants? Why?" I asked in amusement.

"Because elephants have really, really big brains," she said, holding her hands up and spreading them wide around her head. "They never forget anything, and I want to remember everything just like they can."

I smiled again, entertained by her animated passion about elephants. I was pleased at how quickly she'd climbed out of the quiet shell she had been in this morning. She'd been a chatter box ever since seeing the first animal. Taking her to the zoo had been the perfect thing to break the ice between us.

"I like your purple shirt, Mrs. Stone," she said, reaching up to finger the material at the hem.

"Thank you very much, but you don't have to call me Mrs. Stone. It sounds too formal. Why don't you just call me Miss Krys?"

"Miss Krys?"

"Yes. Or just plain old Krys. It's short for Krystina. It's what my friends call me."

"Are we friends?" she asked curiously.

"I'd like to be."

She seemed thoughtful for a moment before saying, "Miss Madilyn said if I was lucky, you'll be my new mommy."

"Oh, she did, did she?" I mused, not sure what to think about that revelation. That was the second time she referred to Madilyn suggesting I would replace Eva's mother. I wondered what else Madilyn had said. "Well, I think we should try being friends first. All good things come with time, Eva. Let's work on being friends first and see where that takes us. How does that sound?"

I didn't add that there was the business of family court to deal with. I didn't even know if I'd be allowed to be Eva's new mother. But that was a grown-up problem, and it was nothing a five-year-old needed to concern herself with.

"That sounds like a nice plan," she agreed with a nod, almost as if it were her idea. "I always wanted a friend. I didn't have any because mommy didn't like me playing with the kids on the street. She said they were no good. And Alejandro and Enzo were always mean to me, so they couldn't be my friends."

I considered her words as we walked. I didn't like to hear that Madilyn's boys mistreated Eva in some way. If they'd been unkind to her, I was even more happy to have removed her from that situation. I thought back to something Hannah once told me. She'd said that she managed to keep Eva sheltered and away from anything that could tarnish her. While I understood Hannah's reasoning, it made me sad to know this poor little girl had never experienced friendship because of it.

"I hope that changes for you soon, Eva. You'll be starting kindergarten soon. I think you'll like the school I picked out for you. I need to call tomorrow and see about getting you registered, but hopefully you can start in a few days. You're sure to make lots of friends there."

"Maybe," she said absently, looking around as if she was bored with the conversation.

As much as I wanted to keep her focused on the details about herself, I needed to remember that she was still so young. Her attention span for serious discussions probably wasn't all that tolerant. Everything was going to have to happen in small steps. Still, she'd given me more than enough to contemplate. This child was a mystery to me, and I couldn't wait to solve all her riddles.

The afternoon flew by, and when Eva asked if she could have some ice cream, of course I said yes. After we got our cones, a vanilla chocolate twist for me and a plain vanilla with sprinkles for Eva, we found a bench in the shade and ate our ice cream in quiet contentment.

Hale sat on the bench next to mine and Eva's, begrudgingly eating a chocolate cone that I'd insisted he order. There was no sense in following Eva and me around all day if he couldn't enjoy even the simplest of pleasures.

I tried not to think about Alexander, who was probably simmering with quiet resentment after our argument last night. There was no use dwelling on it. He'd come around eventually —or so I hoped. Pushing my worries about Alexander aside, I finished the last bit of my ice cream cone and sat back to watch the people passing by. After a while, it seemed as if all I saw was a montage of mommy and me moments.

A mother pushing a stroller walked by. She glanced at Eva and then me. I quickly looked away, unable to meet her eyes as the strangest feeling came over me. It was as if she knew Eva wasn't really mine, but worse, I felt like she knew the reason I didn't have my own stroller to push. It was ridiculous to think that way. Of course, the strange woman had no idea who Eva was to me or why I couldn't have children. Still, my inability to have kids felt like a scarlet letter broadcasting the failure and shame that made me less of a woman.

Still, as the stroller crossed my path, I couldn't help but peek inside. Delicate little fingers flexed around the edge of a pink fuzzy blanket, while wide eyes stared with wonder at the sky. My heart constricted, just as it always did whenever I saw a baby. The tiny infant was a reminder of what I would never have—and it also reminded me of all the steps I would be missing with Eva.

Late night feedings.

Her first steps and her first words.

The first time she had a fever.

I wondered if she was prone to sickness.

I hoped not.

I didn't know her favorite foods or most loved cartoon characters. I'd missed years of watching *Blue's Clues*—or whatever it was a five-year-old watched these days. I wasn't sure how I felt about missing so many firsts. I hadn't even thought about it until now. All of that seemed even worse because I also didn't have anything ready for her. Everything had happened so fast. There wasn't a room made up and I didn't have any toys. In fact, I didn't even know what kind of things she normally played with.

I wanted to feel excited about bringing Eva home, which I was, but I realized I was also scared to death about so many things—the unknowns, life adjustments, new worries. Then there was the issue of telling my mother about Eva.

What would she think about all this?

I liked to think she would be accepting, but my mother was hard to predict. I suddenly began to concern myself with work and other life responsibilities.

I have to update the employees at Turning Stone Advertising about my possible schedule changes. Kids required time and energy from their caregivers. I'll need to coordinate with Regina about my schedule, and carve out space—

I shook my head. I was approaching this like it was business —as if making time for Eva was an appointment that needed scheduling.

Maybe Alexander was right. Maybe this is all a huge mistake.

I swallowed and forced myself to tamp down the panic. I'd been so certain I could handle moving forward without Alexander's help, but now I just felt lost.

But this is what I want, isn't it?

Sure, it wasn't a baby, but it was my chance at having a family.

A family.

It was then that I realized why I was suddenly so afraid. I wanted to experience all these joys and worries with Alexander. Eva and I couldn't be a family as long as Alexander was a missing piece in our puzzle.

Sighing, I closed my eyes and counted to ten. When I opened them again, I glanced down at where Eva sat next to me. She was almost finished with her ice cream. A few stray candy sprinkles stuck to her upper lip and cheeks, evidence of her summer treat. She was looking around, seeming happy and content.

I smiled softly, her young and carefree innocence reminding me that things would only be complicated if I allowed them to be. I needed to stick to the basics and focus on my original plan. Everything surrounding Eva would need to be taken in small strides.

Baby steps.

First and foremost, I had to get Eva settled—in a new home first, and then in a new school. A lot of changes were going to be thrown at her and I wanted to make sure each transition went as seamlessly as possible.

"Eva," I began. My lips curved up in a grin when her wide, expressive gaze met mine. "When I was little, I loved my bedroom because it was a place I could call my own. I have a bedroom picked out for you at my house—your new home—but I want to make sure you're comfortable there, surrounded by all the things you love. So, to help that, I think you and I need to go on a little shopping spree."

18

Alexander

I stood patiently in one of the elevators in Cornerstone Tower as it ascended to the fiftieth floor. When the doors opened, I was greeted with the extravagant waiting area devoid of its usual hum of staff coming and going as they went about their workday. I wasn't surprised to find the floor completely empty, as I was almost always the first to arrive. I glanced down at my Rolex as I walked past the slate gray leather sofas and down the corridor toward my office. It was six-thirty. Laura wouldn't be here for another half hour.

I pushed through the frosted glass door and headed straight for my desk. I barely noticed the view of the Manhattan skyline through the floor-to-ceiling glass windows as I shrugged out of my suit coat. I slung the jacket over the back of the desk chair and sat down.

As was customary, Laura had printed today's schedule

before going home yesterday and had left it face up on my desk. I barely glanced at it, knowing it was most likely changing anyway. I had very little interest in what was happening today. All I seemed to think and care about was this rift between Krystina and me.

Too many days had gone by without talking to my wife. I'd never gone this long without speaking to her. She hadn't come to work yesterday, so there had been no chance run in on the elevator. There hadn't even been a single text message. I'd expected her to call after I left the house on Sunday night, but now it was Wednesday morning and I still hadn't heard a word from her.

I could have called, but ultimately decided against it. Krystina needed this lesson and calling her wouldn't help her learn. Hale had given me an update and I knew she had brought the child back to our home. I didn't like it—not one bit —but I knew it wouldn't be long before she figured out that I was right. Any kid who came from that part of town was bound to be nothing but trouble for her. Stereotypes weren't stereotypes if they always proved true. I just needed to wait this out a little longer.

I moved the mouse to wake the computer, then clicked on my inbox. I shook my head when I saw the new emails that had come between the time I'd left the penthouse and when I arrived at Stone Enterprise. It didn't matter if I'd just sorted through them earlier that morning. There were another forty-eight that needed my attention.

Jesus. Doesn't anyone sleep?

And here I'd thought I was the only one who started my day at such an ungodly hour.

I scrolled through the ever-growing list but stopped when I saw an email that Hale had sent five minutes ago. The name of Krystina's father was typed in the subject line. Without hesitation, I clicked on it.

To: Alexander Stone
From: Hale Fulton
Subject: Michael Ketry Profile

Mr. Stone,

Please see the attached PDF. It's the dossier I put together on Michael Ketry. I'm waiting on a link from Alliance Security System for the CCTV footage surrounding the penthouse. They have a clip of Ketry loitering outside the main entrance to the penthouse building. Once I have it, I'll forward it to you.

Also, we lost Ketry. The PI that I had tailing him saw him go into a local drug store two days ago, but he never came out. We haven't had eyes on him since. Please let me know how you wish to proceed.

Hale

I wasn't happy to hear that the private investigator Hale had hired somehow allowed Ketry to disappear. That wouldn't do. Frowning, I clicked on the PDF. Since I was already familiar with Hale's formatting style from previous background checks, I was able to quickly skim through.

FULL NAME: Michael Francis Ketry
AGE: 59
DOB: August 28, 1963
PLACE OF BIRTH: Albany, NY (Sisters Hospital)
PHYSICAL DESCRIPTION:
Height: 6' 2"

Weight: 200 lbs.

Hair: brown, some gray

Eyes: brown

ADDRESS & CONTACT INFORMATION:

Current address: 237 East 3rd Street, Apartment 18, New York, NY (August 2021 – present)

Previous address: Fishkill Correctional Facility, 18 Strack Dr, Beacon, NY (May 2014 – July 2021)

Phone: Unknown

Email Address: Unknown

I paused, directing my eyes back up to his previous address. I was skimming so quickly, I thought I'd misread it, but I hadn't. Ketry had spent time in jail. I hadn't expected to read that. I continued reading, knowing that Hale would have found out why.

PARENTS:

Father: Francis John Ketry (DOB November 21, 1940, Deceased January 5, 2006)

Mother: Evelyn Rose (DOB April 2, 1942, Deceased May 12, 2017)

SIBLINGS:

None

EMPLOYMENT:

Current Employer: unemployed

Previous Employer: Albany Department of Human Services

Gross annual income: unknown, last tax filing was in 2008

EDUCATION:

Pace Elementary School (gr. K-6)

Pace Middle School (gr. 7-8)

Eastwood High School (gr. 9-12)

College: None

SOCIAL MEDIA PLATFORMS:

Facebook, account inactive since 2014
Twitter, no activity
BANK INFORMATION:
Current Bank: None
Previous Bank: City Trust, overdrawn balance ($436.42), average daily balance ($7.24)
CRIMINAL BACKGROUND:
Grand larceny, forgery, perjury, and identity theft
Sentenced 10 years, granted parole after serving 7 years and 6 months

So that's why he did time. Ketry had quite the rap sheet. Interesting.

At the bottom of the PDF, there was link to a news article. Clicking on it, a boldface headline followed by a lengthy article dating back to 2014 filled the screen.

Albany Man Charged With Litany of Crimes for Decade-Long Scams

Michael Ketry, 51, was charged with multiple crimes for allegedly pulling off numerous scams over the course of more than a decade. The crimes include grand larceny, forgery, perjury, and identity theft. The Albany County District Attorney's Office issued a statement alleging crimes going back to at least 2004. In his statement, Albany DA Terence Straus said: "As alleged, Ketry used every trick in the book to pull off illegal scams over more than a decade. He preyed on the clients he was supposed to assist while he was employed by the Department of Human Services. He used his access to Albany County files to steal the identities of more than ten children. He used their information to file fake tax returns, henceforth defrauding New York State of tens of thousands of dollars in tax

refunds. My office commits to working with our law
enforcement partners to hold him accountable."

I'd been right to keep my limited knowledge about him
from Krystina. She wouldn't want to know this. It would only
hurt her to find out her biological father was nothing but a
lowlife criminal who preyed on the vulnerable. I vowed to only
tell her about him if I absolutely had to.

The article went on to list the details of each crime, but
before I could contemplate what any of it could all possibly
mean, Laura poked her head into my office.

"Good morning Mr. Stone," she said.

"Laura," I replied with a nod, and then glanced at the clock.
It was seven on the nose. "Right on time, as usual."

"I have an updated schedule for you, sir. The meeting with
the Stone Arena board members has been rescheduled for
three o'clock this afternoon. Bryan assures me it should be a
quick one, as the members are all very happy with the new
State contract."

"Good, good. The less time I need to spend assuring them
on the future of Stone Arena, the better," I mused as I
skimmed through the schedule she'd handed me. My day was
lighter than usual and for that, I was grateful. I couldn't help
but think that Laura may have noticed how distracted I'd been
yesterday and had rearranged today's schedule because of it. It
wouldn't surprise me if she had. My secretary never missed a
beat. "I have an hour free between eleven and noon. Block that
off for The Stoneworks Foundation and schedule a call with
Justine. I need to get with her on a few things, but I'm not sure
how long the call will be. An hour should be more than
enough time."

"Yes, sir. Anything else?"

"No. That will be all, Laura. Thank you."

She left the office, and I turned back to the computer to fire off a quick response to Hale.

To: Hale Fulton
From: Alexander Stone
Subject: RE: Michael Ketry Profile

Hale,

Get rid of the PI you hired for Ketry and put Greyson Hughes from the Stone Enterprise security team on it. I hate the idea of starting with someone new, but Greyson is loyal and I can trust him not to fuck this up. Ultimately, I just want Ketry found. That's the priority. After reading the background check, this isn't sitting well with me. He's up to something. I want a status update as soon as he's located.

Alexander Stone
CEO, Stone Enterprise

Three and a half hours later, I was engrossed in a property acquisition contract when a knock sounded on my office door. The door opened a moment later and my sister breezed in. I frowned, wondering how she was able to get in unannounced.

"Justine," I said with surprise. "I was expecting a call in about thirty minutes. I told Laura to block—"

"She called me, but I wanted to talk in person." Justine paused and glanced down at my desk. "I know I'm early. I hope I didn't interrupt anything important. Laura was on the phone when I got here, so I just let myself in."

I smirked. I could only imagine Laura's irritation over that. Justine had a habit of conveniently showing up at my office at the precise moment Laura was tied up. She'd barged in here on more than a few occasions. It annoyed me, but I never blamed Laura. My sister, if nothing else, was persistent, and she hated going through others to get to me. The fact that she managed to do it today pissed me off. I was distracted and miserable about the situation with Krystina, and I had no desire to be around people—especially those with an agenda. And if Justine came all the way here from her newly acquired condo in Westchester, it was for a reason.

"I was just reviewing a contract," I told her. Frowning, I shoved the stack of papers into my desk drawer and leaned back in my chair. "I'll finish going through it later with Stephen. I never sign anything without his legal opinion anyway. Now, I know we have Foundation business to discuss, but it's nothing pressing. What made you feel the need to come here in person?"

Pulling out a chair, she flipped her long black hair over her shoulder and sat down opposite my desk. She crossed one leg over the other, her perfectly manicured toes poking out from the ends of her red sling-backed heels. The shoes matched her business suit, and I wondered if she hadn't been in Westchester this morning after all. She looked as though she may have come directly from The Stoneworks Foundation office building.

"Yes, you're right, Alex. We do have Foundation business to discuss, but it's going to have to wait. I have other things I want to talk to you about first."

I raised a curious brow. "Such as?"

"I spoke to Joanna Cleary yesterday afternoon," she began, and I winced at the mention of my mother's live-in nurse. I knew what was coming.

"And?"

"She told me you hadn't been to see mom in over a week, and she was starting to worry. She said that wasn't like you. I agreed. After all, you were the one who insisted our mother live with you, and I know you're in the habit of visiting her rooms daily."

"I was in Las Vegas for part of that time and—"

"Yes, I know. Vegas for three days, and then MIA for another three," she interrupted. When she began to speak again, her tone was lecturing, and I knew then that Justine had only just begun. "You're entitled to a vacation, Alex—although I do wish you had told me because I would have visited her in your absence. Anyway, I digress. After speaking with Joanna, I decided to pop over last night to see mom and maybe visit with you and Krystina. When I got to your house, Vivian answered the door. Imagine my surprise when she said she hadn't seen you since Sunday night, and Krystina wasn't home because she was out with a little girl named Eva—a child who recently moved into your house!"

My jaw tensed, not liking the accusatory tone Justine was taking with me. My back went ramrod straight, ready to jump on the defense. Instead, I focused on keeping my cool. I didn't owe Justine an explanation. The situation with my wife was none of her business.

"Did Vivian say where Krystina went to?" I asked tersely, refusing to rise to her bait, yet curious about the outing my wife had gone on. Hale hadn't mentioned it to me.

"She said something about Krystina taking the girl to the movies—said she'd never been to one before or something like that. I don't know, but does it really matter? Did you hear anything I said? What in the ever-loving hell is going on, Alex?"

"None of your business. And remind me to have a chat with Vivian and Joanna about their gossiping."

"Oh, come on, Alex. Don't be ridiculous. It's me. They weren't chatting it up with a stranger. Stop trying to deflect." She stopped and waited a beat for me to say something. When

I didn't, she eyed me knowingly. "I suppose I could just call Krystina. I'm sure she'll tell me what's going on."

Standing abruptly, I slammed my palms on the desk.

"Goddammit, Justine! Why do you always have to push?" I snapped, then turned away from her to stare out the glass wall in my office.

There were times when I'd swear my sister was as fragile as a wallflower. Given our past, I could understand it. But there were other times when she'd get up on a self-righteous high horse with nerves of steel, ready to challenge the world over an injustice. Apparently, she decided to choose this as one of those times.

Sighing, I raked a hand through my hair. I shouldn't be upset with my sister. If I could confide in anyone about what I was thinking, it would be Justine. I was sure she remembered the filth we'd once lived in. She would understand. Hell, maybe she'd even help me talk some sense into Krystina.

Turning back to Justine, eyes that matched mine met my gaze. She sat patiently, as if she knew I needed a moment to sort my thoughts. I considered how much Justine knew and realized I would have to go back to the beginning.

"Do you remember Hannah Wallace, the women who held Krystina, along with nearly two dozen others, hostage at Stone's Hope just before Christmas last year?" I asked as I returned to my seat behind the desk.

"Of course, I remember."

I went through the explanation about Krystina's promise, the call she received in Las Vegas, and ended with our argument on Sunday night.

"Krystina just doesn't get it. She's being stubborn. We don't know what kind of emotional trauma this kid experienced. I mean, her father is in prison and her mother killed herself. She hasn't really had a great start in life. I don't want to take on the responsibility of fixing a broken child," I finished.

Justine remained quiet through my entire explanation with an impassive expression right up until my last sentence. She tried to mask it, but I caught the way she flinched. I tried to read what she was thinking, but her expression had gone blank once again.

"It seems like you have a lot going on," she remarked.

"You could say that."

She remained thoughtful for a moment before seeming to come to a decision.

"Look, I've been thinking about taking mom for a long weekend to Niagara Falls. She always seems happiest in nature and the weekend weather forecast is perfect for it. I would bring Joanna with us, too, of course. Maybe with her out of the house, you could give Vivian the weekend off. It will give you a chance to work things out with Krystina without so many prying eyes."

"You're welcome to take our mother for the weekend. I think she would enjoy that. But I'm not going back to the house. Not as long as the child is there."

Justine frowned.

"I'm curious. What does Ally think about all of this?" she asked evenly. "Krystina tells her just about everything. Does Ally agree with her or you?"

"Allyson? I have no idea. I don't even know if she knows. When we left Vegas, things were tense between them."

"Those two are like peas and carrots. What happened?"

I pinched the bridge of my nose, still unsure of what I thought about Allyson's impromptu marriage to my best friend.

"Allyson and Matteo got married when we were in Vegas."

Justine's eyes went wide. "Whoa! Are you serious?"

"Very. Krystina didn't know anything was even going on

with them. Neither did I. They sprung the news of their nuptials on us the morning after they tied the knot. They'd always been flirty with each other, but I never would have predicted what happened. Although it wasn't discussed, I can read my wife. I'm sure Krystina feels incredibly betrayed."

"And rightly so. God, she must feel so alone right now," Justine said, shaking her head in disbelief. "Alex, you need to go home. All things considered, this business of taking in a stranger's kid is a lot for one person to handle. Just talk to her."

"No, I'm not caving, Justine. My position is firm. This child comes from the gutter. I've come too far to be associated with that life."

I saw Justine visibly bristle.

"Since when did you become such a pretentious jerk?" she quipped accusingly.

"Excuse me?"

"You heard me. Not everything is about you, Alex. If you looked past your ego for two minutes you might be able to see things differently. When you said that little girl was broken, I didn't say anything even though the same could be said about me. Yes, we know what it's like to live in poverty. We never had a choice until our grandparents stepped in. They gave us a different life and a second chance. Don't you think this child deserves that chance just as much?"

I pressed my lips together in a tight line at the turn in conversation. This was not going as planned. Not at all. Justine was supposed to be on my side about this.

"It's not that I don't think she deserves it. I just can't be the one to give it to her. She's not my blood, Justine. I owe her nothing."

"There's your ego talking again. Not your blood," she muttered with disdain. "Now I know what this is really all about. Krystina can't have children, so you are going to allow your arrogance to ruin the chance to have a family through any alternative means simply because you didn't plant the seed. Unreal. I expected better from you, Alex. I really did."

I closed my eyes. Her indignant tone cut me to the core, but I refused to show it.

"You're overstepping, Justine. Like I said—this is none of your business."

"It is my business because I love Krystina just as I would if she were my flesh and blood sister, and not a sister through marriage. Blood isn't always thicker than water, Alex. I can love Krystina just as easily as she can love Hannah Wallace's little girl. And have you considered Frank? He raised Krystina as his own even though not a drop of his blood runs through her veins. This isn't about Krystina's stubbornness. This is about your own stupidity. Your wife acts as if you hung the moon, and this is how you treat her when she's at her most vulnerable. Leaving her alone right now is wrong and it's selfish. After Liliana, don't you think the two of you have been through enough? You took a vow—for better or for worse. It's time you swallowed your pride and went home."

And with that, she stood and slung her white Louis Vuitton purse over her shoulder. When she turned to walk out, I could only sit there in shock, having never in my life been told off by my sister. But what was worse—I'd allowed it.

What the fuck is wrong with me?

Shaking my head, I stared at Justine moving toward the door and focused on the only thing that made sense at that moment. Business.

"Justine, wait," I ordered. "I appreciate your flare for the dramatics, but you can't just storm out of here. We still need to talk about the Foundation. There are events coming up, and I need you to coordinate with Harper on a fundraiser for the Women Rise division."

Pausing, she angled her head to look at me through frigid eyes.

"You can consider it done. No need to talk about it. Anything else? Boss," she added, voice dripping with sarcasm. Her eyes, however, were filled with disgust and disappointment.

I tilted my chin up in defiance, as if I were challenging her to push just one more of my buttons.

"That will be all, Justine."

"Fine. I'm going to arrange a van service for mom and her wheelchair. No need for you to worry about anything. I'll coordinate with Joanna about the details."

Then she was gone. And for the second time that day, I slammed my hands on the desk, causing the computer monitor to wobble on its stand.

Fucking Justine.

I wanted to wring her neck and ignore the little voice in my head that was telling me every single thing she'd said was right.

I was about to stand and pace the room, needing to do something—anything—to vent my frustration, but paused when I heard an email ping. Glancing at the computer screen, I saw it was an email response from Hale. Clicking on it, I began to read.

To: Alexander Stone
From: Hale Fulton
Subject: RE: Michael Ketry Profile

Boss,

See the link below from Alliance Security System for the CCTV footage of the penthouse lobby. I was a bit surprised by what I saw, and I expect you to be as well.

Also, the PI has been terminated. Greyson Hughes is now on the job. I'll keep you apprised of any updates.

Hale

I clicked on the link that would take me to the Alliance Security Systems CCTV video footage and located the file Hale referenced. Sitting back in my chair, I waited for it to load. Once it did, I narrowed my gaze. This was the first time I'd seen Ketry and I wanted to memorize every line of his face so I'd be able to spot him if he was ever near. Thankfully, we upgraded security a couple of years back. The grainy black and white footage was gone, having been replaced by clear, high-definition video.

Ketry was tall, with thinning brown hair streaked with gray on the sides. He was slightly overweight, with a round protruding belly that caused the buttons of his shirt to strain. It appeared as though it had been a few days since he'd last shaved, and the dark stubble cast menacing shadows on face.

About ten minutes into the feed, a woman walked onto the screen. Her back was to me and I couldn't see her face. Still, there was something about the woman's posture that was familiar. When she finally shifted so her face was angled in front of the camera, I sucked in a breath, shocked to see the face of Elizabeth Long.

"Well, this day just gets more and more fucked up with each passing minute," I mused aloud to the empty office. "What the hell is she doing?"

As far as I knew, Elizabeth didn't talk to Krystina's biological father. I didn't even know if Elizabeth had ever been married to him. If she had, it didn't show up on the background check that Hale conducted. I wondered if Frank Long knew his wife was still in contact with Ketry.

None of this made any sense, but it was clear that if I wanted answers, I'd need to talk to Krystina's mother. Picking up my cell from the desk, I dialed her number and waited for her to answer. Her voice came through the line after the third ring.

"Hello?"

"Elizabeth, it's Alex."

"Oh, you just caught me. I was on my way out to the dealership. Frank wants me there because Channel Four is coming to interview him about the skyrocketing price of used cars. Frank says it's gotten out of control," she added.

I was happy to hear her time was limited because I wasn't up for a lengthy conversation.

"So I've heard. Since you're on your way out, I won't keep you and get right to the point. I need you to tell me everything you know about Michael Ketry." Silence filled the line and I half wondered if she'd hung up. "Elizabeth, are you there?"

"I'm here," she finally said. "Alex, why are you asking about Michael Ketry?"

"I think the bigger question is, why did you meet with him in the lobby of my penthouse last week?"

19

Krystina

E va and I stepped onto the grounds of Dalton-Hewitt Academy on Thursday morning. Hale had just dropped us off and was waiting at the curb for me to return once Eva was settled. This was her second day in the new private elementary school that I'd chosen for her, and so far, so good. The only thing I didn't like was that my office was an hour away from her school. I worried that if something were to happen, it would take me too long to get to her.

If the court granted me permanent guardianship, I might have to consider moving Turning Stone Advertising to a building facility closer to home. I considered discussing it with Alexander, but the constant twisting ball of anxiety in my belly quickly reminded me that I hadn't spoken to my husband in days. We'd never gone this long without speaking, and I was miserable without him.

Still, despite my angst over my marriage, I felt relatively good about how things were progressing with Eva. We still had so far to go, and Alexander's concerns about Eva's psychological state were never far from my mind. If there were underlying issues with her, nothing had revealed itself. So far, Eva had been nothing cheerful, sweet, well-mannered, and full of curious questions that I could barely keep up with. Hopefully, no trauma would arise, and all would be fine.

I'd been in touch with Child & Family Services and had already petitioned the court for guardianship of Eva. Thankfully, my connection to Thomas Green at the DA's office came in handy. He was able to pull a few strings and got my case seen by a judge right away. The judge granted me temporary custody of Eva that same day, and I was set to go back to court in October to hopefully make it permanent.

Once I had the paperwork showing I had temporary custody of Eva, Dalton-Hewitt Academy made the registration process a breeze, and allowed her to start on time with all the other fresh-faced kindergarteners, many of whom were gathered near the swing set in the recess yard at the school at this very moment.

"Have a good day!" I called to Eva as she took off toward her classmates. I liked that the kids were allowed time each morning to enjoy a moment of socialization before their teacher called them inside.

"Thanks! Bye!" returned Eva's tiny voice as she waved to me over her shoulder. She ran off with her purple unicorn lunch box swinging in her hand and matching bookbag bobbing on her back. As much as she loved her new school bag, it seemed much too large for her little body.

I shook my head and smiled to myself.

I'm forgotten already.

I was happy to see her adjusting so quickly, but I couldn't

help but feel a little envious of her teacher over the amount of time she got to spend with Eva. I'd only been able to spend a few short days with her before school began. A part of me wished I'd allowed her a late start, but I also knew how important the first day was for integration into a classroom. School had to come before my selfish desires.

Already missing her, I decided to walk around to the back of the school where I could watch her for a few minutes before she had to go inside. When I got there, I quickly learned that I wasn't the only one with that idea. A dozen or more adults stood along the fence watching their little ones at play. I joined them but couldn't shake the imposter syndrome I felt over being there. I hoped that would go away with time.

"Which one is yours?" asked a male voice. Looking to my left, I saw an older man had come up beside me. He looked like he was around sixty years old, with brown graying hair.

"The one with the curly brown pigtails," I told him. "You?"

"The dark-haired boy with the red t-shirt. It's my grandson. They grow up fast, don't they?"

"They sure do," I replied, making that imposter syndrome return with full force. I silently cursed, and then decided to just speak truthfully. I had nothing to hide after all. "Eva recently just came under my care. Her mother died unexpectedly and I'm hoping to get permanent custody of her."

"Is that so? So, she isn't yours. I see," the man replied, sounding overly curious and just a tad judgmental.

Damn it.

"Not yet," I said hurriedly, wishing I hadn't revealed so much.

The man angled his head as if to get a better look at the children playing, and that's when I noticed a strange odor emanating from him. It smelled like a combination of garlic and sweat. I took a small step back, hoping my attempt to get away from the smell wasn't too obvious.

"You said her name is Eva?" he asked.

"That's right," I confirmed. I took another step back, but the stench just seemed to follow me. As nonchalantly as I could, I raised my hand to bid him farewell. "Well, I hate to end this chat so quickly, but I have to run. My ride is waiting for me. Nice talking to you!"

I hurried back to where Hale was waiting with the car. Whether or not I felt the need to escape the smelly man was irrelevant. I really had no business dawdling at the school. I'd barely been to work at all this past week, and I had a lot of catching up to do. Even my commute had become precious time. Since taking in Eva, I hadn't been able to go to the cemetery to visit Liliana, so I'd established a new routine of watching the video Alexander had made for me each morning.

Of course, it wasn't the same as being there in person, but I didn't think it was right to bring Eva to a gravesite—at least not now while everything was so new to her. She was young and going through so many changes, but I hoped I'd be able to take her to visit Liliana one day.

After watching the video and pressing an air kiss to the screen with my two fingers, I used the rest of the time in the car to sort emails. By the time I arrived at Turning Stone Advertising nearly an hour later, I'd put a plan in place to best manage my time efficiently. With any luck, I'd be caught up on everything before the end of the day tomorrow.

Pushing open the door to my office, I stepped inside. My gaze scanned the length of the room that I'd fallen in love with so many years ago. The space had been a surprise from Alexander shortly after we started dating. Designed by Kimberly Melbourne, a renowned interior designer in New York, the room was wide and traveled the entire length of the building. Floor to ceiling windows flanked the north and south walls, with a desk made of reclaimed antique hardwoods centering on the west wall. A sitting area furnished with plush armchairs and a glass-topped table was off to my right, while a mini bar complete with a state-of-the-art coffee machine was to my left.

However, my favorite part of the office was the artwork on the wall behind my desk. It was a mural of a single white lily against a black and gray backdrop. The simple color palette swirled together in a downward pattern, creating a waterfall effect with the lily as the focal piece. Above the lily, a quote was inscribed.

"There's something which impels us to show our inner souls. The more courageous we are, the more we succeed in explaining what we know."
-Maya Angelou

At first, I'd simply been drawn to the artworks stunning beauty. But now I was drawn to it for a different reason. After losing Liliana, I'd experienced countless mornings of walking through the office on autopilot, feeling desolate and despondent after spending time at the cemetery. But when I stepped foot into this room, I was able to find peace by looking at the mural and studying the quote. The cascading, fluid design was calming. It reminded me that life, despite its many trials and tribulations, goes on. It never ceases, is constantly moving, and only those who were truly courageous could withstand the tests of time.

I'd survived the hardest test of all—losing a child. Because I'd persevered, I now had the opportunity to experience a different kind of fulfillment with Eva. I only hoped I could convince Alexander to look at it that way. I'd said I'd do this with or without him, but I didn't want to. I'd survived losing Liliana, but I knew I wouldn't be able to survive losing Alexander. He had to come around. I needed him—perhaps now more than ever.

Draping my purse across the back of the desk chair, I sat down and woke the computer. I'd been so pre-occupied with Eva since returning from Las Vegas, I'd completely lost touch with what I had going on at work. As soon as I saw the slew of emails populate on my screen, I resigned myself to a long day ahead.

I drummed my fingers on the desktop as I scrolled through my list of emails, sorting them by priority. As I neared the end of the list, the phone on my desk buzzed. I glanced at it and saw the line from my secretary was lit up. I frowned, wondering what Regina wanted. I'd explicitly emailed her before I arrived at Turning Stone Advertising this morning, informing her that I didn't want to be bothered while I played catch up. It was unusual for her to not follow a direction.

Reaching forward, I pressed the intercom button.

"Yes, Regina," I said into the speaker.

"I'm sorry, Mrs. Stone. I know you said you didn't want to be bothered, but there is a man on the phone insisting that he speak with you. He says he's your father."

"Frank? That's weird. I wonder why he didn't just call my cell. Go ahead and put him through." I waited a moment for the call to switch over, and then picked up the receiver and said, "Hi, Frank."

At first, I was greeted by silence. But then a rough voice that sounded nothing like my stepfather came through the line.

"Krystina," said a man in a gravely tone. "This isn't Frank. I'm ah... I'm not sure how to say this. It's been a long time coming."

I pressed my lips together in a tight line, feeling thoroughly aggravated. I'd been through my fair share of prank calls after the paparazzi debacle where my cellphone number was leaked. I was certain this was just residual fallout from that, and I had zero patience for it.

"I'm sorry, but who am I speaking with?" I asked impatiently.

"This is your father, Krystina."

I nearly laughed. Whoever this was needed to do better.

"You're not my father. I'd recognize his voice."

"No. Not that dim whit your mother married. This is your real father."

The strangest sensation washed over me. I didn't know why, but my heart suddenly began to race. Call it a sixth sense or whatever, but it was as if I sensed truth in his words even though they had to be impossible.

No. It can't be him. And after all this time?

If this was in fact my biological father, he'd given up his chance to know me a long time ago. I wanted nothing to do with him. Frank was the only father I'd ever known. He'd provided for me in more ways than one and my memories were with him—not this stranger on the phone.

Neither the man nor I spoke, and the silence felt heavy. I could hear his heavy breathing combined with ticking second hand on the large black iron-framed clock hanging above the minibar. My heart began to pound harder in my chest until all other sound was drowned out by the pulsing in my ears.

I had to end this call.

Now.

"I have a father, and you're not him," I barked into the receiver before slamming it back onto the cradle.

My hands were trembling. I clamped them together and placed them in my lap where they restlessly began to fidget. Attempting to calm myself, I inhaled a shaky breath. I continued to focus on my breathing, slowly inhaling and exhaling until I felt steady once again. Then I shook my head.

"You're being ridiculous," I whispered to myself in the empty room. "It was nothing more than a prank call. You've got yourself all worked up for nothing."

Swiveling in my chair to face the computer once more, I went back to the task of sorting my inbox. As I dragged the last email into a file labeled for follow up, the anxious feeling returned. I didn't know why, but I had a sinking feeling that today wouldn't be the last time I heard from the stranger. Questions began to populate in my head, with the answers dangling like carrots just out of my reach. I needed to know more.

Reaching down into my purse, I pulled out my cellphone and dialed my mother. As the phone rang, I concocted a story about the purpose of my call, knowing my mother wouldn't even entertain a conversation about the phone call I'd just received. Talking about the sperm donor had always been off limits. It was too upsetting for her, although I'd never asked why. I'd just never cared to. He was like a ghost, invisible to me, and had never once mattered. I didn't even know his name— hence the reason for the call to my mother. I couldn't learn more without a name and I was now kicking myself for not asking him for it before I hung up. At the very least, I could have used it to confirm or refute his claim about being my biological father.

As my mother's phone continued to ring through the line, I realized I should have thought this out better before calling her. I supposed I could just tell her that I was going to take one of those family DNA tests, and I wanted to head off any surprises. It was simple and it made sense. I could use that to segue into why I needed his name.

When the call was sent to her voicemail, I grunted in

frustration. I hung up without leaving a message. I wasn't sure what to say. It was probably for the best anyway. Even with feigned innocence about a DNA test, I knew the conversation would undoubtably be awkward. It may even result in an argument. There was no sense in looking for trouble when I already had enough on my plate. All my focus had to be trained on Eva and fixing everything that was broken with Alexander. They were all that truly mattered.

20

Alexander

I brought the Tesla to a stop on the semi-circular driveway in front of the house in Westchester. The choice to park in front rather than drive around back to the multi-car garage was a strategic one because I didn't know if I was staying. Whether I did would all depend on if Krystina would see reason.

It had been five days since I last spoke to my wife—five long, fucking miserable days. I thought for sure she would have come to her senses by now, but clearly, I was wrong. There was no use having a battle of wills with her. If I thought taking her over my knee would make a difference, I'd do it. But she was too tenacious, and I wasn't going to budge on this one. All I knew was that I missed my wife. We had to talk sooner rather than later. If she was too stubborn to see her foolishness, so be it.

But I was done waiting.

Climbing from the driver's seat, I glanced up at the massive Georgian Colonial that Krystina and I had built for us after we were married. Tall pines flanked the handpicked stone exterior walls of the Chappaqua mansion, creating a picture that would make any experienced painter weep. The house had never been my style, but it had grown on me. It fit Krystina and, just like her, there was no denying its beauty.

I opened the front door and stepped over the threshold with purpose, bracing for the fight that was sure to ensue once I was inside. I was greeted with silence, but I'd expected as much. I had planned my return home for later in the evening, hoping Krystina would have put the child to bed. It would allow me to talk without distraction.

Being that it was well past the dinner hour, Vivian had most likely retired for the night, and if I went looking, I knew I would find Hale in his residence on the East side of the property. While he'd been staying in one of the guestrooms while I was at the penthouse, I'd called him to let him know I was returning and instructed him to go back to his place. I wasn't sure how my conversation with Krystina was going to go and I didn't want an audience for it.

Crossing the foyer, I poked my head into the living room only to find it empty. Going back to where I'd just come from, I made my way up the grand staircase to the second floor. Most likely, I'd find Krystina in her office or our bedroom.

When I didn't find her in either place, I frowned and glanced down the hallway leading to the guest bedrooms.

Shit.

A run-in with the child had not been on my agenda tonight. In fact, I'd wanted to avoid it all together. A feeling of resignation settled over me as I slowly made my way down the hall. Only one door was open, and the faint sound of Krystina's voice filtered to my ears as I approached. When I reached the doorway, I paused when I saw her sitting in a plush chair reading a book to a little girl cradled in her lap. By the looks of her, the girl was sleeping.

Krystina glanced up and her gaze locked on mine. Something unreadable flashed in her deep chocolate brown eyes. Before I could determine what that might be, she raised a finger to her lips, motioning me to be quiet. Then, without a word, she closed the book and set it on the side table. Slipping her arms under the girl, she stood and carried her to the bed.

I did a double take, suddenly noticing the changes to the room. The guest bedroom that was once decorated with modern contemporary décor had been completely transformed. The charcoal gray satin comforter and matching window dressings had been replaced by purple frills and lace. The queen-sized bed with the quilted headboard was gone, and a four-poster canopy bed sat in its place. Sheer purple curtains hung from the rails, pulled back at each corner. A white lamp with a pale purple lampshade sat on the nightstand next to a mountain of stuffed animals. She'd even had the walls painted a light purple. The room, in all its obnoxious purple glory, was virtually unrecognizable to me.

What had she done?

I pressed my lips tight together and frowned. Redecorating an entire room from top to bottom and giving this child what appeared to be her own personal space was the complete opposite of everything I'd wanted. Her being here was only supposed to be temporary until Krystina came to her senses.

But this...

This was all so permanent.

Turning my attention back to my insolent wife, I watched as she pulled the blankets over the sleeping child. I froze, completely mesmerized by the touching scene playing out before me. I had a sense of déjà vu before quickly realizing why this looked familiar to me. It wasn't anything I'd actually seen before, but something I'd imagined—a vision of Krystina tucking our child into bed and pressing a gentle kiss to their forehead. Except in my vision, it was Liliana five years in the future, and not this... this imposter.

The girl in that bed wasn't ours and she never would be. I had to remember that no matter how much my resolve wanted to crumble after seeing Krystina this way. This was not our reality.

Once the little girl appeared secure in the bed, Krystina stood, smoothed out her shirt, and made her way toward me. I stepped back to allow her to pull the door closed behind her. When she turned to face me, relief was plain on her face.

"I'm so glad you came home," she said. Her voice sounded hesitant, almost as if she were weighing her words carefully. Reaching for me tentatively, she slipped her arms around my waist. "I was starting to worry that we might not get through this, but I should have known better."

"Angel, we need to talk," I said stiffly, trying to ignore how good her arms felt around me.

"I know, and we will. But let me just have a moment." Angling her head back, she met my gaze. Reaching up with one of her hands, she began to trace the outlines of my face as if committing them to memory. "I missed you so much, Alex. But your eyes. I think I missed those sapphire blues the most."

I cocked up one eyebrow. "My eyes?"

"Mm, hmmm. And your lips. I missed those, too."

Pushing up on her tip toes, she surprised me by pressing a chaste kiss to my lips. I expected her to be angry when I returned. Never had I anticipated a greeting such as this. When she began to pull away, I stopped her, and almost involuntarily, found my lips begin to move against hers. I shouldn't have kissed her back. Not now—not while I was so conflicted about everything. But I couldn't help it. It had been too long since I last tasted her.

I ran my tongue over her bottom lip, prodding her mouth open. She opened willingly and brought her hands up to grip the back of my neck. I growled my approval and deepened the kiss, pulling her body tighter to mine. Our tongues lapped and danced urgently and desperately. It was so good, as if both of us needed this more than the air we breathed after so many days apart.

I moved my mouth over the line of her jaw, working my way down her neck as she hummed with pleasure. Sliding a hand down until I found the hem of her T-shirt, I navigated my palm under and up, cupping the side of one of her breasts. It was covered in smooth satin, a barrier that I wanted erased.

Pulling one of the cups down, I allowed a breast to spill free. I twisted the nipple for a moment, appreciating the way it pebbled so quickly under my touch, and then pulled down the other cup to give each hardened peak equal attention.

I suckled her neck and she gasped as I pinched and teased, tilting her head back to give me easier access. I savored the feel of her pulse hammering beneath her skin as I breathed in her scent. She smelled like sun-kissed plums and jasmine, an aphrodisiac to my senses. Moving up to claim her mouth once more, I pushed my tongue past her waiting lips and devoured her. She moaned, the vibration from her lips sending electric shock waves to my groin.

"I want you," I growled, pushing her until her back was against the wall. Looping an arm down under her knee, I pulled her right jean-clad leg up to wrap around my hip. I nipped her neck, moving to capture her earlobe between my teeth. "You have no idea how many nights I lay awake wanting to touch you, to feel your sweet pussy milking my cock."

Following my lead, she brought up her other leg until both

legs were scissored around my waist. Despite the barrier of her denim and my shirt, I could feel the heat of her sex pressing against my abdomen. I crushed my mouth to hers once more, kissing her senseless and fueling the need that was already burning hot. Her hands clung to my biceps, moving up to grip my shoulders as if she were hanging on for dear life. And in a way, that's exactly what we were both doing—fighting to keep hold of our fragile relationship in any way we could. The Fates had been cruel, but now it was time for us to take back our destiny. I couldn't spend another day without my angel. I wanted to tear the clothes from her body right there in the hallway, and drive into her brutally and possessively.

But then she spoke, and reality came crashing down around me.

"Alex, oh God, I need you. I knew you'd come back to me. Take me to bed, and when we wake in the morning, you'll finally have a chance to meet Eva and start getting to know her."

Immediately, I pulled back. Our lips hovered over each other's, allowing our breaths to mingle with every pant.

Get to know her?

Krystina still didn't get it. I had no intention of getting to know that little girl.

Ever.

Pushing her legs down until her feet were safely planted on the floor, I took a step back. Confusion spread into her wide, chocolate brown eyes, and it killed me to speak my next words because I knew they would crush her.

"No, Krystina. There will be no getting to know her in the morning. I won't be getting to know her at all. Tomorrow, we need to take her to the Office of Child and Family Services. They can handle her from there."

"Wait, what? But I already spoke with OCFS. Everything

goes through family court. For the time being, I have temporary guardianship. I thought you came back here to..." She shook her head in bewilderment. "Alex, why *did* you come back?"

Sighing, I closed my eyes and pressed my forefingers to my temples. When I opened them again, I saw darkness in Krystina's expression. In the short time since I'd been back, I watched her transition from happy and content to relieved and passionate. But now, all I saw was that familiar anger and a hurt that cut so deep, I wondered if it was a permanent part of who she was now.

"Angel, staying away was one of the hardest things I ever had to do. I had hoped that you would use that time to see reason. Imagine my surprise when I came home to find a room completely remodeled for a child who was never supposed to be here in the first place. It's clear that you've made your decision—and you made it without me."

Angling her chin up stubbornly, she pushed her mussed hair back from her face and eyed me coolly.

"I could say the same about you. You made the decision to never adopt without me. And I'm not just talking about Eva, but about any child. You decided adoption was off limits without so much as a brief mention to me. My feelings about it never mattered to you."

"You make it seem like I deliberately hid my feelings when that wasn't the case. It just never came up."

"I'm not going to argue this in the hallway and risk waking Eva. If you want to talk rationally, we can do so in the living room." Without another word, she walked down the hallway and descended the grand staircase.

I fought the urge to slam my fist through the wall. I didn't know when Krystina decided it was okay for her to call all the shots. That wasn't how things were supposed to work. I didn't operate like that. I was in charge—always—and it was high time she remembered that.

Moving to the steps, I made my way down, reaching the bottom as she was crossing the foyer.

"Stop walking away and look at me," I ordered. My voice boomed, echoing off the tall ceilings.

Stopping in her tracks, she slowly turned to face me. We stared at each other for a long moment, neither one of us speaking. The air was wrought with tension, and while I was supposed to be reminding her who was boss, I instead found my tongue thick and heavy in my mouth.

"I'm not a dog who can be ordered about, Alex."

My jaw tightened.

"In my absence, you seem to have forgotten who's in control."

"And you seem to have forgotten that I've never allowed you to control me—at least not outside the bedroom. I don't know what gave you the idea that something had change. If you want to talk, then that's fine. But it will be a conversation between equals. None of this caveman shit, Alex. I've had a very busy week, and I'm in no mood for it. I urge you to consider your words carefully," she finished in a warning tone.

My eyes narrowed.

"Is that so?"

"Yes. I won't entertain any conversation that involves turning Eva over to the State. If that's where you're going with the talk, you can save your breath. She's staying, and I would like it if the two of us could come to a mutual agreement about it."

"And if I'm not willing to have the conversation you want?" I asked, testing her.

Krystina sighed and shook her head.

"This doesn't need to be a fight, especially because the basis for your argument revolves around an assumption. I remember Hannah once telling me that Eva was good, and that she hadn't been tainted by her environment. I think she was telling me the truth. Eva is good, pure, and so very sweet. She's smart, too, but you won't even give her a chance because in your mind, she's already a lost cause. She isn't—she's far from it."

"It's been less than a week, Krystina. There are things that manifest and reveal themselves with time."

"That's your psychology degree talking. Have you ever considered that there might not be anything nefarious under the surface at all?"

I hadn't returned home for this. Clearly, Krystina needed more time to come to terms with reality.

"You seem to have made up your mind. I'm leaving. Let me know when you want to see reason. But I will say, I never thought I'd see the day when you'd choose a stranger's child over me," I added bitterly. The hurt I felt over that fact was vicious and real.

"That's not fair and you know it. I want you both. The difference is, Eva isn't asking me to choose. You are."

I stared at her, a silent battle of wills raging between us. The dark look in her eyes was something that had become all too familiar. It was the direct result of too much sadness and loss. The last time I saw that look was when we were at Club O— when she'd been desperate to escape her pain by any means possible. This child was just another way at escapism.

Or was her pain brought on by something else entirely?

I had no idea when we'd reached this place of isolation. It was as if each of us were standing on our own lonely rock, our emotions like an angry river rushing around us, yet neither of us were willing to bridge the gap or attempt to step across. I had no words to explain how I felt—at least none that she would understand.

Knowing I needed to get away, I turned and stormed out of the house. My anger was near boiling, and it wouldn't bode well for either of us if I erupted. Krystina didn't follow me, nor did she call out to try and stop me.

I stalked toward the Tesla with hurried steps until I saw movement out of the corner of my eye. I glanced over and saw Hale had just rounded the corner of the house. He paused when he saw me, and then changed course to head my way.

"Boss," he said with a brief nod. "I was just heading down the drive to make sure the security gates are locked for the night. Everything okay?"

"Not particularly," I responded, my words dripping with sour taste. "Krystina is as stubborn as a fucking mule."

Hale's brows arched and I saw one corner of his mouth twitch.

"Oh, you don't say?" he said, not bothering to mask the amusement in his tone. I ignored him and continued on.

"It's brutal. She has to be out of her mind to want this child. She has no idea what she's taking on. When I look at that kid, I see myself and all the bad shit from my past. Krystina is in for a world of fucking hurt, Hale. And it comes at a time when we've already been through so much. I can't control the shitstorm this little girl is sure to bring. Krystina and I have something good here, and I don't want all that ugliness in our home. Mark my words. The child is going to have problems."

"So, you think Eva is the problem then?"

"Yeah," I said slowly, suddenly noticing the knowing lilt in his voice and the way he said the little girl's name with too much familiarity—like he was privy to something I didn't know. "What's with the tone, Hale?"

He frowned and shook his head with seemingly fake innocence. "What tone?"

"That tone. You act as if you know something."

"I'm not taking a tone. I'm just confused by the situation."

"Cut the shit, Hale. If you have something to say, then say it."

"Oh, I have things to say. I just don't know if you'll want to hear it. Do you want brutal honesty?" he asked.

"I'm sure you're going to give it to me regardless."

"Perhaps."

"Fine, have at it. But I'm not in the mood for a long-winded lecture. I've already gotten one from Justine and I don't need another one."

"When have you known me to be long winded?" he said with a sardonic half smile.

"True," I admitted, knowing that Hale had always been a man of few words. But when he spoke, people listened.

"Your past is messing with your compass. You're losing sight of true north by looking at this all the wrong way. I've been watching Krystina with little Eva for the past week. I'm not going to lie—she's as sweet as can be. I'm pretty sure she's already stolen Vivian's heart. I caught them baking cookies in the kitchen a couple of nights back."

"Oh, really?" I said, not bothering to hide my annoyance. I thought I could trust Vivian to keep her distance, but apparently, she'd betrayed me, too.

"Yep. It was hard to miss the twinkle in Vivian's eyes," Hale added with a small, reflective smile. "But mostly, it's the drastic change in Krystina that really made me pause. She's been a shell of herself since losing Liliana—always sad. I've begun to see some of that sadness dissipate. She hasn't been happy in too long and it's good to see a genuine smile on her face again. She's good with Eva. I think you'll see that if you give it time."

"I have no doubt that Krystina is amazing with her. She's a kind and giving person. I would have expected no less."

"You know your wife, that much is true. She really is an

angel, just like you call her. But you don't know that little girl. You say you do—that you can see yourself in her eyes. You think she will bring you nothing but trouble. Maybe that will be the case, but just think of what you could bring her. Your souls have experienced the same emotions and the same fears. And both of you have tragically lost your parents, even if the situations are different. It takes one to know one, boss, and I can't think of anyone better suited to be a father to that little girl than you."

"I've only ever fathered one child, and she's buried in the ground at Westwood Hills Cemetery. There won't be another one," I stated flatly before turning to walk back to the Tesla.

"One more thing, boss," Hale called out. I slowed my stride, but didn't stop until he said, "I hadn't thought about it until you just mentioned it. Liliana's grave."

"What about it?"

"Krystina hasn't been to the cemetery since Monday morning."

My back went ramrod straight, not sure what to think about this revelation. I wanted to tell Hale to fuck off, blame Krystina's change in morning routine on coincidence that had nothing to do with Eva, and say his implication was baseless. But there was truth to every word he'd said tonight, and that truth was why I didn't turn to face him. I just wasn't ready to admit—even to myself—that Hale could be right.

21

Alexander

Despite trying to shut out Hale's voice, his words rang in my head during the entire drive back to the penthouse. He acted as if I hadn't considered everything he'd said. Little did he know, every moment shared with my wife over the past year was on an endless loop in my mind. Countless times, I'd watched from the shadows while Krystina cried, absolutely powerless to make her pain go away. When she stopped talking to me about it all together, I feared she didn't need me, and it was a paralyzing feeling.

There were times when my brain refused to go quiet. I thought I was doing the right thing, but Hale still made me doubt my instincts. I couldn't deny the way Krystina had looked tonight when she was tucking the little girl into bed. She looked content and happy for the first time in far too long. Her actions were so tender and loving, it couldn't possibly have been faked. It was more real than anything else, and I knew without a shadow of a doubt that my wife already had feelings for this stranger's child.

Who am I to rob her of that?

Yet I did exactly that during our argument. The happiness I'd seen in her just a short time earlier had vanished, only to be replaced by darkness. And I'd been the one to do it.

Perhaps I'd been the problem all along.

Feeling more conflicted now that I ever had in my entire life, I did the first thing that came to mind.

"Call Dr. Tumblin," I instructed the car. I didn't care if it was after nine at night. He was well compensated, and he knew it. So, when my long-time psychologist answered the phone after the second ring, I wasn't surprised.

"Alex, how are you?" he said as a greeting.

"Not great."

"Considering the late hour, I figured as much. Tell me what's going on."

"It's Krystina. I don't even know where to begin. She brought a child home and now we aren't speaking... I think. I don't really fucking know what we are at the moment."

"Hang on. Slow down. A child?"

I sighed. There was so much he didn't know. Resigning myself to a lengthy phone call—and a hefty bill at the end of the month—I brought Dr. Tumblin up to speed on everything. I told him about Hannah and the promise Krystina had made to her, and then Hannah's recent suicide. I filled him in on the trip to Vegas, including Allyson and Matteo's unexpected marriage, and about how Krystina was drugged that very same night. I explained our fight over my suspicions that she took drugs on purpose, and then transitioned to the phone call she'd received that prompted our early return. I laid it all out, not holding a single thing back, and didn't slow down until I finished recapping what happened when I went home tonight.

Dr. Tumblin stayed quiet the entire time, and by the time I finished explaining everything, I'd felt like I'd run a marathon.

"I won't negotiate with her on this," I said vehemently. "Right now, the girl is just living at our house. Krystina said something about temporary guardianship, but I know it's only a matter of time before she pushes for something permanent, like adoption. I don't want to adopt, and I need you to help me get my wife to see reason."

"You aren't alone, Alex. Many men don't want to adopt. Some fear that they won't be able to love a child that isn't biologically theirs, while others are simply afraid of the unknown. The path to accepting the idea of adoption typically requires one to face their fears and concerns. So, tell me. Why are you afraid of adoption?"

I bristled at the implication.

"I'm not afraid of it. It just isn't for me."

"Yes, but why isn't it for you?"

"Look, you know where I came from, and the horrors I'd seen at a young age. That little girl comes from the same place I did, yet Krystina hasn't even tried to understand this. If she did, she'd be able to grasp my reasoning and wouldn't be so quick to make rash decisions. I've finally put that baggage behind me, and I refuse to rehash it—or worse, relive it. It took me two decades to get past it all and become the man I am today. I don't want to bring that into my home—not when I worked so hard to escape it."

"It sounds to me like you haven't gotten over your past at all. Perhaps that's why you're so resistant."

"I'm over the past, but you can't blame me for not wanting it to return."

"That will only happen if you allow it. I think you should try to talk to Krystina again, Alex, but work to keep the emotion out of it. Or, we can schedule a group session if you think you need a mediator, but I won't push either way. I won't try to talk her out of adoption, just as I won't push you into it. You know that's not my role. Only the two of you can work this out. She is your partner, and the decision to adopt needs to be agreed upon by both of you. There cannot be a compromise."

"Why not? I might be willing to meet her halfway. Perhaps we could adopt a newborn baby that doesn't come with a lived history. I never thought it would be for me, but now I'm not so sure. I wouldn't promise anything, but I think I could at least be open to the discussion after seeing the way Krystina looked tonight when putting the girl to bed."

"What is the little girl's name, Alex?"

"What girl?"

"The name of the child Krystina brought into your home. You haven't told me."

I hesitated. It was as if saying her name aloud would make her too real. I knew that was a ridiculous way to think, but it was my reality all the same.

You're being a fucking pussy. It's just a name.

"Eva," I said quickly, as if the three letters would burn my tongue from my mouth if I said them too slowly. "Her name is Eva."

"Have you noticed any changes in Krystina since she brought Eva home?"

"Her routine is different. Hale told me that she hasn't been to the cemetery to visit Liliana since Monday morning."

"Why did you have to find this out from Hale?"

"Because Krystina and I haven't spoken much. I've been staying at the penthouse," I admitted.

I heard Dr. Tumblin sigh through the line.

"This is a very complicated matter, Alex, and it's one that deserves more than a quick late night phone call. I'll have my secretary call in the morning to get you on my calendar. In the meantime, you need to keep one very important thing in mind. The life of a child hangs in the balance. You and Krystina need to be all in, or nothing at all. Remember, most adopted children have already felt the sting of rejection in some way or another. This little girl doesn't need to experience more rejection from an adoptive father. Not to mention, it could be disastrous for your marriage. Many marriages fail because one person makes an adoption decision that the other spouse can't support. If you truly can't accept this, Krystina has to understand. Forcing it will be no good for all parties involved."

"That last part is something we can agree on. Now, I'll let you go for tonight. I'll anticipate a call from your secretary in the morning."

"Have a good night, Alex."

I ended the call just as I pulled into my parking space near the penthouse. After climbing from the car and alarming the security system, I pulled out my cellphone once more. This time, it was to send Samuel a quick text. I'd given the security detail the night off, assuming I'd be staying in Westchester—or at least, that's what I'd hoped I would be doing. Now that I was back, he'd have to adjust his morning schedule accordingly.

Today
10:13 PM, Me: *Just pulled into the parking garage. I'll be at the penthouse for the night.*

Immediately, I saw three little dots appear, signaling he was responding.

10:13 PM, Samuel Faye: *I'm in Hale's old apartment. I can be with you in just a few. Should I meet you in the lobby or the parking garage?*

10:14 PM, Me: *Neither. I'll let myself up. I just wanted you to know I was back here and not at the house in Westchester.*

10:14 PM, Samuel Faye: *Okay, sir. Just let me know if you need anything.*

I pocketed the phone and pushed through the doors leading to the building's upscale lobby. I crossed the marble floor and passed the security desk. Jeffrey, the once overzealous doorman who'd I recently promoted, nodded a greeting as I walked by.

"Mr. Stone," he said politely. "I hope you are well this evening. If you'll just allow me one moment, I'll pull your keycard."

"No worries. I have mine."

"Very well. Have a good night, sir."

"Same to you, Jeffrey."

I stepped up to the elevator, feeling depressed and frustrated over the current state of my life, and swiped my keycard through the penthouse's designated slot. After the lift doors closed and I began my ascent, I thought about my recent decision to promote Jeffrey. At least that was one thing that seemed to be going well as of late.

Jeffrey started working for me fresh out of high school. Back then, he'd been a clumsy kid who became frazzled easily. He'd significantly matured with age, and with that maturity, his loyalty grew. I knew I could trust him, and it was why I'd promoted him to building manager after his old boss retired. So far, he was working out just fine.

When the doors for the penthouse opened to the spacious

main foyer, I walked straight past the dining room table to the wet bar. When I was in this state of mind, I usually reached to my dominant side to cope. Having total control over a naked woman's body was an unexplainable high, one that had gotten me through some of the worst parts of my life. However, things had changed. Any warm body wouldn't do. I only wanted my wife, and with her in Westchester, sexual domination wasn't on the menu tonight.

But whiskey was.

Reaching under the cabinet, I poured two fingers of whiskey into a lowball glass. I took a slow sip, then another, swirling the tepid amber liquid in my glass between swallows. When it was half gone, I threw back the remaining contents of the glass. The liquor burned on the way down, but I barely noticed it. My mind was too busy replaying all the advice I'd received—solicited and unsolicited—from Justine, Hale, and Dr. Tumblin.

The problem was, not one of them had gone through what Krystina and I had. This was about more than just decades long past. It was about the present. Losing Liliana caused a seismic shift in our world. Krystina would always feel sadness because of it, and no adopted substitute would erase that.

My eyes burned from lack of sleep over the past week. Perhaps if I could get a good night's rest, I'd be able to think about this in a different light. Right now, I was exhausted.

Making my way to the master bedroom, I quickly stripped down to my boxer briefs and tried not to think about how cold the sheets felt without Krystina beside me as I climbed into bed. I closed my eyes, and it wasn't long before fatigue took over my body and I surrendered to sleep.

I APPROACH *the Chappaqua mansion in Westchester.*

My steps are slow and sluggish as I walk, making my feet feel like they're stepping in quicksand. I struggle to bring a leg up to step forward, and I realize I can't move.

I look down.

The blacktop beneath my feet is no longer solid. Sticky black tar surrounds me. My feet are stuck in it, and I'm unable to move.

I glance back up at the house.

I need to get to Krystina to warn her about the tar. I don't want her to come out here and get stuck in it, too. She could be hurt.

My legs fight against the suction of the sticky, black goo, and I all but will my feet to move forward.

The ground rumbles, almost like an earthquake.

I look up at the house again. It's shaking.

The tall pines flanking the outer walls begin to drop. They disappear into the earth and I gasp.

A sink hole maybe?

I can't be sure.

I focus on the house again.

The glass windowpanes begin to shudder. Then, to my horror, every window in the house shatters in a loud explosion. Glass shards fly in every direction.

"Krystina!" I scream.

She appears in one of the glassless window frames in the upstairs of the house. She's holding a young child.

It's Eva.

She looks so small in Krystina's arms. How had I not noticed how tiny and fragile she was before?

I try to move forward again but my legs are still immobile in the tar.

"Krystina!" I call out again.

She doesn't answer. Instead, she just stares at me with sad eyes.

And then the house begins to crumble.

It's slow at first, the topmost point of the roof seeming to collapse in on itself in a slow wave. But like an ancient roman statue of mother and child, neither of them moves. It's as if they are frozen in time.

Shingles, stone, and mortar break apart, the debris falling all around Krystina and Eva, creating a plume of dusty smoke.

Just as I'm about to call out to her for a third time, the entire house goes down, taking Krystina and Eva with it.

"No!"

I JERKED AWAKE, quaking from the shockwaves echoing through my system. It took me a moment to realize the shaking was coming from my own body, and not from a house that was crumbling to the ground.

It was just a dream.

Nevertheless, my heart pounded, seeming to beat a gaping hole through the center of my chest. I felt sick and I tried to shake off the nausea as I collected my bearings. All I could see was Krystina standing perfectly still with little Eva in her arms. I looked to the side of the bed where she normally slept. I knew I wouldn't see her, but I couldn't stop myself from hoping. My wife was always the best medicine after an unsettling dream, and I missed her now more than ever.

I needed my angel.

Once my heartrate calmed to a more normal rhythm, I swung my legs over the side of the bed. I tried to shake the image of a sad Krystina in the glassless window, but the more I tried, the more I thought I might throw up. The house collapsing was symbolic of my life. It was crumbling around me, disappearing into an abyss. And if I allowed it, Krystina would go right along with it. I would lose her if I stayed on this path, and I would have nobody to blame but myself.

Justine was right. I'd been a fool.

The problem had been me all along. Not Krystina. And it went well beyond the recent issue with Eva. The reality was, ever since Krystina's first miscarriage, I'd felt like less of a man. With each subsequent loss, that feeling grew. My failures to give her a viable pregnancy had made me an echo of my former self. It was as if the protective, dominant side of me had vanished, believing that I was too weak to deserve her submission. In my dream, I'd been the house—too pathetic and frail to hold up and support my wife during her greatest time of need.

I thought back to our exchange during our last visit to Club O.

"YOU'VE HAD ENOUGH, ANGEL."

"I'll know when I've had enough. I'll use my safeword if it becomes too much."

"I'm not convinced that you would, and I won't make you bleed, Krystina. I would never do anything that could leave permanent marks. You know this, so why are you asking me to?"

"I'm fine. I'm not going to bleed. Go again."

BUT I'D REJECTED her demands. I thought she just wanted me to physically hurt her in order to mask her mental pain—at least that's what I'd told her and myself. I'd refused her my dominance even when she begged. While I hadn't recognized what I was doing at the time, I knew now that it had really been about denying myself the dominance I craved. It was my way of punishing myself. Thinking back on something else she'd said, I realized that Krystina knew what I'd been subconsciously doing.

. . .

"I NEED THIS, Alex—we need this. Please."

WE NEED THIS.

She wasn't begging me to erase her pain. She'd been trying to save us. Yes, she had been sad about losing Liliana, but she wasn't in a dark place like I'd thought. I'd been the one who had retreated into darkness, not her.

"Talk about a middle of the night epiphany," I said aloud to the empty room.

But that was truly what it was—an epiphany. Dr. Tumblin believed dreams were our subconscious helping us solve problems in our lives. Perhaps he was right because everything was suddenly so clear.

Impulsively, I threw on a T-shirt and made my way to the office space I kept in the penthouse. Pulling out a pad of paper and a pen from the desk's top drawer, I did the one thing I was fairly certain I'd never done before in my life.

I wrote a handwritten letter.

Krystina,

Handwritten notes aren't usually my style, and I'm unsure about why I've opted to write one now. Maybe this is simply a form of therapy to hash out my thoughts, and you'll never read this at all. Or perhaps I'm just feeling nostalgic after a long night of reaching for you, only to find a fistful of cold sheets. I had a nightmare tonight. It was different from the others, but just as terrifying. When I woke from it, the empty pillow next to mine may have been the most depressing thing I'd ever laid eyes on.

I miss you, angel. I miss seeing how you look in the morning, and I couldn't help but think back to the morning we'd left for Las Vegas. It was the last time I woke with you in our bed. I remember how I gazed upon you sleeping. You were my very own sleeping beauty. Your lips were slightly parted, and your steady breathing created a gentle rise and fall of your breasts. I wanted nothing more than to lose myself in you. Your peaceful and angelic face had calmed the raging beast inside of me—the beast that wanted to lash out at everyone because of the cruelties life bestowed on us.

But now you're gone, and I'm alone, scribbling in a notebook and trying to find answers to an enslaved truth.

When I first met you, solitude had been my companion. You changed that by being everything I didn't know I needed. Despite our challenges, you trusted me enough to give me your submission, and you loved me enough to give me your heart. It was a gift like no other. You were perfect for me, and at times, I wondered if you were really mine—as if your beautiful soul couldn't possibly be attached to someone like me.

You're the reason shadows and nightmares no longer haunt me. You taught me how to feel by chasing away my demons and daring me to dream. Your mind stirs my soul, your touch soothes me, and I've always found strength in our love.

I need you to know this despite all the pain and conflict between us. Our problems are so complex, and I wish I knew the solutions. I've only just begun to realize how badly I've failed you, but I refuse to believe all is lost.

I can't breathe without you. Come back to me, my angel. My body aches to feel you. Let me share your pain, breathe your breath, and I

*promise to give you all that I am. You're my addiction. My
everything—my past, present, and future.*

*All my love,
Alexander*

I pulled the pen away from the paper, surprised to notice
that my eyes felt moist. I blinked. A part of me thought I was
going soft, but another part of me knew this was a necessity. I
had to give Krystina my whole heart on a gold platter, and then
hold my breath as I prayed for her to accept it.

The letter I wrote wasn't an apology. That deserved to be
given in person. But what I'd written was a plea, one meant to
hopefully bring my wife back to me. Krystina's unhappiness
was all on me. I should have been better—much better. From
my unwillingness to compromise to my failures to dominate
her, I alone was creating a great gaping chasm between us. I
considered the past few months, suddenly seeing her patience
and acceptance all too clearly. Every time there had been a
problem, I'd been the one to create it.

She tried.

I had not.

I pushed and pushed, not trusting simple truths. I'd made
unfounded accusations, including alleged drug use. I had to
have been out of my mind. I knew my wife, and I knew she'd
never do such a thing. The problem with my marriage was on
me and only I could fix it. The first step to doing that would be
to accept Eva. I wasn't sure if I could do it, but I was going to try.

I leaned back in the chair and considered how to go about
it. Accepting Eva would be a leap of faith off a cliff so high, I
couldn't even see the bottom. I didn't know where I would land,
but Krystina was worth it. She would always be worth it.

Tearing the sheet of paper from the pad, I folded it and

stuffed it into an envelope. Then, moving my hand to the computer mouse, I woke the screen and pulled up the web browser. I had an idea—one that I hoped would send Krystina a strong message. The letter was only the beginning.

In the internet search bar, I typed in the name of a well-known graphic design program for novices. Whenever I had something of this nature to be done, I would ask Laura to do it for me. It never took her long to whip something up, so I assumed making a simple design wouldn't be that hard.

I was wrong.

An hour later, I looked at my amateur creation. I was a man of many talents, but apparently making attractive graphics was not one of them. Still, the invitation I'd created got the point across, even if Hallmark designers would be outraged at the atrocity. Sitting back, a scanned my work for typos or any other adjustments.

To Krystina and Eva
Your Presence Is Requested Aboard The Lucy
When: Saturday, September 10th
Time: Noon
Your Host: Alexander
What To Bring: Pack swimsuits and clothing for a possible overnight

I debated whether to remove the little yacht clipart at the bottom. It looked like a five-year-old had designed it, but it would have to do. Time was of the essence.

After printing out the invitation, I stuffed it into an envelope with the letter, then hurried back to the bedroom to throw on a pair of gym shorts and sneakers. Grabbing my keys, I headed out. It was the middle of the night, and I was sure the security guard at Cornerstone Tower would think I'd lost my mind when I showed up. It didn't matter what he thought. He knew not to question me. The only thing that mattered was making sure this letter was on Krystina's desk before she arrived at work in the morning.

I wanted to surprise her—and this would only be the first of many.

22

Krystina

On Saturday morning, Eva and I sat in the back seat of the Maserati as Hale maneuvered down the winding road leading to Montauk Marina, the exclusive resort where *The Lucy* was docked. When he reached the parking area, he pulled to a stop near the walkway leading to the main entrance. Climbing from the front seat, he came around to open the back door for Eva and me.

"Shall I leave you to it, or would you like me to walk you to the boat?" he asked.

I looked at him in surprise.

"You aren't coming with us?"

"No, ma'am. The marina is gated and safe, and the boss says he wants alone time. I also think he knows how much you dislike having Samuel or me hovering about," he added, but I saw the teasing humor in his eyes.

"I love you both, and you know it," I told him. "But I do appreciate the privacy. I think Eva and I will be fine heading to the boat on our own."

"As you wish," Hale said with a small nod.

"It's just you and me, peanut," I said to Eva as I slung my Cartier handbag over one shoulder, and a duffle bag full of clothing and a few toys for Eva over the other.

Anxious butterflies danced in my stomach as we walked down the stone pathway toward the main entrance. Eva's fingers were threaded through mine as we approached an intricately designed iron gate. There was a small placard welded to it, reminding visitors that this area was for slip holders and their guests only. I let go of Eva's hand to pull my access card from my wallet, swiped the card through the electronic card reader, and then pushed the gate open.

Eva reached for my hand again immediately after I gestured her inside. The feel of her warm grasp sent a little thrill through me as it was the first time she'd initiated holding my hand without being prompted.

"Where are we?" she asked curiously while looking around at the buildings flanking the path we walked on.

"Where I told you this morning we were going. This is the marina. We're going on a boat."

"But where's the water?"

I smiled at her acute observation. She really was smart as a whip.

"The buildings are blocking the view to help maintain the privacy of the boat owners. You'll see the water and the boats in a moment."

When we reached the building's edge, we rounded the corner and Eva gasped.

"Oh, look at all the boats! It's so pretty!"

"It is," I agreed, allowing us a moment to look around and appreciate the beauty.

The landscape, as always, was impeccably maintained. The boutiques and cafes that followed the long winding pathway to our right had only a few patrons coming in and out. During peak season, the walkways bustled with people and golf carts transporting slip holders to various parts of the resort. This time of year, the marina was quiet and peaceful. It was why Alexander preferred the end of the season, when only the diehards were left soaking up every last bit of summer they could get. It was private, and Alexander valued his privacy above all else.

Eva and I walked toward the main dock to the rows of slips that seemed unending. Being that it was just past Labor Day, most of the boats were still in the water even if their owners were absent. But it wouldn't be long before the boats were either stored in drydock or shipped south for the winter.

"I like those little houses," Eva said, pointing to the white gazebos lining the waters edge.

I chuckled. "Those aren't houses, Eva. Those are gazebos. Maybe we can have a picnic there one day."

"Oh, yay! I've never been on a picnic before."

"Well, then. We'll have to rectify that as soon as we can."

When we reached the slip where *The Lucy* was docked, my nerves returned with a vengeance. The letter Alexander had written, along with his invitation, was tucked into my back pocket. I smiled to myself when I thought about the invitation. It was a nice touch, one that I was surprised to see from Alexander. Cutesy wasn't typically his style, and I'd seen Laura's work before and knew she hadn't made it. It had to have been him. He was extending an olive branch, and I was more than ready to accept it. I missed my husband desperately.

He'd instructed us to come at noon. It was five minutes to,

but I hesitated. I worried about how Eva could be hurt if things didn't go well. But then I thought about everything Alexander had said in his letter. I believed him—every word.

My eyes swept the expansive open deck of *The Lucy*. I didn't see Alexander, but he had left the small gangplank down for us to board. A gentle breeze danced off the waves of Lake Montauk, causing water to lap against the docks and boats at the marina. It was rhythmic and relaxing, and I found it calming as Eva and I stepped onto the boat.

I led Eva toward the center of the boat where the spiral staircase led down to the living area. I stopped short when Alexander came around from the front of the boat. My breathing hitched and I faltered, feeling as if I were transported back in time. He stood only a few feet away from where he'd been standing on our wedding day at the precise moment I emerged from the deck below. He'd been under a trellis covered in thick ivy and white lilies. While there was no trellis today, he was every bit as breathtaking as he was on the day we promised forever.

It had only been two days since I saw him last, but it might as well have been a lifetime. It was hard to believe, but I missed his hovering and checking to make sure I had three square meals a day and eight hours of sleep.

I took a moment to take him in from head to toe. My husband was always a feast for the eyes, covered in muscles and tan skinned from our days spent on *The Lucy*. He wore khaki shorts and a navy polo with the top button loosened at the collar. There was beauty and power in the way he casually strolled toward us with his perfectly chiseled features and square jawline. He was brutally handsome, and he left me breathless. I would never tire of looking at him.

He stopped just a few feet from me, but rather than embrace me like I thought he might, he simply clasped his hands in front of him instead. His stance was slightly parted, accentuating the broad span of his shoulders. His blue gaze was piercing, assessing, and devastating—a force of nature that I would have to reconcile with.

"Angel, I'm happy you came."

"I'll always come when you call, Alex. I hope you know that."

He gave me a short nod, then looked at Eva.

"And you must be Eva. Everyone has been telling me all about you. My name is Alex. I'm happy to meet you," he told her, bending slightly at the waist to extend his hand to her. His voice sounded stiff and formal, but his expression was concentrated. It was as if he was going to great lengths to ensure he said the right things.

She looked at his hand strangely for a moment before suddenly realizing what she was supposed to do. A wide smile spread across her face as she pulled her little fingers from mine. Then, in a way only a five-year-old who thought they were doing something highly important could do, she shook Alexander's hand with overzealous enthusiasm.

"I'm happy to meet you, too," she replied in the cutest voice imaginable. "I'm five years old and I like elephants. Purple is my favorite color. What's yours?"

Alexander raised his brows, his expression amused.

"I never really thought about it, but I'll have to go with blue."

"Just like your eyes."

"That's very observant of you, Eva. Yes, just like my eyes."

"I have blue eyes, too," she pointed out. "We could be twins!"

A ghost of a smile played on Alexander's lips, and I was grateful for Eva's precociousness and easy-going personality.

"Eva," I began. "Why don't we go downstairs and put your things away?"

"Are you planning on spending the night?" Alexander asked.

"We'll see." When I saw Alexander tense, I quickly added, "Eva and I are packed appropriately for an overnight. I just assumed we'd see where the day takes us first."

He eyed me curiously for a moment, almost as if he were trying to read my mind. What he was looking for, I wasn't sure. I'd told him the truth—I really did want to see where the day took us. Alexander and I had been anything but predictable lately, and I didn't want to make a single commitment that I couldn't keep.

"That makes sense," Alexander finally said. The tension in his shoulders eased as he looked back and forth between Eva and me. "I got with Vivian about what Eva likes and set up the guest cabin accordingly. She should be comfortable sleeping there."

My brows arched in surprise.

"You did?"

Focusing his attention on me, I watched countless emotions swirl in his sapphire blues—anger, caution, relief, understanding, patience, and curiosity. But what I saw more than anything was love. When he spoke, his voice was low and full of meaning.

"Consider this a leap of faith, angel."

Without another word, he turned and began to walk toward the door leading to the spiral staircase. Placing my hand on Eva's shoulder, the two of us followed Alexander's descent. Once below deck, we walked through the lavishly decorated entertainment area, complete with a large flat-screen television and lounge seating. Eva looked around with curious eyes, absorbing every detail about her new surroundings. When we reached the guest cabin, I barely had a moment to take in what Alexander had done to the room when Eva let out a loud gasp.

"It's my elephant!" she cried out. Running to the bed, she picked up a purple plush elephant and clutched it tightly to her chest. Alexander and I looked at each other in confusion.

"What do you mean by it's your elephant?" I asked.

"It's the one I lost. How did you find it?"

I frowned at first, but then remembered the first time I'd met Eva. Hannah had come into Stone's Hope Women's Shelter with Eva in tow. Eva had been carrying a purple stuffed elephant—one that looked remarkably like the one she now held. I recalled Hannah telling me later that Eva lost it and had been devastated over it. The odds of Alexander picking up a duplicate of the same elephant had to be slim to none.

"Eva," I began. "I don't think it's the same one you lost."

"Maybe it's her sister!" she suggested gleefully, and I laughed.

"Could be."

"It's just something I picked up at Sal's Toy Shoppe on 7th Avenue," Alexander said, then motioned to the cabin space. "That's where I got most of this stuff."

Turning my attention to the room, I finally had a moment to see what Alexander had meant when he said he prepared a room for Eva. White fairy lights hung from the ceiling, twinkling like stars above our heads. A fuzzy throw blanket covered with purple monkeys was folded at the foot of the bed, with a matching purple monkey pillow at the headboard. A wide array of toys and books were piled in a corner, including puzzles depicting various wildlife and so many stuffed animals, I was sure there was one to represent every animal in The Central Park Zoo.

"Wow," I breathed, not sure what to think about the lengths he'd gone too. "You're going to spoil her."

"Vivian said that she's big into animals, so I stuck with that theme."

"I can't believe you did this—and on your own? As in, you went shopping for all of this yourself?"

"Well, I brought Laura with me. I figured a woman's input would help. Those twinkle light things were her idea."

Looking up at my husband, I thought I might burst with my love for him at that moment. I knew this room and all it contained could mean absolutely nothing, but it could also mean everything. At the very least, my husband was trying. And for that, I was grateful. I'd committed to taking things slow —baby steps—but this felt like a giant leap.

Pressing up on my toes, I placed a soft kiss on my husband's cheek.

"I love you, Alexander Stone. I really, really love you."

23

Krystina

Alexander had pulled out all the stops. Rather than stay within the confines of Lake Montauk, he called in a small crew so we could leave the inlet and take *The Lucy* out into the open water. We cruised through Fort Pond and Tobaccolot Bay, making the loop around Plum Island, before stopping to anchor a mile off the shores of Gardiner Island.

While there, he prepared dinner on the boat—grilled salmon for us, and Scooby-Doo shaped macaroni and cheese pasta for Eva. I'd learned on day one with her that macaroni and cheese was her favorite food. I wasn't sure when Alexander had spoken to Vivian to learn so many details about Eva, but I made a mental note to thank her.

Things felt normal between Alexander and me in ways they hadn't in so long. The way we talked and laughed was reminiscent of how life used to be. Before everything changed.

Before the pandemic. Before I lost Liliana. To a time that seemed like a lifetime ago. I would have thought having Eva around would have created moments of awkwardness, but it didn't. She seemed to fit right in, as if she'd been there all along.

Music played quietly while we ate, the sounds of Israel Kamakawiwo'ole giving our day trip a tropical oasis vibe. Alexander regaled us with mysterious tales about Gardiner Island, a six-mile-long private paradise that had been owned by the same family for nearly four hundred years.

"You can only get to the island by boat," Alexander told us.

"You have a boat. Let's go," Eva suggested between mouthfuls of macaroni.

"We can't. Outsiders are strictly forbidden."

"How come?"

"History tells us that they are private people who want to live a private life. Others believe the rumors that say the family is secretly hoarding a part of Captain Kidd's treasure."

"Who's Captain Kidd?" Eva asked, soaking up every word Alexander said with rapt attention.

"Captain Kidd was a pirate."

Eva's eyes went wide. "A pirate?"

"That's right. He buried his treasure on that island a long time ago."

"Wow," she breathed in awe.

Alexander looked at me and lifted his glass as if in toast, "Yo ho, yo ho!"

"A pirate's life for me," I sang, finishing the song lyric with a laugh.

After dinner, Eva and I cleaned up the dishes while Alexander worked with the crew to navigate us back to the waters of Montauk Lake.

It was dark by the time we tied up in the slip at the marina. The night sky was lit only by a sea of crystal stars for as far as the eye could see. Eva yawned as we watched Alexander moving about the dock to ensure the boat was secure.

"It's been a busy day. You look tired, peanut. Are you ready for bed?" I asked her.

"Can I please have a story first?"

"Of course, you can. Wait here, and I'll be right back," I told her, pointing to one of the lounge chairs on the deck. I probably should have chosen to read to her in her bed in the guest cabin, especially since she almost always fell asleep while I was reading to her. However, it was a beautiful night and I wanted her to experience as much of it as possible. Winter would arrive before long, and we'd be prevented from doing this again until the Spring.

Doing as I'd asked, Eva waited patiently on the chair while I went down below to retrieve a throw blanket and a book. Rifling through her duffle bag, I picked out the book that was quickly becoming her favorite, *Guess How Much I Love You?* When I returned, the two of us cuddled under the fleece, and I began reading the tale about Little Nutbrown Hare.

At some point, Alexander joined us on the deck. He stayed quiet, but I felt his eyes on me, assessing everything in a way that only he could. When I finished the book, I quietly closed it and glanced down at Eva.

"She's asleep," Alexander whispered.

"Lots of fresh air tuckered her out. I'm just going to carry her downstairs to bed, and then I'll be back up."

"I can carry her," Alexander offered.

Before I could protest or say he didn't have to, he was already bending in front of me, slowly slipping his arms under Eva's tiny body. Together, the three of us went down to the guest cabin, with Eva cradled against Alexander's chest while I followed closely behind.

"I'll need to put her into her pajamas," I said in a hushed

voice once inside the room. "I should have thought about that before I started reading to her. It slipped my mind."

I quickly moved to the bag containing her clothes and pulled out a light purple ruffled hem nightgown. When I turned back to Alexander, I froze, feeling rooted to the spot as I watched him carefully lay Eva on the bed as if she were a fragile porcelain doll.

The entire scene reminded me of Daddy Warbucks and little orphan Annie—when he took Annie to the movies, and then brought her home to tuck her into bed with the help of Grace, his secretary. Everything was exactly the same, yet in a different time and place.

And Alexander had more hair.

An image of a bald Alexander Stone flashed in my mind. I snorted at the thought, causing Alexander to cast me a confused look.

"What are you laughing at?"

"I was just making mental comparisons."

"Of what?"

"You and Daddy Warbucks."

"Who?"

I shook my head. Even if I clarified and said Albert Finney, he still wouldn't know who I was talking about. My husband's lack of movie knowledge really was embarrassing. I should have known better.

"Never mind. It's just a movie."

Stepping up to the bed, I carefully slipped Eva's shirt off, taking great care not to wake her. Then I pulled the nightgown down over her head before moving to remove her shorts and sandals. Once I'd successfully maneuvered the gown down her body, Alexander lifted her slightly so I could pull down the comforter and sheets, but it was my husband who brought them back up, tucking her in tightly up to her chin.

Seeing him do this simple act made me smile wistfully.

Snug as a bug...

Alexander returned to standing, keeping his gaze cast down on her.

"She's so little," he murmured quietly, and I couldn't be sure if he was speaking to me or himself.

"She is." I bit my lower lip, afraid to say what else I was thinking. In the end, instinct won out and I said, "You could be a good father to her if you let yourself, Alex."

He didn't respond but moved to exit the bedroom instead.

Damn, I shouldn't have said that!

I worried that I'd pushed him too far, but I couldn't help it. My heart wanted to burst after watching him with her today. Never in my wildest dreams could I have predicted what had happened.

And it had only been one day.

We could have a lifetime of days like today if only he would allow it.

I followed Alexander up to the main deck and watched as he prepared each of us a drink from the mini wet bar near the hot tub. His was a mixture of sugar, bitters, and bourbon to make an old fashioned, while mine was just a simple glass of German Riesling.

Turning, he handed me my glass and said, "I assume you're planning to stay the night."

"Yes, of course. It was a wonderful day—truly, it was."

"I agree, which is why I texted Hale and told him that he didn't need to come back for you."

"Of course, you did," I said with a smirk. His presumptiveness never ceased to amaze me.

Seeming oblivious to my sarcasm, Alexander went on. "Let's get in the hot tub. We can soak for a bit and talk about a few things."

Suddenly, all my apprehension from earlier that morning came rushing back.

Talk. What could that mean?

"I'll need to go change," I pointed out, working overtime to keep my voice even so as not to reveal my nerves.

"You don't need a suit. I've dismissed the crew for the night, Eva is asleep, and there's no moon. You'll have plenty of privacy."

I shook my head and sighed. I was pretty sure my husband would say anything to get me naked. But I began to strip out of my clothes nonetheless while he moved to the hot tub control panel. He pressed the buttons that would raise the cover, then started the jets a moment later.

The steaming water bubbled. It was crystal clear and inviting, especially now that I was naked in the cool night air. I quickly climbed in, and almost instantly, piping-hot water erased the chill and some of my unease about the pending conversation.

Leaning back, I took a sip of my wine and waited for Alexander to climb in. As I did, I couldn't help but admire his elegant and masculine physique as he shed his clothes. His lean, hard body was incredibly powerful. From the wide breadth of his shoulders to his chiseled abdomen, not a scar marred his flesh. Deft hands unfastened the button at his waistband, and I couldn't help but think about the many miracles those hands had performed on my body. I flushed thinking about the way they felt running up the insides of my thighs as he looked up at me with penetrating sapphire blue eyes that could see through to my very soul. He was absolute perfection from head to toe, and he set my world on fire.

I didn't speak once he was in the water, knowing he needed to take the lead for this conversation. I'd made a lot of moves over the past week and I was sure he had a lot of questions to match. He deserved my honest answers—especially after the efforts he made today.

"Eva is an interesting girl," he finally said after we'd been soaking for fifteen minutes in silence. My eyes had been closed and my head was back. Lifting it, I opened my eyes to meet his astute gaze.

"She is," I agreed.

"She's precocious and funny, and not at all what I'd expected. What are your plans for her?"

"I have a lot of tentative plans. What do you mean specifically?"

"I want to hear everything, but specifically your long-term custody plans. Is your end goal adoption?"

"Hopefully, yes. That's what I want *us* to do more than anything," I replied, emphasizing the word 'us' to make sure I was clear about wanting his involvement.

"Have you considered potential obstacles, such as her father?"

"There's no need to worry about that. He died in prison. I don't know the details though."

"And grandparents?"

"I'm not sure at the moment. I have a key to Hannah's apartment. I have until the end of the month to go through it. I may find answers to a lot of questions there."

"Indeed, you will. I want to be there when you go through everything."

"Of course."

"Angel, setting aside all the things that could go wrong for a minute, are you sure this is what you want?"

I took a deep breath, then slowly exhaled, appreciating Alexander's worries more than he thought I did.

"Look, I know the risks just as well as I know why you're driven to face hard realities at all costs. You're determined, and you like to manage things head-on. You have a right to. Just like you have a right to worry about emotional or psychological issues with Eva. I'd be lying if I said I didn't share your concerns. But..."

"But what?"

"But the difference between you and me is that I'm willing to accept the challenges and face whatever the future has to bring. I won't pretend to know what your life was like all those years ago. The simple fact is, you persevered and made a better life for yourself. It's one of the things I admire most about you. If you were able to overcome everything and change the course of your life, who's to say Eva can't do the same? She has a chance with us. We are it for her, Alex. I can't think of anyone better suited to give her the life she deserves."

Alexander was thoughtful for a moment before saying, "Hale said something similar to me the other day."

"Yet you still seem hesitant. If you still have so many reservations, why did you do what you did today?"

"Are you really asking me that?"

"I am, and for good reason. I can't bear for you to pull away from me again, Alex. I need to know that what happened today on this boat was real."

He looked at me then and my breath caught from the intensity of his gaze.

"Today was real, Krystina. And I did it all because I love you."

"Alex...I—"

"I don't know what the future holds, but I know that I'll do anything for you. You're mine, angel. Forever."

He angled his head toward me, and his lips parted slightly. His eyes were a violent inferno of desire, causing something to stir deep in my belly. Leaning in, he pressed his mouth to mine.

I parted my lips, welcoming the pungent taste of whiskey on his tongue as we lapped and danced.

His lips moved over the side of my face, stopping to take my earlobe between his teeth, tracing the outline with the tip of his tongue. His breath was hot as he nipped down my neck. A rush of heat crashed between my thighs and a shiver ran through me. We went from zero to one hundred in three seconds flat— that's how we always were.

Using one hand, Alexander positioned my arms behind my head, holding them at the nape of my neck. The maneuver caused my breasts to lift, making my hardened nipples peak out over the surface of the bubbling water. He worked his way around my collarbone, using his free hand to softly brush over the side of my breast, down my belly, then back up to flick at a rigid peak. When he began to roll it between his thumb and forefinger, I moaned.

Oh, how I'd missed him—missed this. Only Alexander had the ability to stir my blood and make me feel alive in the most unimaginable ways.

Shifting to straddle my hips, he pinned me in place and continued circling a thumb around one of my nipples—teasing, playing, and driving me absolutely wild. I felt his hard cock bobbing in the water against my stomach, and I pushed up with my hips. I strained against him, but that only served to send another rush of heat to the junction of my thighs. I groaned with desire.

Capturing a nipple between his teeth, he whispered, "You want something?"

The way his lips formed the words over my hard areola sent a jolt of pleasure between my legs.

"You know I do, Alex. Give it to me," I shamelessly begged, and I felt the vibration of his low chuckle against the curve of my breast.

But he didn't—at least not right away.

Instead, he moved up, pressing kisses to my wet shoulder and ear before pulling back to look at me. There was a serious set to his jaw as a million emotions swirled in the depths of his sapphire eyes.

"Angel, never forget that you are mine and I am yours. Whatever happens, we do it together. No more with me or against me bullshit, and no more separations. Promise me you won't forget that."

"I promise."

Then his gaze shifted to something primal, causing my sex to throb and pulse. Alexander pulled slightly back, allowing himself room to pull my knees apart, spreading my legs wide.

"Put me inside your body, Krystina."

I did exactly as he asked, and when our bodies slid together as one, I gasped from the instant pleasure. Despite our pent-up heat from being apart for so long, he took me soft and slow. It was a reunion of souls like I'd never experienced before.

And it was an assurance that we were us again, and that everything was going to be just fine.

24

Alexander

I awoke early to sunlight streaming through the sheer curtains of the cabin window. Krystina lay naked and still beside me, a peaceful look on her face while she slept. I watched her for a moment, content to listen to the soft, even sounds of her breathing. I knew I'd missed her during our time apart, but I hadn't realized exactly how much until this moment. A part of me could have watched her sleep for hours, and I vowed to never walk out on her like I did ever again.

After a time, I carefully climbed from the bed, taking care not to wake her. I gave in to a silent yawn, exhausted from restless sleep, and threw on a pair of gym shorts. I'd woken several times over the course of the night, disturbed by dreams of ice blue eyes—Eva's eyes. They were so similar to my own, but a shade lighter. It was strange. At this time yesterday, I'd felt nothing toward this little girl, yet I couldn't deny how my heart surged at seeing Krystina and Eva together. The girl was adorable and charming, softening me in ways I'd never imagined she could.

Making my way out of the bedroom, I grabbed my sunglasses off one of the side tables in the entertainment room and continued up the spiral staircase. I climbed to the top and stepped outside onto the main deck. Squinting at the wash of sunlight, I slipped the sunglasses on and inhaled deeply.

The crisp morning air felt good in my lungs. When I considered everything that I'd ever owned in my lifetime, from the expensive sports cars to the penthouse in Manhattan, *The Lucy* would always be my most prized possession. I loved the time I spent on her, away from the chaos of the city, enjoying the serenity I could only find here. And when I navigated her out of the confines of Lake Montauk, away from everything and everyone, there wasn't anything quite like the salty Atlantic air when I opened up the throttle.

Moving over to one of the deck storage boxes, I popped the lid and scanned the contents. Inside was a plethora of handheld exercise equipment, including resistance bands, various sized kettle balls, NordicTrack Speedweights, and a jump rope. Selecting the weights and the jump rope, I moved to the decks state of the art stereo system and put on some music. I made sure the volume was low so as not to wake Krystina and Eva, and stepped to the center of the deck where I'd have more room for a workout.

The latest Bishop Briggs release filtered through the speakers as I warmed up with the jump rope. Not bothering to count repetitions, I focused my mind on the events from yesterday. I found they were blending with my dreams and it was unsettling.

Before I could begin to analyze anything, a tiny figure in a purple nightgown appeared from below deck. Eva shuffled toward me, rubbing her eyes and yawning. She made her way over to the bench against one of the siderails, laid down, and appeared as if she might fall back asleep.

I chuckled, walked over to where she lay, and sat down next to her.

"Good morning, Eva. You still look a little sleepy."

She didn't reply, but crawled into my lap instead. She reached up and wrapped an arm around my neck. When she began to twirl her tiny fingers in the ends of my hair, I froze. Her touch was foreign, unexpected, and... nice.

What the hell?

I went back to thinking about yesterday, and all the laughs shared between Eva, Krystina, and me. To the average outsider, we probably looked like a happy family. Nobody would guess that it was the first time I'd been in Eva's company.

The day had started off a bit awkward, but that feeling had disappeared more quickly than I'd ever anticipated. The natural banter between the three of us felt real. I thought accepting Eva was going to be hard—that I would have to slowly talk myself into it. As it turned out, getting used to her presence wasn't anything near what I thought it would be. It was much, much easier—and that was because Eva made it easy.

A nagging voice in my head wanted to remind me that it had only been one day, but that one day turned out to be the most fulfilling I'd had in a long time. Krystina was right when she said Eva was pure, good, and sweet. There was just something about her little voice, or about the way she was twirling her tiny fingers in my hair at that very moment, that made my heart surge in a way I couldn't explain.

The intuitive grasp on what my future could look like was illuminating yet mind-boggling. I realized I wasn't only going to accept Eva because I needed to if I wanted to hang on to my wife. I was going to do it because I *wanted* to.

Visions of what could be played in my mind, and I found that they made me... happy.

There was no other word to describe it.

I heard Eva's belly give a loud growl and looked down at her. Sleepy eyes stared back at me.

"I think someone is hungry. How does breakfast sound to you?"

Suddenly, the sleeping beauty was wide awake. She shook her head energetically.

"Yes, please! I'm very hungry. Can we—" She stopped short, and her eyes widened. If I wasn't mistaken, I thought I saw a hint of panic in her expression.

"What's wrong, Eva?"

"I'm not supposed to ask for food," she said quietly.

I felt my heart skip a beat and my jaw clenched. I knew why she wasn't supposed to ask for food without her explaining the reason. She wasn't supposed to ask because there was probably never any food to be had. I'd been in her shoes before, where the hunger pains were so bad, I'd thought I might gnaw my own arm off.

The tragedy with my parents pushed us to live with my grandparents. After that, I wasn't hungry anymore. It was a new life and new routines. I'd once thought it was all out of necessity, but now I found myself subscribing to Krystina's school of thought in that everything happened for a reason. I considered how much my life had changed and thought about the experiences afforded to me because of my grandparents— especially my grandfather. He'd practically moved mountains to make sure Justine and I were protected. I wondered what he would think of me now.

I wondered what he would think of Eva.

"When I was young, my grandfather used to make omelets for breakfast. Do you like omelets, Eva?"

Her thin brows pushed together in confusion. "What's that?" she asked.

"It's eggs with good stuff mixed in."

"I like eggs," she said thoughtfully after a few seconds. "I guess I'll probably like omlies, too."

I laughed.

"Omelets, not omlies," I corrected. I stood, bringing Eva with me, and balancing her on my hip. "Let's go to the kitchen and whip some up."

As Eva and I made our way to the kitchen, I couldn't stop the flashes from the past. After my sister and I moved in with my grandparents, regular meals that had once been a luxury had suddenly become part of our everyday lives. My grandfather ceded most kitchen responsibilities to my grandmother, save doing the dishes after she cooked dinner. He hated cooking—except for breakfast.

Breakfast was his thing.

He made it for Justine and me every day—and not just toasting bread or giving us a bowl of cereal. My grandfather made hot breakfast, his specialty being omelets. Like him, I wasn't much in the kitchen, but I did inherit his omelet making skills.

Setting Eva down on a chair in the small kitchen, I went to the refrigerator and pulled out all the fixings I would need. I got bacon sizzling in a frying pan, then cracked a few eggs into a bowl. As I whisked together all the ingredients, I couldn't help but feel like something was missing.

And then it hit me.

Music.

My grandfather always had Frank Sinatra playing while he cooked breakfast. Sure, I'd prepared eggs plenty of times without The Sultan of Swoon being present, but putting it on today seemed appropriate.

Taking my phone from my pocket, I pulled up one of my subscription music apps. I did a search for Sinatra and voilà. When "Summer Wind" began to play, I pulled a wooden spoon from the drawer and turned to face Eva.

"*The summer wind came blowin' in from across the sea,*" I sang into the round end of the spoon. Eva giggled. "*It lingers there to touch your hair—*"

"Well, good morning," said an all too familiar voice from behind me, interrupting me mid-tune. I spun and saw Krystina entering the kitchen with an amused expression.

"Morning, angel. I made you coffee," I told her, handing her a cup of fresh brewed.

She took the mug from me and breathed in the steamy aroma.

"Thanks. Now, do you want to tell me what all this is about?" She motioned to the mess on the counter with a sweep of her hand, and then pointed to the make-shift microphone that I still held near my mouth.

I grinned, imagining what this must look like to her. I wasn't exactly the type to be caught singing into a spoon. The entire scene was incredibly domestic and just downright silly. It didn't seem like something I would have ever envisioned happening in my life, yet it also felt perfect.

Absolutely perfect.

Glancing down at Eva, I replied, "This is the start of a really good day."

25

Alexander

Krystina, Eva, and I arrived back at our Chappaqua mansion later that night. After another full day in the sun, Eva had fallen asleep quickly on the car ride home. Once we put her to bed, Krystina went to the master suite to take a shower, and I headed out to sit near the pool in the backyard.

With a glass of bourbon in hand, I stared out at the velvet night sky. The moon was just a waxing crescent tonight, allowing the stars to stand out like spilled sugar on black marble. The cool air felt heavy with dew, and it was quiet. So quiet. Bugs hummed in the massive trees that hugged the still night, and the sound of crickets was the only noise that could be heard.

The tranquility was welcome after so many months of turmoil and chaos. Or perhaps the calm had always been here, and I just hadn't allowed myself to appreciate it. All I knew was that something had shifted in me over this past weekend. It wasn't gradual or slow moving, but seismic and powerful. I suddenly felt like I was seeing things clearly for the first time in years.

It seemed as though Krystina had experienced the same, although a bit sooner than I had. She seemed stronger than she had in a long time, unlike the fragile bird that I'd tried to keep caged and protected from the pain life threw at her. There was confidence in the way she held herself. But more noticeable was the way she looked at me. The affection and love in her wide chocolate brown gaze was back, no longer overshadowed by anger and resentment. In no uncertain terms, I felt like I had my wife back.

Now it was time to get *us* back.

I swirled the remaining amber liquid in my glass before tilting the glass back to finish it. Then, pulling my cell phone from my pocket, I typed out a text to Krystina.

Today
9:36 PM, Me: *How much longer are you going to be?*
9:38 PM, Krystina: *Maybe ten minutes. Why?*
9:39 PM, Me: *Because tonight I want to show you pleasure beyond your imagination.*
9:39 PM: Krystina: *Is this the start of sexting? Because if so, I'll settle in.*

She ended her sentence with a devil emoji, causing me to chuckle.

9:40 PM, Me: *No sexting. This is the real deal. I want you naked in the playroom in ten minutes.*

There was a pause as I waited for her response, and I smiled. My request had thrown her, just as I thought it would.

9:43 PM, Krystina: *Are you sure?*
9:44 PM, Me: *Angel, I've never been more sure about anything else in my life.*

Walking back toward the house, I made my way upstairs to the master bedroom in the East wing. I heard Krystina moving about in the bathroom as I pushed aside the bookcase that concealed the hidden staircase down to the playroom. I'd never forget the look on the architect's face when I told him about the modifications I wanted made to the blueprints of the house. It was priceless. However, I'd given him plenty of work over the years, and he knew better than to ask questions about my less than conventional request to add a secret sex room to the master suite.

Maneuvering down the narrow staircase, I entered the playroom and looked around. It had been nearly two years since I had last asserted domination over my wife in this room. There had been attempts in between then and now, but with little success. Tonight would be different. I could feel it in my veins—that intense need for control. Domination was a natural instinct for me. It was something I'd lived for, even though Krystina had often blurred the lines.

But there would be no question about who was in charge tonight. I would show no mercy when demanding my wife's submission. Her body was mine.

A king bed was positioned on the far end of the room, the red comforter contrasting against the dark slate-colored walls. A suspension system hovered above it, just waiting for me to shackle Krystina to it. The wall to my left was lined with pleasure tools. Some were meant for pain, but all ultimately brought gratification of some form. Opposite the wall of sex paraphernalia was a state-of-the-art sound system—a must have depending on my mood.

I powered on the stereo but didn't select a playlist just yet. That wouldn't be determined until I lay eyes on my wife. I'd allow my first instinct after seeing her naked body to set the tone for the night.

Krystina didn't enter the playroom until thirty minutes later. She was wrapped in a black silk robe, balancing on black stilettos. Something about the way her curves punctuated that tight body beneath the black satin caused my sharp mind to lose focus.

I blinked and then frowned after I regained control. I was slightly annoyed that she'd taken this long to get down here, but more annoyed that she'd come down here wearing a robe —no matter how good she looked. I'd specifically told her I wanted her naked.

But then again, my wife never could follow directions, so this shouldn't come as a surprise.

"Take it off," I ordered, not needing to explain what I was referring to. She knew.

When Krystina slid the silk off her shoulders until it pooled on the floor around her feet, my intake of breath was palpable. I hadn't expected her to be wearing anything underneath, but what she had on was unlike anything I'd ever seen her wear before. My initial plan to have her kneel before me was thrown to the wayside because it would have obstructed the view of the sultry vixen standing before me.

Black thigh-high stockings wrapped her long, lean legs. The nylon stopped near her upper thighs, attaching to a black garter belt worn bare with no panties beneath. I hummed my pleasure, loving that she'd chosen to leave her pussy exposed for the taking. A black corset sinched her tiny waist, accentuating curves that no other woman could ever compete with.

Her long brown hair streamed over her shoulders, framing her face and the triskelion necklace I'd given her, giving me only a hint of her full, lush tits. I stepped up to her, allowing my hand to graze her arm, just lightly touching her skin. I fingered the necklace left warm from the heat of her flesh, then pushed her long locks of hair aside to reveal hardened nipples protruding from a strappy open cup black bra.

She was by far the sexiest woman I'd ever seen.

And she was mime.

"So fucking hot," I murmured, all but growling my appreciation. I didn't know what provoked her to dress in such an outfit, but the sight of her like this in our playroom made my cock harder than I thought possible. It strained uncomfortably in my pants, my erection pushing against the tight zipper, wanting to break free and take turns with every single tight hole in her body.

She looked down at the floor as she was taught to do, her expression demure. However, her chest rose and fell at a quicker than normal pace, signaling that she was just as turned on as I was.

"I'm yours, Alexander. I'm ready to submit to your every desire."

My blood heated. While she'd given me her submission countless times in the past, this was a new kind of thrill. The euphoria I felt tonight was unlike anything I'd felt before.

Moving to the stereo system, I selected the playlist I wanted for the night. The compiled list of songs had a rougher edge and were anything but sensual. Tonight wasn't about seduction. It was about satiating pure, unadulterated lust and primal need.

I waited for the music to start playing, and then adjusted

the volume. Natalie Taylor's version of "In the Air Tonight" began to play.

Perfect.

In a way, the moment echoed the song lyrics. It felt like I'd been waiting a lifetime to be in this place and time with Krystina. It had been far too long.

I turned back to her.

"Stand in the center of the room," I told her.

She did as I commanded without hesitation. I followed behind her, watching the seductive swing of her ass as I did so. Stepping in front of her, I reached up to wrap my hand around her neck.

"Do you remember the night at the club in Vegas?" I asked. Worry clouded her expression momentarily until I clarified what I was specifically referring to. "Not everything. Just one part about that night. The choke drop. I saw your reaction to it."

Her eyes widened at first, but then went dark as her pupils dilated with a sultry and provocative glow.

"I remember. It was..." She trailed off, sounding breathless. "It was sexy. I remember thinking that I wanted you to do that with me."

My lips curved in a knowing smile.

"Mmm, that's what I thought. You have a strong core, so I think you can do it. Just squeeze your stomach muscles, hand on my arm, and focus on keeping your back straight. I'll do the rest." I tightened my grip on her neck, careful to avoid crushing her windpipe while still applying just enough pressure to slightly restrict her airway. I wasn't into asphyxiation or edge play, but I wanted to push the limits a bit tonight.

Krystina gasped and gripped the arm that had a hold on her neck, but I didn't drop her. Not yet. Using my free hand, I brought it up to pinch one of her exposed nipples. She sucked in a raspy breath and her head dropped back as she enjoyed the sensation.

"That feels so good. Your fingers, your hand around my neck." She moaned. "I never thought the threat of strangulation would be so arousing."

I pressed a kiss to her shoulder, inhaling her scent that drove me wild as I continued to pinch and pull.

As the song neared its crescendo, I said, "Get ready, angel. And hang on tight."

Once she had a firm grip, I lowered her body to the floor in a fast, sweeping motion. I dragged her a few feet, then brought her back up. Stepping forward swiftly, I guided her to the wall and pressed her up against it. Without giving her a single moment to react, I reached between us and plunged a finger into her already soaking wet pussy.

"Ahh! Oh, God!" Her scream was immediate, as were her fingernails that dug into my arm. I grinned, her reaction exactly as I'd planned it. The choke drop was a distraction and nothing more. I needed her turned on while also sending her mind elsewhere, allowing for the element of surprise before I finger-fucked her.

I eased a second finger into her tight hole, curling them into the warm, ridged flesh of her g-spot. She bucked against me, her need hot, but I had no intention of letting her come. The night was still young, and I had so much more planned.

When I knew she was close to climax, I ruthlessly yanked my fingers from the clutches of her body and stepped away. She nearly doubled over in shock from the way I viscously denied her release.

"Alex, what the—" she began between pants.

"Shhh. No talking."

Walking over to the wall of crops, whips, and floggers, I ran my hand slowly over the selections before choosing a red dragon tongue whip.

This will do nicely.

I studied Krystina for a moment, watching her reaction to my selection. Her eyes widened and I smiled. I loved seeing that expression of frightened arousal.

I smiled to myself, deciding I wanted to torture her with more than just the whip tonight. On the table with the stereo system, there was a little black box containing two small, weighted balls. Opening the box, I slipped the balls into my pocket and then turned back to Krystina.

My dick twitched as I stalked toward her, fingering the tongue of the whip as I approached. The smooth leather was cool against my fingers, but it would deliver a brutal sting without leaving an ounce of damage to her perfect skin.

"Tell me your safeword."

"Sapphire," she immediately replied.

"I'll only stop doing what I'm doing if you use it."

"I know."

But I knew she wouldn't use it. She craved my dominance—true dominance, and not the vanilla orders she'd been given over the past two years. She'd been too long without it to risk using her safeword now. There was no doubt that my wife would willingly take everything I gave her tonight, no matter how far I pushed.

"On the bed, near the edge, with your ass in the air," I demanded.

She moved to the bed, positioning herself near the end. On her hands and knees with just her feet dangling off the edge, she was a glorious sight to behold. The scent of her arousal filled the air. I wanted to taste her—to bury my tongue in that sweet pussy and lap up every ounce of her divine nectar. But not yet. I had other ideas in mind for her first. After all, she was in my playroom, and I wanted to take advantage of all the pleasures it had to offer.

Still, a little taste wouldn't hurt. I paused to stare at her magnificent ass for a moment before positioning my head between her legs. I took one swipe with my tongue across her pink folds, then another, before stepping back and licking my lips. Krystina's breathing was rapid and uneven, with the occasional desperate whimper.

And that was exactly how I wanted her.

Desperate.

Reaching into my pocket, I pulled out the small silver balls. I rolled them in my fingers for a moment before inserting each inside her wet canal.

"Ben Wa balls, angel. Squeeze your pussy. Hold them in your body, and don't let them fall out. If they do, I'll punish you."

"Yes, sir."

My hand tightened on the handle of the dragon tongue whip. I loved it when she called me sir.

I saw the moment she clenched her muscles to keep the balls in place, and I groaned as I imagined her tightening that way around my dick.

Lifting the whip, I didn't give her any warning before delivering the first lash to her naked ass. She cried out, the sound music to my ears. I snapped the whip again, leaving a matching stripe across her other cheek.

Krystina's back arched, and she collapsed to her elbows while still keeping her perfect ass in the air. I walked a circuit around her, peppering her ass, clit, and legs with strikes of the leather. My cocked throbbed at the sight of so much red blossoming across her skin, but not because I was inflicting pain. It was about the power. Knowing my wife trusted me unequivocally was an inexplicably heady feeling that would compare to nothing else.

Over and over again, I showered her body with stinging blows. By the time I finished painting more than a dozen stripes over her back and ass, her pussy was glistening with juices that had now begun to run down the insides of her thighs. Framed in an arching garter belt, it was a beautiful display to behold. The friction of the balls inside her and the bite of the whip had her writhing with need.

Reaching under her, I found her clit. She deserved release after the lashing she just took. I circled around the hard nub, spreading her body's natural moisture. My heart was racing and sweat began to collect on the back of my neck. I wanted her —desperately—but I wanted her orgasm first.

"Come for me, angel."

Instantly, her hips pushed against my hand, searching eagerly for release. I could feel her rippling heat as I pumped my hand. It drove me wild, but I didn't slow the speed as I waited for her to get there. It wasn't long before I felt the clench of her orgasm. She went off like a rocket, and I thought I might explode if I didn't get inside her soon.

"Alex!"

"That's it, angel. Say my name. Fucking scream it!"

I added a third finger, pumping into her, manipulating the Ben Wa balls deep inside her to prolong her orgasm. Her juiced dripped over my whole hand, slathering it with her creamy essence. Her eyes rolled back, and her moans turned into screams before giving over to one last fantastical cry of release.

I gave her a moment to come down. When she eventually gave me her eyes, they were glazed and unfocused.

"I don't know how you can make me feel so good," she said sluggishly.

"I promised you, angel. Tonight would be pleasure beyond

imagining. This is only the beginning, and I never, ever break my promises."

Pushing her over onto her back, I climbed onto the bed, hovering above her before taking her mouth in a deep, feral kiss. When I pulled back, her cheeks were flushed with arousal causing my core muscles to tense and coil in reaction to her satiated look.

Moving from the bed, I yanked off my shirt and tossed it on the floor. I watched Krystina's eyes rake up and down my torso as if I were a feast she couldn't wait to eat.

And who was I to deny her of that?

My hands moved to my belt. I unfastened it and allowed the heavy buckle and pants to fall to the floor with a thud. My dick sprang free, curving up with pre-ejaculate already glistening at the tip.

"On your knees, on the floor. Clench that pussy tight, holding in the balls as you suck me off." My tone left no room for debate, but my angel had no issues obeying.

Sliding to the side of the bed, she planted her feet on the floor and stood. Moving before me, she dropped to her knees and wrapped her perfect, lush lips around my cock. Pushing forward, she suckled teasingly for a moment before taking me deep. When my head hit the base of her throat, I moaned.

She moved slowly, never taking her eyes off mine while allowing her throat to adjust to my girth. It was both tender and searingly erotic. My thighs tensed as I gathered her hair in my hands, pushing and pulling her head over my length, dictating the pace. I fucked her mouth like I owned it, thrusting forward until saliva dripped with every pump and tears sprang into her eyes.

I shoved my head in hard, aggressively hitting the back of her throat. To her credit, she never gagged. Not once. Instead, she kept her tongue flat, wrapping her slim fingers around the base of my cock, seeming as though she couldn't get enough.

When I reached the precipice of what promised to be a blockbuster orgasm, I forced myself to pull out of her mouth, not wanting to end this prematurely. Krystina licked her lips, then kissed the tip of my cock in a teasing fashion until I stepped completely away.

"Play with yourself," I commanded.

Leaning back so her ass balanced on her heels, Krystina spread her knees wide and brought her eyes up to meet mine. Using her middle finger, she began a slow and deliberate circular motion over her clit. I grabbed my cock, stroking myself as she played. I loved watching my wife pleasure herself almost as much as I loved being the one who gave it to her.

I took in the rise and fall of her breasts, a show of how rapidly she was breathing. When her breaths began to quicken, I turned my attention to her face. Her eyes were glazed, and she looked drugged from a high that could only come from intense pleasure. She was close to orgasm, but I had to stop her. That orgasm belonged to me.

"Stand. I want you back on the bed, face up," I told her.

Rising to her feet, she climbed onto the bed. Taking my time, I took hold of her legs and removed her stockings one by one to expose smooth, tanned skin. I unhooked the garter belt and the clasp of her bra, sliding both from her body until she was completely bare. The only thing left was the triskelion necklace.

Spreading her legs apart, I used a finger to pluck the balls from her body. Then I pressed my mouth to her, wanting my tongue to be the only thing giving her pleasure. She was soaked, and I couldn't wait to consume every last drop of her desire. I loved her taste and her smell, easily losing myself in my very own personal heaven. She moaned quietly as I explored her. My tongue was soft, knowing she wouldn't be able to handle too much pressure after the bite of the whip and my merciless fingers.

"Grip your knees, angel, and pull back. I need to taste more of you."

Looping her arms around the back of her knees, she spread herself even wider for me. Everything was on display—her perfect pink pussy and her tight little asshole. I planned to take both before long.

Using the moisture dripping between her two openings, I spread it back and slowly slid a finger into her tightest hole. Krystina gasped from the initial shock of my invasion, but I knew it was a gasp of pleasure. I'd turned my wife into a naughty, dirty girl, and we'd been here plenty of times before.

"Is this where you want me, Krystina? Hard and deep?"

"Oh, God," she moaned. Soft, pleading sounds poured from her throat.

My mouth curled in amusement.

"Tell me you want it," I whispered, blowing softly against her clit. "You're so wet and needy for me. All you have to do is call my name and tell me what you want."

"Fuck, Alex. I want you every way imaginable. Fuck me hard—my pussy, my ass. I want you everywhere," she begged.

I smiled at her filthy language. It wasn't often that she used such words, but when she did, I became harder than stone.

Sitting up, I climbed from the bed and moved over to the large cabinet that held every sex toy available on the market. My fingertips grazed the clamps and anal beads before I eventually settled on a medium sized silicone butt plug. The blue jewel adorning the wider flared end would stare back at me before I brutally penetrated both holes.

She wanted it all, so that's exactly what I would give her.

26

Krystina

"Lift up," Alexander ordered, tapping the side of my hip.

Knowing my obedience would bring me ultimate pleasure, I did exactly as I was told. I lifted my hips from the bed, allowing him room to slide a cushioned wedge beneath me. With my arms still locked in place behind my knees, I was fully exposed. Before the end of the night, I knew my skillful husband would have me twisted into knots.

It didn't take long before the plug was deliciously stretching my behind. The devil in my subconscious squealed with delight as I felt a tease of pleasure that promised dark enticement and decadent corruption. When Alexander notched the head of his cock at my entrance and slid inside, he stilled for a moment and waited for my body to adjust to having both holes filled to capacity. His sapphire eyes gleaned with intent, causing my core to clench.

"It's just us in this room. There's no history to get in the way or hold anything back," he said vehemently, almost as if he were saying it more as a reminder to himself. The intensity in his eyes, however, seemed to convey so much more than just his words. It was something huge and profound, solidifying our connection. "There's nothing here but you and me—*we* are all that matter."

He pressed his lips to mine, kissing me forcefully and hungrily, pushing his tongue inside my mouth with persistent aggression. When he began to move inside me, a soft whine fell from my lips.

Alexander took me brutally, the rigid lacing of his abs flexing with every thrust. He pushed impossibly deeper, filling what little space was left inside of me. I was panting and gasping for breath, absorbing the deep spasmodic tremors in my core. When he took me this way, it was both painful and pleasurable, neither one outweighing the other.

Dark, edgy sensations crawled hot through my veins, propelling me into a state of rapture as he savagely thrust deep and hard. He was truly dominating me, demonstrating his power forcefully as only a true alpha could.

I relished every touch, every sensation. Alexander unlocked my most secret places, unleashing my darkest desires—filthy thoughts of being taken, used, and controlled. Tonight was exactly what I wanted—what I had been missing. My husband was back in every way possible, and I would never get enough of his power and domination.

Grabbing my wrists, he pushed them back until my hands were pinned to each side of my head. Using the weight of his body, he pressed my knees to my shoulders, taking full and complete control. I was helpless to his every desire, relishing the vulnerable state he put me in as he drove hard into me. It was an addicting feeling, like the kind experienced with the most euphoric drug, calling to the most secret and darkest parts of my soul.

I pushed against him, meeting him thrust for thrust. My body bucked and spasmed. My core tightened. I was close to the breaking point, my orgasm just within my reach. The room began to blur around me. I cried out in abandonment, giving in to the passion burning between us.

"Alex!"

But Alexander didn't stop moving. Over and over again, he pumped his hips forward, the power of his possession overwhelming.

"Fuck, Krystina," he said in a rasping tone, and I could feel his chest vibrating with a deep groan. "You're so tight and wet."

Just as I thought it would be too much, another intense wave of pleasure rocketed through me. Battling tears and euphoria, I exploded like a firework. Closing my eyes, I let my head lull to the side as I was overcome with a pleasure so powerful, it caused stars to dot my vision. I shook violently, buzzing from the most inexplicable high as I crested and spiraled into an abyss of mindless ecstasy.

"Ah!" Alexander thundered. His body jerked, plunging so hard into me, his balls tapped the jewel at my rear. With one final pump, he collapsed down on top of me, completely and utterly spent.

A rush of breath escaped my lungs as my hammering heart worked to return to a normal rhythm. We were sweaty and messy—and delightfully satisfied. When Alexander finally pulled out, he shifted to lay alongside me. Reaching up, he began to tease one of my nipples.

I tossed him a teasing look.

"Round two already?" I asked.

"Oh, angel. That was only a warmup. No part of you is going

to go unexplored tonight. I have you in my playroom. Did you really think I'd let you out so easily?"

TIME HAD no meaning while we were in the playroom, and I had no idea how long we'd been down there. It could have been two hours or four, but it was more than enough to leave my body limp and satiated. I felt somewhat delirious, struggling to string together a coherent thought as my body hummed.

After multiple rounds of some of the most powerful sex we'd ever had together, Alexander carried me up the narrow staircase back to our bedroom. Setting me down on the bed in the master suite, he said, "Lay on your stomach. I'll be right back, angel."

I didn't need to be told twice. Sprawled face down on the bed, I lay there with my eyes closed on the verge of succumbing to sleep. A moment later, I felt a shift on the bed and heard the pop of a cap, prompting me to peer with one eye at Alexander. I watched as he squirted aloe into his palm, and then began to rub the soothing gel over my backside.

He circled his hands over the curves of my back, ass, and legs, massaging the cool aloe into all the places that had felt the sting of the whip throughout the night. Alexander had always emphasized the importance of aftercare, making today not unusual from any other time I fell into subspace. I sighed, loving the way he doted on me after a round of intense, borderline maniacal, sex.

"That feels nice," I murmured.

"I'm glad," he said, rotating his fingers up my spine. "God, you're exquisite. Absolutely perfect."

After he finished with the aloe, Alexander slipped his arm

under my head, nestling me between his chest and arm. With the softest parts of me against the hardest parts of him, we lay there quietly as he softly traced his fingertips around the curve of my shoulder.

Now that I'd come down from the tremendous state of bliss, I was able to think more clearly. I ruminated on what had happened this weekend and Alexander's unexpected desire to use the playroom tonight.

I'd often compared our chemistry to a lightning bolt. It sizzled and sparked with every look and every touch. But tonight had been different. The intense intimacy I'd experienced made it feel like we were new lovers again. It was as if we were discovering each other anew, but with a level of trust that could only be shared between two souls who'd experienced as much as Alexander and me. This was the start of something new. I could feel it in my bones. I just wondered how far I could push.

Angling my head up to look at Alexander, I decided to test the waters.

"I was wondering," I began.

"Oh? What about?" Alexander replied lazily, still circling his fingers around my shoulder.

"I was wondering if you could bring Eva to school tomorrow."

He hesitated.

"I probably should know this, but where do you have her enrolled?"

"Dalton-Hewitt Academy."

"I know where that is. Is there a particular reason you can't bring her?"

"I want to go to the cemetery to see Liliana in the morning. If I go after I drop off Eva, it means getting to work really late. I haven't been there since the day after we got back from Vegas, and I don't know...I just feel compelled to go. I don't want to get back into the habit of going there every morning, but I'd like to shoot for once a week whenever possible."

His arm tightened around me with understanding.

"Okay, angel. What time does Eva need to be dropped off?"

"Hale usually has us at the school by eight, and I walk her in. Class starts at eight-thirty. Which reminds me of another issue I have. I'm considering moving the Turning Stone Advertising offices closer to Westchester. Not getting to the office until nine-thirty every morning isn't going to cut it for much longer."

"Damn! That reminds me. I didn't even think about the commute," he said, scrubbing a hand over his head, then dragging it down to rub his jawline. "I'm sorry, but I can't drop her off. I have a meeting with Kent Bloomfield and Walter Roberts at nine to go over blueprints for a Wally's store remodel. I'll never make it on time to the meeting if I bring Eva to school. It's already been rescheduled twice, so I don't want to push it off again."

"Oh, okay," I said quietly, already flooded with disappointment over not being able to visit Liliana tomorrow.

"Hang on. I have an idea. I know you've already been getting to work late because of school drop off, but do you think you can sneak out of work early tomorrow?"

"Maybe. Why?"

"So we can go to the cemetery. I can go without an issue later in the afternoon. I'll talk to Clive about it and ensure he makes it work for you, too."

I pressed my lips together in a frown. I might love it when my husband dominated me in the bedroom, but I absolutely hated when he tried to brandish his dominance over my company.

"You will do no such thing," I quipped. "Clive is my

marketing coordinator. He works for me. I don't need his permission to leave early any more than I need you to manage him or any other member of my staff. I just needed to know why you wanted me to leave early. I can handle the logistics."

"Fair enough," he agreed easily, which shocked me. But when he spoke again, his tone was different—more subdued. "I've been thinking about this a lot, angel—about all the ways I've failed you since losing Liliana. For starters, I should have gone with you more to the cemetery."

"Alex, it's okay—"

"No. My number one job is ensuring your well-being. In my effort to stay strong, I abandoned you. I won't do that again, nor will I allow you to go to our daughters grave alone anymore. From now on, I will always be with you. So, what do you say? If we leave Cornerstone Tower by two, that should give us plenty of time to visit Liliana and still make it to Eva's school on time to pick her up at the end of the school day."

I snuggled in closer to his chest.

"That sounds like a perfect idea. Thank you, Alex."

"Why are you thanking me?"

"For getting it—for getting me. I love you so much."

He didn't respond right away, but when he did, my breath caught.

"When you go to court in October for permanent guardianship of Eva, I'll be there with you for that, too. You have my full support. I'll get with Stephen about arranging legal representation, and I'll make sure Bryan puts together a financial statement for the court. We're partners in life, angel, and it's time I started acting like it. Plus, there's just something about that little girl that..." He trailed off as if searching for the right words. "Something about her just feels right. I should have given her a chance—should have given you a chance. I'm sorry I didn't right away, but I'm with you now. I love you. Always."

Tears glistened in my eyes when I reached up to cup his cheek.

"And forever."

27

Krystina

I inhaled deeply as I walked down the front steps of Dalton-Hewitt Academy, appreciating the fresh air in my lungs as I made my way back to the Maserati where Hale was waiting. New York mornings in late September were always cooler, and this Autumnal Equinox was proving to be much like so many others in years past.

I had just dropped off Eva, and was happy to know she'd get to spend the first part of her morning outside, enjoying the beautiful day with her fast-growing list of friends. The sun was bright, and the air was crisp. The trees had not yet started to change, but it was only a matter of time before the vibrant gold, orange, and red leaves filled their branches.

Hale stood at the ready as I approached the car, holding the door open for me to climb inside. As I stepped onto the sidewalk, I paused when I saw something bright flash out of the corner of my eye. My head snapped to my left and located the glare. There was no mistaking what I saw poking out of the window of a nondescript car parked across the street.

Damn it!

It was a telephoto lens.

I'd become all too accustomed to them after I'd married Alexander. However, to my knowledge, the paparazzi hadn't successfully nabbed a picture of me since before the pandemic. Alexander had made sure of that. Why they would choose now to come around was beyond me, but their timing couldn't have been worse. I was hoping to keep Eva a secret for a little longer.

But then again, perhaps the paparazzi was here for someone else. After all, Dalton-Hewitt Academy was a prestigious school. They could be taking pictures of any number of celebrities. I was low in the pecking order by comparison. They probably weren't even here for me at all, and I was just being paranoid.

"Is everything okay?" Hale asked.

I quickly looked back at him and hoped my expression was blank. The last thing I needed was to alert Hale to possible paparazzi activity. He'd report to Alexander and all hell would break loose.

"Everything is fine, Hale. Let's make a quick stop at La Biga before heading to Cornerstone Tower. It's been a week since I was there last, and I'm sure Maria and Angelo will give me hell for it."

"Sure thing, Miss."

I climbed into the car and settled back in my seat, feeling more content today than I had in at least a year's time. All in all, things were going well. They weren't perfect, but as well as could be expected given everything. After the weekend on the boat, followed by the night in the playroom, Alexander and I seemed to have found our stride again. Marriages are comprised of peaks and valleys, and we were on the upswing from our lowest point.

It helped that Alexander and I developed a new routine over the course of the past two weeks. He went to the cemetery with me on the days I thought I needed it, but I was able to make do with the video he made for me on most days. The mornings we actually went to Liliana's grave was a different experience than it used to be. Alexander's presence made things easier because I was able to draw on his strength.

Alexander and I had plans to go through Hannah's apartment at the end of the month, and I'd begun the hunt for new office space closer to home. Keeping my employees' commute in mind, I was hoping to find something somewhere between Westchester and the city. Until I relocated, Alexander and I had agreed to take turns bringing Eva to school, as it wasn't conducive to either of our jobs to be showing up late every day. Sure, we could have had a member of our staff or security team take her, but I didn't want to lose out on those valuable moments in the car with her—especially the moments Alexander got to spend with her.

My husband was really trying with Eva, and the drive to school was precious time that allowed him to get to know her better. Watching their relationship slowly transition made my heart soar. He made regular time for her, often including her in moments that he held most dear, such as the time he spent with his mother. I'd once caught him with Eva on his lap, reading *Hop On Pop* to a smiling Helena. She was mostly non-verbal, but it was easy to see her happiness whenever Eva was around.

Whether Alexander realized it or not, I knew every smile Helena granted during those visits was another brownie point scored for Eva. He tried to hold the appearance of keeping his guard up, almost as if he was afraid of getting too close to Eva, but I saw him when he thought I wasn't looking. His expression was curious, and I knew he was attempting to unpack her little mind.

True to the meaning of her name, I believed Eva breathed life into Alexander and I during a time when we were feeling the most deflated. I wondered if she was also part of the reason going to the cemetery seemed easier to endure. I couldn't be sure. All I knew was that I was grateful to have her sweet and curious disposition in our lives. There were still so many unknowns, but I truly believed she came to us for a reason. This was going to be a long series of baby steps and I was ready for every single one.

I felt a vibration against my thigh and recognized it as my cellphone pulsating in my purse. Reaching down, I opened the clasp and pulled out the phone. Allyson's name showed on the caller ID. I hesitated, not sure if I wanted to answer.

We hadn't spoken since Las Vegas. She had called a few times after she and Matteo returned from their so-called honeymoon, but I'd been avoiding her. It wasn't that I didn't want to talk to her. Allyson had hurt me deeply by hiding her relationship with Matteo, and fixing things with her was important. However, I didn't want the distraction when so many other things needed my attention. My marriage and the life of a young girl were on the line, and I had to prioritize.

Sliding my finger across the screen, I answered the phone.

"Ally, hi."

"There you are, stranger! I've been trying to reach you since last week."

"I know. Things have been hectic," I explained. I kept my voice even yet chose not to go into too much detail about why things had been so busy for me. Eva was big news and I wanted to tell her later when, hopefully, things felt less awkward.

"I thought we could catch up and get drinks soon. How

does a night out at Murphy's sound? We haven't been there in ages."

"Maybe," I replied noncommittally. "Evenings are tough for me right now, but I'm sure I can figure out something. When were you thinking?"

Ally fell silent for a beat before saying, "Krys, look. I'm really, really sorry. I know you're upset, and you have every right to be. I should have told you about Matteo."

"It's fine, Ally," I lied.

"No, it's not. I can tell by the sound of your voice that you're hurt. Matteo and I were just really complicated for a while there. I didn't know how to explain us to myself let alone anyone else."

I hesitated with my response, trying to decide whether I wanted to have it out with her over the phone, or save if for when we were in person. But another part of me didn't want to go a round with her at all. Yes, she'd hurt me. But she was my best friend and I wanted her back. All the turmoil between Alexander and me seemed to have taken all the fight out of me, and I didn't have the energy to argue anymore—with anyone. In the end, I went with honesty.

"It really did hurt, Ally. Hiding that you were together was one thing, but then you got married without including me. I feel like you didn't trust me enough to confide in me."

"Oh, no! Krys, it wasn't like that at all. It wasn't that I didn't trust you—I didn't trust me."

I frowned. "What do you mean?"

"There has always been this undercurrent of sexual tension between us. But Matteo is... Well, he's just not the kind of guy you have a fling with. He's the settle down, for better or for worse type of guy. That's why I never let it go beyond flirting."

"Except you did."

"Yes, but it wasn't planned. It began back when everything

was in lockdown during the pandemic. Matteo's restaurant was only open for takeout. I popped in there to get something to eat, we talked for a bit, and then I went home. Afterward, Matteo called to tell me he'd been exposed to the virus and had to quarantine. Considering our close proximity when we were talking, he thought I should do the same. It was right before Christmas, around the time you and Alexander left for Vermont."

"Ally, that was nearly two years ago! I can't believe you've kept this hidden for that long," I said, feeling a fresh wave of hurt.

"I know and I said I was sorry. But let me finish." Through the phone, I heard her suck in a deep breath. When she let it out, it wasn't quite a sigh, but more like she was preparing for what came next. "We talked on the phone every day for the first few days of isolation. Three days in, we both began to get stir crazy. Plus, the idea of being alone on Christmas was really depressing. So, I had the notion to quarantine together. Matteo agreed to the suggestion, packed a bag, and headed to my place. A few days later, one thing led to another... and, well. You know. Pandemic sex."

I pressed my lips together in a frown.

"That still doesn't explain why you both hid it from Alexander and me."

"I didn't tell you because I regretted it almost immediately after it happened. Remember what I said about Matteo being the settle down type of guy?"

"Yeah."

"He told me that he loved me the morning after we slept together. He confessed to having feelings for me for a long time and I panicked. I was terrified that I'd break his heart, and I thought for sure I'd ruin the dynamic we all had together—you, me, Alexander, and Matteo. We always had so much fun and I thought I foolishly fucked it all up. I didn't believe that I was built for marriage, kids, the white picket fence, etcetera. So, knowing I couldn't give Matteo what he deserved, I asked him to leave my house. I kept my distance, which wasn't hard because of the pandemic. But once everything started opening back up, and we began to resume normal life again, I found myself around him more and more. The attraction never died, no matter how I tried to fight it. Then Vegas happened. It was spur of the moment. Impulsive. I mean, have you ever known me *not* to be impulsive?"

I laughed. "No."

"I didn't mean to exclude you. It just wasn't ever supposed to happen."

"But it did happen."

"Yeah, it did," she said with a wistful sigh. "But you aren't the only one upset about it. My parents aren't too happy, and Matteo's family is furious. I'd never heard so many Italian swear words in a single sentence until Matteo broke the news to his mother over the phone after we got back from Vegas. She railed on and on about not getting married in a church for what seemed like forever, but by the end of the phone call, she'd had an entire traditional wedding planned for us. We have a meeting with Father Daniel next week."

"You're getting married—again?" I asked incredulously.

"Apparently," Allyson said with a laugh. "Besides, wasn't it you who said Vegas marriages weren't real? Matteo's mother basically said the same thing. I want what I have with Matteo to be real, and if that means a traditional wedding, I'm all for it. And to be perfectly honest, I'm looking forward to it."

I shook my head as I processed everything. Allyson sounded grounded, level-headed, and nothing like the flighty friend I'd known since grades school. But most of all, she sounded happy—truly happy. I couldn't begrudge her for that. My friend deserved all the happiness in the world.

"Wow, Ally. I guess I can finally say congratulations."

"We haven't set a date yet. I told Matteo I wouldn't set one until I checked with you."

"Me?" I asked, frowning in confusion.

"Yes, silly. I need to make sure my Matron of Honor is available for the big day."

The smile on my face was instant.

"Of course, I'll be available!"

Allyson and I chatted for a while longer about wedding plans. I didn't tell her about Eva. I would eventually, but I wanted to tell her in person. After deciding on a date to meet at Murphy's Pub for drinks, I ended the call feeling a bit lighter than I had when I woke that morning. My friendship with Allyson had stood the test of time, and if felt good to know that this latest thing had merely been a speedbump in the long road we were committed to traveling together.

I glanced out the car window and saw that we'd arrived at La Biga at some point during my phone conversation. Hale sat patiently in the front seat. When he caught my eye in the rearview mirror, I gave him a short nod.

"I didn't realize we were here. I'll be right back," I told him, reaching for the car door handle.

"I'll accompany you," he said, climbing from the driver's seat before I could protest. When he came around to open the car door for me, I gave him a pointed look.

"Hale, really. It's La Biga. I'll be fine."

"I'd just assume not take a risk. I allow you to go into little Eva's school without me, but only because I understood the concern about drawing too much attention to her. I won't be making any more exceptions."

"Fine," I mumbled, thoroughly annoyed even though I

knew Hale wasn't only just following orders. He actually cared about me.

Once on the sidewalk, I breathed in the aroma of espresso and fresh pastries coming from La Biga. I'd been coming here for as long as I'd lived in New York, and the owners, Maria and Angelo Gianfranco, had become friends over time. They were fabulous people who I couldn't help falling in love with—along with their cozy café that I loved almost as much as I loved them.

I pushed through the entrance door and looked around at the simple interior modeled after the original Café La Biga in Rome, Italy. The sound of espresso beans in the grinder mixed with chatter from patrons sitting at the small tables filled my ears. Dean Martin was playing through the overhead speakers and, as always, Angelo was whistling to the tune. I walked up to the counter and gave him a huge smile.

Looking up, he caught my eye and quickly had a grin to match mine.

"*Ciao, bella!* Where have you been? We have not seen you in a long time!" he said in his thick Italian accent.

I laughed.

"You know you say that every time I come in here. It's only been a week," I pointed out in jest. It was a little game we played. He would make it seem like I hadn't visited the café in eons, and I would remind him how long it had actually been.

"A week is too long to go without seeing your beautiful face," he quipped, and I laughed again, having already known what his response was going to be.

Angelo began making my favorite drink—a cappuccino with two packets of raw sugar.

"How is everything?" I asked.

"Good, good. I just found out I'm going to be a grandpa again. My daughter-in-law is expecting another *bambino!*"

"Oh, that's wonderful news," I told him while trying to tamp down the pang of jealousy I felt over another woman's pregnancy. I wondered if that feeling of being inadequate and flawed would ever go away.

"Ah, I thought I heard your voice!" Maria called out, interrupting our conversation as she exited from the back stock room.

"Hello, Maria," I greeted as the aging Italian walked around the counter to give me a hug. After kissing both my cheeks, she pulled back to look at me.

"You look well, Krystina. You have a little sparkle in your eye. You are happy, no?"

"Things are going good."

"*Bravo, bravo!* Now, tell me," she said, leaning in conspiratorially. "Did they catch that man that's been hanging around?"

I blinked in confusion. "Man? What man?"

"Maria, *basta così!*" Angelo hissed, then began speaking in rapid Italian. I couldn't understand a word he said. I glanced at Hale just in time to see him shaking his head at Maria.

"Hale, what is she talking about?"

"It's nothing."

I knew Hale and his response came just a little too quick. I could tell whatever was going on wasn't just nothing.

"Maria," I said, interrupting Angelo's tirade. "Can you please tell me what this is all about? What man were you referring to?"

"Maria," Angelo said in a warning tone.

"*Non mi dire!* She should know," Maria countered, then turned to me. "Look here."

Going back to the other side of the counter, Maria reached under it and pulled out an eight by ten sized photo. By the angle of the candid image, it appeared to have been taken by a security camera. I recognized the man featured.

"I know this guy," I said, pointing to the image. "Well, I don't actually know him, but I've talked to him a couple of times."

"You've spoken to him? When?" Hale asked.

"Outside Dalton-Hewitt Academy, near the fence surrounding the playground. He said that he has a grandson who goes there."

I watched Hale visibly pale—an unusual reaction from him to say the least. My heart began to race, and I looked to Maria and Angelo. Both had worried expressions on their faces, but neither said another word. Instead, Angelo handed me my cappuccino, and looked toward Hale as if waiting for permission before saying or doing anything else.

"I can assure you, that man does not have a grandson at that school," Hale said gruffly. "Come now. I need to get you to Cornerstone Tower. Mr. Stone will want to know about this."

He took hold of my elbow, but I shrugged his hand away.

"Hale, tell me what's going on this minute. Who is that guy and what does he have to do with Alexander?"

"It's not for me to say. You'll have to ask Mr. Stone."

"Fine. Let's go then," I snapped, turning to march toward the door.

I didn't even think to say goodbye to Maria and Angelo. I was too pissed about being left in the dark yet again. Who knew what it was about this time? With Alexander, it could be anything, and my personal safety was almost always cited as the reason.

No matter what it was, I would get to the bottom of it—I always did.

28

Alexander

I was walking from the conference room toward my office when I spotted Krystina stepping off the elevator on my floor in Cornerstone Tower. Hale was behind her, but I only had eyes for my wife.

Dressed in a burgundy jumpsuit, she strode toward me on nude pumps with an air of sophistication and a naturally seductive sway to her hips. The capped sleeves left most of her arms bare, revealing smooth, tanned skin. Silver hoops dangles from her ears, accenting the light rose colored sunglasses on her face. The obstruction brought my attention to her mouth— and to the full lips that had been wrapped around my cock just that very morning.

Any other day, I would have met her halfway, unable to keep from touching her for a moment longer. However, when she removed her sunglasses, there was no mistaking the fury in her eyes.

"We need to talk. Now," she stated harshly. Thin eyebrows pushed together over furious chocolate brown eyes.

"Excuse me?" I questioned, not sure why she was taking such a punitive tone.

"I don't know what's going on, Alex, but I'm sure it's some nonsense about safety. You can't always keep me in the dark."

Several heads turned at the commotion, each one able to see the anger written plainly on Krystina's face. I raised my eyebrows in surprise at her brazenness. Nobody spoke to me like that in this building—in my empire—and especially in front of my staff.

Not even my wife.

"Sir, let me explain," Hale began, but Krystina silenced him with a slice of her hand.

"I want answers, Alex."

My jaw tightened.

"My office. Now," I hissed through gritted teeth.

"Good idea," Krystina agreed.

Squaring her shoulders, she breezed by me, making a beeline for my office door. I pressed my lips together in a tight line, having little choice but to follow her. After the three of us were in my office, I quietly closed the door and turned to face them. My temper simmered just below the surface, ready to erupt at any moment.

"Now, what is the meaning of this?"

Krystina opened her mouth to speak, but Hale beat her to it.

"Maria Gianfranco showed her a picture of Ketry. Come to find out, he already made contact with Krystina. He's been talking to her outside of Eva's school, but never let on who he was."

I felt myself pale.

"Ketry? Who's Ketry?" Krystina demanded.

I still didn't know what Ketry was up to, and I briefly toyed with the idea of not telling her. The information I had wasn't going to be easy for her to hear for more reasons than one. I didn't know how she would react to learning about her birth father—or that he was a criminal—after all this time. However, Hale seemed to read my thoughts.

"Boss, it would be easier for me to keep her safe if she was aware of the threat."

I looked at my security detail and longtime confidant. We'd had our share of ups and downs, but we'd worked through them and I trusted him with my life. If he thought my wife should know who Ketry was, I valued his judgement.

Turning to Krystina, I said, "We don't really know how significant of a threat he is—or if he's even a threat at all. However, given his background, there's a high probability that he is. Does the name Michael Ketry ring a bell to you?"

She shook her head. "No. Should it?"

I sighed, knowing there would be no easy way to do this. It was best to be as straight with her as I possibly could.

"Have a seat," I told her, pointing to the plush seating area in my office. "There's something you need to see."

Moving to my desk drawer, I pulled out a manila folder containing a printed version of the dossier Hale had put together. Along with it was any documentation pertaining to Hale's research and several photos of Ketry in the penthouse lobby, La Biga, and other places my wife frequented. I tossed the entire folder onto the low table in front of where Krystina sat.

"Michael Ketry is your biological father," I stated flatly.

Confusion flashed quickly on Krystina's features.

"What?" she asked incredulously.

"This is a comprehensive background check that Hale put together. You need to read it, angel."

She glanced between me and the envelope before slowly reaching to pick it up. I watched her eyes as they followed the lines of text, rapidly turning the pages and reading every bit of the dossier. The perplexed look on her face slowly morphed into one of shock.

Shoving the papers back into the envelope, she looked at me, and then to Hale.

"But how can you be sure this is my father? There's nothing in here that connects me to him, and I've seen my birth certificate. There's no name listed for the father."

This time, it was Hale's turn to speak.

"As you know, when you first started coming around, I conducted a background check on you. Your name appeared in the last will and testament for a woman named Evelyn Rose Ketry. She died in 2017 and listed you as a beneficiary in her will. If you look in the folder, you'll find a copy of it. The will cites you as her granddaughter. However, her estate never went to you as she intended, although I wasn't able to find out why. It defaulted to a man named Michael Ketry, Evelyn's only child. That's how I was able to deduce that he was your father."

"Your mother also confirmed this for me," I added.

Krystina snapped her head in my direction.

"My mother? You spoke to her about this?"

The betrayal in her eyes was real and fierce. It flayed me. We'd promised no more lies and no more secrets, yet I'd kept an important truth from her for months. I wasn't sure if she'd forgive me after this.

"Yes, I spoke to her, but not many words were exchanged. She was pretty tight lipped about him, saying it hurt too much to talk about. She only confirmed Michael Ketry was, in fact, your biological father. She didn't say much else before hurrying off the phone with me."

"That's typical," Krystina sarcastically mused. "My mother—"

Whatever she was about to say was cut off by the ringing of my desk phone. Glancing down at the caller ID, I saw it was Laura.

"Laura, this isn't really a good time," I informed her after I activated the speaker.

"Mr. Stone, I've very sorry to bother you. Cameron Duncan is on the phone. He says he's the assistant to Paul Glower from ESI, and he insists it's urgent. Should I put him through?"

As much as I didn't want to be bothered at that moment, I'd told Laura that anything related to Empire State Innovation was to be given priority. The partnership was still too new and needed to be nurtured carefully—especially considering the lukewarm reaction the deal received in the press. It wouldn't be wise for me to put off taking the call. Hopefully, whatever Cameron had to say would be quick.

"Put him through, Laura," I told her. When the light on the conference phone flashed green, I knew he was on the line. "Cameron. Alexander Stone here. What can I do for you today?"

"This isn't Cameron, although I did enjoy reading all the criticism you've been receiving from the press about your deal with the devil, or should I say, with Paul Glower and company. I thought someone with your success would know better than to get in bed with the government."

"Who is this?" I demanded.

"Oh, I think you know who this is. You've had a tail on me for months."

My head snapped up to look at Krystina and Hale. Krystina's brows were pushed together in confusion, but I saw the moment she began to connect the dots. Hale, on the other hand, had gone remarkably still, and I knew his acute instincts had silently kicked into overdrive.

Pressing my finger to my lips, I motioned for them to be quiet and turned my attention back to the phone.

"I know you've been following my wife, Ketry. What do you want with Krystina?"

"Five million dollars," he breezed.

I nearly snorted with amusement, while becoming angered at the same time.

"Try again," I challenged.

"Come now, Stone. That's a drop in the bucket for someone like you."

"Not a chance."

"I think I could get you to change your mind. You see, I know all about you—including how you get your kinks at a special place called Club O."

I only had a brief moment of panic before deciding to call his bluff. If Ketry really had something, he wouldn't get far with it. I'd make sure of it. At the end of the day, he was nobody, and I had amassed connections all over the city and several parts of the country. Ketry was nothing more than a bug who needed to be quashed.

When I spoke, I made sure to keep my tone even and unruffled but inside I was seething.

"You can threaten all you want but nobody will believe you," I told him. "I've been around this block before."

"You think so? Turn on the TV to Channel 7."

"No."

"Don't be difficult, Stone. It ruins all the fun—and I had a lot of fun during my interview this morning. I wouldn't want you to miss it. The reporter was very excited to talk to me. I think you'll find what you see and hear enlightening."

I narrowed my gaze and turned to the three large flat-screen television panels hanging on the wall to my left. As was customary, one of the TVs was tuned to Bloomberg TV with the volume muted. Another displayed stock tickers, but the third one was powered off.

Grabbing the remote from the top drawer of my desk, I pointed it at the blank screen until Channel 7 came on. *Good Morning New York* was on, a show focused on local events, celebrity gossip, and anything else that might be interesting to the local population. To my surprise, Ketry was on camera being interviewed by a journalist.

And not just any journalist—it was Mac Owens.

"Jesus fucking Christ," I muttered. Mac Owens had been obsessed with me for years. Every time I thought I'd fallen off his radar, he'd turn up. He was like a bad penny, and I wondered when he landed himself a position on television. Last I knew, he was still working at *The City Times* newspaper.

I quickly turned up the volume and glanced at Krystina. Her shock mirrored mine. Focusing my attention back on the television, I could barely believe what I was hearing.

Mac Owens: *It's hard to believe you never knew about her until now.*

Michael Ketry: *Her mother kept her from me. As soon as I found out she existed, I came straight to New York. Reuniting with her was really great.*

Reuniting?

I looked to Krystina, but she just shrugged with bewilderment. Whatever Ketry's angle was, it was all a lie.

A series of photos flashed across the screen. Many were of Krystina when she was younger, until they fast-forwarded to after she had met me. Quick flashes of us in various places filled the screen. Some were pictures taken by the tabloids while we were unaware. Others were of us at various charity events or galas.

However, I did a double take when a photo appeared of Krystina and me in Vermont. It was a selfie taken a couple of years back, and it had been one of Krystina's favorites. She'd framed the picture, and it was currently on display at our home. As far as I knew, the only digital copy of it was on Krystina's phone. Just as I began to wonder how *Good Morning New York* had gotten a hold of that particular photo, the screen transitioned to another image of Krystina. This one was taken on *The Lucy*.

I froze.

I knew for a fact there was only one copy of that picture because I had taken it. It was my favorite photo of my wife, and it sat on the fireplace mantle in my home office in Westchester. The only possible way they could have that photo is if someone in our household had given it to them. Or worse—a person who'd trespassed in our home had stolen it.

My stomach tightened when the camera panned back to Ketry. As I stared at his face, a terrifying realization came to me.

It had been him—he'd been the one in our house.

I quickly looked at Krystina. From her expression, it seemed as though she had reached the same conclusion I had. My heart began to race in my chest as I wondered how many times Ketry invaded our personal and most private space. Considering the security we had in place, it seemed impossible that he could have gotten in without notice, yet I couldn't deny the obvious.

Turning my attention back to the interview, I focused on what they were saying. The pictures flashing on screen were disturbing in more ways than one, but what Ketry was giving

Mac Owens was hardly newsworthy. I wondered why Owens gave him the time of day. There had to be more to it.

Mac Owens: *We at Good Morning New York are excited to hear about the news of your grandchild, too—or I should say, soon to be. I have to wonder how the Stone's kept her a secret. Tell us more about her, Michael.*

My stomach dropped.

Eva.

That was why Owens was interviewing Ketry. Eva was newsworthy and prime content for the show's celebrity gossip segment—especially if it was pitched that we'd been keeping her hidden. After this interview, there was sure to be a media frenzy.

Fuck!

When the television screen panned to a picture of Eva playing on a swing set at her school, I felt all the blood drain from my face. Not only had he been stalking Krystina's whereabouts, but he'd been watching Eva, too. I slammed my fist on the desk, causing the conference phone Ketry was on to rattle.

"Why, you son of a bitch!" I roared.

"She really loves the swings, doesn't she?" he replied gleefully.

"You stay away from her!" I warned, not caring one iota about watching the interview anymore. I could watch it later online if I needed to—when I didn't have Ketry chirping in my ear.

"You know my price, Stone. Pay up and I'll go away."

"I'll sue that network for everything they're worth for using that picture without permission. You think you've got it all figured out, but you have no idea who you're dealing with. I'll—"

"Oh no, no. I *know* I have it all figured out," Ketry interrupted. "You see, there's something called public records, and there was a court filing in my dear daughter's name. You can't do anything about that picture—and Owens knows this, too. The records show that a little girl by the name of Eva Wallace isn't yours at all. But you want her to be. Finding that out was an unexpected surprise. What do you think a judge would say if they knew the potential legal guardians or adoptive parents were regulars at a sex club?"

"Fuck off!"

But Ketry ignored me and continued.

"The court date is in October, right? Five million doesn't seem like a lot to pay now, does it?"

We weren't regulars at Club O. In fact, our visit there a few weeks back was the first time we'd gone in years. So again, I tried to call Ketry's bluff.

"You have proof of nothing," I dared, hoping this was in fact the case.

"Don't I? Check your inbox. You'll find a few pictures of the two of you exiting the club on August twenty-sixth of this year."

I didn't hesitate.

"Fucker," I hissed under my breath. He was playing us like puppets, knowing we'd jump with only the slightest tug of the string.

Moving quickly, I went to the computer and opened my inbox, furious that he was calling the shots. There was an email from an anonymous sender. Clicking on it, I waited for the images to load. When they did, I sucked in a sharp breath.

In vivid detail, the series of pictures that populated showed Krystina and me walking down the steps from the massive stone building that housed Club O. My arm was around her and she appeared extremely disheveled. Black smudges were under her eyes and her shirt was only partially buttoned. The strap to her purse slung haphazardly over one shoulder, with her bra left dangling over the gusset of the clutch.

We'd left in a hurry that day, which was why she was braless with her shirt in disarray. The black under her eyes was mascara smeared by her tears. However, to anyone who didn't know what really happened that night, the images painted a picture of a couple who'd had more than just a good time. In fact, by the way a half-dressed Krystina clung to me on the steps, she could easily be perceived as an intoxicated woman who needed me for support.

I shifted my gaze to my wife. She was standing next to me, a look of horror plastered on her face.

"Alex..." she whispered. She saw what I saw, and we both knew these pictures could not be made public.

"Now, about that five mil," Ketry said, as if to remind us he was still on the phone. "You've got two days. I want unmarked bills in two nondescript black duffel bags. Be in the parking lot at the corner of Shea Road and Seaver Way in Queens on Saturday night at ten-thirty. I hope you aren't afraid of the dark."

"And if I don't show?"

"I'll give the pictures taken outside the club to Mac Owens. He'll pay for it—not as much as you of course, but it's better than nothing. That guy really hates you, doesn't he?" he added with a chuckle. "And Stone, unless you want to lose the kid, no police. You need to come alone. If I get arrested, my one phone call will be to Mac Owens. Don't forget—Saturday, ten-thirty. I'll find you once I see that you're holding up your end of the deal. Wait for my call. If I so much as sniff a hint of cop, I'll leave and call Owens."

Then the line went dead.

We all looked at each other.

The idea of losing Eva made me feel sick. I'd barely had time to get to know her, but the thought of anything happening to her made my stomach turn, and I thought I might throw up right then and there. Eva was too sweet and innocent to get caught up in the greed-driven charades of a crazy man. I had to protect her.

The room was silent for another solid ten seconds before I jumped into action.

"Hale, did you get a trace on that call?"

"Yes, sir. The security team was able to pinpoint his location to a payphone in New Rochelle. He's nowhere in the vicinity."

I nodded, then turned to my wife.

"Krystina, call your mother and tell her we'll be in Clifton Park early this evening."

"We can't just leave. Eva is at school."

"We'll go after she gets out. We should pick her up early anyway. Now that her existence has been made public, the media will be circling. She can come with us to your moms. Since she's going to be a permanent part of our lives, it's time she meets Frank and Elizabeth. Hale, we'll need to take the Bell 407GXP helicopter. Can you secure a flight plan with Air Pegasus?"

"Yes, sir."

"Good. I want to look Elizabeth in the eye and ask her about Ketry. I want to know what motivates him and what makes him tick. No more of her avoiding my questions and claiming it hurts to talk about the past. I want to know exactly who we are dealing with, and she's the only one who knows."

Krystina didn't ask questions, but immediately pulled out her phone.

While she busied herself with calling her mother, I

instructed Hale to contact Greyson Hughes, the man charged with finding Ketry's whereabouts.

"Update Greyson on what's going on and set up a meeting with the entire security team for after we get back from Clifton Park. I'm going to call Stephen and Bryan and bring them up to speed."

Not waiting for a response, I picked up my desk phone and dialed Stephen first. While I waited for him to pick up, I looked at Hale. In all the years I'd known him, never had I seen this level of worry in his expression before. It matched the uneasiness in his voice when he spoke.

"Greyson, we found Ketry," Hale said into the phone. "We have a serious problem."

After all the calls were made, Hale left to meet with Greyson, Samuel, and the rest of the security team to try and come up with a preliminary plan.

I looked at Krystina after she ended the call with her mother and found her expression devoid of emotion.

"Krystina, what is it?"

"Nothing. Everything is fine."

The flatness in her tone and vacant look in her eyes put me on high alert.

"Talk to me, angel."

"I recognized his voice when you were on the phone with him, although, not as the man I met at the school. He called me before at Turning Stone. He'd claimed to be my father, but I dismissed it as a prank. I just didn't realize the person on the phone and the person I'd met were one in the same."

I noticed a slight tremble to her hands, and she was pale, her cheeks lacking their normal rosy hue.

"Krystina, come here," I said, moving to the sofa. I sat down and pat the seat beside me. "Sit down, angel. I think you're in shock. Talk to me."

She moved toward me like a robot, her motions stiff as she sat down. But when she angled her face to look up at me, a lonely tear slid down her cheek. The sight of it flayed me.

"He's not just stalking me—he's stalking Eva, too. Those pictures of us look really bad. We can't lose Eva, Alex. I... I won't be able to survive this again."

Pulling her tight into the crook of my arm, I cradled her head against my chest and intertwined my fingers in her hair. I pressed a hard kiss to her temple, my love for her never fiercer than it was at that moment.

"I know, angel. I know. We won't lose her. I promise."

29

Krystina

Like most suburban homes, Frank and my mother's house sat in a cluster of other residential properties. Their neighborhood, the place where I spent my formative years, was a bit more upscale, with an eclectic variety of home styles. Tudors had been popular when they were house hunting, which is what they had ultimately settled on. Me, being just shy of eleven years old at the time, had thought the house looked like something out of a storybook. The old-world aesthetic was comprised of steep roofs and gables, brick fronts, and timber accents, reminding me of an oversized fairytale cottage.

With Eva's hand in mine, the two of us walked next to Alexander, up the steps to the home from my youth. Hale and Samuel followed close behind, looking up and down the street for anything out of the norm, and appearing more alert than I'd ever seen. After the call from Michael Ketry, Hale and

Alexander both agreed that we would all have double security until "the threat was neutralized."

I thought their verbiage was a bit dramatic, but I wasn't going to balk. Eva's safety was more important than anything.

"Do you want to ring the doorbell, Eva?" Alexander asked when we reached the top step. He'd been going to great lengths to make sure nothing seemed out of the ordinary in front of her.

She nodded excitedly and reached up on her tiptoes to depress the small button to the left of the door. Alexander slid his arm around me and brushed his lips over my temple, flexing his fingers into my waist as he did so.

"Are you ready for this, angel?" he asked quietly.

I wasn't sure if I was. After all, I was about to learn about my biological father for the first time. I had no idea what to expect or how to feel, but my husband's look of heated intensity and ferocious love relaxed me enough to have the confidence I needed.

"I'm ready," I said, offering him a small smile as reassurance. No matter what I discovered today, I would get through it because he was with me.

A few moments later, Frank opened the oak front door. My mother stood just behind him.

"Hello, there! Welcome to our humble abode!" Frank greeted, and I smiled. The four thousand square foot home was anything but humble, but I knew why he said what he did. Compared to the home that I shared with Alexander in Westchester, this house was modest.

"It's good to see you," Alexander said.

"Likewise," Frank agreed. "It's been a while."

"It has indeed," I remarked, feeling somewhat nostalgic to be back in my hometown. Despite the distressing circumstances, I was truly happy to see my mother and stepfather.

They stepped back to allow us inside. Hale stayed out front guarding the door, and Samuel made his way around to the back of the house.

My mother, Frank, Alexander, and I exchanged hugs before my mom squatted down so she was eye-level with Eva.

"You must be Eva," she gushed. Eva smiled brightly in response.

When I called earlier to tell my mother and Frank that we would be coming, I gave them an abbreviated version of how Eva came to be in our care. I didn't wait for my mother's reaction to the news before diving right into our plans to visit. I didn't explain the exact reason for why we were coming, but I think the urgency and abrupt timing of our trip is what made my mother pause. Normally she'd be full of opinions, but I suspected she knew the true reason behind our impromptu visit.

"Did you eat dinner?" my mother asked. "I can heat some leftovers if anyone is hungry."

"We're fine, Elizabeth. We grabbed a bite to eat before getting on the copter. But thank you," Alexander told her.

"Well, there's always dessert. We can go out to the back patio and—"

"Elizabeth, we aren't here for pleasantries. I think you know that. And Frank," Alexander added. "I think you know why we're here, too."

"I do."

My mother pressed her lips together in a tight line before nodding her head in resignation.

"Very well. Why don't the five of us go to the living room?"

We moved to the formal living space, where Alexander, Eva, and I sat on a cream-colored leather sofa, while Frank and my mother sat in matching armchairs across from us. I looked around the spacious room, realizing that not much had changed since I moved out at eighteen.

The walls were still a pretty, muted mint green. The bold colors of the oriental area rug stood out against the light furniture, but it was the grand piano that drew the eye more than anything else. Frank had inherited it from his grandmother when she passed, and it had sat in the far corner of the living room for as long as I could remember. Both Frank and my mother had hoped I would want to learn to play one day, but I was never any good at it. In hindsight, I wished I'd put forth more of an effort. The cherrywood antique piano just sits there now, its beauty wasted.

"Elizabeth," Alexander began. "We have questions that I hope you can answer. However, before we jump right in, I need to know if there will be anything unsuitable for young ears."

My mother looked hesitantly at Eva, then to me.

"We need to know everything, Mom. You can't hold back anything," I maintained. Looking to Frank, I motioned with my chin to Eva. "Frank, would you mind? Maybe find something for her to do in another room just in case the conversation gets a bit too intense for her curious little brain?"

"Of course," my stepfather agreed, although he seemed hesitant to leave my mother.

"That won't be necessary, Frank. There's nothing to tell. It was a long time ago," my mother insisted, her voice a little too high pitched. It told me she was nervous.

"Elizabeth, you owe it to her. It's time," Frank said, the resignation clear in his voice. "I'll be right in the next room if you need me."

"But Frank, I—"

"You'll be fine," he asserted, cutting off my mother's

protests. "Alexander, let's give Krystina and Elizabeth some privacy. Follow me into—"

"No. I'm staying right here," Alexander said resolutely.

Frank's eyes scanned the room, falling on each one of us. Always the peacemaker, he seemed to be deciding if leaving us alone together was a good idea. Finally, he sighed.

"Well, then, Eva. I guess it's just you and me. I think I might have some mint chocolate chip ice cream with your name on it. Come with me into the kitchen." Frank extended his hand to her, and Eva glanced at me for approval. I nodded and she smiled, excited to be getting a sweet treat.

After they were out of earshot, I turned to my mother.

"Okay, Mom. You have the floor."

"Krystina, really. I don't know what you expect me to say, or even where to begin."

"How about the beginning? Such as, where did you first meet Michael Ketry? I mean, no detail is too small. I literally know nothing about the guy." I tried to keep the bitterness out of my voice. I was mad that she'd kept everything about my biological father from me, but I'd also never wanted to know anything about him. It was a fine line, but one that made being upset with her over not telling me any details rather difficult.

My mother stayed quiet with her hands twisting in her lap. I frowned, noticing her nervous habit for the first time. I wasn't sure how I'd missed it all these years, but I'd apparently inherited my anxious fidgeting from her.

"Elizabeth, please," Alexander implored. "He's trying to extort five million dollars from us. He's been stalking Krystina and Eva. Anything you tell us could give insight to what we are dealing with."

Worry flashed in my mother's eyes as she glanced between Eva and me.

"He's dangerous, Krystina—a criminal," my mother whispered.

"I know. But that's about all I know."

My mother closed her eyes and breathed deep. It seemed as if she were gathering her thoughts. Or perhaps she was gathering strength. I couldn't be sure.

"Frank is right. I need to tell you everything. As much as I just want to forget that it all happened, I should have told you everything a long time ago. Or, at the very least, told you as soon as I discovered he was snooping around."

"It's okay, Mom," I said earnestly. All that mattered was that she came clean now.

"When I met Michael Ketry, I was barely seventeen years old," she began. "He was nine years older. At twenty-six, he was good looking, charming, funny, and a great storyteller. After only minutes into our first date, he had me doubled over in laughter. My father had recently passed, and Michael was the best medicine to keep the sadness away. I fell for him instantly."

She paused and took on a faraway look, as if transfixed by a moment in her past. She appeared almost wistful. It was strange to see her this way.

"So you dated and fell in love. What happened next," Alexander prodded, clearly anxious to find out everything there was to know about Michael Ketry. I looked up at my husband and reached out to squeeze his hand, feeling grateful that he was here with me for this.

"He was an insanely jealous man. Within weeks of dating, he started making remarks about the clothing I wore to school. He'd say it was too revealing or too tight. If I wore too much makeup, he'd say I looked like a whore. I took it, thinking I was a bigshot for dating an older guy, and that his negative comments were only because he worried about me. He made sure to pick me up from school every day. I told myself it was because he couldn't wait to see me. In retrospect, it was just one of the ways he kept tabs on me. My mother never liked Michael, but as a recent widow, she was going through the grief process. She didn't have the energy to push her concerns on me, but I wish she had. Maybe then..." She trailed off, seeming lost in thought again.

Everything she was saying struck a nerve. It was so similar to my own past with Trevor, the abusive boyfriend I was with before meeting Alexander.

After a minute, my mother collected herself and continued.

"I graduated high school, and Michael and I dated for another few years. I thought we were inseparable, but somehow during that time, he managed to lead a whole other life. To this day, I still don't know how I missed it."

"What do you mean?" I asked.

"We were having fun, and I enjoyed his many compulsive tendencies. We were living in the fast lane. Money never seemed to be an issue for him, even though he never kept the same job for long. Everything he bought had to be the latest and the greatest, regardless of price. He was a collector of things and seemed to experience a high whenever he acquired something new. But the more things he bought, the less satisfied he seemed. He always wanted what others had." My mother paused again, this time to look pointedly at me. "I began pushing him to get married. He refused, citing various reasons that are irrelevant now. At the time, I was extremely naïve and believed all his excuses. But then I got pregnant with you, and everything changed."

I did the mental math.

"You were about twenty-one at the time, right?"

"That's right," she confirmed. "He promised to take care of me and our baby. He still refused to marry me, but I agreed to move in with him. It was when I was living with him that weird things started to happen. When I was around six months pregnant, he suddenly became irrational and paranoid about everything. I didn't understand it. He started stock piling guns. He wasn't sleeping and would stay up late into the night guarding the door."

"You say he was paranoid. How so? Could there have been mental illness at play?" Alexander asked, but my mother waved him off.

"No. It wasn't anything like that, although I had no idea what to make of his behavior at the time. Later, I'd find out that he'd gotten in over his head with some bad people. He was right to be paranoid."

"What did he do?" I pressed.

"The day after you were born, I got a visitor in the hospital. The visitor was Michael's wife."

"His wife?" Alexander queried.

"Estranged, but yes," my mother explained. "Her name was Carol, but I don't recall if she ever told me her last name. Legally, Carol and Michael were married, which is why he couldn't marry me. Learning about her existence crushed me. But she opened my eyes to things that had been right in front of me all along. That piece of paper between them saved me in ways I'll probably never know."

"That's odd. I had a background check done and there wasn't any record of a marriage," Alexander mused.

"No, you probably wouldn't have found one. She filed for divorce around the same time she came to visit me. Carol told me she planned to ask a judge to seal the marriage and divorce record for her protection. She wanted no connection to Michael, claiming that she'd been receiving death threats from people who he owed money. Drug dealers—serious ones who wanted to see him dead. However, they couldn't kill Michael because then they'd never get their money, so they were looking to send a message to him instead by harming the people he cared for. Listening to Carol was like listening to crazy talk—like the stuff you only see and hear in movies—but she insisted the danger was all real. That's why she came to see me. She'd heard about me through mutual connections, and when she discovered I'd had a baby, she felt obligated to warn me for the sake of the child."

I sat there feeling relatively stunned, almost unable to comprehend what I was hearing. My mother—Elizabeth Long —the woman who acted as if she was a pillar in the Clifton Park community, had once been connected to drug dealers. It was unfathomable. Her story seemed like something from another person's life.

"I didn't want to believe anything Carol told me," my mother continued. "I was young and in love, and also a little bit jealous of the woman who had gotten Michael to legally commit to her. Could you blame me? I mean, he refused to even entertain the idea of marriage with me. Still, her words got to me. I hadn't filled out the birth certificate yet, so when the nurse brought me the paperwork for it, I left the space for the father's name blank just in case. If Carol's wild tales about Michael's debt and drug dealers were true, I didn't want them to make a connection to you. I thought that with only my name, Elizabeth Cole, listed as your parent, you would be safe."

"But you still stayed with him," I pointed out. "You've never told me much, but I know he was around for about a year after I was born."

"Like I said, I was young and in love—and incredibly stupid. Yes, I was upset to learn about Carol, but I believed all his many excuses about why he lied, and I forgave him. However, something shifted after that. Carol's words affected me more than I realized. I was constantly afraid. I hated guns, yet I found myself taking one of Michael's and sleeping with it in the nightstand next to my bed. It was a false sense of security because I had no idea how to use it. I began to share Michael's paranoia and jumped at every little sound. Sometimes days would go by and I wouldn't hear a word from him. The phone would ring at all hours of the day and night. It was maddening. I was constantly walking on pins and needles, trying to take care of you while Michael broke my heart a little more each day. Eventually, I couldn't take it anymore, and I knew I had to get you out of there. So, when you were eight months old, I left Michael and moved back home with my mother."

"I'm sorry you went through that, Mom. But at least you got out."

She smiled bitterly.

"That isn't the end, honey."

"Oh?"

"I told you that Michael was extremely possessive. He wouldn't just let me leave him."

"What did he do?" I asked, almost afraid of the answer.

"Oh, he tried everything to get me back. He even tried to kidnap you to try and get me back—if you can believe that. I won't go into the details, but just know that my mother—your grandmother—was a force to be reckoned with. I might have been clueless about how to use a gun, but she wasn't. Michael stopped bothering me after that—at least until your grandmother died. You see, Michael was smart, and he was always watching. He knew I'd be vulnerable after losing my mother, making it easy for him to schmooze his way back in. He was around just long enough to cash your grandmother's life insurance check. Then he was gone, and I was penniless."

I recalled how much my mother struggled when I was growing up, trying to make ends meet. There were so many nights when I'd hear her crying in the kitchen over a pile of bills. As a small child, I'd tried to comfort her, but she would tell me not to worry and say it was grown-up problems.

"What a bastard," I whispered. It was no wonder she had a hard time trusting men. I understood now why she never wanted to talk about him. My biological father had really put her through hell.

"I'm sorry I didn't tell you all of this sooner, but you have to understand, Krystina. I was broken-hearted and embarrassed. I wanted to pretend like it never happened, so I never spoke a word about that time in my life to anyone. I never even told Frank until years after we were married, and even then, it was only because I didn't have a choice."

"What forced your hand?" Alexander asked.

"The police showed up at our house asking questions about Michael. They had an arrest warrant regarding all the trouble he got into when he was working at the Department of Human Services. Forgery, identity theft—all kinds of crazy stuff. It was all over the news. They only came looking at our house because I had been listed as an emergency contact at one of his previous jobs. They thought maybe I was still in touch with him."

I frowned, trying to recall a time when the police came to our house for a visit.

"Where was I for all of this?" I asked.

"It was your freshman year of college and you were away at school. That might have been the only time I was grateful you pushed so hard to go away to NYU," she said wryly.

"Elizabeth, let's fast forward to now. We all know Ketry did time in prison, but now he's out. Why did you meet with him?"

"To protect Krystina," she said, as if the answer were just that obvious.

"I figured as much. Try to elaborate, please," Alexander said with a slight edge of impatience.

"Michael Ketry is a dangerous, desperate man. He's impulsive and greedy and will do anything to get what he wants. Right now, he sees dollar signs. He saw Krystina's picture in the tabloids and knows she's married to a very rich man. He contacted me in an attempt to reach her. I didn't want him anywhere near you, so I'd hoped to pay him off so he would leave you both alone. I thought ten thousand would do it."

"You paid him ten thousand dollars?" I asked incredulously.

"I did. I talked to Frank about it, and he agreed it was the right move. However, knowing Michael's possessive side, I knew it would be best if I met with him alone. I also knew Frank would never agree to that, but I couldn't take the chance of doing anything that might rile Michael's jealous tendencies. So, I considered the state-of-the-art surveillance system Alex has at the penthouse and decided that would be the best place to meet. The cameras are obvious, and I thought they'd detract Michael from doing anything stupid. And in the off chance that something did happen to me, it would be recorded. Needless to say, Frank wasn't happy with me when he found out."

"I watched the video of your meeting," Alexander said thoughtfully, as if he were piecing things together in his mind. "There are a couple of areas in the lobby that are out of range for the camera. You were careful to avoid those dead spots."

"Yes. Like I told you—he's dangerous and can't be trusted. It was a hard lesson that I was reminded of the day I gave him the money. After he took it from me, he thanked me for the down payment. I knew right then that he wasn't going to go away, and it was only a matter of time before something like this happened."

"You should have come to me, Elizabeth," Alexander snapped harshly, shocking me with the forcefulness in his tone. He was normally very placating when it came to my mother. "If I had known what kind of threat Ketry posed from the beginning, I could have put safeguards in place. Now he's had time to stalk our every move. He knows too much about us and is using Eva as leverage."

Frank returned to the room then, holding Eva on his hip. She was brushing out a nylon mane on a small plastic pony that used to be mine when I was little. I wasn't sure where Frank procured the toy from, but it sparked another wave of nostalgia.

"So, what are you going to do about it, Alex?" Frank asked.

My husband stared at Frank for a moment before focusing his attention on Eva. He frowned and studied her for what seemed like a long while. Stress lines etched his beautiful features, and for the first time, my husband looked old to me. It was as if the idea of losing Eva was just too much.

When he finally spoke, the gravity in his tone sent chills down my spine.

"That little girl is the definition of everything that's good in the world and I won't let Ketry mess things up for us. I'm going to give in to his demands and pay him. Every last penny. Eva is worth it—my family is worth it."

30

Alexander

Late Saturday afternoon, I paced back and forth in my office like a caged animal. I plunged my hands thorough my hair as rain slashed against the floor-to-ceiling windows in an angry torrent. The storm that blew in an hour ago brought with it fierce winds that matched my mood. A crack of thunder clapped outside. It felt like an omen.

After the call from Ketry, the choice was clear. I had to meet his ultimatum and give in to his demands. But I also knew I couldn't handle this alone. So, I'd asked trusted confidants to meet with Krystina and me at Cornerstone Tower. The people in this room—Hale, Samuel, Bryan, and Stephen—were in the know about everything. Greyson Hughes, the newest high-ranking member of the security team, was also here. He had been brought up to speed on everything relevant to the situation, but everyone else here had lived through most of it.

There was only one person missing who I wished was here —Matteo. I wasn't hurt like Krystina was over finding out the truth about him and Allyson. Ultimately, who he was screwing —or marrying—wasn't any of my business. While Krystina and Allyson were now on the mend, nothing was ever really broken between Matteo and me, and I wanted my friend here to offer me his assurances. The problem was, he and Allyson didn't know about Eva yet. After multiple painstaking discussions, Krystina and I thought it best to keep them out of the loop for several reasons. For one, we didn't want their first experiences with Eva to be tainted with this ugliness. We also didn't want the distraction of explaining Eva's backstory while we had so many other things to worry about.

Stephen, my attorney, had been given a front row seat into my sordid past after the attempted blackmail by Charlie Andrews, and there were no secrets between us as a result. Now here we were again—another blackmail situation. I would have scoffed at the odds of it happening to me twice if there was anything even remotely funny about what was happening.

As for my accountant, Bryan, even if I'd wanted to, there was no hiding much from him. Money always left a trail.

Then there was Hale. I wholly trusted him, and I needed his acute awareness now more than ever. I glanced up at my security detail. He was on the other side of the room, pacing just like I was. We were six hours away from the deadline set by Ketry and the consensus in the room about what to do was split.

"Hale, your thoughts?" I asked.

"I don't like it, boss," he replied.

"The situation is far from ideal, but I'm not opposed to the plan," Greyson Hughes mused.

Turning toward him, I considered the security officer. With his cropped hair and impeccably ironed white button-down shirt, he looked every bit the part of someone who had spent time in the military. He was here today providing valuable input, but most importantly, he was one of the few who didn't have a personal connection to Krystina or me. It allowed him to be more objective.

"It's a good one," I agreed.

"It's the best plan we've come up with so far," Greyson added.

"How do you figure?" Stephen chimed in.

"The Rolling Loud Festival is happening all weekend at Citi Field," Greyson explained. "The concert goers should start dispersing around the time you're scheduled to meet Michael Ketry. I'm sure he planned it that way deliberately because it will give him the opportunity to disappear into the crowd. But that also gives us the same advantage. I can have my guys dress in Busta Rhymes t-shirts and they'll blend right in. This way, if Ketry tries anything stupid, we'll be around to offer protection."

"I'm with Hale. I don't like it," Bryan said from his place on the sofa where he sat next to Krystina.

I noticed how he cast his gaze down toward the large duffel bags sitting on the floor in front of my desk. Each one contained two and a half million dollars. It wasn't easy to get our hands on so much cash with such short notice. Thankfully, Bryan was a stickler about diversifying my liquid funds to comply with FDIC rules, so we were able to collect the money needed from various banks throughout the city without drawing much attention. I might be a rich man, but even to me, seeing that many greenbacks in one place was intimidating.

"You just don't want me to hand over all that money," I said, knowing how hesitant he was about any large transaction—legal or illegal.

"That's not fair and you know it," Bryan retorted. "It has

nothing to do with money. You're my friend, and I think getting in bed with this guy is dangerous."

"Look, Alex. I'm trying to back you up, but I've got to stick with Bryan and Hale on this one," Stephen added. "We should get the police involved."

Krystina vehemently shook her head. "No police. He was very specific about that."

"If you give into him, what's to say he won't come back for more?" Stephen challenged. "It's not like you're making an exchange of some kind. You're just handing over cash. Even asking him to delete the pictures means nothing. We're long past the days of actual film. With digital images, there's no way to know how many copies there are."

Stephen was right to be suspect—Ketry might come back for more. He was a vulture, just like so many others. It was why I kept very few friends. Most people I knew were acquaintances, and even that was a term I used loosely. At the end of the day, almost everyone wanted something from me, and I knew to be cautious. One mistake, or trusting the wrong person, could cost me everything. This knowledge lived in a cold, dark corner of my mind at all times, pushing forward only when instinct warned me of imminent danger.

However, this was different. If Ketry came back, so be it. I'd deal with it when the time came. There was no other option. It didn't matter how much money I had—no court would give us custody of Eva if those pictures were leaked. Setting aside that we were caught at an underground sex club, the media frenzy that was sure to ensue as a result would have a dramatic impact on a child. That fact alone would make any judge pause. Losing Eva now would break Krystina, and after everything we'd been through, I knew it would break me, too. I'd move mountains to protect her.

I wasn't sure when it happened, but I'd come to care a great deal for Eva. Her sweet smile and curious mind had brought life into the darkness. Her innocence was refreshing, and I found myself looking forward to our interactions more and more every day. I knew I'd eventually love her just as Krystina did. She'd already created countless fissures in my heart, and it was only a matter of time before it burst apart completely.

"There's no more debating this. We're doing it," I announced. "Hale, Samuel, and Greyson, get your team in place. We'll leave for the meeting point at nine-thirty, and then wait for Ketry's call."

THE RAIN HAD ENDED hours ago, leaving behind hazy and damp air. The night was cool with a gentle fog rolling in, giving way to wispy patches that floated by the car windows during our drive to Queens. Hale was at the wheel and Krystina sat beside me in the backseat of the Porsche Cayenne Turbo S. I wished she'd stayed behind where I knew she would be safe, but she had insisted on leaving Eva with Vivian for the night so she could be with me. After a lengthy argument, the guilt I felt over keeping Ketry from my wife in the first place won out and I gave in—but only if she agreed to stay in the car while I did the drop.

Krystina squeezed my hand, and I could feel her nerves. Glancing down, I gave her a reassuring smile.

"Everything will be fine, angel. Just relax."

"I'm trying, but I'm starting to have second thoughts. What if Hale, Bryan, and Stephen are right? What if this is a mistake? There are so many things that could go wrong. I feel like we are doing this blind. Outside of what my mother told us, how much do we really know about Michael Ketry?"

"I have confidence in our security team. Greyson knows

what he's doing, and Hale would never let anything bad happen. We're surrounded by guards," I assured her, motioning a circle in the air with my finger. Samuel was in the lead car with Greyson at our back, and two additional vehicles carrying more security personnel followed on neighboring streets.

"Maybe it's just because everything is happening so fast. I feel like we didn't have time to think it through."

I didn't respond as I ruminated over her words. Although I wouldn't voice it aloud, I shared her sentiments. But my instinct was to protect Eva, and my instincts were never wrong. When I thought about how our privacy had already been intruded upon, I shuddered.

Late Thursday night, I'd made the mistake of looking online after Ketry's interview with Mac Owens had aired. There were already conspiracy theories and wild speculation for why Krystina and her father had been estranged for all this time. I'd mastered the art of staying off the press's radar, but they were relentless with Krystina. They were obsessed with her, and she never stood a chance. Eventually, I had to stop looking at the online search results, having been filled with helpless fury after only getting through page one of a basic search.

Then there was what we were confronted with when we brought Eva to school yesterday morning. Friday was my day for drop off, but given everything that was going on, Krystina and I had opted to drive her together. When we arrived at Dalton-Hewitt Academy, paparazzi swarmed the sprawling green lawns of the school.

I refused to subject Eva to that, so she spent the day at Cornerstone Tower instead. Her presence at Stone Enterprise had been anything but a burden. In fact, it gave me peace of mind knowing she was close by while I worked through a game plan for Ketry with Krystina and the security team. The staff was more than happy for the distraction from their mundane work routine. They'd fallen instantly in love with Eva's sweet disposition and doted on her all day.

It wasn't an ideal situation, but it solidified my decision to cooperate with Ketry. The world would be looking at us and scrutinizing our every move for months to come. The sooner he was out of the picture, the sooner the tabloids would lose interest.

I looked out the window as Hale pulled into Lot A, just down the street from Citi Field. The lot was jammed with cars, but the lot attendant was able to point us to a spot on the far end. There weren't a lot of people about, as most were still inside for the concert. However, I did spot a few raucous groups partying from their car back bumpers with music blasting from the car speakers.

Samuel and Greyson had peeled off a quarter mile back. We didn't want Ketry to see us arrive with an entourage and risk spooking him. I didn't know where the other members of security were, but I was sure they were somewhere nearby.

After the car was parked, Hale climbed out and began to survey the area. I stayed inside with Krystina. I glanced down at my phone. It was nearing ten-thirty. Michael Ketry should be calling within the next few minutes. He'd said he would call once he saw me.

"Sit tight, angel. I'm just going to get out of the car for a minute. Ketry needs to see I'm here without any cops."

Climbing out, I stood beside Hale. The sounds were drastically different outside the car. Music poured out of Citi Field, filling the air with some of the best hip-hop music to date. I wasn't a fan of it myself, but I could appreciate it if the talent had a strong, rhythmic beat and solid vocal track.

"I don't see him," Hale said as his eyes continued to scan the lot.

"He's here somewhere."

As if on cue, my cell began to vibrate with an unknown number. Holding my breath, I slid my finger across the screen.

"Hello?" I answered, even though I already knew who would be calling.

"I said come alone," Ketry said.

"Alone to me meant no police. I never travel anywhere without security. Only Hale, my security detail, and my wife are with me," I said, refusing to give him the privilege of even hearing Krystina's name.

"Fine. But they both stay behind from this point on. Start walking North along the fifth row of cars in the lot," Ketry told me. The background noise over the phone matched what I was experiencing, so I knew he was close. "Stop when you get to the street, then turn right on Shea Road and walk to the intersection. There's an auto repair shop across the way. Wait there."

Then, the connection fell silent.

Taking a deep breath, I climbed back into the car and looked at Krystina.

She threw her arms around my neck and squeezed tight.

"Be careful, Alex."

"I will."

"I love you."

They were just words, but they were three words I would never tire of hearing. Emotion clogged in my throat as I realized how much I needed them right now.

"Love you, too, Krystina."

Pulling away, I refocused on the task ahead and reached behind me to retrieve the duffle bags of cash.

A part of me wanted to worry about carrying so much cash out in the open. This was New York after all. No one looked your way in this city—even if you were doing something crazy. They simply put their heads down and kept walking. I just wasn't sure if that fact was comforting considering the circumstances.

After lugging the bags over into the backseat, I glanced at Krystina one more time. Her beauty never failed to take my breath away. She was perfect—like a goddess from the heavens.

And she was mine to protect.

"I'll be back soon, angel."

31

Krystina

I watched as Alexander walked away from the car toward the main road. I spotted Greyson and Samuel tailing him, each with a Solo cup in hand and acting as if they'd just come from a concert tailgate party. Seeing them didn't make me feel any better. Despite my initial agreement with Alexander about this being the only way to handle Michael Ketry, I now had a sinking feeling about all of it.

It was that sensation of dread that compelled me to open the car door and step out.

"Ma'am, what are you doing?" Hale asked hurriedly, jumping to come to my side.

"Something isn't right, Hale. I can feel it."

"I agree, but the boss has made up his mind. There was no convincing him otherwise."

"I know. I was on the same page as him at first, but now I'm not so sure. I think there's a different angle we could have played, but I didn't think of it until now."

"What angle is that?"

I pushed my brows together and tried to work out my thoughts. I hadn't had time to think anything through yet, so when I spoke, it was more like I was thinking out loud. I only hoped it made sense to Hale.

"What if I played on the whole rich daughter thing while also pretending that I want a relationship with Ketry? You know—one big happy family, as if there's been something missing without him all this time. If I could convince him that becoming a regular in my life would be more beneficial to him, maybe he'll back off."

"Is that what you want?" Hale asked, seeming genuinely perplexed.

"Of course not! I don't want anything to do with him, and I especially don't want him anywhere near Eva. But if he believes my pitch, it could buy Alexander and I time. We just need to put him off until everything is settled with Eva and family court. Once we are either Eva's legal guardians or adoptive parents, we don't have to worry about judges and court decisions, and we could cut Michael Ketry loose. We may even be able to prosecute him for extortion, although that would need careful consideration. A court case would be fodder for the media."

Hale rubbed his jaw with this thumb and forefinger as he considered my words.

"There's still the issue of the picture with you coming out of the club," Hale pointed out.

"If the picture gets out, so be it. It won't be easy dealing with the fallout in the press, but at least Ketry won't be able to use Eva as leverage. She's all that matters." I paused and glanced nervously over my shoulder. "Hale, if I'm going to do this, I need to catch up with Alexander now."

"He'll never go for it. Neither will Greyson Hughes, and he's leading this op. I could get in touch with him, but a last-minute change—"

"I know, I know. They won't like it. But the clock is ticking." I would have just taken off in the direction Alexander had disappeared if I didn't think Hale would tackle me to the ground.

"So what do you propose?" he finally asked in a resigned voice.

"Let's walk so Alex doesn't get too much further ahead of us, and I'll tell you my plan."

HALE AND I FOLLOWED ALEXANDER, keeping a safe distance yet still keeping him within our line of sight. When he crossed Seaver Way and entered a rundown car repair shop, my stomach dropped.

"Hale, why is he going in there? I thought Greyson said Ketry would want crowds to disappear in."

"I don't know, ma'am," Hale replied with a shake of his head. The worry in his voice matched what I felt, and we both quickened our pace.

As we got closer to the automotive shop, I began to wonder when it was last opened for business. Paint flakes peeled from the clapboard siding and the two large garage doors were streaked with rust. The windows no longer allowed light inside since dust and cobwebs covered the glass, blocking any sun that would dare try to penetrate. The front door appeared as if it had once been a bright cherry red, but just like the siding, the paint had peeled, littering the front step with flecks of red, salmon pink, and dingy white.

Hale and I paused just outside the door that we saw Alexander disappear behind. We could hear voices coming from inside, but I couldn't make out what was being said.

The sound of footsteps behind us made me turn. Greyson and Samuel fast approached, each with a confused expression on their faces. Greyson opened his mouth as if to speak, but Hale silenced him by bringing a finger to his lips, then pointing toward the inside of the building.

"I'm going in," I whispered. Hale violently shook his head, but I ignored his silent warning. "I have to do this alone. If you come in with me, it could provoke a negative reaction from Ketry."

Without waiting for a response, I turned and gripped the door handle. I pushed it open, causing the hinges to moan and echo against the steel beams that fought the sagging roof above. Once inside, I quickly closed the door behind me as quietly as I could, then turned the deadbolt to the locked position. I did it to keep Hale, Samuel, and Greyson from following me, but from the amount of rust particles that flaked off the lock, I was sure they'd be able to get in with minimal effort.

The voices I'd heard from outside were louder now, but still a distance away. I recognized Alexander's muffled tones and followed the sound toward the back section of the building.

The smell of urine permeated the air, and I scrunched my nose in disgust as I walked. My heart raced and there was a buzzing in my ears. I couldn't help but feel like I was living in a horror movie. I was the reckless girl who entered an abandoned building, all while the audience watching the scene unfold held their breaths, waiting for a gruesome monster to jump out from behind her.

I reminded myself that there were no monsters in real life. Just evil people.

A part of me wished this were, in fact, all just a dramatic movie. It certainly felt like one. If only I could call on the mafia and order a hit on Michael Ketry, essentially eliminating my problem just like I'd seen on *The Sopranos* or in the movie *Casino* with Robert DeNiro.

It was a foolish notion, but one I had all the same as I slowly walked across the dust and debris covered concrete floor. I didn't even feel guilty for wishing death on my biological father. He was a threat to me and all who I held dear, and there was no love lost there.

I rounded a corner, passing through a narrow entryway, when Alexander and Ketry came into view. They were facing each other, standing about fifteen feet apart. The bags of money were at Alexander's feet, and he looked murderous. Ketry, on the other hand, appeared cocky and self-assured—as if this were just another day at the office.

Alexander's head whipped around when he heard me approach.

"Krystina! Goddammit! I told you to wait in the car," he snapped.

I shook my head. "No. I thought it was important to come. I want to talk to my father."

Alexander gave me the strangest look, as if he thought I'd lost my mind. Perhaps I had. I didn't pay him any attention but kept my focus on Ketry.

He was dressed in a green, grease-stained, button-down shirt and a style of black stonewashed jeans I hadn't seen since the early nineties. I could see how he'd once been handsome but time had been hard on him. Even now, he was messier and more disheveled than he had been when I saw him loitering about the school, yet somehow managed to stand there with arrogance.

"There's nothin' to talk about, sweetheart. Just tell your husband to hand over the cash and I'll be on my way."

"Do we really need to do this?" I asked. "I mean, I literally just found out about your existence. I thought we could try getting to know each other. I am your daughter after all."

"Krystina, what are you doing?" Alexander hissed, but I didn't take my eyes off Ketry.

"If I wanted to get to know you, I would have done so a long time ago," Ketry said.

"What about my mother? You had a relationship with her a long time ago, and it resulted in me. Doesn't that mean anything to you?"

"No, actually. It means nothing to me at all."

He stared at me with so much hatred, it was as if I could feel the evil burning in his very soul. I shuddered. The sudden realization that this man's vile blood ran through my veins was revolting.

"Michael—" I began to implore, but stopped short when he pulled a gun from the back of his waistband.

He pointed it Alexander and then at me. We both froze, and I could only pray that Alexander would stay put and not do anything reckless that might provoke Ketry to put a bullet in one of us.

He moved the gun back and forth between Alexander and me, slowly advancing toward us until coming to a stop in front of Alexander.

"Now, I'm going to pick up these bags," he informed us. "No funny business. Ya hear me?"

Alexander gave him a slight nod.

Ketry slowly bent down and unzipped the duffels to check their contents. Seeming satisfied, he slowly stood back up. He slung one bag over the arm that held the gun while carrying the second in his free hand. He walked backward toward the narrow door where I'd just come through, never once taking the trained muzzle off us. As he reached the door, he grinned and raised one of the bags.

"Thanks for this. I'm sure I'll be seeing you again soon."

Then, he was gone.

I exhaled the breath I hadn't realized I'd been holding. However, the relief I felt over not having a gun trained on my chest was short lived when Alexander rounded on me. He grabbed hold of my shoulders, his grip so tight, I winced.

"What in God's name were you thinking by coming in here? For fucks sake, Krystina! You could have been killed!"

"And so could you have," I snapped back, not appreciating the way I was being manhandled. I shrugged out of his grip. "Ketry wasn't going to kill anyone. You heard what he said at the end. He said he'd be seeing us soon. He's going to be back for more. I came to hopefully buy us time to—"

A loud crack came from somewhere behind me, causing Alexander and me to jump. Turning, I saw a large piece of sheet metal had fallen lose from a makeshift wall. The cracking sound had been the metal hitting the concrete floor.

"I'm not arguing with you here," Alexander said briskly. "This place is in shambles and will blow over with the slightest gust of wind. Let's go."

Grabbing my arm, he all but dragged me back to the main entrance. Right before we reached it, the door burst open. Hale, Greyson, and Samuel came rushing through. All of them appeared to be fuming, but Hale looked downright furious.

"Why did you lock the damn door?" he asked angrily as soon as he saw me.

"We'll discuss it outside," Alexander responded. "This building is falling apart, and it isn't safe."

Once we reached the street, I yanked my arm free from Alexander's grasp. "I can walk just fine on my own, thank you very much."

"Krystina," Alexander responded in a warning tone. I ignored him and turned to head back to the car. Alexander was upset, and perhaps he had a right to be, but at least he could have let me explain.

I was crossing the street when I heard a loud commotion to my left. People were yelling and tires screeched. I followed the direction of the noise and saw a car appear from around the corner, barreling down Seaver Way and plowing through the crowd of people coming from the concert. Some managed to get out of the way, but others flew into the air as if they were nothing more than bowling pins in the way of a ball searching for a strike.

"Oh, my God," I whispered. "That car hit those people. All those people are..."

I barely had time to process that the moving car was headed straight toward me before I was violently shoved to the ground. My head smacked hard against the asphalt, and I rolled. My stomach pitched. I glanced up to find Greyson covering my body, and I thought I might vomit all over him. I tried to move —to breathe—but it was as if my lungs couldn't expand. Dizzying stars dotted my vision, and then the world went black.

32

Alexander

S irens and flashing lights were everywhere. We were surrounded by firetrucks, police cars, and ambulances, all vying to make their way to the worst of the scene. I barely saw any of it as I focused on keeping Krystina flat on the ground. Thankfully, she'd only been knocked out for a few minutes, but her deathly still body had been enough to scare the life out of me. She'd been unresponsive to my touch, and until she woke, her strong pulse was the only indication that she was alive.

"Alex, let me up. I'm fine!"

"You're not fine! You have a five-inch gash across your forehead, and who knows what else is damaged? You aren't moving until someone looks at you. Hale!" I called out over my shoulder. "What's taking the paramedics so long?"

I wanted to be pissed at my wife. The intense need to lash out at her for not staying behind like she was supposed to was real. I didn't know how one woman always managed to find so much trouble. She'd put herself in direct danger just by being... by being Krystina.

Again.

And she made me fucking crazy in the process.

As much as I wanted to lock her in our bedroom forever after today, I was just grateful she wasn't more seriously injured. When she'd hit the ground, I'd felt my heart stall. With the way that car came barreling through the crowd, I shuddered to think about how much worse it could have been.

If Greyson hadn't been so close by...

Greyson Hughes was newer to the security team, but I made a mental note to give him a raise. He was proving to be more of an asset each and every day.

"I was told a paramedic will get here as soon as they can," Hale said. "All of them are just tied up right now. A lot of people are seriously hurt."

"Are you saying that my wife isn't?" I barked irritably.

"I'm not saying that at all but..." He hesitated, forcing me to turn my attention away from Krystina and look up at where Hale stood. "Quite a few are dead, sir. It's chaos. The police are trying to process the scene."

"Dead?" Krystina asked, struggling to sit up again.

I followed Hale's line of sight and saw what he was looking at. I'd been so wrapped up with worry over Krystina, I hadn't bothered to assess the severity of what had happened.

Police were taping off sections along the street, enclosing areas that contained bloodied, unmoving bodies. They were working their way down the block, but still had a way to go before they reached us. The maniac behind the wheel of the car had traveled at least eight hundred feet at high speed before coming to a stop, and only then it was because they had hit a parked car only a few feet from where I sat.

I turned my attention to the vehicle, wondering what the situation was with the driver, but stopped and did a double take when I saw a familiar figure laying in the middle of the road. His round belly protruded between a green shirt and pair of black stonewashed jeans. There was no doubt who it was.

It was Michael Ketry.

He lay sprawled out and perfectly still, his limbs extending at odd angles and blood pooling beneath his head. His eyes were open and vacant. There was no question that he was amongst the dead. If it were another place and another time, I may have thanked the Fates for resolving this threat to my family, but not today. Not when there was so much more loss of life all around me. This was nothing short of a tragedy.

Standing just a few feet behind Ketry's body was Samuel. He was in his concert t-shirt, looking no different from any of the other bystanders. I saw Hale give him a quick nod, and then watched as Samuel casually strolled past Ketry's body and picked up the two duffle bags containing the five million in hush money. By the grace in which he moved, nobody would have noticed what he did if they hadn't been watching him closely. Within seconds, Samuel disappeared into the crowd lining the street.

"Less questions if that isn't found lying around in the middle of all this," Hale said quietly. "I trust Samuel to put it someplace safe."

"Good call," I agreed. I wondered if I should feel relieved that I wasn't out all that money, but all I seemed to feel was shock. It was hard to process the chaos and carnage around me.

Once again, I turned toward the vehicle that caused so much destruction, trying to make sense of it all. Firemen surrounded the vehicle, using the Jaws of Life to remove the driver's side door. I watched as they worked, until eventually the door was removed completely. The EMT's were no more than seconds behind, pulling the male driver from the car and placing him on a yellow backboard.

His body was limp as one arm fell free from the board, dangling until a paramedic reached to lay the arm across its owners chest. From my vantage point, I couldn't tell if the driver was dead or alive, but he looked fairly young.

"Oh, no!" Krystina suddenly gasped.

"What is it?" I asked hurriedly. She wasn't looking at the driver as I had been, so I wasn't sure what put the horrified look on her face.

She brought a trembling hand to her mouth, and then pointed with her free hand toward the street opposite of where I'd been looking. I knew what she was pointing at without her having to say. Krystina was seeing Michael Ketry's lifeless body for the first time.

"He's dead," she whispered. "It's my fault. I did this."

"What do you mean? You had nothing to do with what happened here."

"But I wished it. I wanted him dead for threatening our family. I *wanted* something like this to happen." Her voice was shrill, and I worried she might be going into shock.

"Krystina, look around you. You did not wish for this."

"But I wished it for him. What kind of person would want to see another person dead?"

I pressed my lips together in a tight line, bothered that she'd shoulder any guilt whatsoever for this horrific scene. It was a case of being in the wrong place at the wrong time, and it had nothing to do with any kind of wishful thinking.

"A lot of people wish death on others. I wished my father dead, too. What sort of person does that make me?"

She stared at me for a long moment before saying, "But that was different. You were—"

"What? A child? It makes no difference. If he were still alive now, I'd still wish him dead after what he did to my mother. But that's just it, angel—it would have been a wish. Nothing more. You had no control over what happened here. Don't blame yourself."

She pushed her brows together in concentration.

"I hear you, but still. I can't help but think..."

"Think what?" I prodded, trying to discern her conflicted expression.

"I don't know how to explain it. I mean, I just found out who my father was, and now he's dead. I don't know how to feel about that—or any of this. Alex, what is going on? All these people..." Her voice cracked and she trailed off again, her eyes brimming with unshed tears as they traveled across the incomprehensible scene.

It was too much. I needed to get her out of here.

"Hale, we don't know how long the paramedics will be. We'll get Krystina to a hospital faster on our own at this point. Head back to the parking lot and see if you can get the car to the corner of Roosevelt Avenue. Krystina and I will meet you there."

"Yes, sir."

After he walked away, I turned to Krystina. My gaze traveled the length of her body, inspecting her for any injury I may have missed before.

"Are you okay to walk?" I asked.

"I already told you. I'm fine."

"Alright then. Take my hand—carefully. I don't want you moving too quick."

"Alex, really—"

"Everyone okay over here?" asked a voice from behind me.

Slipping my arm around Krystina's waist, I pulled her to a standing position. Angling to see who was addressing us, I saw a uniformed police officer approaching. I recognized him immediately as one of the cops who'd responded to the hostage situation at Stone's Hope last year. It was Officer Bailey, the cop who'd shoved me down to the cold, snowy pavement in front of the women's shelter to stop me from going inside.

"We appear to be okay, officer. Thank you," I told him.

"Hey, don't I know you?" he asked.

One corner of my mouth twitched in a wry smile.

"Sort of. You made me eat concrete outside of Stone's Hope Women's Shelter last year."

He frowned, then looked at Krystina before recognition flooded his features.

"Well, well. So I did. Small world. I'm sorry to meet again under these circumstances."

"It's awful," I agreed. "Do you know what happened?"

"I shouldn't say until there's an official statement, but I know an opioid overdose when I see it," he said with a shake of his head. "Blue skin, shallow breathing. We gave him some Narcan to revive him. Once he sobers up, that boy is going to find himself in a world of trouble."

Officer Bailey looked down the street and I followed his gaze. The crowd had begun to thin, and the bystanders who remained were illuminated by a sea of flashing red and blue lights coming from at least a dozen emergency vehicles. I took in all the taped off areas—yellow lines that represented so much death. The driver who caused all that loss was most likely going to face life in prison.

"How many are dead?" Krystina asked, her thoughts traveling to the same place as mine.

"Four confirmed so far, and too many are in critical condition," the officer said grimly. Sighing, he looked back to us. "If you're okay, I'm going to continue my checks. Is anyone else in your party injured? Or is it just you two?"

I couldn't stop my gaze from flicking to Ketry. I didn't linger, but only held long enough for me to make a split-second decision.

"No officer. It's just us. We don't know anyone else here."

Wrapping my arm around Krystina's waist, I turned and the two of us began to walk up the street, leaving all the madness behind us.

EPILOGUE

Krystina
5 months later

I reached behind my back to pull up the short zipper of my dress. It was a snug enclosure designed to keep the back from dropping too low, running from the curve of my ass to just above the base of my spine. At the top of the zipper was a hook and eye closure. Unable to see it, I struggled with connecting it. Stepping out of my walk-in closet, I went to search for Alexander's help. I didn't have to look far.

Polished to perfection in his black tuxedo, my husband stood on the opposite side of the bedroom looking shamelessly handsome. His stunning good looks and charisma was potent to my system, and when he flashed me a smile, it made my heart flip and pitter-patter.

"Would you mind hooking the clasp?" I asked, stepping up in front of the full-length mirror.

Alexander came up behind me and slipped the j-hook through the loop.

"This dress is too revealing," he told me.

I looked at my reflection. I liked the dress Allyson had chosen for me to wear as her Matron of Honor. It was a gorgeous, blood-red gown with a beaded bodice and lightly layered skirt that billowed behind me when I walked. The top came up in a high-neck halter, giving way to a deep plunging V in the back. My entire spine was exposed, and it was most likely the cause of my husband's ire.

"I didn't pick the dress. Ally did, and it's her big day. I think the bold red is perfect for the Valentine's Day theme she and Matteo chose. Plus, it's fitting for Matteo—always the hopeless romantic."

Just then, Eva came bounding into our bedroom. Her light brown hair was pulled up and separated into two curly pigtails that bobbed when she moved. The red ribbons tied around them were the perfect accent for the white and red flower girl dress she would soon be wearing.

"Can I watch TV in your room?" she asked, peering up at me with those wide, curious blue eyes.

"Sure, peanut," I agreed. "But only for a little while. You need to put on your pretty dress soon."

"Come on over here and sit on the bed with me," Alexander told her as he sat on the edge of our king size mattress and patted the spot next to him. Picking up the remote from the nightstand, he pointed it at the television. "What would you like me to put on?"

Smiling, I left the two of them to discuss morning cartoon options while I went to the master bath to finish getting ready.

As I applied the color combination for the smokey eye effect, I sighed with contentment. Things had calmed down over the past five months, allowing us to develop an easy routine, but it was one that hadn't come without a few bumps along the way.

After weighing our choices, we decided to deny the claims Michael Ketry made on the news about being my father. My mother was more than happy that we decided to go that route, as it allowed her to truly put that part of her life behind her once and for all. However, we didn't do it for her. We did it for Eva. She seemed happy and settled, and she was doing well in school. We thought it was best if she had no connection to the man who never cared to have a relationship with me until he saw an opportunity to extort money. He was a criminal and nothing more. When reporters asked questions, we simply said we had no idea who he was.

Of course, the press sniffed around for a bit despite what we said, but they could look all they wanted. Short of a DNA sample—which I would never concede to—there was no proof he was anything to me all thanks to my mother's decision to leave him off the birth certificate. I thought I might feel a twinge of guilt for denying the man whose blood ran through my veins, but I felt nothing. My indifference made me pause, but only for a brief moment. He was a stranger to me, after all. Frank was the only true father I ever knew, and I loved him with my whole heart.

I unscrewed the cap to my tinted gloss, applied a touch of it to my lips, then tossed it into my clutch. I rifled through my makeup bag, removing anything else I might need throughout the day and adding it to the small purse. Stepping back, I looked at my reflection. The only thing left was to put on the diamond and pearl teardrop earrings Alexander had bought for me just for this occasion.

Going back into the bedroom, I made my way over to my jewelry stand and pulled the earrings from their velvet box. As I applied the back to the post of the first earring, I heard Eva giggle at something. I turned to see what was so funny. Her attention was on the television, where a cartoon of a famous dog with long black ears was battling with an angel and a devil perched on opposite sides of his head.

Alexander laughed as well, and then leaned down conspiratorially to whisper in Eva's ear.

"She has an angel and a devil, too. Just like the dog," he said, pointing at me and making sure his whisper was loud enough so that I could hear.

"Oh, hush now. Don't be telling her all my secrets," I teased.

"What do they do?" Eva asked, her eyes full of wonder.

Feeling playful, I went along with the narrative.

"They act as your subconscious, telling you what's right and wrong," I told her. "The angel is good, but the devil tempts you to do bad things."

"I want and angel and a devil, too!" she declared.

"Maybe Krystina will share hers with you," Alexander chimed in with a wink.

I rolled my eyes and shook my head. "You're incorrigible."

"I've been thinking hard about something," Eva said, suddenly taking on a very serious tone.

"Oh, have you now," I said with amusement as I picked up the second earring that belonged on my other ear. "What have you been thinking about?"

"I don't want to call you Alex and Krys anymore."

I angled my head to look at her, not sure what she would say next. She was a very thoughtful child, and when she said she was thinking hard about something, she probably was.

"So, what do you want to call us?" Alexander prodded.

"Well, I have this friend at school," she began in a matter-of-fact way. "Her name is Jenna, and she has two moms. She calls one of them mommy and the other one mama. I think I have two moms, too—you and the mom in heaven. I called the one in heaven mommy, so I thought I could call you mama."

I froze, not sure what to say. Alexander and I had been to court, and we were granted legal guardianship. The next step was adoption. We'd discussed whether we should ask Eva to call us mom and dad but decided not to push the issue. She rarely brought up Hannah anymore, but I knew her birth mother still played on her mind from time to time.

"Mama. I like that. It's perfect actually," I told her, mulling the four letters around in my head.

"And what about me?" Alexander asked.

"You can just be daddy, silly," Eva said with a grin. "I don't have another one, so why would I need to find a new name?"

She said it as if it was so simple. And for her, it probably was since she'd never had a father figure before now. It was just one of the many things that we'd discovered when going through Hannah Wallace's apartment.

We'd found bottles of pills with Hannah's name on them—medications that were used to treat bipolar disorder. All were empty, and the dates on the bottles showed that she'd been out of her medication for at least a year before her suicide. She'd also kept multiple journals, giving us insight into her mental state. We'd given her notebooks to Dr. Tumblin, and he deduced with limited knowledge that Hannah most likely suffered from bipolar schizoaffective and had been battling demons none of us could possibly understand.

I thought Alexander would panic over this discovery, but he took it in stride, saying it was good to know Eva's family medical history. When the time came, we would tell her the truth, making sure she understood that she was always loved, and that it was not rejection but mental illness that took her birth mother from the earth.

But the most important thing that we'd found in Hannah's

apartment was Eva's birth certificate. Eva Eloise Wallace, born on the twenty-eighth of February, appeared to be fatherless. Hannah hadn't listed a name for the father. We also found no evidence that Dante, the man who was killed in prison, was her biological father as was told to me by Madilyn Ramos. It may have been him, but there was no way for us to know for sure. There were no pictures of Eva with him or any other man, making the identity of her biological father anyone's guess.

However, seeing the way Alexander beamed when Eva called him daddy was enough to make none of that matter.

I smiled as I watched him plant a kiss to the top of Eva's head. He would be her father now. And just like Frank was to me, my husband would be the only one who ever truly mattered to her. They'd already established a groove, falling into some of the most adorable routines. My favorite was the way they prepared breakfast together each morning. Music was always playing, and they'd often be caught singing. Eva rarely knew the words, but hearing Alexander change the lyrics from "Jack and Diane" to "eggs and fried ham" was utterly priceless.

"There you are!" announced an exasperated Vivian from the doorway to the bedroom. She looked pointedly at Eva. "I've been looking all over for you, little one. I believe I told you it was time to get dressed. I did not say it was time to watch cartoons in bed."

I inwardly smiled at Vivian's fake outrage. While I knew there was no real heat to her words, Eva took them to heart and bowed her head sheepishly.

"I'm sorry, Miss Vivian."

"Oh, now. Nothing to apologize for. Come with me. Let's get you all prettied up!" Walking over to the bed, she reached for Eva's hand.

I grinned, loving the easy relationship our doting housekeeper had with Eva. "Thank you, Vivian. I'll be right along to help. Ally is expecting us in two hours. The ceremony isn't until one, but Eva and I are going to help her get ready."

"I can't wait to see her," Vivian said with a bright smile. "Allyson is going to make a beautiful bride!"

After they walked out, Alexander came over to where I stood and raked me head to toe with a scorching look.

"Since I have you alone," he began. "Let's talk more about this very revealing dress. There's something about it that doesn't look right."

"Don't start on this again. The dress is fine. Besides, even if I wanted to swap it out for a different one, I can't. You know that."

"Who said I wanted you to change the dress?" he asked, cupping my face in his hands and lowering his voice just enough to make my toes curl.

"It seems to me like you're not pleased about the revealing back."

His elegant brows arched slightly, as if what I said couldn't be further from the truth.

"Or perhaps the dress is just missing something."

Then, to my surprise, he reached into the breast pocket of his tuxedo jacket and produced a string of diamonds. He brought them up, securing the dazzling gems around my neck before turning my body to face the mirror.

With my back to him, I took in the gorgeous, glittering, one-inch-wide choker. There was a lone pearl at the center, nestling between my clavicles. It was a perfect compliment to the diamond and pearl earrings Alexander had already gifted me earlier that morning.

"Alex, it's beautiful!" I reached up and touched it with a trembling hand, marveling over its exquisiteness.

"Only because it's on you. You're radiant when you smile, angel."

"Listen to you pulling out the smooth lines—and it's not even nine in the morning yet!" I laughed.

"It's not a line. It's the truth. And when you laugh, you're more breathtaking than any diamond."

I blushed as he wrapped his arms around my waist and leaned down to press his lips to my bare shoulder.

Turning in his embrace, I pressed up on my four-inch red stilettos and brought my lips to his.

"Thank you," I murmured.

I felt his mouth curl against mine.

"When we get back from the wedding reception tonight, I'm going to fuck you wearing my diamonds and those high heels —and nothing else."

"Mmm," I crooned as his tongue darted out to lightly trace my lips teasingly.

"But I'm not done here yet. I have another surprise for you, angel."

I pulled back, feeling slightly shocked. The cost of the necklace and earrings was enough to feed a starving country. I couldn't fathom what more there could be.

Moving over to a tall dresser, Alexander pulled open the top drawer. From within, he removed a small box and a cream-colored legal sized envelope. He handed me the envelope first.

"What's this?" I asked as I took it from his hand.

"Just open it."

Doing as instructed, I opened it and scanned the contents of the first page.

"Adoption papers. How did you... Alex, I thought we had to go to court again," I said in confusion as I flipped through the other pages, making sure I was reading everything correctly.

"I managed to pull some strings. All you need to do is sign."

My heart pounded in my chest, hardly able to believe this was real—that this was really happening.

Eva would become Eva Eloise Stone.

Ours.

Now and forever.

Tears welled in my eyes as I processed the gravity of this moment. A year ago, I never thought I'd be here. But now, I no longer felt sad when I saw a mother pushing a stroller. Instead, we shared knowing smiles, acutely aware that we were both part of something bigger than ourselves.

"Give me a pen," I said, my voice thick with emotion. Tears were threatening to spill over but I blinked them back, not wanting to have to redo my eye makeup.

Alexander reached into his breast pocket and procured a pen. I signed my name with a flourish, not wanting to waste another moment to make it official.

"I'll have Stephen file them first thing Monday morning."

Taking the papers from my hand, he walked a few steps to set them back on the dresser. I'd barely had a minute to process the adoption before Alexander returned to me and opened the small velvet box. A ring was nestled against purple satin.

"Oh, wow..." I breathed, unable to find better words to describe the stunningly unique design. The platinum setting held a single pearl with an intricate silver swirl bent into the shape of a triskelion. Accenting the design were three small gemstones.

"Each of the stones in the triskelion is a birthstone—yours, mine, and Eva's. I want today to be considered the first day of the rest of our lives—as a family. Let this ring be a symbol of that."

Tears welled in my eyes as Alexander slid the ring on my finger.

"Alex," I said hesitantly. I felt so many emotions all at once —elation, love, but also worry. I didn't want to ruin this precious moment, but I couldn't ignore the fears I'd been harboring for quite some time. "You and I... we've talked about the dark place I'd fallen into after losing Liliana. We both did in our own way, and we lost a bit of ourselves. Things are going so good now, but I feel like I'm waiting for the other shoe to drop. It's like there's this part of me that's unwilling to believe that everything is okay. What if something bad—"

"Angel," Alexander interrupted, pulling me to his chest. "Nothing bad is going to happen. Stop focusing on the negative. There's too much good in our lives right now to dwell on what-ifs."

"I know, but...oh, God. I just realized how much I must sound like my mother. She's so negative," I told him, feeling somewhat appalled that her negativity might be coming out in me as I aged.

"Maybe that's because you're a mother now. Perhaps it's never been negativity, but simply a mother's worry. Maybe you're experiencing the same worries she had. If that's the case, is sounding like her so awful?"

I took a half of a step back, slightly surprised by his words.

"Well, I suppose not. I just never looked at it that way. I just thought she was negative about everything."

"Could be, but I don't think she's as bad as she used to be, especially now that she's faced her demons. Just think about how she is with Eva. She slid right into the role of grandma without skipping a beat. Sometimes, I don't think you give her enough credit. You're more like her than you want to admit."

I frowned. "How so?"

"Moving on takes strength, and it took a considerable amount of strength to move on from what Michael Ketry did to her. You inherited that same strength from her. Just think about all you've overcome. You are very different from your mother— very different—but you're also very much the same. And that isn't a bad thing. Things haven't been easy, but I'm proud of you, angel—I'm proud of us."

I stared up at my husband, seeing nothing but love in his gorgeous sapphire eyes as he leaned in to press his lips to mine. His mouth sealed over mine, and he kissed me with a fierce intensity that only two • people who shared our lived experiences would understand.

In his arms, I thought about his words. He'd spoken the truth. I'd experienced grief before—friends or relatives who passed away or grief from a romantic relationship gone wrong. There were different levels to grief, but nothing held a candle to the grief I felt after losing Liliana. There were some wounds that would never completely heal, but they could make us stronger if we allowed it.

Losing our first born had changed Alexander and me, but I could finally see how, through that experience, we'd discovered new strengths and who we truly were as a couple. We were no longer just two people heavy in lust and in love. We were truly partners.

And now, we were parents.

People linked by destiny would always find each other. When we took in Eva, our little peanut, she filled in pieces of our hearts that we hadn't known were missing. She brought hope—that feeling deep inside your gut that makes you willing to try again.

She was a blessing and a miracle.

Our miracle.

THE END

AFTERWORD

If you loved *The Stone Series*, check out a some of the other books in my catalog!

The Sound of Silence
Meet Gianna and Derek in this an emotionally gripping, dark romantic thriller that is guaranteed to keep you on the edge of your seat! This book is not for the faint-hearted. Plus, Krystina Cole has a cameo appearance!

Fade Into You Series
What's your favorite trope? Second chance, secret baby, suspense, enemies to lovers, sports romance? *Untouched, Defined, Endurance* will give you all that and more! Prepare to be left breathless!

MUSIC PLAYLIST FOR BREAKING STONE

Thank you to the musical talents who influenced and inspired *Breaking Stone*. **Listen on Spotify!**

"Possession" by Sarah McLachlan
"In the End" Mellen Gi Remix by Tommee Profitt, Fleurie, and Mellen Gi
"I Dare You" by Kelly Clarkson
"Gold on the Ceiling" by The Black KeyS
"Easy On Me" by Adele
"Hearts on Fire" by ILLENIUM, Dabin, Lights
"Play with Fire" by Sam Tinnesz (feat. Yacht Money)
"Don't Blame Me" by Taylor Swift
"Iris" by Natalie Taylor
"Falling" by Harry Styles
"Somewhere Over The Rainbow" by Israel Kamakawiwo'ole
"White Flag" by Bishop BriggS
"Summer Wind" by Frank Sinatra
"In the Air Tonight" by Natalie Taylor
"War of Hearts" by Ruelle
"On An Evening In Roma" by Dean Martin
"Hold On: by Chord Overstreet
"I Know What You Want" by Busta Rhymes & Mariah Carey (feat. Flipmode Squad)
"Reckoning" by Alanis Morrissette
"What a Wonderful World" by Kina Grannis & Imaginary Future

OFFICIAL WEBSITE
www.dakotawillink.com

BOOKS & BOXED WINE CONFESSIONS

Want fun stuff and sneak peek excerpts from Dakota? Join
Books & Boxed Wine Confessions and get the inside scoop!
Fans in this interactive reader Facebook group are the first to
know the latest news! JOIN HERE: https://www.facebook.com/
groups/1635080436793794

NEWSLETTER
Never miss a new release, update, or sale!
Subscribe to Dakota's newsletter!

SOCIALS

ABOUT THE AUTHOR

Dakota Willink is an Award-Winning and International Bestselling Author. She loves writing about damaged heroes who fall in love with sassy and independent females. Her books are character-driven, emotional, and sexy, yet written with a flare that keeps them real. With a wide range of published books, a magazine publication, and the *Leave Me Breathless World* under her belt, Dakota's imagination is constantly spinning new ideas.

The *Stone Series* is Dakota's first published book series. It has been recognized for various awards, including the *Readers' Favorite* 2017 Gold Medal in Romance, and has since been translated into multiple languages internationally. The *Fade Into You* series (formally known as the *Cadence* duet) was a finalist in the *HEAR Now Festival Independent Audiobook Awards*. In addition, Dakota has written under the alternate pen name, Marie Christy. Under this name, she has written and published a children's book for charity titled, *And I Smile*. Also writing as Marie Christy, she was a contributor to the Blunder Woman Productions project, *Nevertheless We Persisted: Me Too*, a 2019 *Audie Award* Finalist and *Earphones Awards* Winner. This project inspired Dakota to write *The Sound of Silence*, a dark romantic suspense novel that tackles the realities of domestic abuse.

Dakota often says she survived her first publishing with coffee and wine. She's an unabashed *Star Wars* fanatic and still dreams of one day getting her letter from Hogwarts. She enjoys traveling and spending time with her husband, her two witty kids, and her spoiled rotten cavaliers. During the summer months, she can often be found taking pictures of random things or soaking up the sun on the Great Lakes with her family.